Hard Day's Knight

Hard Day's Knight

Katie MacAlister

A SIGNET ECLIPSE BOOK

SIGNET ECLIPSE
Published by New American Library, a division of
Penguin Group (USA) Inc., 375 Hudson Street,
New York, New York 10014, USA
Penguin Group (Canada), 10 Alcorn Avenue, Toronto,
Ontario M4V 3B2, Canada (a division of Pearson Penguin Canada Inc.)
Penguin Books Ltd., 80 Strand, London WC2R 0RL, England
Penguin Ireland, 25 St. Stephen's Green, Dublin 2,
Ireland (a division of Penguin Books Ltd.)
Penguin Group (Australia), 250 Camberwell Road, Camberwell, Victoria 3124,
Australia (a division of Pearson Australia Group Pty. Ltd.)
Penguin Books India Pvt. Ltd., 11 Community Centre, Panchsheel Park,
New Delhi - 110 017, India
Penguin Group (NZ), cnr Airborne and Rosedale Roads, Albany,
Auckland 1310, New Zealand (a division of Pearson New Zealand Ltd.)
Penguin Books (South Africa) (Pty.) Ltd., 24 Sturdee Avenue,
Rosebank, Johannesburg 2196, South Africa

Penguin Books Ltd., Registered Offices:
80 Strand, London WC2R 0RL, England

First published by Signet Eclipse, an imprint of New American Library,
a division of Penguin Group (USA) Inc.

ISBN 0-7394-4942-7

I knew the minute I read about the International Wenches Guild that the members were sisters of the heart. How could anyone resist an organization whose motto is "Bigger, better, faster, more"? This book is dedicated with much gratitude to all my Wenchly sisters, as well as the Rogues who adore them.

Chapter One

"Right, so where are all the good-looking men in formfitting tights?"

"Probably rehearsing. You can set that down next to the cooler."

"Rehearsing? Rehearsing what? Hunky men in skintight clothing don't rehearse! They're far too manly for such a sissy thing. *Actors* rehearse. Men in tights . . . well, they just don't. Unless . . . hey! You wouldn't drag me out here to the middle of nowhere by promising me really handsome, dashing guys in extremely cool knight getup without telling me they were all gay, would you?"

CJ grinned as I deposited a box of toilet paper, napkins, and assorted towels on top of the red plastic cooler. "I'm sure some are, but not all. Don't worry; you'll have lots of manly-man guys to slobber over."

"I'd better," I muttered darkly as I stomped off to the car to fetch another load of camping accessories. Twenty minutes later I returned from the wilds of the parking lot. "You know, I always imagined ye old days of medieval yore had a whole lot more dashing, daring knights hanging around, and fewer steaming piles of poop." I stepped carefully over the huge pile of fly-bespecked horse manure, and staggered toward the ever-growing collection of bags, boxes, coolers, food hampers, and suitcases that contained those items my cousin deemed vital to our continued existence.

"Oh, no, poop was everywhere back then. Open sewers, you know," CJ answered from where she was on her knees digging into a rucksack, muttering to herself as I dropped a box of canned beans and packages of freeze-dried hiking food next to her.

"I still haven't seen even one man in tights. There's a couple of women a few tents down who are dressed like knights, but that's it. So help me, Ceej, if you dragged me out here on false pretenses . . ."

"I didn't!" CJ all but climbed into the rucksack, her voice muffled as she tried to placate me. "They're rehearsing, I promise. Everyone rehearses before opening day. The vendors are probably vendoring or setting up their booths. And the jousters are doing practice runs."

"Okay, but I'd better start seeing some soon. You promised me great big herds of manly guys being knights and rogues and swashbuckling pirates." I peered around at the sea of tents that surrounded us. The flat, open field adjacent to the fairgrounds housing the Faire served as a tent city of Faire performers, vendors, employees, and joust participants. Most of the tents were blocky squares and rectangles of dull gray or green, like the one CJ had provided for us, but at the far end of the tent city were clustered beautiful striped tents of all colors, some with pennons and flags bearing coats of arms waving lazily in the late afternoon summer breeze. Other than the two women I'd seen coming from the car, the tent city was strangely devoid of human life. "I'm not seeing even a small flock of manly knights, much less a herd of them. In fact, there doesn't seem to be anyone here at all. Are you *sure* that this Faire is a hotbed of romance and dishy guys?"

"Would I lie to you?" CJ pulled herself out of her rucksack, a smile lighting her happy gray eyes. "I personally know of six couples who met because of the Faire in the last two years, and they're all happily married. So don't worry; there are oodles of manly knights here, all of them dashing and daring and wildly romantic, just like my lamb."

I rolled my eyes as I started back toward the car, located a hot, sweaty half mile away in a distant field. "Oh, yeah, your lamb, the man known to everyone as the Butcher of Birmingham. I said I wanted a modern-day personification of knightliness, Ceej, a man who's not afraid to laugh triumphantly in the face of death, a man who lives for adventure and excitement—*not* a guy who scares the crap out of anyone who gets a good close look at him. I'll go get the last of the stuff. If I'm not back in half an hour, find the bravest, handsomest jouster you can and send him after me. Maybe you'd better make it two. I'm feeling like I'll need a lot of resuscitating."

CJ waved an acknowledging hand at me as she dug through the canvas bag. "Right. After you get back you can slip into the garb I brought for you."

I sighed a sigh of the soon to be martyred, and staggered off toward the car. By the time I collected the last items, locked up CJ's VW Beetle, and returned to our tent, sweat was rolling down my back, soaking the light gauze shirt I'd put on before we left my aunt and uncle's house in London—the town midway between Detroit and Toronto, not the English capital.

"Whew!" I set down the box of kitty litter, kibble, tiny little cans of premium cat food, bottled water, three different kinds of cat treats, a bag of dried catnip, assorted cat toys, and one huge domed litter box with infrared beams and automatic clump removal. "Criminy dutch, the things this cat . . . Moth! Come back here; that isn't yours! *Ceej!*"

My cousin CJ looked up at my whine. "Hmm?"

"Your parents' cat is eating someone's tent." I

pointed at the huge white cat with four orange stockings that was gnawing on the black canvas tent set up next to ours.

"Oh. Probably isn't best that you let him do that. He'll just puke it up later. I wonder where I put my side-lacing bodice?" Ceej walked on her knees over to where three suitcases were stacked neatly in front of the humongous pea-green tent it had taken us a half hour of sweating (and swearing) to erect.

"Me? He's not my responsibility anymore. My job was to get him from Seattle to Ontario in one piece while your parents did the cross-country thing. I did that, not that it was easy, since he insisted on yowling and trying to claw me through the cat carrier the entire flight. But we're here now, and that means he's your responsibility."

"Nope, sorry, I've got too much to do, what with the official Wenches' Conference and all. Besides, Mom paid *you* to take care of him."

"Only for the flight!" I dug through the ice in the cooler and extracted a chilled bottle of water. "They were supposed to be home by now to receive the horrible beast with open arms."

"Yeah, well, you know how Dad is. Once he gets an idea in his head, there's no changing his mind. He's always wanted to see the Klondike."

"He's the only man I know who'd feel it necessary to drive from Seattle to Ontario via Alaska," I grumbled as I swigged the cold water. "Moth, dammit . . . argh! No! Spit it out! Bad cat!"

"You really should keep a closer eye on him," CJ said as I grabbed the cat and pulled out of his mouth the bit of tent he was gnawing on. "Mom's really attached to him. She'd never forgive you if anything happened to him."

Moth shot a slitted, yellow-eyed glare at me as I picked him up.

"The feeling's mutual," I growled, and lugged him over to the pyramid of stuff in front of our tent. I checked the snap on the long leash that was tied onto a lounge chair, adjusted his harness so he couldn't slip out of it again, and tethered him to the chair so I could put stuff away. "There isn't enough money in the world to pay me for having to babysit him for two whole weeks."

"Well, it's not like you have a lot of other options, is it?" CJ asked.

I froze in the act of hauling the sleeping bags into the tent.

"Oh, Pepper, I'm sorry. That wasn't nice of me. I didn't mean it. It's not your fault that unemployment is so high in Seattle."

I shrugged the sting of her comment away and tossed the sleeping bags inside the musty, faintly mildew-scented tent. "It may not be nice, but it's the truth. I don't have anything else to do except sit around and watch my unemployment benefits run out." That wasn't really the truth; my days were very busy, what with job-hunting and all the volunteering I did to keep myself sane—I didn't even have time to date, let alone sit around and do nothing—but still, her point was taken.

"Maybe if you went to California? I always heard that was a good place for software engineers."

"It *was,* which is why when so many of us were laid off two years ago, everyone moved to Silicon Valley and its environs. I figured with the mass migration south, I'd have a better chance at finding a job where I was, but . . ." I shrugged, unwilling to dwell on my increasingly desperate situation. This was supposed to be my vacation, my man-hunting, romantic, "fall madly in love with some gorgeous guy" vacation. I wanted to forget the depressing life I would have to face if it all came to nothing.

"Isn't there anything else you can do?" CJ asked, her brow wrinkled as she sat on her heels watching me. "You've got a degree; surely there must be some job—"

I shifted a few more boxes into the tent. "You'd think so, huh? But since there were some fifty thousand other people let go by the local airplane company, there's *nada* job-wise. Squat. Zilcho. Not even a McDonald's fry-jockey job."

"Boy, that is hard." CJ sucked her lower lip for a moment as I flopped down exhaustedly on the cooler, brushing at the trickles of sweat snaking down the valley between my breasts. "I guess you don't really have any other option but to find yourself a man, fall in love with him, and live happily ever after. Fortunately, I'm here to help you."

My shoulders slumped as the full realization of what I was doing hit me. I'd been in delusional mode ever since my cousin had convinced me that she'd be able to hook me up with a veritable God of perfection, courtesy of the local Renaissance Faire and international jousting competition. And now here I was, actually believing her promise of finding me a man, a soul mate, someone who would fill my empty, lonely life. It was all so . . . sordid. Unrealistic. *Stupid.* I let my damp forehead drop into my hands as I moaned. "Oh, Ceej, what am I doing? Why did I let you talk me into this? Your plan is ridiculous, utterly ridiculous! What was I thinking? I'm thirty-six, unemployed, have a degree in programming and half of one from the vet school I quit before I got eaten by something big with sharp teeth, and guys don't even look twice at me. Why on earth did I imagine that you can find me a man in two weeks when I haven't in sixteen years of concerted searching?"

"Because I can!" She tipped her head to the side as I rocked miserably on the cooler. "I told you that Butcher and I met at the Faire last year, and we were madly in love after just a couple of days."

"He lives in England. You live here," I pointed out, wondering if I shouldn't just give in and have an indulgent wallow in self-pity.

"But I see him every couple of months, and just as

soon as I get that job at the BBC, we'll be set. And then there was Fairuza Spenser, Cathy Baker, and Mary Denhelm."

I looked up, having decided against the wallow. "Who are they?"

"Wenches in my local chapter whom I introduced to their respective husbands last year at various Faires. You'll meet them later. And the year before that there were three others whom I also found hubbies for. I'm a matchmaker extraordinaire, so relax and place yourself fully in my capable hands. Before the Faire is over, I will have not only found you your perfect man, but you'll be deeply in love and well on the way to happily-ever-aftering."

"Life is not a fairy tale," I said morosely, wanting to believe her, but knowing that things like that just didn't happen to people like me.

"No, it's better," she said calmly, then frowned as her brows drew together. "You have to help, though, Pepper. You can't just stand around waiting for the love of your life to swoop you up and carry you off."

"Why not? We're surrounded by knights in shining armor."

Her frown deepened. "I just want to make sure that you're totally committed to the idea of finding a guy."

"Committed like to a madhouse?"

"Pepper!"

I held up my hands in mock surrender. "Okay, okay, little joke. I'm committed; I really am."

"I hope so, because once I find a guy for you, you're expected to keep him. I just worry that you're not really serious about this. After all, look what you've done at home."

I stood up and glared down at where she sat poking through the bag. "What do you mean, what I've done at home? I haven't done anything!"

She grabbed a handful of jeans around my knee region and tugged me down to the cooler. "Stop looming over me like a great hulk. You're too tall. I can't bend my head back far enough to see you. And that's exactly what I mean—you seem to expect the perfect man to drop into your lap without your lifting a single finger to find him, but that's not going to happen unless you get proactive. You have to admit that until now, you haven't actually expended any energy in dating."

I grabbed her ear and peered in. "Hellooo, anyone home?" She slapped my hand away. "Didn't you hear me on the drive up here? I've looked and looked and looked, but all the guys back home are either unemployed plane mechanics or likewise unemployed software geeks. The first group hang around bars ogling women and having competitions about who can pee the farthest, while the second thinks a wild time is getting drunk and creating dirty computer animations."

"Maybe your standards are too high," CJ said thoughtfully as she eyed me up and down. "There's nothing really wrong with you. You're pretty, in a general sort of way. You have nice thick red hair. And freckles—guys like freckles. And if you're a bit . . . well . . . solid, guys like that, too. Some guys. *Most* guys. And you're smart; that's a plus."

I paced the length of the tent, avoiding Moth as he lunged for my ankles when I passed in front of him. "You try it, cat, and you're going to find yourself locked into the tent for the next two weeks. Thank you for your so reassuring assessment of my many fine qualities, CJ."

"You're also stubborn, very set in your ways, and you like to argue, but that's okay, I think we can work around those points." She gestured expressively with her tiny little hands. I added that to the list of injuries I was nursing. In addition to being gainfully employed by the Canadian Broadcasting Corporation as a researcher—a job that allowed her to travel to England several times a year—CJ was graceful, delicately built, and had a charming little heart-shaped face and a fragile manner that left most men prostrate before her. I, on the other hand, was built along the lines of a brick house, or so my mother always used to tell me. Big-boned, tall, and gawky—that was me. The only way a man was going to be prostrate before me was if he accidentally ran into me and was knocked out cold. I knew it wasn't fair to add CJ's genetic makeup to my list of ways the world was picking on me, but I was too crabby to care.

"I don't know, maybe it's me. Maybe something's wrong with me." I avoided Moth's lunge at my shoelaces and plopped down to snag another bottle of cold water. "It just seems to me that guys today don't have any *cojones*. They sit around and whine and don't *do* anything. At least I'm out trying to find work. And when I'm not, I'm volunteering. I don't spend my day watching soaps and complaining and trying to pee farther than anyone else."

"It must be frustrating to be unemployed," she said, accepting a bottle of water. "And yes, you're doing more than just complaining. It's too bad that the women's shelter or the literacy center can't hire you, although honestly, Pepper, I think you're being a little overly rough on the guys you know. Maybe you should just cut them a little slack? They must feel as helpless as you do at being in such a bad situation."

I waved her explanation away. "It's not just that; it's the *sort* of men who are being produced these days. They're all so wimpy! No guts to them, no balls! Whatever happened to the men of old, the men not afraid to stare death in the face and laugh a mocking laugh at it? What happened to their sense of adventure? Where are all the bold, daring men who would risk anything for the woman they loved?"

"Alpha males."

"Huh?"

"They're called alpha males, and you've been reading too many historical romances," she answered with a smile. "Real men like that don't exist. Well, they do—my lamb is one—but they're few and far between. In reality, most alpha males are jerks. Butcher just happens to be a shining example of a delicious one."

"Yeah, well, it seems to me that you've matchmade all the good guys already. There's probably nothing decent left over." I watched Moth as he dragged the aluminum-framed canvas chair over and tackled my left tennis shoe, viciously biting at the hard rubber of the shoe's front. "I want a little romance, Ceej. I want a guy who will like me for the person that I am. I just want someone to love. Is it asking so much to find Mr. Pepper Marsh?"

CJ snickered for a second. "Mr. Pepper. Sounds like knockoff soft drink or a swishy hairdresser."

"Ceej!"

"Is now the time to make a Sergeant Pepper's Lonely Hearts Club Band joke?"

"No!"

She put on a suitably sincere face. "Sorry. No, it's not asking too much. You just have to have faith in me, Pepper. I'll find him for you, I promise."

"Before the end of the Faire," I reminded her, feeling once again the brief flare of hope deep within me. Say what you will, CJ did seem to have an extraordinary talent in matching up her friends and acquaintances. Maybe my luck was about to change. Maybe it was my turn to have something go right. Maybe—*Ow!* "Cat, I swear to you by all that is holy, if you do not release the flesh of my ankle, I'll be wearing a cat stole!"

CJ snickered even harder as I squatted to disengage Moth's claws from where he had attacked my naked ankle. "He's just expressing his affection for you. He doesn't like many people, you know. He tolerates Mom, but that's because she's the only one who feeds him. He pees in Dad's shoes."

"He's about to use up one of his nine lives," I said grimly as I plopped the cat down onto the chair he was tied to. "Sit. Stay."

"You really don't like animals, do you? No wonder you didn't become a vet."

"It's not that I don't like them; I just don't trust them. You never know what they're thinking," I said, glaring at the huge orange-legged cat until he curled up into roughly the shape of a meat loaf, his front legs tucked under his big white chest. I wasn't at all fooled by the air of innocence the cat wore—I knew from experience that he had a particularly creative and vengeful mind. "You're up to something; I know you are. Just don't try it when I'm around," I told the cat, then looked back at my cousin. "Beastly things, animals."

CJ giggled at my pun. "There speaks the daughter of a vet. How on earth could you grow up with animals all over your house and not love them?"

"You have no idea what it was like having a mother who was more interested her four-legged clients than in her only child, but I know all too well how innocent-looking, cute, adorable beasts are really bloodsucking leeches that demand constant attention."

"Whatever." CJ clearly wasn't buying my sob story. She didn't look the least bit sympathetic as she straightened her bloodred Irish dress and strapped on a long leather belt and tapestry pouch. "If it gives you pleasure to think you were abused, go for it. Just don't say anything about not liking animals. Faire people are gaga over them, and that goes double when we're talking about the way the men here adore their horses."

I shuddered and plucked the water bottle from where I'd set it, reveling in the icy cold as I guzzled thirstily. I had had the erroneous idea that because Ontario was farther north than Seattle, it wouldn't get at all hot. I was very, very wrong. "Horses are the worst," I said, tossing the now-empty water bottle into one of the cardboard boxes used to hold bottles for refilling from the big ten-gallon water cooler CJ had lugged in. "They're big, smelly, they step on you, and they eat your hair."

"Just because when you were a kid your mom had a horse that used to snack on you doesn't mean that all of them—"

"That horse was trouble on four hooves," I interrupted, the memory of the indignities I suffered from the brute wonderfully clear in my mind. "But it wasn't just him, monster that he was. They're all like that. They're big and pushy and they do whatever they want and stomp all over you while they're doing it. Do you know that I still have scars on both feet from being run over by horses? At least with a cat you can confine it to a room. Horses are just impossible."

CJ pulled a suitcase toward her. "*That* is most definitely an opinion you should *not* share with anyone here unless you want to be lynched. Now, where did I put your garb?"

"I don't need any," I said a bit petulantly, immediately feeling ashamed of myself. It wasn't her fault my life was a disaster, and she *had* promised to do everything she could to match me up with my ideal mate—not that I was convinced she could do any such thing, even if I was the sort of a girl who'd fall for the kind of man who wore tights and a funny jester's hat. Then again, some of the jousters that CJ had told me about on the trip up sounded intriguing, very masculine, filled with a dashing sense of adventure, with just a tiny smidgen of the thrill seeker. . . . Maybe I should think positive. I made a resolution right there to not be a clinging, whiny pain in the butt. So I was stuck with Moth watching and had to dress up like a medieval harlot—I could deal with that. The perks—hunky guys in knight clothes, one of whom could potentially be *him*—were sure to outweigh the drawbacks of the next two weeks.

Or so I told myself. My Wise Inner Pepper was reserving judgment.

"Here." CJ extracted some garments from the suitcase and shoved them into my arms. "Go put your garb on. It'll make you feel better."

"I hardly see how," I muttered, but obediently ducked my head to enter the tent, chastising myself that ten seconds into my resolution, I'd already broken it. "Being self-conscious because I'm strapped into a harlot's outfit is not generally known to make me feel better."

"Everyone wears garb at the Faire. You'd stand out if you didn't. Besides, you're a Wench, an official representative of the League of Wenches. It's a violation of LOW bylaws for you to appear in street clothes at a Faire."

"You're the one who signed me up," I pointed out as I let the front flap fall so I could peel off my sticky clothes. I used another bottle of ice water to give myself a fast sponge bath as CJ puttered around outside the tent, shivering at the delicious feeling of the cold water on my sweaty flesh. No doubt I'd be refilling the big water cooler from the fairground's water main frequently, but it was a small price to pay to cool down. "I didn't even know there was such a thing as a League of Wenches, let alone that you were one of the Wench Pimps."

"That's Madame Wench, missy! Charter members are all Madames. Newbies like you are Harlots until you prove your Wenchness and move up to Temptress status."

I slipped into a thin ankle-length cotton chemise before lacing up the black bodice with gold embroidery that CJ had presented to me.

"How very—cheese on rye, how tight is this bodice supposed to be? My boobs are flowing over the top!— flattering to be known to all and sundry as a Harlot."

CJ popped her blond head into the tent and gave me the once-over. "Can you still breathe?"

I straightened up and tried to take a breath. My lungs didn't expand any noticeable amount, but I was still standing. "Yeah."

"Then it's not tight enough. Hurry up; I want to get this gear stowed so we can go Wench Butcher and his team. He promised to bring his kilt, and I'm dying to do an official LOW kilt check on him."

The lascivious glint in her eyes told me everything I needed to know about just what a kilt check consisted of. "I can't go out like this, Ceej. Look at my boobs!"

She frowned as my hands fluttered around my chest. "What's wrong with them?"

I thinned my lips. "Well, for one, I no longer have individual breasts; I have a bosom shelf. This bodice is too small. My boobs are practically touching my chin."

She rolled her eyes and started to back out of the tent. "Don't be silly; all boobs look like that in a properly fitted bodice. Guys love it. They'll offer to drop grapes down your bosomage and do a grape dive. Don't forget to put on your Wench pin. I have some favors you can give away, too."

I eyed the mound of breasts that rose like overflowing bread dough in a too-small pan. "I don't think a grape would fit in there."

"Fine, you stay and fuss with your breasts. I'm going to go see what's happening in the jousting field. Butcher and his team should be there practicing with their loaner horses. See you there. And don't forget Moth. You'd better get your skirt on quick; he's eating someone's pennant now."

"Oh, lovely, he'll probably barf all over me when I pick him up. God almighty, how am I supposed to bend in this bodice?" I asked as I shook the wrinkles out of a black-and-gold cotton ankle-length skirt and slipped it over my head, then spent five minutes twirling around ineffectually trying to see over the breast shelf to fasten the skirt's buttons. "All I wanted was a chance to get away for a bit, a chance to find some nongeek potential husband material, and where do I end up? Cinched into a bodice with a four-legged, hairy companion who has a taste for canvas. Moth!" Skirt in place at last, I stepped out of the tent to find

that Moth had dragged the chair over to a neighboring
tent. I swore under my breath and ran out to get him.

Right in front of a massive thundering herd of deranged killer horses.

"Jesus effing Christ!" a male voice bellowed.

I froze into a nearly six-foot-tall, begarbed, soon-
to-be-trampled pillar of terror as a huge white horse
screamed, rose up on his back legs, and pawed the air
with razor-sharp hooves just inches from my head. The
man on the horse's back yelled something else, but I
was too stunned and horrified to understand it. Just as
the white devil's hooves made the downswing straight
toward my face, a black shape loomed up from the
side of my vision, and suddenly every last molecule of
air was driven from my lungs as a heavy arm grabbed
me around the waist and swung me up and out of the
way of certain death and dismemberment.

Still stunned, my brain operating sluggishly, I turned
my head at the same time I was slammed down hard
on top of pair of muscular thighs, my right leg ram-
ming painfully against the front of a deep, leather-
covered wooden saddle.

The man looking back at me was dressed in medieval clothing—a long, gorgeous red tunic embroidered
with three golden dogs, black tights, and knee-high
leather boots tied on with leather garters. The man's
eyes were a beautiful pure, unblemished gray ringed
with black, and made positively devastating with the
thickest black lashes I'd ever seen.

"Wow," I breathed as my mind suddenly came to
life, realizing that the man had just saved me. "Rescued from certain death by a brave, dashing knight.
It's just like something out of a romance."

"You bloody idiotic fool!" the handsome dark-
haired knight swore, his eyes narrowing in anger.
"You stupid git! What the hell do you think you were
doing? You could have killed someone! Are you completely daft, or do you just look it?"

Well, it was *almost* like something out of a romance.

Chapter Two

"What the bloody hell were you thinking? You could have seriously hurt someone!"

How mortifying. My first half hour at the Faire, and I was being yelled at by a big, handsome knight. On a horse.

A really *big* horse.

"Argh!" I clutched the angry knight's arms as it suddenly struck me that I was perched a good six feet off the ground. "Look, I'm sorry, but this cat I'm babysitting ran out, and I just wanted to grab him before he ate someone's tent."

The knight glared at me for a second. "I'm not talking to you."

"You're not? Oh." It took me a minute to realize that he was narrowing his eyes at the man facing us on the murderous white horse, the one that had almost run me down. I turned to add my glare to his. "Yeah! I could have been seriously hurt, not to mention what would have happened to Moth, and if you think I want to explain to my aunt that her precious baby was murdered by a horse, you can just think again."

The man on the white horse unhinged his metal helmet and took it off, pulling off a soft white cloth cap before shaking out a glorious mane of shoulder-length golden hair. Even red-faced from riding in full armor under the broiling August sun, he was handsome, handsome, handsome—tanned face, sun-streaked hair, vivid blue eyes, and one of those chis-eled chins with a dimple in the middle. He didn't even give me a glance as he fought to control his slobbering-all-over-the-bit, almost-bucking horse. "Walker, what a completely unexpected surprise. I had heard that the motley group of misfits you call a team had registered for the competition, but I never thought you'd actually have the balls to show up. That's not really your forte, is it? Actual jousting, I mean, not just hulking around the fringes reliving the distant, vague images of your former glory."

"Farrell, I might have known it was you," Walker rumbled. A little shiver went down my back at the sound of his voice. He was English (my favorite ac-cent!), and his vocal cords must have been wrapped in velvet, because the words that emerged—when he wasn't bellowing them—had the same effect on me as if I were being stroked by the softest touch imagin-able. "No one else would be so arrogant, so self-centered, so *stupid* as to gallop a green horse through the tents."

"Green, but fully under my control," the blond man named Farrell snapped. Evidently he didn't like being called stupid by the rich velvet rumble that came deep out of Walker's chest. I had the worst urge to lean back against him to listen to its source, but managed to keep myself from cuddling into his broad chest. This wasn't the moment to investigate the interesting man behind me; this was the moment to request that he put me down—very slowly and carefully. Before I could ask, though, Farrell smirked and slapped Walker with a zinger. "Perhaps you've forgotten what it's like to have a prime piece of flesh between your thighs, but I assure you that I am more than capable of con-trolling any ride."

"Ooooh, that was a low blow," I told Walker. "You're not going to take that, are you?"

He turned his narrowed gaze to me, and I saw again

just how pure his eyes were. They were like silver discs edged with black. "Do I know you?"

"I'm the damsel in distress you dashed in and rescued in the very best brave-knight manner," I answered.

"In other words, I *don't* know you."

I offered him a perky smile. "No, but I *am* sitting on your lap. That's gotta count for something, don't you think?"

"No," he said, and tried to swing me off the side of the horse. Evidently the black monster he was riding didn't care for the act, for it tossed its massive head in the air and snorted that warning snort that horses always give before they start doing things like trampling little girls, or eating their hair, or knocking them down, or any of the gazillion other things that loomed up out of my nightmares as the torments I used to suffer with my mother's horses.

"Don't drop me!" I screamed, and twisted my body around so I could cling to Walker. I got one leg wrapped around his waist as I clutched at his head, struggling to free my other leg from where it was confined in the yards and yards of cotton that made up my Wench skirt. "Please, whatever you do, don't drop me!"

"What is wrong with you, woman?" Walker asked. His voice was a bit muffled because, straddling him as I was, his face was smooshed into my overflowing breasts. Beneath us, his horse shifted sideways.

"There's nothing wrong with me that can't be cured by being off this horse!"

"I'm *trying* to get you off, blast it!"

"You're going to drop me! I'll fall and break something!"

"Having a bit of trouble with your Wench?" Farrell asked. He managed to get his hooves-of-death horse under control and rode over to my side.

"I'm not his Wench, and I'm— Argh!" The black horse evidently took exception to the white horse's nearness, because he snorted again and did a little sideways dance that had me shrieking and clawing at Walker's back when he tried to peel me off him.

"For God's sake, woman, I can't breathe." He gasped as he strong-armed my overflowing chest off his face. His gaze dropped for a minute to my bosom (heaving, in the proper Wench fashion), and he added in a much softer voice, "Not that I don't appreciate the wubby, but I'd prefer one that isn't conducted on horseback."

"What are you talking abo—oh, my god, he's going to rear! Don't let me fall!"

"Marley is too well bred to do any such thing, but he doesn't like you squirming around," Walker said as he pried me off his chest. "Sit still, will you? Marley, stand!"

"Clearly the lady wants away from you, a fact that illustrates her obvious good taste and intelligence. My lady, I am your humble servant. If you will allow me to remove you from the knave Walker's slug of a horse . . ." Farrell reached for my arm as he maneuvered his horse even closer. He grabbed my wrist and tugged me to the side, nearly making me fall off.

"Augh!"

"Let go of her, you damned fool," Walker snarled as he nudged the black horse in the opposite direction.

"Help!"

"*You* let go of her! It's obvious she doesn't want to be near you." Farrell pulled me harder toward him until the top half of me was draped over his lap, while my lower half was held tight by Walker's arm around my waist.

"Someone, please, help me!"

"It is *not* obvious; she just admitted that I saved her. And she shoved my face in her breasts. Which she certainly wouldn't have done if she didn't want to be near me. Now let go of her!"

Farrell jerked at my arm. "She said she wanted off—"

"*I* will put her down if you just let go of her," Walker said stiffly.

Oh, lovely, they were fighting over me. Why couldn't they do it when I wasn't strung between two horses? I stared down at the ground that seemed a long, long way down, and swallowed hard. "Hey! Guys, I feel like a really big human wishbone here, and I don't think either horse likes having me half-on, half-off him—"

"Let go of her before you hurt her," Farrell demanded, the white horse doing a nasty little up-and-down move that made my teeth rattle. Farrell's grip slipped a bit as the horse sidled, leaving me hanging by my wrist between the two men.

"I had her first," Walker said, tightening his hold on my waist.

"You didn't want her," Farrell said. "You tried to throw her off that slug you call a horse."

"*Throw me off?*" I screamed to the ground.

"Whether or not I want her is not the issue. I had her first, so she's mine to put down. I realize that you don't have a shred of chivalry in your sun-bleached soul, but if you did, you'd know that the finders-keepers rule applies here, and let go of her."

"Okay, I'm starting to seriously panic now," I felt it wise to inform them, trying to quell the note of increasing hysteria in my voice. Whitey turned his head to give me the evil eye, then tried to bite my arm. "He's trying to eat me! Let me down, let me down, let me down!"

"Screaming like that isn't going to help," Walker lectured me. "Horses like calm, confident people. Screaming and yelling and whinging just upsets them."

I lifted my head and glared back over my shoulder at him. "Do you think maybe we could save the horse etiquette until a time when I'm not doing an imitation of a badminton net?"

"I was just trying to point out—"

"I know what you were trying to point out, but dammit, look at me!"

Both men eyed me stretched out between them.

"She doesn't look very comfortable. It's ridiculous for you to keep her when she wants away from you. Release her, Walker," Farrell ordered.

"Oh, for God's sake," I muttered.

"She's safer with me than with your ill-mannered stallion. Here, you, whatever your name is, let me have your arm." The white horse snapped at my head again as I clung with one hand to Farrell's leg, the other still behind held in his iron grip. "Christ, Farrell! Can't you control that loose cannon you're riding? Will you stop screeching, woman? You're not going to fall. My horse is too well mannered to do anything to harm you."

As the words left his mouth, a white-and-orange streak shot from the shadows of a tent to a stack of boxes about four feet high. The premonition of what the cat was going to do left my blood turned to ice, my jaw dropped open, and my heart in my momentarily speechless mouth. "Moth, no—" I screamed just as all twenty-four pounds of massive cat hit Marley's rump, feline claws extended to give him a better grip on the glossy, well-groomed horse.

Marley, not unreasonably, I'm willing to admit, took exception to such treatment. He rose up on his back legs, let out a disgusted snort, and slammed back down to earth with a teeth-jarring buck.

"Oh, very well, have it your way," Farrell said at the exact same moment, and released my arm as the white horse tossed up his head and jerked Farrell's leg from my tenuous grip. I did a beautiful half gainer off Marley as Walker released me in order to grab at the reins.

"Too well mannered to do anything to harm me, huh?" I asked as I lay on the ground and did a silent inventory of my arms and legs. My wrist stung, and my hip hurt from where it had been crushed against Walker's saddle before being pounded into the ground, but other than a few bruises, everything seemed to be in working order.

"Really, Walker, there are gentler ways of removing a woman from your lap," Farrell said, a self-righteous, solicitous smile touching his lips. "But I forget, you have so little experience in dehorsing people that I suppose one must make allowances. Please, my dear, I will help you—"

"No!" I screamed as the white horse's hooves danced toward me. I stopped checking my limbs and scrambled to my feet, absently brushing off my butt as I backed away from the white monster, now snorting and rolling its eyes at me. "You've done enough to help me, thank you."

"What the hell?" Walker, who had been busy controlling a fussy Marley, realized the cause of the problem. He turned in the saddle and scooped Moth up from where he was clinging to the horse's broad rump. Moth meowed a protest as Walker faced me with flared nostrils and a disgusted look that almost exactly matched the one on Marley's black face. "I take it this cat is yours?"

"No, he's not mine," I said feeling trapped between the huge black horse and the high-strung white one. I edged my way out from between them. "But I'm cat-sitting him for the next two weeks. Moth, you are a very bad cat! No kitty num-nums for you tonight!"

"Moth?" Farrell asked.

"It's short for Behemoth," I told him. He rewarded me with a flashy smile, but I refused to be swayed by the smile of a man who'd drop me just when I needed him.

"How amusing."

"You wouldn't be laughing if you were stuck with him." I turned back to Walker, who was trying to pull Moth off from where the cat was now riding his shoulders. "Moth! Come down here this instant."

"Farrell, are you all right? I heard yelling and

thought Lancelot might have run away with—" A
shortish, chunky young man with carroty red hair and
big round Harry Potter glasses dashed around the side
of one of the tents, skidding to a stop at the sight of
a cat riding on top of Walker. His eyes widened before
he shot a look out of the corners of them to where
Farrell was once again trying to gain control of his
fretting horse. "Eh . . . everything okay?"

"Get out of the way, you idiot," Farrell yelled as
the white horse (Lancelot? How trite could you get?)
tried to take a bite out of the red-haired man's shoulder. "Can't you see he's nervous?"

"Untrained is more like it," Walker said in his
lovely smooth English accent. My knees, which
wanted to go all swoony at his voice, were reminded
by my abused hip that he, too, had dropped me, and
after promising me I wouldn't fall. "You're a fool to
be racing him through here like that."

"When I want the opinion of a has-been farrier,
I'll ask for it." Farrell's mouth was tense, which was
probably the reason his words came out like icy little
bullets. He swung the demon horse's head toward the
cringing red-haired man. "Claude, you waste of oxygen, get the hell out of my way! Can't you see you're
making Lancelot nervous?"

"S-sorry. I thought you might need help. Oh, there's
a TV crew at the arena, and Simon thought you'd like
to know—"

"Television!" Farrell's head snapped around as he
looked toward the big buildings of the fairground.
"Why didn't you tell me that before? Here I sit wast-
ing my time with this third-rate shield tagger—if I've
told you once, I've told you a million times, the press
always comes first!"

"S-sorry," Claude stammered again, hurrying out of
the way as Farrell dug his heels into Lancelot's side.
The horse screamed, tossed his head, and lunged forward, barely missing Claude. I helped him up from
where he had stumbled.

"I was just trying to help," Claude mumbled as I brushed the dirt and dried grass from his navy-blue tunic. "I thought he might need help because of the new horse."

"That was very thoughtful of you," I said, picking from his shoulder a discarded candy wrapper. "Nice . . . er . . . outfit."

"It's our uniform," he said as he wiped his glasses on the hem of his tunic. "The Team Joust! uniform, that is. I'm a squire."

"Ah. A uniform," I said, walking around him to eye the many-colored patches on each arm and the front. "I guess that would explain all the sponsorship labels on it, huh? I mean, most medieval garb didn't have ads for iced tea companies, or equine supplements, or four-wheel-drive trucks."

"Team Joust! is the Californian team headed up by Farrell Kirkham, CEO and self-proclaimed world champion," a dry English voice informed us. "While all of the other teams perform at fairs and other venues in order to fund their appearances at competitions such as this, Farrell and his group don't have to sully themselves with anything so tawdry. Their corporate sponsors ask for nothing more strenuous than occasional appearances in commercial advertisements. If you wouldn't mind taking your cat now, I do have work to do. Real work, not preening myself in front of television cameras."

I looked up at the dark-haired, yummy-voiced man on the huge black horse. "Jealous?"

One glossy black eyebrow rose. "Of Farrell? No. I wouldn't wish to be him for all the sponsorship money in the world. If you will excuse me . . ." I stepped back, grabbing Moth as Walker rode by.

"Hey, I wanted to thank— Well, poop. He could have at least waited around for me to thank him."

"That's Walker for you," Claude said.

I turned to give him the eye. "You know him?"

"Walker McPhail? Sure, I do. Everyone on the

jousting circuit knows Walker. He's like one of the grand old men of the sport."

"He didn't look that old to me," I said, frowning. He looked to be my age, mid to late thirties, with dark hair, tiny little lines around his eyes, and one of those long English faces that are so fun to watch. He wasn't drop-dead gorgeous (except for his eyes), but he made a nice contrast to Farrell's over-the-top handsome, young, blond good looks. "So he's a jouster?"

"Nope. Gotta run. Farrell will have kittens if I'm not there to squire him in front of the press. See ya 'round."

Before I could ask anything more about Walker, Claude took off at a fast jog.

"Well, that was exciting," I said to Claude's disappearing figure. Moth meowed and bit my wrist. "Ouch! You monster. Fine, you want down? You can just walk on your own pudgy little legs."

I stuffed Moth back into the harness he'd slipped out of three times now, tightened the belly strap another notch, and snapped on the lightweight lead my aunt had given me with the promise that Moth loved to go on walks.

I grabbed a bottle of cold water, rubbed my hip, and gave Moth's leash a snap. "Come on, cat; we're going to go find us some more knights in tights. I wonder where Walker went?"

For those of you who've never been to a two-week-long international jousting competition held in conjunction with the world's largest Renaissance Faire, the environment can be a little overwhelming until you learn to just take everything with a really large grain of salt.

"Prithee, my fair lady, a good after the nooning hour to ye and your fine cat. Canst ye direct me to the nearest porta-privy?" A middle-aged, bearded man in a purple-and-green jester's hat stopped me as we came to the end of the field holding the tents.

"Sorry, I can't; I'm new here. But I imagine there

are bathrooms . . . um . . . privies over there, by . . .
uh . . . yonder snack bar."

"Thank ye, gentle lady," the jester man said, making a wobbly bow.

"Been at the mead a little early, no doubt," I said
as he staggered off toward one of the fairground snack
bars, now being run by a number of specialized food
vendors. The fairgrounds themselves had been given
over entirely to the Ren Faire and sporting competitions. Moth and I wandered down a row of wooden-
sided, open-fronted shelters that were being used by
vendors to hawk their wares. Since the Ren Faire itself
wasn't due to start until the following day, the vendors
now were laying out cloths, setting up their items, and
arranging very fanciful displays.

We walked past tables of scented candles in a jar,
wrought-iron jewelry, ceramic dragons, a chain-mail
and steel-plate armorer, a place that sold the tall, medieval pointy princess hats complete with sparkly veils,
and a dizzying array of shops featuring just about anything you could imagine: Wiccan magic, henna painting, temporary tattoos, real tattoos, a piercing booth,
leather clothing, medieval clothing, Scottish clothing,
swordmakers, glassblowers, and jewelry for your
hands, head, ears, wrists, ankles, bodice, waist, and
just about anywhere else you could hang something
from. Boomerangs sat alongside Viking gear, which
was next to a medieval candy maker selling pynade,
sugared violets, gingerbread, and cinnamon almonds.
There were people who would take your picture in
garb, people who would paint your face, back, and
arms with intricate Celtic designs, people who would
write you a sonnet and inscribe it on a piece of parch-
ment, people who would rent you garb for the duration of the Faire, people who would sell you a bodhran
(Celtic drum), guitar, or bagpipes, depending on your
preference. There were jesters and jacks-of-all-trades,
jugglers, fire-eaters, rogues and wenches, lads and
lasses, knights and their ladies, louts, wastrels, tarts,

alewives, noblemen and peasants, lords and squires, mercenaries, scoundrels, cads—all there with the intention of having fun, indulging in a little harmless playacting, and if the length of the line at the mead and ale tent was anything to go by, guzzling huge quantities of alcohol while doing so.

"Ceej was right about one thing," I told Moth as we stepped around a huge black Great Dane in a jester's hat that was relieving itself against a shrub. "Everyone here seems to love animals. The poor saps. Moth, no! Leave it! You can't possibly be hungry; you ate three times on the ride up here. Spit that out! Oh, all right, I'll buy you your own Ye Olde Corn Dogge."

Victim to the cat's demands, I stood in line at one of the more contemporary food booths and shared a corn dog with Moth before asking directions to the sports area.

"What sports are you wanting?" asked a man with slicked-back hair, a stylish goatee, and a purple silk shirt covered by a black pirate vest. He was in the act of setting up a booth of metal breastplates, both women's and men's. The women's had spikes for nipples, I couldn't help noticing. "Jousting, running the rings, swordplay, quintain, archery, spear placements, distance throw, Saracen's head, or the gauntlet?"

I blinked a bit stupidly. I thought there was just going to be jousting? I clung to the one thing that was vaguely familiar. "Um . . . jousting."

He pointed past a big building with red metal siding to a fenced field beyond. "Jousting is out in the practice field today. Tomorrow it will be in the arena. The swordplay and archery practice rings are to the left of the arena. The rings, spear work, and gauntlet are over there, by the racetrack."

"Thanks." Moth, who it turned out really did like going for walks (even if it was while he was strapped into a harness), strolled along happily next to me as we made our way past a couple of practice rings, normally used for horse shows and the like, now set up with archery butts, and circles for the swordplay. Moth wanted to investigate every pile of horse poop, but I kept him on a firm line to the big fenced practice oval behind the arena.

"There you are," CJ said as we walked toward the small stand of wooden bleachers that sat outside the ring. The ring was empty, and the bleachers bare except for CJ. She was standing next to a box of equipment—swords, chain mail, and helmets. "I wondered where you had gotten to. You don't have your Wench pin on! How will people know you're a Wench without it? Honestly, Pepper, I can't take you any-where!"

"How, indeed. What a great tragedy that would be. Oh, stop muttering threats; I have it right here." I tucked Moth's leash under my elbow as I rooted around in the small leather pouch attached to the long leather belt that hung at a rakish angle around my hips. "Here, see!" I held up the small brass pair of lips that was the official League of Wenches pin.

"Well, put it on, silly!" I didn't do it fast enough, because CJ grabbed the pin and affixed it to my bod-ice. "Do you have your favors?"

I peered into the pouch. "Are those the little wooden sheep and bee and horse pins?"

"Yes. You give the sheep pins to new acquain-tances, the bees to any vendors who let you have free samples of their wares—honey, get it?—and the horses to any rogues and knights who catch your eye."

"Ah. Okay. What about these?" I pulled out a small laminated set of cards bedecked with the LOW logo and the words *Entitles bearer to one free smooch from originating Wench.* "What am I supposed to do with them?"

"Give them out to people you want to kiss, stupid!" CJ rolled her eyes as a thin, small woman with shock-ing pink short-cropped hair strolled over. She was dressed in a knee-length forest-green leather jerkin, cream linen shirt, black leggings with green cross garters, and fringed ankle boots. Strung over her shoulder was a beautiful oak bow and a leather quiver filled with green-tipped arrows. "Hullo, CJ. Glad to see you again. Have you seen Patrick anywhere? Little rotter disappeared on me when I wanted him to mend my mail."

"Vandal?" CJ shook her head. "He was here, but he ran off after one of the ale girls. This is Pepper Marsh, my cousin from the States. Pepper, this is Fenice Carson. She's part of Three Dog Knights."

I did a mental double take. "Huh?"

"Three Dog Knights. It's the name of our jousting company," Fenice explained, offering her gauntleted hand. I shook it, wondering if someone else liked old 1970s music. "Pleasure to meet you. Nice cat. We're performance jousters," she added, as if that explained everything.

"Uh . . . okay." I looked at CJ. She sighed and tugged me over to where Moth had gone into meatloaf mode on one of the bleacher seats.

"There are two kinds of jousters—competition and performance," CJ said quickly. "Most jousters you see here are performance jousters—men and women who put on scripted shows, work the Ren Faires, etcetera. The others are competitive jousters—they don't do shows; they only compete for the purses and titles."

"Ah. So the competition guys are the real jousters."

"Real, my arse," Fenice said, plopping down on the bench at my feet. "We train just as long and hard as the competition crowd—longer and harder, because we have to know how to unhorse someone without harming them, how to fall while wearing a full suit of armor, and how to hit marks. That lot just *thinks* they're better than us."

I looked to where she was waving a scornful hand. Beyond the nearest stable a collection of RVs was clustered around a huge white-and-blue striped tent. Emblazoned across the top of the tent was a pennant bearing one word: *Joust!*

"Farrell Kirkham and his team?" I asked.

"They're the worst of the lot," Fenice said with a disgusted curl to her lip. "Think their shite don't stink. Think they're better than us. You know what they call us? Ground pounders. Shield taggers."

"Yeah, I heard him say that. What's it mean?"

"A jouster who can't stay in his saddle," CJ answered. "It's not very nice."

"And not at all true. Every time we come up against the competition crowd, we clean their clocks," Fenice added. "They're just smug bastards because they don't have to perform to pay for their travel or horses or gear. They have *sponsors*."

She said the word like it was dirty.

"Ah. And your team . . . ?"

"Three Dog Knights—so named because of Walker's three dogs—performs at a number of fairs and schools. We also do corporate retreats. We have seven different shows," Fenice said proudly.

"Wow. So, you're part of the team with Walker McPhail?"

CJ, who had been standing on the seat next to me, peering around with a hand shading her eyes (sunglasses were verboten to Wenches unless they had a medical excuse), looked down with an odd look on her face. "How do you know Walker?"

I grimaced and rubbed my hip. "I . . . uh . . . ran into him on the way in from the tent city. I met Farrell, too. He seemed a bit intense." *Intense* was the nicest thing I could think to say about him.

"He's a snake in the grass," Fenice said. "Oh, there's Patrick. *Patrick!*" Fenice bellowed the name and waved her arm at a man in knight's garb who was leaning against a fence railing and flirting with a woman holding a tray of empty beer steins. "Damn him, he's got another Wench. . . . Patrick!"

Fenice took off at a lope toward the duo.

"Husband?" I asked CJ, who was back to peering around the area.

"Hmm? Oh, no. Brother. He prefers to be called Vandal. He's her twin brother, actually, although you wouldn't know it. They don't look at all alike. There he is! My lamb!" CJ pulled an embroidered triangle of cloth from her poofy chemise sleeve and waved it in the air. Across the ring, Walker—on foot this time—had opened up the gate into the ring. A man in a full suit of jousting armor (the heavy plated stuff) rode into the ring on a big piebald horse, followed by another armored man on the black horse named Marley.

"That's Butcher there," CJ said excitedly, waving her cloth favor. The man on the piebald gelding lifted a hand and waved back. "Isn't he the yummiest thing you've ever seen?"

"Well . . . I can't actually see him," I pointed out. "He's in full armor. All I can see is that he has to be very strong to wear all that. How much does that weigh?"

Walker and another man with spiky blond hair entered the ring, each bearing a number of long wooden lances.

"CJ! It's been forever, luv." A woman approached us from the other side, stopping to give CJ a kiss on the cheek and a big bear hug. "Is this your cousin? Hello, I'm Bliss."

"Pepper," I said.

"That your cat?" Bliss, an older woman with an ash gray pageboy, bent to pick up Moth. She was in sweats, the first person at the Faire I'd seen who wasn't in garb, but Moth didn't seem to mind. He gave her his patented slitty-eyed look for a few seconds, then graciously lifted his chin and allowed her to scratch his neck. "Nice puss!"

"No, he's not, and no, he's not. He's CJ's mom's cat. We're stuck with him for the next two weeks."

"*You're* stuck with him," CJ reminded me. "Oh, good, they're going to do the heavy-armor jousting. The plate armor weighs about thirty pounds, Pepper.

But it looks good on Butcher, don't you think? He plays the Fearsome Black Knight."

"Doesn't do as good a job at it as Walker did," Bliss said, sitting down next to us, a contented, purring Moth in her arms. I toyed with the idea of offering her money to take over cat-watching for me, but realized the few bucks I had wouldn't go very far in buying her off.

"That's because Butcher is an inherently sweet lamby-pie, and Walker is . . . well, Walker."

"Why isn't he jousting now?" I asked, watching as the men in the ring set the lances along one side. The two men on horseback were walking their horses around to calm them, each keeping to one end of the oval. Down the center a long white wooden fence had been set up. I figured that must be the list, what they called the actual area the jousters used. As a dedicated reader of medieval romances, I thought it was kind of cool seeing one in person. I summoned up the memories of every medieval I'd ever read as Walker and the blond man separated, each taking a lance to one of the jousting knights.

Bliss gave me a long look, her brown eyes almost black as she examined me. "It's a long story," was all she said.

I was about to tell her I had the time to listen to it, when CJ stood up and started jumping up and down, yelling, "Go, Butcher, go! Knock him on his ass!"

I didn't see a starting signal, but all of a sudden the horses were thundering down the list, the two jousters swinging their lances from an upright position to a horizontal one angled above their horses' necks, the almost ten-foot-long wooden poles bobbing up and down for a few seconds as each was aimed dead-on to the man riding toward it.

"Oh, my god!" I gasped, sucking in my breath a moment before the lances connected. There was a great *crack!* as both lances struck the curved metal plate on the approaching knight's shoulder, splinters flying off of both shattered tips. CJ's boyfriend, Butcher, was thrown backward in his saddle by the impact, but he held on. The other man wasn't nearly as lucky. He was flipped backward like Butcher, but unlike the bigger knight, he lost his grip on the reins, his broken lance flying over the horse's rump as he sagged drunkenly off the right side, the animal's momentum throwing him further off balance until he hit the ground with a tremendous crash.

Chapter Three

"Ouch on rye!" I winced in sympathy when the cantering horse stepped on the downed man's leg as it continued to the end of the list where the spiky-haired man caught it. "Is that what jousting is really like? How . . . how . . . *manly!* Is that guy hurt? Are the lances supposed to break like that? And I thought they jousted with shields? My God, that must hurt like hell to have those lances plowing into your chest like that. Oh, look, he's moving!"

CJ was still jumping up and down waving her cloth favor, blowing kisses to the armored Butcher, who had ridden back to the other end of the list, tossing his broken lance into a corner. "Yay, Butcher! You're the best, snuggle-bunny!"

"Yes, that's what jousting is really like," Bliss answered, watching with amazing calmness as Walker strode over to the twitching fallen man. To my surprise, rather than calling for an aid unit or even checking him for injuries, Walker just stood over the guy, asked him a couple of questions, then hauled him to his feet. "It's not really that manly—lots of women joust very successfully. I do. It's all a matter of timing, you see. You can take down even the biggest opponent if you have the speed and skill to do so. It's rather like martial arts, but on horseback."

"Is he all right?" I asked as the downed knight staggered sideways toward Walker. "Shouldn't someone be doing something?"

"Oh, trust me, Walker is," Bliss said with laughter in her voice. "He's letting Bos know in no uncertain terms exactly what he did wrong."

I stared at her for a moment with my jaw hanging down around my knees, then I pointed toward where the two men were walking toward Marley. "Walker is lecturing the guy who got hurt?"

"Reaming him up one side and down the other," CJ agreed as she sat back down next to us. She must have seen the appalled look on my face, because she patted my hand. "That's his job, silly. He's the team coach."

"And squire, and farrier, and groom, and stable hand, and harness cleaner, and medic, when it's needed. The only thing Walker doesn't do is mend the costumes, and that's only because Bos and his partner Geoff do them," Bliss said with a nod to the spiky-haired man who was standing next to Marley as Walker helped the knight named Bos back into the saddle.

"That's a big horse," I said, distracted for a moment by the fact that Geoff's head just barely reached Marley's withers.

"Seventeen hands. He's half Percheron. Walker's been training him the last week. Says he's a real goer," Bliss answered, her fingers still working their cat magic on Moth.

"So Walker and Geoff are squires?" I asked, still trying to work it out in my mind.

CJ shook her head while Bliss nodded.

"They are, but everyone on the team acts as squire at one time or another," Bliss said, attempting to explain the confusion. "We don't have enough team members, you see. There's just Walker, Butcher, Fenice and Vandal, Bos and Geoff, and me. Seven, not ten, but Walker doesn't joust anymore, so it's really six."

"Uh . . ." I hated to sound stupid and ask to have everything explained, but there was no help for it.

"Most teams have ten members," CJ said, obviously taking pity on my confusion. "Each team has to produce four jousters, four swordfighters, and two archers. All the teams but Three Dog Knights have one person for each competition, plus the support staff of grooms, squires, and varlets."

"We're short, so everyone doubles in the sports, and also works as squires, etcetera," Bliss added. "Butcher jousts and swordfights; Fenice is the best archer in northern England and is just as good with a sword; Bos jousts and is the backup swordfighter, although he's not really very strong in either, which is why Walker has been working so hard with him. Vandal jousts and hacks away at people with a sword, and I joust and also participate in the archery contest."

"I had no idea women could be jousters," I said, watching as the two men rode to opposite ends of the lists. Walker called out some instruction to Bos, but I couldn't hear anything other than a threat to have his guts for garters if he did something foolish like he did the last time. "Wow. Walker is really mad at him, huh?"

"He should be," Bliss said, handing me Moth as she stood up. "Bos let his lance dip. He came close to harming Butcher's horse. Walker was just letting him know that if he did it again, he'd be off the team."

"Ouch. I don't think it's right that a horse should be hurt, but it seems like kind of an ironic thing to be mad about when the whole point of jousting is to knock the other guy off."

"Do you know what they used to do to a knight who hit a horse with his lance?" Bliss asked as she stepped down over the bleachers.

I shook my head.

"They'd shoot him with crossbows. The first rule of any joust—performance or competition—is that if you hit a horse with a lance, you're history. Drummed out of the jousting community. No second chance, no appeal, nothing. It's all over." She smiled at both me and CJ, then headed off toward the stables behind the practice ring, pausing by the rails to have a quick word with Walker.

"Wow," I said, watching as the men prepared to joust again.

"I told you they loved their animals," CJ said smugly, then stood up and yelled out encouragement to the big man in black armor.

They ran another course, but this time I was prepared for what was going to happen. Both jousters kept their seats, although Bos lost his lance. Walker went out to both men and evidently told them what they did right and wrong. I felt a little sorry for Bos — Walker spent just a minute with Butcher, who nodded his head several times, but Bos got a lengthy lecture before Walker clapped a hand on Bos's leg and gave Marley a pat.

Over the course of the next half hour, they jousted five more times, with Butcher going over his horse's butt once, and Bos being tossed three times. You'd think watching the same thing over and over again would be boring, but it was just the opposite. Each time the great horses jumped forward, each time the lances were leveled at the opponents' chests, my heart jumped into my mouth.

"Now I know why tournaments were so popular in the Middle Ages," I said as I sat down after a particularly spectacular crash on Bos's part, having just stood and screamed my support for him (I felt it only polite, since CJ was yelling like mad for Butcher). "This is fabulous stuff!"

"If you think so now, you should see us in all our finery," a smooth English voice said. "Then we're not just fabulous; we're spectacular. CJ, what a delight it is to see you again." The handsome dark-haired young man named Vandal stood with one booted foot propped up on the edge of the bleacher. "You look lovely as ever. Might I hope that you have seen the error of your ways and are ready to bestow upon me your fair hand and fairer body?"

His eyes danced wickedly as their gaze lingered first on CJ's bodice (her bosom had distinct hemispheres, unlike my shelf of solid breast), then on mine. His eyes bugged out a bit when he got to me, but eventually he managed to drag his gaze off my shelf.

"Not on your life, Vandal. You know my heart and all the other parts belong to Butcher," CJ answered, blowing him a kiss nonetheless.

He made a show of catching it and sighing dramatically. I had to give him credit: He was a really handsome guy, just my idea of what a knight should look like: tall with waist-length black hair pulled back in a ponytail, a charming goatee, not in the least bit effeminate in a worn leather jerkin and green tights. . . . Oh, all right, it was the way the tights clung to his long legs, and the jerkin opened to expose a smooth, muscled chest that *really* had me paying attention.

"Butcher is an infidel. I can only hope the time comes when you realize just how cruel you are to wrong one who has sworn to you his eternal love. You must be Pepper. My darling sister told me there was a new toothsome Wench on the grounds. My lady, I am your servant." He swept me a low, elaborate bow. "Might I hope that your heart, at least, is not claimed by any knave present?"

"Nope, I'm heart free," I said with an answering smile, sliding CJ a questioning look. I did a little eyebrow semaphore to let her know that I was perfectly willing to entertain the idea of Vandal as a mate if she, the queen of matchmaking, thought it was a good idea. Her eyebrows signaled back uncertainty.

"Lovelier words I have never heard, unless they be 'I name thee tourney champion,'" Vandal said, possessing himself of my hand in order to kiss it. Moth, who had been disgusted with the fact that I kept leaping up to cheer on the jousters, was sitting next to me wearing an extremely pained look on his white face. When Vandal reached for my hand the cat hissed and flattened his ears back. Vandal snatched his hand back quickly.

"I'm sorry," I apologized, clamping a hand down over Moth's head. He glared at me from between my fingers. "He's a very *bad* cat."

"Protective of his lady. An admirable quality in one so . . . erm . . . diminutive," Vandal said, eyeing Moth's rotund sides. "Might I beg for the honor of your company later tonight, say, at the dinner hour? I know of a perfectly divine inn where the mead flows like a honeyed river, and the roast boar is most delectable."

"Does he talk like that all the time?" I asked CJ, amazed that anyone could get so much into his persona.

"Yes. Don't buy that line about honeyed rivers. He uses it in other contexts, too, which has given him the title of Champion of the Medieval Pickup Lines."

"I am beset by a desire in my loins, dearest lady, and only you can quench its fire," Vandal said in a soft, seductive tone, his dark blue eyes going into flirting overtime.

Moth growled at him.

"Alas, brave sir knight," I said, getting into the swing of the thing (when in Rome and all that), "yonder kitty finds your loins unworthy of my extinguishing attempts. Mayhap another time I could tame?"

"*Any*time," Vandal all but cooed, and I think he would have braved Moth's displeasure to kiss my hand, but just then Walker, who was standing a few yards behind him in the practice ring, yelled his name.

"Stop slobbering on the woman and suit up, Vandal. You and Bliss are next." Walker's velvety voice had an underthread of steel that sent a little shiver up my back and down my arms.

Vandal slid him a questioning look, but nodded before giving both CJ and me another bow, excusing himself to go don his mail.

"He wasn't doing anything wrong, Walker," CJ called as Vandal headed at a trot for the stable. "Just flirting. You know Vandal—he doesn't mean any of it."

"He might not with you," Walker answered with a dark look at me, "but that's because he knows Butcher would have his balls on a platter if he touched you. Other women aren't excluded from his less than honorable intentions."

"Wow, a man who knows what honor is," I said facetiously. I don't know what it was about Walker that had me wanting to alternate between a full swoon and teasing the smug look right off his face, but I just couldn't refrain from tweaking his nose a little, so to speak. I've always been partial to a man who can parry words as well as a sword. "I wonder if we can clone you?"

He glared at me. I smiled back. "You wouldn't, by any chance, be feeling protective of me since you saved my life?"

"Hell, no!"

"He saved your life?" CJ asked, looking from me to Walker and back. "You said you ran into him. How did he save your life?"

"He rode in just like a knight saving a lady from a dastardly villain, only the villain was a big, mean white horse. One moment I was a nanosecond away from a horribly painful death; the next I was crushed up against Walker's manly chest. It was very romantic." I sighed, peeking from the corner of my eye to watch Walker.

"It was *not* romantic," he answered, looking disgusted at the very idea.

"Yes, it was." I batted my eyes at him, thoroughly enjoying the horrified look that flitted across his face at my next words. "A lesser woman might have swooned into his strong arms and begged him to make her his woman, but alas, what with him and Farrell insisting on trying to stretch me on some sort of equine rack, I had no chance to swoon and beg. Perhaps later?"

"I'm busy," he said quickly, and almost ran back to where Vandal and Bliss were coming into the ring.

"That was fun." I giggled to CJ as I watched him walk away. My mind went a little girlie on me there for a couple of seconds while it admired the natural saunter in his stride, not to mention the long line of his strong legs. Unfortunately his tunic hid all the good parts, but I allowed myself a moment of fantasy about just what his backside would look like before I realized that CJ wasn't giggling with me. "Wasn't that fun?"

"I don't know," she said, a faint frown between her brows.

"I was flirting, Ceej. You told me I have to be proactive, so that's what I'm doing. Flirting is step one in the hunt for a mate."

"You didn't flirt with Vandal," she said slowly, looking at me as if it were the first time she'd seen me. "Every woman who can breathe flirts with Vandal. Every woman but you."

I shrugged. "He's just so obvious. Where's the sport in that?" I let my eyes drift back to the broad-shouldered, long-legged, smooth-voiced man in the ring. "I prefer my prey to be a little more of a challenge."

"Yes, but—" CJ bit the words off without continuing.

"But what?"

"But Walker isn't . . . he's not . . . he's just . . ."

"What? Married? Involved with someone? Gay? A *eunuch?*"

"No to all of those—at least, the last time Butcher wrote to me Walker wasn't involved with anyone."

"Then what's your objection? Honestly, Ceej, here

you are ready to do the matchmaking thing, and you get all dismal on me when I do a little constructive flirting."

"He's not right for you," she blurted out quickly, clutching my arm. "There, are you happy? You made me say it. He's not right for you. He's not the one you should end up with. He'll only bring you unhappiness. Look somewhere else, Pepper. I don't want to see you hurt, but pain is all you'll get from Walker."

"You can say that again," a smiling, auburn-haired, very tanned woman said as she stopped at the bottom of the bleachers. She wrinkled her perfect nose at CJ. "I know you, don't I? You're one of the British team, yes?"

"No. My boyfriend is," CJ answered, giving me an unreadable look.

"Oh, yes," the woman said. She held out her hand and gave us a bright smile. "I'm Veronica Tyler."

CJ shook her hand politely. "This is my cousin, Pepper Marsh. I'm CJ Brand."

"How nice. Do you joust?" Veronica asked me.

I raised my eyebrows. "Who, me? No! Don't know the first thing about it."

"Oh." Her emerald gaze raked over me, making me extremely aware that I was hot, sweaty, my hair was pulled back in a simple scrunchy, and I had a shelf bosom, whereas she looked cool and stylish with perfectly coiffed short 'do, a green-and-cream-striped tunic with a tiny palm tree emblem over her left breast, matching cream tights, and boots that went up to midthigh. "I assumed if you were Walker's new squeeze that you'd joust."

"I'm not his squeeze," I said, pulling Moth closer to me to make room for her. "I just met him an hour ago."

"No? Mmm. You're just his type. He loves redheads." She touched her auburn hair with a long-nailed hand, then sat on the other side of the cat and watched the ring for a moment. In it, Bliss and Vandal were taking their positions.

I wanted to ask her if she was making such obvious insinuations for any particular reason, but decided that it wasn't cool to be so suspicious right off the bat. Too, it wasn't as if I had any right to be jealous or put out by her obvious (and assumedly ex-) girlfriendhood. I wasn't serious about flirting with Walker.

There's nothing wrong with investigating all possibilities, Wise Inner Pepper said as I thought back to the feeling of being held on Walker's lap. I ignored my inner voice, telling myself I wasn't really *interested* in Walker; I just liked to tease him. I was only amusing myself, indulging in a little light flirtation to pass the time, a way to keep my sadly out-of-practice hand in the action before my knight in shining armor rolled up and swept me off to his castle.

Wise Inner Pepper snorted at that thought, leaving me to distract her with other things. "How come Fenice and Vandal aren't wearing suits of armor? And why do they have shields, but Butcher and Bos didn't?"

"Light armor," Veronica said, leaning forward to prop her chin on her hand. "For light armor you joust in chain mail, and strike your blow on your opponent's shield rather than their breastplate or grand guard. This is French, so they use shields."

"French what?" I asked, wondering if there was a guidebook on jousting I could read.

"French style of jousting. There are seven different styles, each one slightly different. Some use light armor and shields; others use full armor and no shields."

"I take it you do some jousting?" I couldn't help but ask.

She smiled. "Darling, I don't just do *some jousting,* I win."

"I've heard of you," CJ said suddenly. "You're the

woman who organized the team of all-women jousters. Californians, aren't you?"

"The Palm Springs Jousting Guild," Veronica said with a practiced hair flip and another white-toothed smile. She could have been an actress, she was so perfect. "This is our first official international competition. I've competed for the last few years, naturally, but this is the first time the team has competed together. We're quite good, you know."

"Wow, a whole team of women? Good for you!" I said.

"Thank you. I hope I can count on your support when . . ." Her words stopped for a moment as Walker gave the signal, and Bliss and Vandal dug their heels into their horses' sides. There was a moment of a dull rumble as the horses charged toward each other, then a massive crash as the lances met the shields, and the shattered lance tips went flying. ". . . we compete. Bliss is very good," Veronica said, her voice losing a smidgen of its self-confidence. "She must have been training this summer."

"They all have," CJ said proudly.

"Except Walker," Veronica said with another smile.

"Yes, well . . . that goes without saying," CJ answered.

"Why—" I started to ask, but just then a group of laughing men armed with a couple of coolers of beer rounded the end of the bleachers, called out greetings in a number of languages, cracked a few jokes at the jousters in the ring, then took over the bleacher in a swarm of beer-enlivened good humor.

"They're the Norwegian team," CJ whispered before I even had a chance to ask her. One of the men, a big blond Viking sort, shoved a bottle of beer in my hand and plopped down beside me. Moth flattened his ears at the man. "They're very nice, but they do like their beer. Stay away from them after dark."

"Why, do they get grabby then?" I whispered back, nodding and pretending to drink my beer when my seatmate asked me something in a language I didn't understand just before downing the contents of his bottle in one gulp.

A sonic belch reverberated to the left of me.

"No," CJ answered as I glared at the man next to me. He grinned and reached for another bottle. "That's when they take wagers on things, like who can projectile-vomit the furthest. Trust me, you don't want to be near their camp after dark."

"Wagers!" a dark blond, red-bearded Viking beyond CJ cried. "Yes, we take wagers. Tomas, what do you wager that Vandal won't keep his seat the next pass, eh?"

And so they were off. For the duration of the training session, they wagered with extreme good nature on everything—not just whether or not the jousters would unhorse their opponents, but which direction the lance tips would fly, which direction the jouster would lean after a hit, and once, whether or not Bliss's lovely big gray mare was going to poop or not.

Veronica left shortly after the Vikings arrived, inviting us both to visit the Palm Springs team headquarters to meet the rest of the team. "We're in the green-and-cream-striped tents with the big plastic palm trees out front," she said, pointing vaguely toward the tent city. She paused before leaving, her head tipping to the side as she gave me another once-over. "Do come by later. You don't live near Palm Springs, do you?"

"No, Seattle. Why?"

"You've got a jouster's physique—very . . . *sturdy*. You'd probably be a divine jouster if you put your mind to it."

"Sturdy?" I asked the Viking next to me as she strolled off. "Did you hear that? Did she just call me fat?"

He leered at my breast shelf. "Sturdy means strong, yes? Is good?"

"I suppose. At least she didn't call me chunky. Or worse yet, husky."

"That's it, show's over for the Three Dog Knights," CJ said as Walker and his team members left the ring. "I'm going to back to their camp. Want to come, or are you and Torvald there getting it on?"

The bearded Viking leered again and grabbed my knee. I stood up quickly with Moth in my arms (staggering only slightly, which is amazing considering the cat weighs as much as a small Shetland pony). "Sorry, I have to take the cat for his afternoon walk."

Half of the Norwegian team went off to take their turn in the practice ring, while the other half settled back to enjoy the show.

"When do Farrell and his team have their practice?" I asked CJ as she walked back to the tent with me so Moth, who refuses to heed the call of nature while he's on a leash, could use his litter box and have his dinner. "I'd like to see him joust."

"Oh, they use the warm-up ring. All the Americans and Canadians do."

"How come?"

CJ unzipped the tent and did a little makeup repair while I stuffed a cold wet cloth down my bodice and sighed with pleasure. "Quarantine laws. The foreigners can't bring their horses in and take them home again because of quarantine laws. So they get loaner horses from people around the area.That's why they come a week early, to work with the horses and learn their ways and do any necessary training. Because they're at a disadvantage working on horses that aren't their own, they get the bigger practice ring to compensate."

"Ah. I suppose that makes sense." We chatted for a moment with people passing by, heading for their own tents to change clothing or grab food for dinner; then CJ snagged a package of hot dogs, one of frozen hamburgers, and a couple of packages of buns.

"Come on, I'll show you where the Three-DK tents are."

I tried to lock Moth into the tent, figuring he'd be

ready for a postdinner snooze, but he started scratching at the material the second I zipped up the door, so I ended up putting his harness on.

"You're putting a crimp in my style, cat," I said as I scooped him up and ran across the field to catch up with my cousin. "Hey, Ceej, wait up, I'm lugging his majesty."

She stopped and waited for me, rolling her eyes when I set Moth down. "Honestly, the way you coddle that cat . . . I thought you didn't like him?"

"I don't. He deliberately dribbled cat food on my foot and kicked the lid off his litter box so the litter sprayed all over my sleeping bag."

"You sure keep him around you a lot for someone who doesn't like him."

I glared down at the big white cat walking alongside me. "He's a great big hairy pain in the butt."

"Methinks the lady doth protest too much," CJ said in her best Shakespearean voice.

"Methinks the lady hath no other choice. Hey, what do you know about Veronica? Was she really . . . er . . . you know. With Walker?"

CJ shrugged and raised her hand when a couple of people sitting around a campfire called out a greeting. "They're minstrels from Ottawa. Nice people, but never get into a singalong with them. They don't know the meaning of the word *enough*."

I smiled and waved at the minstrels, following as CJ weaved her way through the seemingly endless tent city. Smoke from various barbecues mingled with the exhaust from the food vendors, making my stomach growl. I dragged my mind from the need for food to the need for information. "You said you've heard of her. Veronica, I mean. What have you heard?"

CJ looked a bit evasive, which really made me curious. "Not much, just that a bunch of rich society babes had formed their own jousting troupe. Word is they do a lot of charity stuff, and donate all their winnings to a children's organization. There they are! Lamby-pie!" CJ squealed and launched herself at the man who was sitting in a lawn chair.

Moth lunged forward, all but dragging me into the circle of people collected around a couple of barbecue grills and coolers.

"Moth, stop it! Heel! Excuse me, I hope I didn't hurt your toe— Moth! Get down off him!"

Clearly unaware of how a proper cat maintains an air of dignity and uninterest in the people around him, Moth hauled me through the group of people and leaped up into a startled Walker's arms. He dug his claws into Walker's tunic, quickly scaling him and alighting on his shoulders, just like Walker was some sort of human scaffolding put there for feline entertainment.

"I'm so sorry; he seems to have a little crush on you," I said, tugging on the leash to get Moth down. "Come along, you horrible beast."

Walker grimaced as Moth fought the leash. "It's all right; he's not doing any harm there."

"Oh." I unsnapped the leash, then stood looking at Walker, more than a little awed by what I saw. On a horse he was impressive. In a practice ring, he was intimidating. Standing just a few feet away from me, the setting sun turning his hair a glossy ebony, he was magnificent. He was a few inches taller than me, and had shoulders big enough for a monster like Moth to settle onto comfortably, and a long, angular, English sort of face with extremely expressive eyes. He wasn't handsome the same way Farrell was, but his face was interesting. I liked watching his eyes, and the way his lips moved when he talked. I also liked his softly blunted squared chin, the sharp angle of his jawline, the faint shadowing of whiskers darkening already tanned skin. I had the worst urge to just taste that lovely spot where his jaw connected behind his ear. . . .

"Why are you staring at me?" he asked, the low voice rubbing against me like the softest silk. It took me a minute to stop fantasizing about nibbling on his neck to realize what he had said.

"Oh . . . uh . . . am I?"

His brows pulled together in a frown. "Yes, you are. I'd like to know why."

I gave him my best smile. "I like looking at you."

His eyes got huge at that, and I would have said more, I would have told him about how I liked the shape of his jaw and chin, but CJ was trying to get my attention.

"Pepper, this is my lamb. Isn't he the most gorgeous thing you've ever seen?" CJ, petite little five-foot-two CJ, hung off the arm of a huge man. He had to be at least six-foot-six, and if I was built like a brick oven, he was an entire bakery. His face was pitted from a severe case of acne in his youth, and somewhere along the line he'd had his nose broken and never set quite right. He held out a huge hand for me to shake. It wasn't until I looked into his soft brown eyes that I saw the gentle man inside him that had attracted my cousin.

"Pleasure to meet you," he said in a low bass rumble that was just as deep as Walker's, but had none of the latter's goose-bump factor. "Ceej has told me a lot about you. Glad you could join us this year."

"Thanks, I'm looking forward to watching the competition. I've never seen jousting before, but it looks like a blast. Is it hard to learn?"

"Not hard, but it takes practice," Butcher said with a smile that turned his face from gruesome to delightful. "A lot of practice, if you'd be noticing all the falls we took today."

"I just assumed that was because you were riding horses you weren't used to."

"Yes, that's it exactly; that's what we keep telling Granddad here, but will he listen to us? No," Vandal said as he emerged from a tent, giving the Moth-clad Walker a wide berth as he took my hand in his, indulging in a little palm tickling before he kissed my knuckles.

"That's because it's not true," Walker said, one hand absently scratching Moth's chest. The big cat's eyes were closed in sheer delight, his purr throbbing in the soft air of the summer evening. "The horses are fine; it's you lot who need the practice."

"Granddad?" I asked Vandal.

"Vandal," Walker said with an obvious warning in his voice.

Vandal nodded to Walker. "Our fearless leader. We call him that because he's so—"

"Vandal!"

"—cautious," he finished with an insolent grin. "But enough of that knavish one. How charming you look with the fire of the sun dancing in your . . . erm . . . fiery locks."

"You're really good," I told him. "Do you have to practice at that roguish smile, or does it come naturally?"

Everyone around us laughed. Vandal waggled his eyebrows at me and made a pretty bow to everyone else.

"I think you've met just about everyone," CJ said, looking around. "That's Bosworth Bale over there by the stable, and the guy with the water bucket is his partner, Geoff. Fenice you know, and talking to her are Gary and Ben. They're from Whadda Knight, a jousting and steel combat troupe out of Oregon."

The two men sitting in close conversation with the pink-haired Fenice were in chain mail, each clutching a bottle of beer. They nodded a greeting, then went back to their quiet conversation.

"The others you'll meet as they show up. We usually have a lot of fun at night. Kind of a potluck picnic thing, where everyone brings a few bottles and some steaks and hamburgers," CJ said. She rustled around the barbecue grill, chatting brightly with the people who strolled by, most of whom stopped to say hello, a few who dropped into chairs and joined the conversation. Everyone was very friendly and included me in their conversations, but I couldn't help feeling like an outsider. I didn't know the in jokes, and I didn't understand the terminology, who the people were they were discussing, or even what the past tournaments signified in discussion. From time to time I was aware of Walker's silver-eyed gaze on me, his attention itching my skin like an irritating sunburn.

"Do you ride?" Butcher asked me suddenly.

I was standing on the outskirts of the circle, watching everyone laugh and talk and joke, while CJ and Vandal manned the grill, turning out copious quantities of hamburgers and hot dogs. Fenice and her two attendant Americans went out and returned with big tubs of potato salad, beans, and pasta salads, which they were now arranging on a couple of card tables that someone had produced. My stomach grumbled as I turned to face Butcher. "Do I ride? I used to. I was raised with horses—my mother was crazy about them. I haven't ridden in a while, though. Mom had to sell her horses when she moved to Belize to take care of underprivileged animals."

"Ah. So she's one of those charity workers?"

I gave him a wry smile. "No, just a vet who likes to help the underdogs. Literally."

"World needs more people like that," he said with an answering smile, and I thought to myself how lucky CJ was to have found him. "We ought to put you up on a horse. You have the look of a jouster."

Instantly my hackles went up. "Why, because I look *sturdy?*"

Evidently Butcher missed both my glare and the way I spit out the last word. "That, and you look like you could take a hit and not lose your seat. Walker! What do you say we get Pepper up on Cassiopeia after supper? She rides, and she's interested in jousting."

Who, me? *Ack!* "No, I—"

Walker turned to give me a thin-lipped look. "She's afraid of horses."

It was the scorn in his voice that had me nipping my protest in the bud. "Oh! I am not!"

"You are, too. You screamed earlier."

"Well, of course I screamed! I was strung out between two horses, one of which was clearly planning to eat me for lunch."

"Horses don't eat people; they're herbivores," he said patiently, just like I was too stupid to know that.

"Most horses are, but that white monster Lancelot is the exception to the rule," I snapped back.

One glossy black eyebrow rose. "There are no bad horses, only bad owners."

"Oh, that is such bull!"

"You're not a good enough horsewoman to joust," he added with a self-righteous cock to his eyebrows.

Now, that really got my goat. I might not be horse crazy like everyone else at the Faire, but I had been riding for as long as I could remember. "It just so happens that I'm a very good rider. My grandfather rode on the Olympic team in 1952, and he taught my mother and me how to ride. So you can just take that 'not a good enough horsewoman' crap and shove it up your—"

"Pepper!" CJ yelled, waving a spatula at me. "Honestly, can't I leave you alone for two minutes without you picking a fight with Walker?"

I pointed at him. "He started it. He said I didn't know how to ride."

"That's not what I said. I simply pointed out that a woman who screams around horses and falls off them when they're standing still is not a person who should be thinking about jousting."

I whirled around to face him, the urge to wrap Moth's tail around his throat until his face turned red making my fingers twitch. "I fell because you dropped me when that big black monster bucked. He was *not* standing still."

"Marley bucked because your cat attacked him," Walker said, his gorgeous eyes narrowing. He took a step closer to me, probably thinking he could intimidate me with the sheer power of his size. *Ha!* Little did he know that sturdy old built-like-a-brick-oven Pepper didn't intimidate easily. I took two steps forward until we were standing toe-to-toe, madly squelching the part of my mind that was telling me to lean into him and just taste those thinned lips of his.

"Moth isn't my cat, and if your horse is so high-strung that he doesn't allow cats near him—"

"He's not high-strung in the least. He's a very well-mannered horse. It's my experience that horses—all horses—don't appreciate strange cats using them as a perch."

"Oh, so now you're an expert on everything to do with horses as well as jousting?"

He leaned forward, his breath fanning across my cheeks, Moth's slitted yellow eyes glaring at me as his body was slung up against the back of Walker's head. "Yes, as a matter of fact, I am an expert on horses as well as jousting. I'm a farrier. I have a great deal of experience with horses of all types, and unlike some people I could name, am not afraid to be around them."

"Really?" I crossed my arms under my bosom shelf and put on my best knowing smile. "For a man who couldn't control his mount, you're awfully cocksure. Tell me this—if you're such an expert, why wasn't that *you* out there jousting today?"

Everyone, and I mean *everyone* in the Three Dog Knights camp, went absolutely silent at my words. The jokers stopped in midjest, the chatters stopped with words caught on their tongues, Vandal stopped flirting in the middle of telling a pretty passing girl about the fire in his loins. Every single person there turned to statues. It was as if someone had flipped a switch and turned off all animation. The only sound was that of fat hissing as it dripped down onto the coals.

Walker's eyes glittered a silvery fury at me as everyone stared at the two of us standing close enough to be in an embrace. His body was rigid and tight with anger, and I regretted my hasty words. For some reason I didn't understand, they obviously cut him deeply.

"Yes, Walker, please do tell us all why it is you weren't out jousting with the rest of your so-called team," an amused voice drawled from behind me. Heads swiveled as Farrell strolled out from the shadow of a nearby tent. He was all in black: black doublet, black hose, black thigh-high pirate boots, and a black shirt with ruffly neckline and matching ruffles at the sleeves, a dearth of color that highlighted the brightness of his eyes and his sun-bleached long blond hair. He strolled forward, the setting sun turning his hair to molten gold. "The lady is curious, and I for one I would love to hear you admit the truth behind your cowardice."

"Don't you have something else to do, Farrell?" Walker asked in a tired voice. "Like waxing your body hair? Practicing your smile in front of a mirror? Giving yourself yet another meaningless championship title in an attempt to cover yourself in glory?"

The smug smile on Farrell's face held until Walker got to the last bit; then it cracked and anger flooded his eyes. "As a matter of fact, I do have something better to do than waste my time on a bunch of has-beens." He turned to me and flashed me the full wattage of his smile. "I have a damsel to rescue from tedium and mediocrity. My lady, if you will do me the honor of joining me for dinner, I would be happy to escort you from these drab surroundings to more convivial company and cuisine."

"Oh," I said, more than a little flattered by the offer. It wasn't often I had a handsome, dashing blond knight asking me to dinner. "Um . . . that's nice of you, but we were going to have dinner here."

"I'm sure your friends won't mind if I borrow you for a few hours," Farrell said politely.

Everyone in the Three Dog Knights camp stood as silent as statues, their eyes flickering between me and Farrell. No one said a word, but I was very much aware of a wall of hostility that had gone up at Farrell's arrival. He was not one of them, their wary expressions said. He was not welcome there. Despite his bravado, Farrell looked uncomfortable, no doubt aware that his presence had put a damper on things. In a way, I empathized with him—I was a stranger among them, too. But it was the look in Walker's eyes that left me with a clammy, cold feeling deep in my stomach.

"By all means, go with him," Walker said, his beautiful silver eyes positively glacial with scorn. "We wouldn't want to be accused of forcing you to rough it with us when you could be dining in splendor, courtesy of Farrell's many sponsors."

"It really galls you that so many companies have come forward to sponsor my troupe, doesn't it? Oh, but I forget, you've left such crass commercial concerns behind in your new career as a . . . failure, isn't it? Tsk," Farrell said, holding up his hand to stop Walker's protest before he could speak. "My mistake, the word is *farrier,* not failure, although the two can be so alike, can't they?"

"Do you think you two could have your pissing contest somewhere else? Our dinner is getting cold," CJ said in a deceptively mild tone of voice. Her eyes were angry, and Butcher stood next to her with a hand on her arm, as if he were holding her back. I thought she was angry at Farrell until her frown hit me. She glared as if I had done something wrong.

"Hey, I'm innocent here, I didn't do anything—" I started to tell her.

"Oh, just go have dinner with him," she said abruptly, then turned her back to me and poked at the hamburgers grilling on the portable grill, her shoulders twitching angrily.

I glanced around. Everyone's faces were closed, polite masks of disinterest. Obviously none of them cared what I did. They probably wouldn't even blink if I were to drop down dead right at their feet.

"Fine, if that's the way you want it . . ." I reached for Moth. Walker stepped backward so I was out of his reach before he plucked Moth from his shoulders and held the cat out to me, his eyes refusing to meet mine. I had a sudden urge to cry at the implied rejection, but I swallowed back the lump of tears as I set Moth on the ground and gave Farrell a watery smile. "Looks like I'm all yours."

Goose bumps went up my back at the flow of icy chill that emanated from Walker. Farrell flashed him a triumphant look before waving a graceful hand toward the opposite end of the tent city. "My team's rigs are this way."

"I'll see you later, Ceej?" I asked over my shoulder as I followed Farrell.

"I wouldn't count on that," she muttered without even turning around to face me.

The last sight I had of the camp as I left was of Walker's eyes glittering in the dying sun, his long face as unmoving as if it had been hewn out of rock. The lump of tears tightened my throat painfully until I reminded myself that I wasn't *really* interested in Walker, not *that* way, so his willingness to get me off his hands wasn't really a rejection.

It sure felt like one, though.

Chapter Four

"So what exactly is the story on Walker?" I asked Farrell a short while later. We were seated in an air-conditioned black-and-red RV, one of four RVs, all with California plates and the word *Joust!* written in fancy gold script along the sides. Farrell had told me that his sponsors paid for the team's RVs, so they could travel around the country in style and comfort. The sponsorship I didn't doubt for a moment—not only were the squires and varlets (the ground crew) wearing matching garb with sponsor patches on their arms, but the saddle that was sitting on a chair next to where Moth was flaked out also had sponsor emblems on it. I suppose if they could do it to race cars, a horse's tack was fair game as well.

"My sweet, I'm sure if we put our minds to it, we can come up with all sorts of other interesting topics of conversation. No, Claude, not that one, the iced champagne. And bring the salad before the scallops. How is your duck, Pepper?"

Claude shot Farrell an anguished look as he turned and retreated to the rear part of the RV, assumedly where Farrell kept his portable wine cellar. I glanced down at the smoked Muscovy duck appetizer on the hand-painted plate before me. "It's good. I've never had duck with a maple vinaigrette before. You really don't believe in roughing it, do you? And I'm sure

that there are all sorts of things that we can talk about,
but what I'd really like to know is why you keep taunting Walker about being a failure and a loser and all
that."

"You'll like the salad, as well. It's yellow tomato
and buffalo mozzarella with Nicoise olives and a delightful herb vinaigrette from my own recipe," Farrell
said with a knowing smile. "After that, we'll have tian
of grilled scallops—you do like scallops, don't you?—
and Parmesan risotto. As for roughing it, why should I
dine off charred-on-the-outside, undercooked-on-the-
inside hamburgers and canned beans when I can have
a romantic, well-cooked dinner for two?"

Farrell's RV was just as elegant as he was, done in
shades of black and gold. The dining area held a small
linen-covered table with real china and crystal wine-
glasses, embraced by a half-moon curved black suede
seat. Ice clinked in the back of the RV as Claude,
evidently Farrell's body servant as well as squire,
hunted for the champagne.

"I don't think dinner with the Three Dog Knights
would have been as bad as all that, and yes, I like
scallops, and this table is gorgeous, as is the food, but
why are you so anti-Walker? Have you known him
for long? And why are you guys always sniping at
each other?" I kept my tone light to deemphasize the
fact that I was grilling him.

He laughed and raised his hands in surrender, nodding when Claude thumped back with a bottle of
champagne covered in beads of water. "I can see
I will be unable to steer you to more interesting
topics until your curiosity is satisfied. Very good,
Claude, you may pour it. Salad next, when you are
through."

I quickly stuffed a piece of Muscovy duck into my
mouth after Farrell raised his eyebrows at the un-
touched plate before me. "Delicious."

"Mmm. Shall we have a little toast?" He waited
until I lifted my glass. "I believe it is traditional to

toast a lady's beauty when one is dining in such a manner, but in this instance I'm going to toast the winner of the tournament, for surely the lady in question will bestow him with the warmth of her smile and the charm of her presence in such a way that he will not fail to appreciate her beauty."

He clicked his glass against mine, sipping the champagne as I said, "Very nicely done, but you're assuming two things that well may not happen."

He raised his chin in a practiced hair flip that had his golden hair shimmering down his shoulders. "Really? What might those two assumptions be?"

"First, that a man will be the tournament champion. From what I've heard, there are several women jousters."

"True, and although some of them are very good, very good indeed, none have ever won the title of tourney champion when the world's top male jousters are competing."

Such complacency rankled. "You may find yourself surprised."

"Why, do you intend to joust against me?" The amusement in his eyes did a lot to dampen any interest I might have had in him as a prospective mate. *Besides,* the honest little voice in my mind pointed out, *he's much too handsome for the likes of you.*

"No, certainly not. I don't even know how to joust, but I have met Veronica and Bliss, and they both seem to be very confident."

"They might have confidence, but they lack in other areas," Farrell said as he waved the subject of women jousters away. "What is the second assumption?"

I smiled. "That this lady you are referring to gives a hoot who wins the tournament. She may not wish to bestow anything on the champion."

"Ladies always love a winner." He nipped delicately at a bit of duck.

"Unless they're in love with a loser," I retorted before realizing just how stupid that sounded. "Uh . . .

that is, the person who didn't win the tournament, not loser in the sense of a *loser* loser. The nonwinner is what I meant."

"I know exactly what you mean," he answered with a great deal of amusement in his eyes. "But I remain unconcerned that anything so ridiculous could happen."

"You're that sure of yourself?" I asked, leaning back as Claude clumped back into the RV with two plates of salad on a tray.

"Absolutely. Confidence is of much importance to a jouster. One moment of self-doubt, one moment of fear or worry or distraction, and you might as well throw your lance away, because it'll all be over."

"Is that what happened to Walker?"

Claude paused in the act of removing my plate, sliding a warning look my way, but I was tired of people dancing around the issue. There was some secret about Walker's past that everyone but me was privy to, and I wanted to know just what it was.

Farrell leveled a glare at Claude until he gathered up the used plates and left the RV.

"Walker . . ." Farrell leaned back and pursed his lips as if he were remembering something amusing. "Walker doesn't so much suffer from a lack of confidence as he does a lack of skill."

"If he's unskilled, why are you so threatened by him?"

Farrell's nostrils made a little "you hit the target" flare. "Threatened? I'm not threatened by him. He poses no threat to me whatsoever. He never did."

I said nothing, although it was obvious I'd pressed on a sore point. But I knew men and their egos—having worked around male software geeks most of my adult life—so I kept my mouth shut and let him protest at will.

"Walker used to joust. He was fair, nothing great, although he had everyone in England thinking he was the king of the hill. He was all show and no style."

The translation from male wounded-ego-speak: Walker was hot stuff and Farrell knew it.

"But then one day about three years ago he lost his nerve. He took a fall during a competition joust, a hard fall, cracked up some of his ribs. After that, he made all sorts of excuses—his arm was injured so he couldn't hold the lance, his favorite horse was too old to joust in competition, he didn't have the time to go traveling around from tournament to tournament. It was pathetic. Everyone knew what really was keeping him from rejoining the circuit—he had been beaten, and he just couldn't stomach losing. Those ground pounders, they talk big, but the truth is they just don't have the skill or stamina to joust with the big boys. Walker didn't have what it took then, and he doesn't now."

"But he's here with his team," I pointed out.

Farrell shrugged as he chewed a mouthful of buffalo mozzarella and yellow tomatoes. "As a squire only. Oh, he trained the members of his so-called team— he does that because he can't stand to leave the sport altogether—but he's nothing more than a pitiful shell of what he once was. Do you know what they used to call him?"

I shook my head, feeling a little sick to my stomach at the delight in Farrell's sapphire eyes.

"Walker the Wild. He was supposedly known for the fact that he took wild chances, used unheard-of, dangerous jousting moves that no one else could pull off, although I think it was all propaganda he put out. I certainly never saw him do anything the least bit impressive."

Walker the Wild? The man his team members now called Granddad? "That really must have been a bad accident he had if it shook him up so much he stopped jousting," I said slowly, spearing an olive and popping it into my mouth.

"There's no jouster worth his salt who'd stop because of a few broken bones," Farrell said around a mouthful of arugula and cheese. "That was just a convenient excuse to hide behind. The truth is, he didn't like losing. No, not yet, you fool! We just started our salads!"

Claude, who had come into the RV carefully balancing a couple of plates, stopped dead when Farrell snapped at him. "You know, my job title may be squire, but that doesn't mean you can treat me like I'm your damned slave."

I gave him a little thumbs-up, happy to see him not allowing Farrell to stomp all over him, but it was short-lived.

"You are, however, employed to do the tasks I assign you, and if you can't do them correctly, I'm sure we could find someone who can," Farrell said with silken insolence. "Now take that away and keep it warm until we're ready for it."

Claude scowled down at Farrell, and I held my breath, waiting to see what he'd do, but in the end he just stormed off, bearing the plates of scallops. "He'd fit right in with the software-geek crowd," I said sorrowfully to myself.

"What's that?"

"Nothing important," I said, giving Farrell a long look. "It's none of my business, but don't you think you're a little high-handed with Claude? I mean, all this knight and squire business only goes so far, and in the end you're just two guys with the same goal— to do your job well."

Farrell stared at me.

"Right, okay, none of my business. Back to Walker . . ." He rolled his eyes and stabbed at a bit of errant yellow tomato. "What did you mean when you said that the real reason he quit jousting was because he didn't like losing?"

He shrugged again and poured himself another glass

of champagne. "Just that—he is a poor loser. He never jousted again after being beaten."

"Wait a minute," I said, waving my fork at him. "Are you saying that he was unbeaten, and that when he eventually was, he quit the sport?"

"Anyone can *say* they're unbeaten," Farrell said smoothly—a little too smoothly for my taste. Obviously it was his ego speaking. "All it takes is to ensure that you go up against men who have nowhere near your skill. Because there's no one governing organization, anyone can form their own jousting society and give themselves titles, make up rules that benefit them, and so on. It's all unregulated, so claiming you're unbeaten really means nothing. And now I refuse to ruin the rest of the evening with talk of the unpleasant Mr. McPhail. After dinner I'll show you around the stables and let you see what sort of a horse a *real* jouster rides."

I kept my mouth shut after that. I've always maintained that you can learn a lot about a man by allowing him free rein, conversationally speaking. Guys who secretly (or not so secretly) feel that they are the most important thing on God's green earth will talk only about things that have to do with them. Guys who sincerely want to get to know you better will draw you out with questions about your likes and dislikes, your past, your hopes, dreams, and, if they're really good, your fantasies.

Guess which category Farrell fell into?

Farrell waved a hand at a bay horse later, when we visited the stable. "This is Sonora; she's my backup in case Lance or Hellion goes lame. She's very good, for a mare. I rode her earlier this spring at the U.S. Championships despite the fact that I'd just started training her. She held up well. I won that championship by seventy points."

"Ah," I said noncommittally as I viewed the mare placidly munching hay in a stable so antiseptically clean, it could have doubled for my mother's surgery.

"So how hard it is really to joust?" I asked as Farrell walked Moth and me down the brightly lit stable to view yet another horse. Moth, surprisingly, didn't seem to be intimidated by the horses, going so far as to stand up on his back legs, bracing himself against the stall door in order to smell a couple of the horses who expressed a mutual interest in him.

Moth seemed to be having a better time than me, to be honest. Thus far I'd seen Farrell's horses and his specially made, custom-designed tack, met a good dozen of the people who served as squires, grooms, and assorted flunkies, chatted briefly with the other three jousters on his team (they all looked like surfers who'd taken a wrong turn in life, too), and survived listening to tales about the last year's worth of tournament results (all of which Farrell and his team won, of course). I began to envision just how satisfying it would be to plant a lance into his chest and throw him off his horse when he paused for breath. "I mean, I know from what you've said that you've practiced for years and years and years to get where you are—"

"Not that many years," he protested quickly.

"—but how hard is it to learn?" I ignored his interruption. "Is it something that anyone can pick up?"

"Why, do you intend on learning how to joust?" he asked, his blond eyebrows making a mocking sweep upward.

I hadn't—heaven knew I wanted nothing to do with a sport that had to be accomplished on the back of a horse—but his chauvinistic attitude was really grating on my nerves. "Maybe. Is there something wrong with that?"

"Darling." He laughed, putting his arm around me and pulling me tight to his side. Moth gave him a look that said he didn't appreciate having his leash tugged in such a manner. "There's a reason women didn't joust in the Middle Ages."

"But they did," I said, allowing him to walk me down the stable block. "My minor in college was European history, so I know. There *were* instances of women who went to war and who jousted in tournaments. Modern historians don't want to recognize that fact because it goes against their male-dominated view of the times, but the facts are there for people who want to find them."

Farrell waved that away without any difficulty. "Jousting is a time-honored male sport. There's a reason for that—women don't have the strength that men do. They just can't do it properly."

"What about groups like the Palm Springs jousters?"

"Dilettantes. They do performance jousting for charities and such. Their leader is above par—for a woman—but she's not of competition quality." Farrell stopped to point out a speck of dirt on the cement floor to one of the women wearing a Team Joust! tunic. She gave him a look that I wholly sympathized with. In fact, Farrell's overwhelmingly chauvinistic attitude had pretty much pushed me beyond my distaste for horses.

"What's the gentlest, least-likely-to-eat-my-hair horse you have?" I asked, pulling away from him.

His smile was smug enough that I wanted to smack it right off his face. I also formally struck him off my potential spouse list. Even if his ego could be salvaged, he was just too pretty for me. I wanted a man who spent less time on his hair than I spent on mine, and Farrell's carefully coiffed, gleaming golden hair positively screamed expensive hair care products and much time in front of the mirror. "You're serious about this, aren't you?"

"Yep. I'd like to see if it's as difficult as you say it is."

His eyebrows rose even higher. "You're not one of those women who feel as if they can do anything a man can do, are you?"

"With the exception of being able to write my name in the snow, yes, I am. It's put-up-or-shut-up time, Farrell. What's it going to be?"

He shook his head, but turned to snap out an order to another Team Joust! employee. "Saddle up Volcano, and bring a couple training lances to the warm-up ring. Is the quintain still set up there? Good."

"Volcano?"

He turned back to me with a tight smile, holding out a hand for me to take. I didn't really want to hold his hand, but since I was making him and his crew go to a lot of trouble on my behalf, I figured it wouldn't kill me to make nice. "Come along, my fair one. If you wish to play like the big boys, you'll have to do it properly."

"Um . . . about this horse named Volcano . . ."

His hand closed over mine as he led me toward his RV. "A very experienced mare. She's the safest horse I have."

I wasn't convinced. Maybe it was the gleam of amusement that shone so brightly in his eyes, but I doubted if it was likely the description *safe* could be applied to any horse named Volcano. "Oh. Okay. Uh . . . you're not going to make me wear one of those suits of armor, are you?"

He eyed my breast shelf. "No, I don't have any armor that would fit your . . . you. But I think you'll fit into my chain mail."

"Gee, thanks for that vote of confidence."

Ten minutes later I staggered into a large open-air paddock. Next to me was a smug Farrell, who grinned every time I tripped over a clump of grass, and Claude, who was stuck with Moth-watch duty.

"You're sure the mail isn't too heavy for you?" Condescension dripped from every word.

"What, too heavy for sturdy old me? Not in the least. In fact, maybe I should wear a second one, just for safety's sake," I said, full of bravado that I didn't come close to feeling. The mail hung down to my knees, the deadweight of it already making my shoulders ache. *What in God's name am I doing?* the sane part of my mind shrieked as I stumbled again, quickly righting myself to give Farrell a smile that I feared was just as weak as my knees. *Jousting? Me? On a horse?* I gave a mental shrug and pointed out to my shrieking mind that it was too late now to back out, even if I was the queen of stupid to have allowed myself to be so annoyed by Farrell's attitude that I was about to mount a horse named Volcano.

"Really? I'd be happy to send someone back for another coat of mail—" Farrell stopped and looked around for one of his minions.

"No, no, it's already late enough; let's just get this over with," I said, tugging on his arm to get him moving again. "So, who am I jousting against? And do I get a shield? I think I should have a shield. I don't think this mail is going to do much to protect me from a lance hitting me in the chest."

"Squires always start on the rings, then move up to a quintain before they can joust with another person," Farrell said, waving over a pretty pinto mare and her attendant. "Since we don't have the rings set up, you'll have to make do with the quintain."

The mare didn't look at all impressed with what she saw as I staggered forward. She flared her nostrils, and, mindful of years of my mother's horsey dictates, I bent down to Volcano's face and greeted her in the approved manner: by exhaling through my nose into hers. She snuffled my face for a minute, gave me a look that said I wasn't fooling her in the least, and turned her head to beg for treats from Robin, the man holding her.

"Right, a quintain," I said, eyeing Volcano to make sure she wasn't going to reach back and nip me as I scrambled into her saddle. "I know what that is—a swingy wooden thing."

"It's a training tool. The goal is to hit the shield fixed to the top of the beam. If you hit it dead-on, the quintain will pivot. Usually we put a bag of sand

on the opposing arm, which teaches jousters speed
as well as accuracy, but for you we'll just count the
revolutions. All set? Stirrups all right? Jody, the
lance."

I settled down on Volcano's back, the feel of a horse
beneath me sending me back to the childhood years
I had spent hacking around with my mother, but unlike my mother's unholy trio of equine terrors, Volcano didn't seem to mind having me on her. She
tossed her head up and down a few times, but I inter-
preted that more as a "let's get on with it" attitude
than an objection to me personally.

I shoved the mail back off the leather gloves Farrell
had loaned me and carefully clutched the reins, trying
to remember everything my grandfather had drilled
into me about imparting confidence to a horse.

"Here's your lance," Farrell said, handing me a ten-
foot-long black-and-gold-striped wooden pole. It was
about four inches around at the handgrip, and tapered
down to about a third of that at the tip. "Cross it over
your horse's neck, but don't let it touch her."

"Okay," I said, experimenting with the best grip for
the lance. It was counterweighted at the butt end, but
it was still an awkward piece of equipment. "So I just
ride toward the quintain, hit the shield . . . uh . . .
wait a minute, what shield?"

Farrell snapped his fingers. "Jody, find the floodlights!"

The woman who had brought the lances dashed off
to do his bidding.

"No, that's okay. I can see it well enough; you don't
have to turn on more lights," I protested, hating to
have everyone jumping around because of my silly
need to prove something to Farrell.

The sun had gone down by this time, and the yellow
sodium lights scattered around the fairgrounds provided enough illumination to see the stocky wooden
shape of the quintain lurking at the far end of the
ring, although I had a hard time seeing the wooden

shield nailed onto it. But before I could have Farrell
call his employee back, the air was filled with a high-
voltage hum; then suddenly the soft yellow lights were
drowned in the brilliant white and blue floodlights that
surrounded the ring.

"Geez, I bet passing airplanes could see the
quintain," I joked, blinking in the brilliant light. Evidently passing airplanes weren't the only ones, because before Farrell finished giving me a brief
demonstration of how to hold a lance, the bright lights
had attracted a number of people from the nearby
tent city.

"Oh, God, now I have an audience," I muttered,
gripping the lance in the manner Farrell had shown
me. "Lovely. Volcano, I will personally see to it that
you have a bucketful of apples if you resist the urge
to take a bite out of my leg, or any other body part
that might come within reach."

The horse, which had been reaching back to snap
my toes off, snorted disgustedly and pooped.

"Put up or shut up," Farrell reminded me with an
odious grin. I contemplated lancing him for a minute,
then figured it wasn't sporting, no matter how intense
the provocation. He grabbed Volcano's bridle and
pointed her to the nearest end of the ring, slapping
her on the rump to get her moving. "Off you go then.
Take it at a canter; it's easier. And don't mind the
crowds."

"Oh, that's helpful," I said as Volcano walked to
the end of the ring. How could I help but be aware
that everyone within range of the spotlights had come
to the ring to see what was up? There were men and
women in various types of garb, kids running around
behind them, some people perched on the railing, others standing around with drinks in their hands, laughing just like it wasn't them about to make a big, fat
fool of themselves. Which, I guess, it wasn't.

I just thanked my lucky stars that CJ and Walker
and his group were at the opposite end of the tent

city. "At least this way they won't see the lights and come over to witness what is sure to be my downfall. And I mean that literally," I told Volcano as I turned her head to line her up with the quintain. "Let's keep the word *fall* from our vocabulary, shall we?"

A flash of white caught my eye, a familiar flash of white with orange legs, and the form of Claude running after it. I looked ahead to where Moth was racing to, and wanted to sink into the ground. Leaning up against the railing, flirting with one of the girls in an especially low-cut bodice, was Vandal. Next to him Fenice was climbing onto the top railing. Butcher was clearing a space so that tiny, petite CJ could watch the show—namely, me. But worst of all, standing next to the Norwegians (who had brought a cooler with them), a tall, dark-haired, silver-eyed man frowned at me.

"Great, just what I need. Everyone in the world to watch me fail at hitting a stupid target. Okay, Volcano, we have a point to prove here. Let's try to keep Pepper from falling off, and if you could aim so the end of my lance hits the quintain, I'd be eternally grateful."

"Ladies and gentlemen," Farrell suddenly bellowed, turning around in a circle with his arms spread wide, ever the showman. "Team Joust! presents a very special entertainment this evening."

"What a ham," I told Volcano. Her ears twitched as if she agreed.

"Lady Pepper asserts that women are just as capable of jousting as a man is!"

The women in the crowd cheered. Most of the men made disparaging noises, but I knew they were all in fun. I doubted if anyone but Farrell and his all-male team was serious in the belief that only men made good jousters. "Tonight we witness that age-old battle between the sexes, taking the form of a challenge between a lady fair and Sir Quintain."

The crowd, which I noticed with dismay was quickly growing until the entire ring was surrounded by Faire folk, chuckled appreciatively. The Norwegians promptly began to take wagers. I kind of wished I could put a few bucks on Sir Quintain, but figured that wouldn't be kosher.

"Will the lady rise to the challenge . . ." Farrell mimed someone stabbing something with a lance. The crowd cheered. ". . . or will she fall victim to Sir Quintain's tricky nature?" He swept a low bow, and pretended to dust off the dirt around the quintain. The crowd howled.

"My lady, are you ready?" Farrell yelled down to me.

"As I'm ever going to be," I muttered, then waggled the awkward lance as my answer.

The people around the edges of the ring roared their approval.

"Then let the challenge begin," Farrell shouted before sauntering away from the quintain.

Volcano snorted as I adjusted my one-handed grip on the reins, pushed my heels down, and tightened my legs around her sides. "Ha!" I yelled as she jumped forward from a dead stop into what I hoped was a canter.

Evidently Volcano had a bit of ham in her, too, because she didn't canter down the practice ring; she galloped—head down, ears back, tail streaming behind her, a flat-out gallop.

I tried pulling her back to an easier pace, but she was not Farrell's horse for nothing. Bits of dirt flew up from her hooves as she thundered down the ring. It took me a few seconds to remember that my part was not just to stay on her back. I leveled the lance over her neck, keeping it a good foot above her mane so it wouldn't accidentally drop onto her, aimed at the yellow-and-blue shield nailed onto the quintain, and prayed the shock of hitting it wouldn't hurt any of my vital organs.

I needn't have worried. I didn't even come close to hitting it. We zipped past it, and Volcano, an old hand

at the quintain, immediately swung into a wide circle
to head back toward the starting spot. Unfortunately,
I wasn't quite quick enough with the lance, and before
I could call a warning, several people sitting on the
rails threw themselves off just seconds before the
lance tip slammed into the wooden railing, shattering
with an ugly squeal of wood on wood.

The shock of the blow threw me backward and sideways in the saddle, and I have to admit that it was
Volcano's skill as an experienced jousting horse that
kept me on her back. She adjusted her swing to keep
me balanced, even as I dropped the lance and clutched
at the saddle pommel with my free hand.

The crowd groaned.

"Just a practice run, gentlefolk," Farrell said as Volcano cantered past him. I gritted my teeth at his grin,
and shook my still-smarting hand. "We have to give
the lady a practice run. Now we'll see Lady Pepper
regain her honor!"

Volcano stopped at the far end, snorting and tossing
her head as she mouthed the bit, obviously waiting
for me to arm myself again. Jody approached me with
a new lance. "You don't have to do this," she whispered over the din of people making bets on the out-
come of the next pass, advice being called out to me,
and, in the minstrels' case, a rousing song sung in
my honor.

"I'm okay; it just stings a little," I told her. "Can't
let all of womanhood down, now, can I?"

Jody smiled and backed away as I took the lance
in my gloved hand, sliding it down until I had a good
grip. Volcano's body tensed beneath me, her ears forward as she waited for me to give her the signal to
go. I glanced over to where Walker and his team were
lounging. CJ was clutching the railing so hard her fingers were white. Butcher was smiling and giving me
the thumbs-up. Bliss called out some advice about
keeping my lance tip up. Vandal followed after a well-

endowed woman with a bunch of grapes and a promise in her smile as she disappeared into a darkened stable. And Walker . . . Walker was leaning against the railing looking bored, Moth draped around his shoulders like some sort of living fur boa.

"Ladies and gentlemen!" Farrell clapped his hands for silence. He didn't get it, but the din did drop down a level or two. "Now that she's had her practice run, I give you Lady Pepper versus—"

"Time out!" I called, swinging Volcano's head toward the Three Dog Knight team. She didn't want to go, but I didn't grow up riding the most evil horses in existence for nothing.

Walker's eyes got bigger as we headed straight for him. Several people sitting on the railing around him shrieked at the sight of my lance, diving off the railings much as the guys near the quintain had. Everyone within a six-foot radius of Walker peeled off, stopping at a safe distance as I pulled up Volcano to lean toward him. "Any advice?"

"Pepper?" Farrell called. "Lady Pepper, your audience is awaiting you to make good on your challenge to Sir Quintain."

Walker's lips pursed for a moment, and I was distracted by the sudden image of what it would be like to suck one of those lips into my mouth and have my wicked way with it. "Yes. Get off the horse."

"Lady Pepper, your audience!" Farrell bellowed.

I ignored him, keeping my eyes on the man in front of me. "Other than that, any advice?"

One of his glossy eyebrows rose, just as I knew it would. "You're asking me, a has-been, a failure, for advice?"

I gave him a long, steady look. "Those are Farrell's words, not mine. Do you have any advice for me or not?"

"My good people, the lady is a bit shy. Shall we give her some encouragement?"

The crowd screamed their enthusiasm as Walker matched my look for the count of ten; then he asked, "Why?"

I sighed noisily. "Because I get the idea you're the best there is at this. If you don't want to help, then I'll ask Farrell, but to be honest, I'd rather listen to your advice than his."

His eyes narrowed for a second as he thought about this, but in the end he nodded briefly. His voice was low and deep, sending shivers down my arms and back as he quickly rapped out instructions. "Let the horse watch where she's going; you keep your eye on the quintain. Don't lower your lance until the last minute. Aim a little high and to the right. Lean into the hit. And keep your horse at a canter; a gallop is too hard to control. As soon as you make contact, pull your arm inward, toward your body. It will lessen the shock to your wrist."

I smiled and blew him a kiss, something that had him taking a step back in surprise. "Thanks, Walker. Don't let Moth eat any horse poop; it makes him barf."

Volcano was only too happy to head back to the starting point, but this time I had a firm grip on her, her neck arching as she slipped into a flashy trot. The crowd yelled and offered comments and suggestions, all of which I ignored as I lined her up with the quintain, whispered a plea for her to make me look good—or at least not bad—then clamped down tight on her sides with my heels as I gave a little war cry I had no idea I knew.

I kept my attention on the quintain as the horse leaped forward, but she settled happily enough into an easy canter, allowing me to narrow my focus to the simple blue-and-yellow shield. I noticed but didn't pay any attention to the fact that everyone at that end of the paddock cleared the decks. Instead I leaned forward, my eyes on the shield, and when Volcano was a few lengths from the quintain I lowered the lance. I didn't even have time to adjust my aim upward and to the right before it hit the shield, the blow much less a shock as the quintain spun around on its axis. I whooped with joy and hoisted my lance in victory, the people along the railing cheering like mad.

"Atta girl, Volcano!" She trotted toward Farrell, who jumped out to catch her reins, pulling us to a stop in the middle of the ring. I looked for Walker's tall form, intent on sharing my victory with him. He inclined his head at my grin, which I figured was as much as I was going to get from him.

Farrell wasn't nearly so reserved.

"Hear ye, hear ye, manly lords and virtuous ladies! It gives me the greatest possible pleasure to present to such a worthy gathering that brave damsel, that maiden of the lance, the most buxom and beauteous Lady Pepper, champion of the quintain! And what shall my lady's reward be for such a daring act of bravery and strength and a keen eye?"

I gave my lance to Jody as she ran out to get it, then turned to indulge in a little gloating to Farrell as he played up to the crowd.

"I've got a lance she's welcome to try next," someone yelled out.

"She can scale my battlements any day," another joked.

"I've got a couple of crystal balls that need polishing," one of the Americans next to Bos offered.

"No, no, fair knights, this is a *lady* we're speaking of," Farrell said, one hand on my knee. My skirt was wide enough to ride a horse astride without flashing too much flesh, but even so, he managed to get his hand on my bare knee. His fingers tightened around it as Volcano tossed her head. "Her reward must be a treasure as pure as her virtue."

"Have her come over to my tent and I'll show her the largest treasure in the land," one of the Norwegians suggested.

"A kiss!" a woman's voice yelled out. "Let her have the kiss of the bravest knight present!"

I perked up at the thought of that, looking straight at Walker. "Oooh, yeah!"

"It shall be so," Farrell proclaimed, and without giving me a chance to flash Walker the leer I was warming up, he reached up, grabbed the neckline of my mail, and hauled me sideways, planting his lips on me as I slid off into his waiting embrace.

Chapter Five

I'll say this for Farrell—the man knew how to kiss. That thought popped through my mind as he locked his lips on mine. It was a distant sort of thought, and academic analysis of just exactly how his lips were moving over mine, an assessment of his technique from the brush of his lips to the way his tongue tried to tease its way into my mouth.

I thinned my lips, not willing to give him the intimacy he wanted. I was willing to let him end the show with a grand gesture, but a gesture it would remain— empty of meaning and purely for show.

By the time I put my hands up on his chest and pushed him back, the people around the edges of the ring were hooting and hollering advice that was— fortunately for the children present—couched in the worst sort of Olde Medieval Speake.

"Thanks, but no thanks," I said to Farrell. His nostrils did their annoyed flare again, but he stepped back easily enough, sweeping me a bow that rivaled Vandal's for effectiveness. I turned to give Volcano a reluctant scritch behind her ears, feeling she deserved it after treating me so well, and looked around her to find Walker.

He wasn't there. Moth was, an annoyed expression on his furry face as CJ clutched him to her chest, but Walker wasn't there. Damn.

"Pepper," Farrell said behind me. "Wait—"

"Thanks for the loan of Volcano; that was fun. Oh, here's your mail. Maybe sometime you can show me how to joust against a person. And thanks for dinner; it was great." I struggled out of the mail, dumping the heavy set of linked rings into his hands as he tried to stop me. "Thanks for your help, Jody. You're the best squire a girl could have."

She giggled as I walked past, struggling a little in the soft sand-and-dirt mix that made up the warm-up ring. The spectators alongside the ring were dispersing slowly, a small clutch of people gathered around the Norwegians as they doled out money to people who'd bet on me. Several of them called out greetings as I made my way along to the far end of the ring. I waved, thanked the people who yelled congratulations, and hurried as fast as I could over to where CJ and the entire group of the Three Dog Knights—minus Walker—huddled together in a tight circle, clearly talking about something important.

"Hey, guys," I said by way of (an admittedly weak and feeble) greeting. Given the coldness that had come over them before I had left for dinner with Farrell, I decided a happy, joking attitude was the one that was going to win friends and influence people. "That was a lot of fun. What did you think of my form? Am I ready to give up my day job and become a jouster?"

The group broke up and scattered like they were billiard balls struck by an anvil.

"Hi, Pepper," CJ said, looking at Butcher from the corner of her eye.

I looked from her face to the others. CJ avoided meeting my eyes, but the others had no such difficulty. They all grinned big, shark-toothed grins at me.

Instantly I was suspicious. "Uh . . . is something the matter?"

"No, nothing, not a thing, not one single, solitary

thing," Fenice said, looking at her fellow Knights. "Nothing's the matter, is it?"

"No, nothing is the matter. Something is very right," Bliss said; then she reached out and squeezed my hand. "Be at the practice ring tomorrow at seven. I'll take you through running the rings."

"Running the what?" I asked, wondering if everyone was being nice to me because someone had called with bad news. Was my mother dead? Had my apartment been burned? Were CJ's parents going to take even longer coming home, leaving me with extended Moth duty?

"Rings. You'll need to know how to run the rings. Tomorrow, seven." She waved at one of Fenice's Americans, the two of them heading off to where the Norwegians were now toasting their success as bookies.

"Um . . ." I said, totally at a loss. I looked back at the remaining people. "Okay. Rings. Oh, jousting rings, did she mean? I heard someone mention them."

Five heads nodded in synchronicity. Four smiles got brighter. One cousin avoided my eyes.

"Why are you guys being so nice to me?" I couldn't help but ask, my suspicions getting worse with every flash of their piranha smiles. "Has Seattle dropped into the ocean? Has my mother been captured by bandits? Have CJ's parents bequeathed Moth to me?"

"We're just happy," Fenice said.

"Really? Because I hit the quintain?"

"No, because Walker was so angry," Bos said. He was a nice man with sweet brown eyes, not what you'd think of when you imagined dashing knights of old, but he had a twinkle in his eye that had me smiling back despite my confusion. "You ready, honey?"

Geoff, who was standing next to Bos with a bucket of grain and a currycomb, nodded, winked at me, then toddled off with Bos to the far stable, where the Three Dog Knights' horses were housed.

"Okay, maybe you guys would like to explain to me what's going on, and why Walker would be angry that I took his advice and hit the quintain."

Fenice put her hands on her hips and glared as Vandal sauntered out of the shadow of a nearby stable, his mouth smeared crimson. "For God's sake, Patrick, wipe your mouth! You look like you're seven and have been into the jam pot."

"Probably pretty close to the truth," Butcher rumbled to CJ, who giggled. Fenice marched over to her twin and grabbed him by his ear, scrubbing her sleeve across his face. "Piggy, that's what you are, a little pig! I can't leave you alone for a minute, can I?"

"Fenny," Vandal whined as she dragged him off toward the tents, "let go of my ear; you'll rip it off!"

"And a good thing, too. Here you are engaged to my best friend, and you're all over anything in skirts," Fenice snapped.

"Not *everything* in skirts," Vandal argued as she pulled him around the corner of the building. He was still trying to rescue his ear as they disappeared, his plaintive voice reaching our ears. "I leave the guys in kilts alone—"

I turned back to Butcher and CJ. "And then there were two," I said with a meaningful arch of my eyebrows.

CJ looked panicked for a moment, then shoved Moth into my arms and, with a craven cowardice I hadn't known she possessed, said, "Sorry. Butcher and I have to go try to make little Butchers. It's been four months. See you tomorrow, Pep."

Butcher gave me a wry grin, half embarrassment, half resignation, as my tiny little cousin towed him off into the darkness, looking for all the world like a tug leading an ocean liner.

I sighed and glanced down at Moth. He had a jaded look on his face, the look that usually prefaced his eating someone's tent. "I don't suppose you'd care to tell me what that was all about?"

He captured a small insect that fluttered past me, chewing on it thoughtfully.

I looked around us. Someone in a nearby stable clicked off the bright floodlights, leaving me and Moth standing alone in the now-dim puddle of yellow from a nearby security light, the sound of crickets and other night insects taking prominence again as the voices of my audience drifted away. The last few flickers of shadowy forms disappeared as people returned to their tents and the evening's peaceful slumber—or connubial entertainment, as the case might be.

Behind me, the warm-up ring yawned dark with shadows, the quintain a black shape looming at the far end. Not even Farrell hung around to try to hit on me. I was a bit disappointed by that. Not that I was interested in him in a sexual sense, but still, it did a girl's ego good to know *someone* wanted her.

"Oh, well, I'll always have you," I told Moth. His whiskers twitched as he spit out an insect leg. I set him on his feet, looping the end of his leash around my hand. "Yeah, I know; it's not a very comforting thought, is it? Come on, cat; let's get some sleep. Sounds like we're going to need it."

The cloudless, clear blue sky the following morning promised that the day was going to be another scorcher. Being an early riser, I wasn't bothered much by the time difference, so I was up and had fed and watered Moth and given him his morning walk by the time Bliss came into the practice ring that she and Vandal had used the day before.

"Good, you're on time; I like that." She nodded in greeting. Behind her the gray mare she'd ridden earlier bumped her nose against the back of Bliss's head, mouthing her hair. I flinched, knowing just how much it could hurt to have a horse eat your head, automatically reaching for my own hair, now pinned up in a braid. "Geoff's going to help us this morning. Is that all you have to wear?"

I looked down at my wrinkled jeans that were the only riding clothes I had. "It's that or Wench garb."

She made a face, one hand smoothing down her sweats before turning to gently slap the gray mare's muzzle. "It's better than a skirt. This is Cassie. She's a nibbler, but a good girl. Why don't you tie your cat over there, next to those packing crates, and we'll get started."

I hesitated, not because I didn't want to tie Moth up somewhere, but because I had no idea why I was really standing there next to a horse, about to learn how to joust at rings. "Why exactly are we doing this, Bliss?"

She palmed Cassie a bit of carrot, giving me a surprised look. "Thought you had a point to prove?"

"I do. I did. Last night I did, but I proved it. Didn't I?"

She shook her head. "Not if your goal was to prove that women can joust just as well as men. All you proved last night was that out of two tries, you could hit the quintain once."

"Oh." I felt a bit deflated by that realistic assessment of my triumph the evening before, but had to admit that she did have a point. "The thing is, I'm not really dead set on proving that women are just as good as men, at least as far as jousting goes."

She stopped feeding Cassie bits of carrot and looked at me, disbelief clearly visible in her dark eyes. "Do you mean to tell me that you have no intention of honoring the challenge you issued?"

The implied judgment made me a bit uncomfortable. I picked at the hem of my T-shirt, fidgeting despite the fact that I knew I had nothing to apologize for. "It wasn't really a challenge—"

"Did you or did you not tell Farrell that women could joust as well as men?"

"I did, of course I did, and I believe that, but there are a lot of women jousters here, so they really don't need me to help their cause—not that I could, because

I don't know the first thing about jousting," I pointed out quickly, hoping to escape the peal I could see she wanted to ring over my head. "It must take years to work up to this level of jousting, and as you said, all I did last night was hit a target—"

"It doesn't take years to learn, although practice does help. We can teach you all you need to know in a day or two," she said dismissively, waving when Bos trotted out from the stables with a bunch of white rings hanging on a stick. "Come on; up you go. We'll work you on the rings this morning, and after the qualifiers are over this afternoon, Vandal and Butcher will walk you through jousting with a person."

"But I don't want to be a jouster," I protested as she scooped up Moth and walked over to a stack of wooden crates sitting next to the ring. "And even if I did, even if a miracle happened and I was suddenly the best jouster there ever was, there's no use in my learning how to do it now because I couldn't compete. It's too late to join a team, surely?"

She tied Moth's leash to a post and took half the rings from Bos before turning toward the list. Tall poles that marked the dividing line of the list suddenly sprouted wooden arms, each equipped with a long metal rod with a hook in the end. Bliss placed one of the white rings on the hook and shook her head at me. "It's not too late. Teams can add alternates at any time. As long as they pass the initial qualification test, which is basically proof that you can control your horse, anyone can join a team. But that's not the point—you issued a challenge, and now you're honor-bound to stand behind it."

"But it wasn't a serious challenge; I just couldn't stand Farrell being so smug anymore—"

"You don't think defending women's participation in this sport is a serious issue?" Bliss stormed over and shook a ring at me, making Cassie toss her head nervously. I grabbed at the bridle as the horse tried to sidle away. "It may not be to you, but take it from one who has fought long and hard for the infinitesimal amount of respect granted to women jousters that it is *very much* a serious issue. Do you know that most tournaments refuse to allow women to compete with men—if they allow them to compete at all—or that the women's purse is less than the men's? Can you imagine how demeaning it is to be told you can't do something because traditionally it has been a man's sport, and you're not good enough to participate? Do you have any idea how frustrating it is to sit on the sidelines and see jousters whom you know you could beat, but not be able to because of the misguided belief that women who joust with men are nothing more than magnets for accidents and injuries?" She took a deep breath and closed her eyes for a moment, clearly trying to gain control over herself. "If you don't believe what you said about women being men's equals, then it's useless my trying to persuade you."

"I am serious," I said in a soft voice, aware that Bos was hanging the remainder of the rings while keeping one fascinated eye on us. "I meant what I said, but Bliss, this is the twenty-first century. The issue of women's equality is over and done with. We won! We're equals!"

"Not in the world of jousting," she answered in a low, gritty tone. "This is a stronghold of chauvinistic attitudes, and we need every fighter we can rally for our cause."

"You sound like a suffragette." I gave her arm a little squeeze.

"I feel like one. Now are you getting on that horse and learning how to spear rings, or are you going to be one of *them*?"

I looked at Cassie. She sniffled my T-shirt, obviously looking for carrots. I pushed her nose away. "My mother always said I shouldn't turn down an opportunity to learn something new, so I guess it won't kill me to learn how to joust. But don't get the idea that I'm going to do this in competition or anything! I was just lucky to hit that quintain, and I know I'm going to suck at this."

"If you have a losing attitude, you've already lost the battle." Righteousness dripped from her words as she placed the rest of the rings.

"This is ridiculous. How do I get myself into these situations?" I grumbled as I gathered the reins and hoisted myself up and into the saddle. "I'm deranged, that's all there is to—ow! Hey, let go of my sock!"

I leaned down to slap at Cassie's nose. She had reached back and grabbed the scrunchy sock bagging around my ankle while I had my leg stuck forward in order to tighten the girth. "Let go of me, you monster on four hooves! What is it with you Canadian animals eating cloth?"

Cassie took one last swipe at my socks, then nickered when I jerked my foot out of the range of her huge horse teeth.

"Stop teasing the horse and pay attention," Bliss said as she appeared on Cassie's off side, her hand squeezing my right knee for a second to add emphasis to her words. "Your goal is to spear as many rings as you can. We've used the big six-inchers, so it shouldn't be too hard. We'll try it first at a walk, then a trot, then a canter. All set? Stirrups okay? Good. Keep your eye on the rings, your lance up, and your back straight. Good luck!"

You'd think spearing a big white ring hanging absolutely dead still off a pole while at a walk would be a relatively easy thing, wouldn't you? I'm here to tell you it isn't. For some reason—and I can attribute this only to my aforementioned derangedness—I could not for the life of me spear the rings while walking, *or* at a trot, but I nailed all six of the little buggers the first time I urged Cassie into a canter.

"It doesn't make sense," Bliss said, shaking her head as I rode over to her after forty minutes of frustration at a walk and a trot, triumphantly brandishing my lance full of rings.

"Not one single morsel of sense," Bos agreed, scratching his head thoughtfully as he looked down the list at the empty hooks. "Maybe that lance is warped, too, like the one I had yesterday that almost gutted Butcher's horse?"

Bliss rubbed her arms, a frown pulling her brows together. "I checked them all earlier, and they were fine."

"Well, Walker always did say that the harder he tried to aim, the worse he got. Maybe Pepper has the same sort of eye that he has."

The two exchanged looks full of portent.

"I saw that," I said, pointing at them. "Just what was that supposed to mean?"

Bliss pursed her lips and absently patted Cassie when the horse bumped her, looking for treats. "It means nothing."

Bos grinned at me.

"Oh, like I just fell off the stupid wagon? I know a look full of meaning when I see one. What is going on with Walker? Why do you guys smile and look like you've got a secret whenever his name is mentioned?"

Bliss grabbed Cassie's bridle and led us out of the ring past a group of people who were wearing *Knight's Bane World Jousting Grand Championship and Renaissance Faire* T-shirts, busily dragging all sorts of pennants, sound equipment, and assorted banners into the main arena.

"You seem to be very interested in Walker," Bliss said as we walked toward the stable assigned to the Three Dog Knight team, stopping just long enough to collect Moth and sling him up to my lap. "Is there a reason for your questions about him?"

When in doubt, play stupid, that's my motto. "Me? Interested? Do you mean, like, *interested*?"

"Do you think he's hot?" Bos asked, then made a face when Bliss shot him a warning look. "What? I can ask her that, can't I? What's wrong with finding out if she thinks he's attractive?"

Clearly my stupid ploy wasn't going to work. Instead, I'd go on the defense. "Oh, I get it! CJ told you what I said, didn't she? She told you all about my quest to find a dashing, daring, brave man so I wouldn't have to date out of the software-geek pool, and now you guys are trying to match me up with Walker, despite the fact that the man hates my guts."

Bos grinned. "He doesn't hate your guts, Pepper."

Bliss rolled her eyes.

I rolled mine right along with her. "Oh, right, that's why he wouldn't even wait for me to come over and thank him for giving me quintain advice. Look, I appreciate the help, but even CJ thinks that Walker is all wrong for me, so you guys can just stop sending each other those looks full of meaning—hey, you did it again!—and mellow out."

"We don't know what you're talking about, do we, Bliss?"

"Ha! Oh, ha! I laugh at that. No, I scoff, I *scoff* at such a blatant mistruth. You guys are up to something, and it concerns Walker and me, and you can just forget it, because if you'll excuse the metaphor, that horse isn't going to run."

"So you don't like Walker?" Bos asked, walking on my off side, the long tips of the two lances he'd brought bobbing along in time to the muted *clump, clump, clump* of Cassie's hoofbeats.

Bliss stopped outside the big double door that yawned darkly into the stable's interior, and held up an arm for Moth. I plopped him into her grasp and swung down, stepping back quickly out of reach as Cassie whipped her head around to grab at my T-shirt. "Dammit, horse, leave me alone! I'll get you a carrot, okay?"

Bos peered over the saddle at me as Bliss dropped the reins and sat on her heels next to the stable door, stroking Moth's back in a manner that had him drooling from one side of his mouth. I took Bliss's cocked eyebrow to mean that I was expected to give Cassie a rubdown. Lovely. I couldn't think of anything I wanted to do more than to place myself within eating range of a horse who clearly was unable to tell the difference between hay and human.

I fumbled with the girth buckle as I answered Bos. "Like Walker? *Like Walker?* What's to like about him? I may not have known him for very long, but aside from the fact that he did save my life, I'd have to say that he's the grouchiest, crabbiest, most misanthropic person it's ever been my misfortune to be rescued by. He's conceited, arrogant, and obviously doesn't have brains in that melon he calls a head to get out of a sport that has done him so much damage. As if that wasn't bad enough, he's also one of those men who is clearly afraid of commitment, is threatened by a woman who is strong enough to take him on, is too blind to see when someone just doesn't like horses as opposed to being afraid of them"—Bos stared at me with huge eyes—"and . . . and . . . he's behind me, isn't he?"

Bos nodded.

I pulled the saddle and pad off Cassie's back and turned around with a smile plastered to my face. "Why, hello there, Walker. We were just talking about you. Ow! Right, that's it, horse, you're dog meat—"

"Stop threatening the horse. She, at least, is innocent," Walker said, stroking his hand down Cassie's face as I rubbed my butt where she had nipped me.

"Just like a man to take her side," I complained. "Where do you keep the saddles?"

"I'll take it," Bos said, hurrying forward.

"We have a rule—those who use the equipment clean up after themselves. That includes grooming the horses. I'm sure Pepper, with her superior knowledge of both horses and men, can manage to handle a saddle on her own," Walker said, still stroking Cassie's long face. I swear, the man murmured love words in her ear. "The tack room is on the left, fourth door along. Don't forget to wipe the saddle down."

By the time I had found the tack room, cleaned up the saddle, and shaken out the saddle pad, I had worked out most of my embarrassment at being caught by Walker saying things I'd rather he had not heard me say—which, of course, translated into my saying even more nasty things, albeit under my breath so only the horses could hear me.

"The tack is clean," I announced as I stepped from the cool, dark confines of the stable out into the clear morning sun. "Would you care to inspect it, or will you just trust that I know how to clean a saddle?"

Walker was currying Cassie while Moth lay curled up on a nearby wooden bench watching the object of his affection with an avid eye. Bliss and Bos had disappeared, probably off to plot whatever it was they were planning for Walker and me. Ha! I could tell them that *that* would come to nothing. Which was really a shame, when you thought about it . . .

"I'll check the saddle later," Walker said, intent on brushing Cassie.

"I didn't doubt that for a moment. What happened to the 'you ride her, you clean her' rule?" I asked, scooping up a soft finishing brush to go over the side of Cassie he'd already done.

He grunted something that I took to mean he didn't trust me to know how to groom a horse properly.

"Walker."

He looked up, his face in shadow, since his back was to the angled morning sunlight. I don't know if it was the combination of his light silvery eyes and the thick black lashes, or his dark hair, or his enticing mouth and jaw, or the whole package altogether, but just having his attention on me was almost as intense an experience as if he were stroking my bare skin. I shivered, dragging my mind from where it was happily frolicking in a land made up of Walker doing just that, and forced it back to reality. I gestured toward Cassie with my brush. "I *do* know how to groom a horse."

"Bliss told me it wasn't your idea to ride this morning," he said before resuming currying, which I gathered was an apology for his abrupt manner earlier.

Since my own manners were more than a little lacking, I felt guilty enough to continue doing my share of the work. I brandished my brush with enthusiasm, smoothing down her already glossy gray rear quarters, wondering if Cassie would kick me if I tried to comb out her tail. "No, it wasn't my idea, but it was kind of fun, and Cassie only tried to eat me twice, so it wasn't as bad as I thought it was going to be. Well, maybe the first part of it was bad, but the last pass—when I nailed all six rings—was fun."

"You what?" His head popped up over the top of Cassie's back at my words. She had been munching happily out of a grain bucket, but at his unexpected, quick move she did a little sidestep that had her shifting toward me.

"Got all six— Aiiiieeeeee! She's on my foot, she's on my foot, get off me, you damned brute of a horse!" I did a little one-footed dance of pain as Cassie stepped squarely onto my right foot. "I knew it! I just knew it! Horses hate me! They always step on me! *Get off of me!*"

I threw myself at her rear quarters, slapping at her big horse butt in an attempt to push her off, tears pricking behind my eyes. My foot felt as though it were caught in a waffle iron, a red-hot waffle iron. *"Off, off, off,* you great big mean bully of a horse!"

"Horses don't like to be yelled at," Walker said as he strolled around Cassie as if he had all the time in the world.

"Don't they? Well perhaps we can swap horse tips later, while I'm in the hospital having my foot amputated," I snarled as he casually put his right hand on her hip, and reached down with his left to slide his hand down her back leg.

When he got to the fetlock, all he said was, "Up," and—blessed Saint Hippolytus—Cassie lifted her foot off of mine.

"For someone who claims to have lots of experience with horses, you certainly don't seem to know how to handle yourself around them," Walker said as he watched me hobble over to a bale of hay before ripping my shoe off to see how many of my toes were broken. "The first thing any farrier learns is how to ask a horse to pick up its leg."

Fortunately my leather tennis shoes took most of the damage, leaving me with nothing more than a bruised foot. I wiggled my toes just to make sure they were intact. "It may have escaped your notice, but I am not a farrier." I ground my teeth a bit as I crammed my foot back into the tennis shoe, then cursed luridly as the abused limb protested such a cavalier action.

His eyebrows went up when I limped over to him, poking my finger into his chest as I snapped out, "And you can just wipe that 'I'm a farrier; I know horses and you don't' look off your face, because this is all your fault."

"*My* fault—" he started to say.

"Yes, yours!" Admittedly, I was speaking in a bit of a loud voice, but if anyone was deserving of the opportunity to yell at him, I was. "You, Mr. Horse Expert of 2005, purposely jumped up and startled Cassie so she'd stomp on my foot. And you can stop widening your eyes like you can't believe what I'm saying, because I'm not buying your innocent act for one minute. You've had it in for me ever since you rescued me and I told you how sexy you were, and how nice you smelled, and for your information, that's not at all how a real knight acts!"

"Sexy? When did you tell me I was sexy? You never told me I was sexy, you daft woman. All you do is argue with me, and unless you're into some very kinky things, arguing seldom serves as foreplay."

"You think not, huh?" I asked, confused by conflicting emotions. I wanted to be mad at him for the way he refused to challenge me, but with every passing second, my irritation morphed into something much more pleasant. Damn the man—he must have bathed in pheromones that morning, because just being close to him had every inch of me on alert, my body pleading with my brain for permission to do all sorts of wicked, unmentionable things to him. I took a step closer. "You're just saying that because you can't admit the truth to yourself. They have a word for that, you know—it's called denial."

"Denial?" he snorted, his beautiful eyes flashing as he moved toward me, so close that my breasts were just a hairbreadth away from his chest. "I am most definitely not in denial. Denial about what?"

"You're jealous," I said, breathing in the wonderfully spicy scent that I had just realized was Walker, and not an aftershave or soap. It was him, all him, and it went straight to my many and varied erogenous zones. "You're jealous because Farrell kissed me first, and you wanted to do that because you rescued me, and therefore by rights I was yours. Not that I buy into that whole guy-owning-a-woman thing, but I admit that a little bit of possession is kind of sexy. However, you're obviously too much in denial to admit that you want to kiss me."

His hands fisted at his sides as he ground out through clenched teeth, "I am *not* jealous. Farrell can kiss you until the sky falls down, for all I care. And as for denial, Miss Pepper whatever-your-last-name-is, if the shoe fits, wear it!"

"Oh!" I gasped, little thrills of pleasure going through me when my chest brushed against his. "Are you implying that *I* want to kiss *you*?"

"Yes," he answered, crossing his arms over his chest. We both stared down at where his forearms were pressed against my (now heaving) chest. I stared dumbly at the fine, dark hairs that were scattered along the muscles of his arms, knowing I should move back a step so my breasts weren't rubbing on him, but for some reason—sunspots, Mercury in retrograde, acid rain (take your pick)—I was unable to move. "Go ahead, tell me you don't want to kiss me."

"I'm not going to tell you that! I, at least, am honest with myself. I do want to kiss you, McPhail. I think I'll just do it."

"No, you won't," he said, dropping his arms and leaning toward me. His breath fanned over my face, his eyes burning silver deep into my brain. "You don't have the nerve."

"I do, too. Fine, try your reverse psychology. You win. I'm going to kiss you. Right now."

"Fine."

"So you'd better brace yourself. 'Cause I'm going to do it. Right now."

His eyes narrowed as my body—totally without asking me permission first, I'll have you know—swayed against him. "Fine."

"Are you ready? Because I'm going to kiss you."

"Now," he said, his lips brushing against mine as he spoke.

"Yes, now. Right now. Right this second." I swallowed hard, trying to put out the fire that had somehow started deep in my belly and was quickly spreading to surrounding environs. "Obviously you're the kind of man who likes aggressive women, so that's what I'm going to do: kiss you first. Because you want me to."

"I don't like aggressive women," he growled against my mouth, his eyes narrowed into brilliant slits of molten silver. His lips caressed mine in light butterfly touches that he would no doubt fool himself into thinking were unintentional, but I knew better. My entire body went up in flames as his lips touched mine again. "I don't like them at all."

"What?" I breathed in his breath and just touched the edge of his lips. I knew he was talking about something, but just exactly what the subject was had escaped me. All I could think about was what an amazing effect just being near him had on me. I'd never felt so aroused in my life. "What don't you like?"

"I can't remember," he said, his lips parting just a little to swoop down on mine.

"Walker, they're calling for the first teams to— Oh, sorry."

Walker leaped backward at the sound of Butcher's voice, careened into Cassie, and swore mightily as she lashed out with her back foot.

I stood looking at those beautiful lips of his, my entire body one unending ache of unfulfilled desire, tears pricking again behind my eyes because I wanted to wail at what might have been if Butcher had interrupted us just a couple of minutes later.

"I'm sorry," Butcher apologized, his lips twitching as Walker rubbed the spot on his thigh where Cassie's hoof had caught the edge of his leg. "I didn't know you were . . . uh . . . busy."

"I'm not busy," Walker snarled, giving me a heated look that stripped the breath from my lungs. "We were just . . . talking."

Both of Butcher's eyebrows rose as Walker limped toward the stable door, disappearing into its depths. "Talking, eh?"

"He was trying to make me kiss him," I said loudly—loud enough for Walker to hear, if the lurid cursing coming from the stable was anything to go by. "He was using reverse psychology on me because he's too stubborn to admit that he wants to kiss me."

"Is he now?" Butcher asked, rubbing his jaw thoughtfully.

"Ignore her! She's mad with lust for me. She doesn't know what she's talking about," came from the bowels of the stable.

"I think he's what CJ calls an alpha male. You know, leader-of-the-pack mentality, although with Walker, there's some other things going on. Like the fact that he's sexually frustrated. It's clear he's using his natural alpha maleness—not to mention his jealousy of Farrell—as a shield against admitting the fact that he has normal needs and desires, just like any other man."

"Sexually frustrated?"

Both Butcher and I ignored the bellow coming from the stable.

"That's very . . . erm . . . understanding of you," Butcher said.

"It is, isn't it? That's because I'm a woman, and honest with myself. And I know how men think. Walker doesn't want to admit to himself that he's deliberately making himself attractive to me, because then he would have to acknowledge the reason behind his desire to have me make the first move."

"I am not sexually frustrated!"

"Ah, so he's deliberately making himself attractive to you?" Butcher asked.

I nodded, picking up the brush I'd dropped, and carefully stepping behind Cassie to finish brushing her other side. "Yes, he is."

"How is that?"

"Oh, lots of ways," I said, keeping a wary eye on Cassie as I used long, sweeping strokes to brush her side.

"Give me some examples."

"She's deranged, Butcher. Don't listen to a word—Marley, dammit, open your mouth—she says, because she's got it all backward."

"Examples?" I very carefully brushed under Cassie's belly. Some horses are a bit ticklish there and apt to act up when belly brushed. "Well, for one, he smells nice."

"He does that on purpose, does he?"

"Yes, I'm sure he does. Men don't normally smell nice, you know. Either they're overcologned or musky or sweaty or something. But Walker smells very nice, which of course he does because he knows women like it."

"He's very clean," Butcher agreed.

"Oh, for Christ's sake . . . don't encourage her, man!" Walker's shout had Cassie jerking up her head. I edged away from her, leaning as far forward as I could to brush her while still being out of range of her hooves.

"And then there's his jaw. He's got a very nice jaw."

"Manly," Butcher said.

"Yes, exactly, very manly. His beard stubble is very manly, too."

An unintelligible rumble came from the stable. I scooted down to finish the near side of Cassie's rump, Butcher leaning comfortably against her as if he weren't in the least bit worried about her kicking him. I thought for a moment, then said, "And then there's his eyes. He has beautiful eyes, don't you think? All that silver and black."

"Beautiful," Butcher said, the corners of his mouth curving.

We both looked at the stable at the profound swearing that emerged from it.

"He could do with a bit more control," I said thoughtfully. "But all in all, I think he's pretty darn yummy."

"I'm sure the feeling is mutual," Butcher said, his eyes smiling at me.

"Will you stop putting words in my mouth?" Walker emerged from the stable leading the huge black warhorse named Marley. I backed away from both of them, Marley's size intimidating me almost as much as Walker's glare. Unfortunately, the beastly man saw what I was doing, and couldn't resist taunting me. "Oh, no, *you're* not afraid of horses."

I stopped, raising my chin and giving him a look that was meant to scorch the hair right off his head, but which turned to amusement at the look of surprised agony on Walker's face when Moth, evidently feeling abandoned, left his spot on the bench and swarmed up Walker's back, using his leggings and long red-and-gold tunic as a ladder.

"Can't—ow!—you control your cat?" he snapped as Moth hit the summit of Mount Walker, settling himself down with a look of smug pleasure that only a cat could achieve.

"He's not mine," I reminded him. "But I don't imagine he'll be a welcome addition to your team while you guys do the qualifying thing, so I'll take him for you."

Walker muttered something that I thought it best not to hear as he ducked his head, allowing me to pluck Moth from his shoulders. I snapped on the cat's leash, tucked him under my arm, and nodded to Butcher as he brought out the deep jousting saddle and plopped it on top of the saddle pad. "Good luck, Butcher. Break a lance, or whatever it is you say for luck. Walker?"

Walker slid the saddle pad down onto Marley's back before looking at me. "What is it now?"

I was going to apologize for teasing him in front of Butcher, but the petulance in his voice grated on my still-humming nerves. "I just wanted to tell you that I'm sorry for what I said."

Walker narrowed his eyes for a minute; then he nodded abruptly and picked up the big brown Paso saddle that he had used on Marley before.

"I wouldn't want you feeling obligated to finish that kiss you started," I continued, sauntering slowly around Cassie's rear with an extra dollop of hip action, just in case he was watching. "I like a man who can rise to any challenge, not run away whenever someone threatens him, and obviously you were very threatened by the fact that I was going to kiss you, so all in all, it's really better that you are the type of man you are."

His silver-eyed glare truly was a thing of beauty to behold. "Just what the hell is that supposed to mean?"

I shrugged and headed toward the tent city, tossing over my shoulder, "Nothing other than that it's clear you're not interested in me after all. Sorry I bothered you. I wonder what Farrell is doing? Bet he's an alpha male, too. He probably wouldn't be threatened by someone wanting to kiss him."

There was a soft *thump* that was the saddle hitting the dirt, making Marley dance a little dance of objection. As I rounded the side of a nearby barn, Walker stormed over to the bale of hay, kicking it viciously while swearing up a blue streak.

Chapter Six

Moth garnered some interesting looks an hour later as we strolled into the big arena where the jousting was to be held. No one forbade him entrance, however, which was a big weight off my mind, since I had no idea what I would do if they told me cats weren't allowed in the arena. I had him tucked under my arm as we navigated our way through the ground crews and horses waiting at the opening of the arena for their turn at the qualifying runs.

"I heard you ran the rings successfully this morning." Veronica stood smoking just outside the big double doors that led to the practice ring. She waved the smoke away, and smiled as I lugged Moth toward her.

"Trust me, I owe my entire success to accident rather than any sort of skill," I said, setting Moth down on a nearby stack of wooden fence railings. Veronica moved aside as one of the Norwegians rode in from the warm-up ring.

"I wouldn't be so sure of that. I've found through the classes I teach that there are some people who are just born to be jousters. You've obviously got the eye for it, and the requisite level of horsemanship." She shrugged. "Why shouldn't it be due to your skill and not an accident?"

"Because yesterday was the first time I ever tried

anything like that. I know it takes you guys years to learn how to joust."

"No, it takes us years to hone our skills so that we joust with a reasonable amount of success. Anyone can learn to hit a target while at a canter—it just takes practice to be able to do it every time."

Inside the arena the tinny voice of an announcer was calling the first round of jousters to the list, going through an explanation of what the qualifying rounds were. One of the Norwegian ground crew marched through the doors, cupped his hands around his mouth, and yelled to a man on a big bay in the practice ring.

"I think they're about to start," I said, grabbing Moth and moving even further out of the way as the bay charged into the arena. "Shouldn't we go in?"

"In a moment. I'd like to talk to you, if you don't mind. I have a spot for an alternate on my team—one of our members' son is ill and she's had to return home—and I thought you might like to have me put you down for the spot. You could train with us, and even do a spot of squiring if you'd like until you feel comfortable." I started to shake my head. "There's little chance you would have to compete, if that's what you're worried about."

"Thank you, I'm very flattered that you'd even consider me for an alternate position, but I've only held a lance twice in my life. I have no doubt that almost everyone else here is infinitely more qualified than me to serve as an alternate."

She considered me while taking a long drag on her cigarette, allowing the smoke to curl out of her mouth before she blew it away from me. "I've never been one to appreciate modesty. I wouldn't ask you if I didn't think you could do the job—with training, of course. If you'd like the position, it's yours."

"Thanks," I said again, hoisting Moth a little higher as I sidled around her toward the opening of the arena. "I appreciate your confidence, but I'm afraid it just wouldn't be a good idea."

"Are you going to joust for Walker's team? If you are, I'd better warn you—he has a very different training method than I do. He expects perfection from all his team members, and drills them mercilessly until he gets it. He expects the same sort of perfection outside the list, too."

Her cold green eyes took in the forest green Irish dress outfit that CJ had brought for me, saying it matched my eyes and would go far in bringing my dream man to his knees. Although I had to agree that the heavy boning in the bodice that made my waist look smaller than it was (not to mention gave me much more cleavage than I ever imagined possible) and the long, sweeping lines of the skirt that split to open over a fancy gold-worked chemise were flattering even to my *sturdy* figure, I doubted that the men of the Faire were in any danger of falling victim to whatever charms I could claim.

I stopped in the doorway and looked back at her. "You know, if you want to tell me something about you and Walker, you can just come right out and say it. You don't have to do a dance around the issue. I gather you and he were together at one time."

"Together?" Veronica took another drag on her ciggie. "I guess you could call four years of marriage being together. I assure you that I don't dance around any issues, Pepper." She ground her cigarette out, gave me a dazzling white-toothed smile, and strolled off toward a nearby barn.

"Married?" I asked Moth. "Hoo! No one happened to mention that little fact to me. Not that it matters, as long as the divorce is legal and all, but still, you'd think someone would have said something about it."

Moth declined to say anything on the subject, although he did take a moment to bite my hand as I hefted him up. "Stop biting me. If you weren't so fat, I wouldn't have to keep hoisting you up. Oh, good, there's Auntie CJ. You can go bother her for a while."

I made my way down the far side of the arena to a

section of bleachers that CJ and Bliss had claimed, and plopped Moth down on a canvas bag bearing a colorful League of Wenches logo. "Hi, guys! You'll never guess who wants me on her jousting team."

"Veronica, and sit down; you make a better wall than a window," CJ said, tugging on my arm until I sat down next to her, wrapping Moth's leash around my wrist so he couldn't escape.

"Yeah, it was her; how'd you know?"

"Shhh! The Kiwis are on. We haven't had a chance to watch them." Bliss's eyes were narrowed with concentration. She rested her chin on her hand as she watched the people in the big oval ring.

"How'd you know?" I asked CJ in a whisper.

"She was talking to Bliss earlier," she answered, her eyes also on the action in the ring. "She wanted to know what you were doing with Bliss in the training ring. Oooh, that was a good one!"

The crowd—fairly small, and consisting of jousting team members, their crews, and a few Faire folk—groaned as one of the knights went over the side of his horse.

I watched for a minute while the man in a mail hauberk got to his feet, dusted himself off, and walked toward his squire. "Did you know she was married to Walker?"

"Who?" CJ asked.

"Veronica."

"Oh. Yeah, I knew."

I walloped her on her arm. She stopped watching the ring long enough to shoot me a glare. "Ow."

"Why didn't you tell me?"

"That he had been married?" She shook her head. "Pepper, I've told you, he's not the man for you. It won't work, so just let it go, okay?"

"No, it's not okay. I like him. When he's not being obstinate and pigheaded and smart-assish, and all that, he's got kind of a gruff charm that I like. Plus he's smart and sexy and is very, very interesting. He doesn't back down to me, did you know that? And although it's a bit annoying, he appeals to me, so I'd appreciate it if you'd stop with whatever prejudice you have against him, and put that powerful matchmaking mind of yours to work on my behalf."

She shot me a look that more or less shut me up on the subject, at least for the moment. We spent the morning watching the various team members qualify for the jousting matches to come later in the next thirteen days.

"So the guys in the ring now are just showing they can joust?" I asked right before the lunch break as two men took headers from their horses, their broken lances thumping softly on the loose-packed dirt of the arena.

"Yup, that's it. Today is French and Northern Italian qualifiers; tomorrow is the Southern Italian and Realgestech."

"Uh. Okay. Um. Is there a jousting cheat sheet somewhere so I know what's what?"

She pointed to where Vandal and one of the Norwegians were riding into the ring. "Using shields, with the jousters passing left side to left side so their lances cross over the horses' necks, means they're jousting in the French style. No shields, left on left is Northern Italian."

The emcee called out the jousters' names and team affiliations; then both men gave a yell and the horses leaped down the list. Vandal was slower bringing his lance down, but he nailed the Norwegian Tomas's shield dead-on. The tips shattered, but both men stayed on the horses, turning them to return to the starting point.

"Okay. I think I have that."

CJ stood and stretched, applauding lightly when Vandal and Tomas prepared to run the course again. "Tomorrow you'll see Realgestech and Southern Italian. The first is what you saw Butcher and Bos do yesterday morning—jousting with full armor and no shields, left side to left side. The last one, Southern Italian, is the real showstopper."

"Why?" I asked, watching as the two horses thundered down the arena toward each other. There was a moment of breathless suspense as the lances hit the shields at almost exactly the same instant; then the wood tips cracked, and Tomas listed heavily to one side. Vandal stayed steady as a rock. CJ cheered him on, then started gathering up her things.

"Southern Italian is the most dangerous. They joust with no shields, full armor, and right to right." She must have seen the look of confusion on my face, because she added without my prompting her to, "When you ride left side to left side the jousters have to cross their lances over the horse's neck, right?"

I nodded. That much I could see.

"That means they strike their target at a thirty-degree angle, which makes it safer, because the jousters aren't taking the full power of a hit. But when they joust right to right, the lances are held at only a slight angle, and therefore take much harder hits. It's also the most dangerous, because if a jouster goes for a head shot, he can seriously injure his opponent. That's what happened with—" CJ stopped talking and bent down to gather up her cloth book bag of official Wench documents.

"What? What happened with what?"

"Nothing. Come on; you're invited to the Wenches' lunch. We're going to talk about League business, and arrange for our official Promenade of Wenches."

I snapped Moth's leash onto his harness, then scooped him up in my arms to follow CJ as she climbed down the bleacher steps. "Oh, no, you're not getting away with that. What were you going to say?"

"Shh! Watch."

We stopped at the bottom of the stairs next to the angled railing that separated the seating area from the main area of the arena. Vandal and Tomas lined their horses up, and before I could blink, they were off.

This time both men broke their lances, but both remained in their seats. CJ yelled out a congratulations to Vandal, who raised his hand in salute.

"Come on, we're late, and if you're late to a Wench lunch, they nominate you Ale Wench behind your back."

"What's an Ale Wench?" I hoisted Moth higher, ignored his growl, and hurried after my cousin, feeling sorely put-upon. "Why do I have to go to the Wench lunch? And what were you going to say about the jousting?"

She refused to tell me, mumbling something about telling me later, but I hadn't been her cousin for all of her thirty-four years without learning that when CJ had her mind made up, she was impossible to budge.

We left the relatively cool air of the indoor arena and burst out into a totally different world than the Faire that Moth and I had walked through earlier yesterday. "Holy cow, it's a population explosion!"

"You think this is bad? Wait until Saturday, when all the qualifying is over and the team jousting begins." CJ wove her way through a veritable tidal wave of people strolling up and down the vendors row. Most of them were in garb, but it wasn't all medieval garb — there were Middle Eastern dancers (belly and otherwise), a whole flock of women in pink, gold, and green gauze with big pearlescent fairy wings, men in oddly abbreviated outfits consisting mostly of leather, and even a woman in full Queen Elizabeth regalia, complete with eight matching courtiers in red velvet cloaks and starched ruffs.

"Where are we going?" I stepped around a Lab puppy wearing a pair of devil's horns, pausing for a moment to ask the young woman holding the leash a question. She pointed to a nearby vendor. I hoisted Moth higher under my arm, and grabbed for my leather pouch.

By the time I caught up to CJ she was talking to a man in musketeer garb, both of them standing at the

entrance of one of the small red-and-white buildings
that were scattered around the fairgrounds.

"There you are," she said, turning around to glare
at me. Behind her a flowery hand-painted sign reading
LEAGUE OF WENCHES OFFICIAL CATHOUSE hung from
the door. "I was just talking to David the Rogue. He's
married to Fairuza. You remember her— What on
earth? Horns? You bought Moth horns?"

"I thought they were all too appropriate." I smiled
and offered my hand to the handsome musketeer
Rogue. He shook it, grinning all the while at the cat.
"Nice to meet you, David. I'm glad to see one of CJ's
victims looking hale and hearty."

"You wouldn't know it, but she claims she doesn't
like animals," CJ told David with a disgusted look at
me that almost matched Moth's. I adjusted the elastic
that ran under his chin and made sure his soft blue
felt horns were settled comfortably on his head. "She
was almost a vet once, but quit because she was afraid
of being eaten by horses."

"The entire equine race has it in for me," I mumbled, surreptitiously wiggling my bruised toes.

"Are you and Fairuza coming by the Three Dog
Knights camp tonight? We're doing alder-smoked
chicken."

David made a courtly bow with his fancy musketeer
hat. "We would be delighted to join the festivities. I
look forward to seeing you both then."

"Oh, Pepper won't be there," CJ said airily. I
blinked in surprise, more than a little hurt by her
quick assurance that I would be elsewhere. "She's
seeing Farrell Kirkham, and you know how he is—
strictly haute cuisine, and no mingling with the common folk."

"I am not seeing Farrell," I protested, only just restraining myself from pinching her as she deserved. "I
had one dinner with the man. I don't think that qualifies as dating him."

David's friendly smile faded at the mention of Farrell's name. "That was *you* with Farrell last night? With the quintain?"

"Yes, it was," I said slowly. "But that didn't mean anything, either."

"You kissed Farrell in front of half the Faire, cuz; that's proof you are seeing him."

"I didn't kiss him; he kissed me. And will you just stop it with the whole Farrell thing? You're obsessed with him or something. I'm not dating him, I didn't kiss him, and while I don't clam up the way everyone else does around him, he's not the man who turns my crank, and since you know full well who does, you can just let it drop. Okay?"

"Who turns your crank?" David asked, his head tipped to the side just like that dog on that old record company's labels.

"She thinks she has the hots for Walker," CJ told him.

"Ceej! Do you have to tell *everyone* my personal business?"

"Walker? Really?" David eyed me carefully. "I suppose I can see that. You're his type."

"Sturdy," I said, pronouncing the word with loathing.

"Redheaded," he corrected.

"Just like his ex-wife?" I couldn't help but ask.

"*She's* not a real redhead," CJ said smoothly, causing David to choke briefly. She gave me a gentle push toward the LOW building. "It was great seeing you again, David, and yes, please, we'd love it if you could round up a contingent of Rogues to serve as a guard on the Promenades. Come along, Pepper, the Wenches are waiting, and a Wench kept waiting is like a locked door."

"Don't tell me—she needs a firm hand to *pick her lock?*" I asked, waggling my eyebrows at the double entendre as CJ nudged me into the building.

She grinned. "Exactly. You see? You were born to be a Wench."

I had another opinion, but kept it to myself as I sat through the official Wench lunch. The Wenches weren't a bad lot—far from it; they were a group of women who had fabulous senses of humor, enjoyably bawdy without going over the line. They were also a very tight-knit sisterhood, most of whom had met one another many times before. Although everyone was very friendly and pleasant to me, I was once again conscious of being the fish-out-of-water: I was the only one who hadn't been to a Ren Faire before, this was my first time out as a Wench, and I hadn't a clue what exactly Wenches did other than hand out wooden favors.

"Oh, we do all sorts of things," Fairuza said when I expressed my ignorance. She was a buxom brunette, with long curls and dancing brown eyes and, like CJ, was one of the founders of the League of Wenches. "There are the Promenades—those are very popular."

"Very popular," another Wench, a redhead like myself, nodded. "The men love it, especially the Faire folk."

"The Promenade is when a group of Wenches— usually called a harlotry of Wenches—gathers and walks a preset path through the Faire."

"We give out favors," a Wench named Lusty Susan said.

"And we mark Rogues, Cads, and Scoundrels," the redhead added.

"Why do I sense proper names in that list?" I asked.

"Because the Rogues, Cads, and Scoundrels are organized just like the Wenches," CJ answered. "They are our male half."

"Kind of a brother organization?" I asked, feeding Moth the last of my chicken sandwich. I figured I owed him as much since he didn't make a fuss about wearing the devil horns.

The Wenches snorted into their goblets of mead.

"Brothers?" Fairuza grinned. "Not even close."

"Okay, okay, I gotcha. They're a lusty bunch, too."

"Amen to that," Lusty Susan said with a heartfelt sigh.

"So what else is involved in Wenching? Ceej told me about the favors, but what's this marking business? And dare I ask what is involved in a kilt check?"

The ladies hooted, several of them making rather risqué comments.

"Now, now, it's a fair question," Fairuza said, holding up a hand to belay the naughtier suggestions of how to do a kilt check. "Harlot Pepper has a valid question, and she is due a serious answer. All markings are done via lipstick kisses, strictly limited to the waist and above. A kilt check is a simple test to see whether or not the man or woman wearing a kilt is doing so in the proper manner."

I smiled, more than a little relieved. I liked fun as much as the next person, but wasn't sure I had the nerve needed to flip up a strange man's kilt to see what he wore underneath it. "So you just make sure that they are wearing period garb and stuff? Good. I was worried you had to check to see if they were wearing undies or not."

The ladies all nodded.

"That's what we mean," CJ said. "Undies under a kilt just aren't proper."

My eyes bugged out when they explained just how a kilt check was accomplished (and it turned out it was merely a hand run up the outside of the checkee's leg to the hip in an attempt to feel an underwear line, the Wenches being very big on maintaining a PG-13 level of participation at Faires, although I heard mutterings from a few Wenches who swore by a version of kilt check that involved their hands on bare flesh). By the time they explained the rest of the Wench duties—which included taking a turn as an Ale Wench in the ale tent, and singing bawdy ballads when requested—my head hurt.

"You know what? I think I'm just going to be a Wench Lite for a while." We were all standing outside, the rest of the LOW meeting having been devoted to more mundane matters like a treasurer's report, plans for an improved Web site, charitable donations, etc. I adjusted Moth's devil horns (he'd knocked them askew in his frenzy to eat my chicken sandwich) and snapped his leash on. "I'll Wench and learn, but I don't think I'm up to a kilt check or kissing a guy I don't know."

"Both are honorable actions within the LOW guidelines," Fairuza pointed out.

"Yeah, I know, but I feel a bit weird doing them." I tried not to think of just how willing I'd be to do the more daring activities if Walker were the recipient of my attention.

CJ sighed dramatically. "She's just got no spirit. Her side of the family has always been that way, except for Pepper's mom."

"Yeah, and look where that's gotten her—stuck in a third-world country up to her armpits in mud and rabies," I mumbled as CJ made her good-byes. She hustled Moth and me back toward the arena. "So what's up for us now, more jousting?"

"Of course." She frowned at me for a couple of seconds. "Pepper, this thing with Walker worries me."

I patted her on the arm as we strolled through the crowd toward the big arena. There were more people gathering to watch the afternoon runs, although the audience was barely large enough to fill the first couple of rows of benches. "Don't worry; I won't hold it against your matchmaking scorecard if it turns out as you're predicting."

She stopped, her forehead furrowed. "I don't want you to get hurt, Pepper. Walker is . . . he needs a different type of woman. He needs someone who will understand his sorrows, someone who can give him solace and comfort him. He's been through a lot the last few years, and he needs succor, not upheaval in his life."

I smiled a sad little smile and continued on to the

arena. "As it happens, I disagree, but I don't suppose it will matter much if he doesn't rise to the challenge I threw him."

"What challenge?" CJ grabbed my arm and pulled me to a stop as we passed through one of the doors into the arena, oblivious to the fact that we were blocking an entrance. "What did you do?"

I gave an insouciant little shrug. "Nothing much. Just threw down the gauntlet. If he's the sort of man I think he is, he'll rise to the challenge. If he's not . . . well, then it's better I learn that now, before I really fall for the big lug."

CJ slapped her hand against her forehead, moaning softly to herself. "I try to tell her, but does she listen? Does she believe me? No, she just goes on like nothing I say matters. It's like talking to a redheaded clump of dirt."

"I know, I know, you use your superpowers only for good. My cousin the martyr. Oooh, look, there's Bliss ready to joust against one of Fenice's boyfriends. My money is on her."

CJ mumbled more dire warnings, but I didn't listen to them. There was no sense in worrying about something that was out of my control—although I had more or less decided that Walker was worthwhile investigating, a lot depended on him. There was only so much unrequited interest a girl could express without getting really depressed.

We settled down to watch the afternoon's qualifying rounds, Moth happily curling up inside a paper bag that someone had used to bring lunch items. The afternoon jousts were pretty much the same as the morning's courses, only this time the jousters were in armor, with no shields.

It wasn't until the end that the first inklings of something sinister tickled my brain. Bos was up against one of Farrell's men, a slight guy with a weedy moustache and ears bristling with very un-medieval earrings.

"That's . . . um . . . what's his name . . . Allen.

He's the newest member of Team Joust!, according to Farrell."

CJ shot me a look that said much, all without words. Fenice and one of her Oregon jousters had joined us, sitting on the row below, offering commentary on all the jousters—all but Farrell's team members. I felt obliged to fill in the gaps of their knowledge, whether or not they wanted them filled.

"Allen told me his dad used to joust with Farrell, but he's retired."

"Ah," Fenice said.

"Allen has been jousting since he was a kid."

"Has he?" Gary, Fenice's friend, said in a very non-committal voice.

"Yup." I waited for a count of three, then added, "His favorite color is blue, he wears a size-eleven shoe, and was a virgin until he was nineteen."

CJ glared at me for a second. I grinned back at her, then directed my attention to the arena as Bos and Allen lined up, both waiting for their respective squires to place the lances in their hands. Walker was squiring Bos, and I spent a few seconds watching him, asking myself what it was about him that interested me so much. I'd just come to the conclusion that it was equally the sense of loneliness and pain I glimpsed in his eyes, and the challenge his dominating, curmudgeonly attitude presented, when Bos gave a shout and the horses jumped forward. Both men waited until they were halfway down the list before leveling their lances.

CJ and Fenice jumped up to cheer Bos on. I made sure Moth was sleeping in his paper bag before I stood up to add my voice to the cheering section. The two men came together directly in front of us, giving us a ringside view as their lance tips slammed into the target piece of metal bolted onto the shoulder plate of the armor. Just as Bos's lance touched his opponent's shoulder, Marley stumbled hard, almost going down to his knees. The entire length of Bos's lance shattered as he was thrown forward and to the side, causing Allen's lance to catch him not on the special piece of armor meant to take the blow of a lance, but instead tearing across the other side of his chest and down his right arm.

"Oh, dear God," I breathed as Allen frantically tried to pull his lance away from Bos, but the tip caught in one of the metal lames, the overlapping pieces of armor on his arm. Bos screamed as the force of the lance slammed even harder against him, literally ripping him right out of the saddle.

I was down the stairs even before I realized I had moved, CJ right behind me.

"Take care of the cat," I yelled back to Fenice, who had her hands over her eyes, her fingers spread to peek through them.

CJ ran down the length of the seating area to the opening onto the arena floor, but being half a foot taller than her, I didn't bother. I grabbed a handful of my Irish dress and chemise, vaulted the railing, and dropped three feet to the soft dirt-and-sand floor of the arena. Several of the tournament ground crew were running to converge on the downed Bos, who was lying unmoving in the middle of the list. Walker was already at his side as a wild-eyed Marley cantered by me. His neck and flanks were wet, indicating that he was in distress. Quickly squelching the more graphic thoughts of what injuries a horse in pain could inflict on me, I lunged sideways and caught the end of a rein as he passed me.

Marley fought for a few minutes, but finally allowed himself to be calmed. I brought him to a halt, speaking in a low voice, stroking his slick neck until his breathing slowed down. Remembering the stumble in the ring, I slid my hand gently down his near leg, feeling a slight swelling on his cannon bone.

In the middle of the ring, Allen, having dismounted from his big roan mare, stood watching silently as Walker gave way to a pair of paramedics. Butcher collected up bits of the shattered lance, giving them a long, curious look. Walker had peeled part of Bos's armor off to assess the damage, but the bright smear of red on the dull gray metal was enough to tell me that whatever the injuries were, they weren't minor. The paramedics bundled Bos onto a stretcher and carried him off to the hushed murmurs of the shocked audience. Walker, still holding a bloody breastplate, consulted with CJ and Butcher for a minute; then he followed the paramedics out of the arena.

"How badly is he hurt?" I asked when CJ walked slowly toward me. "Is he going to be okay?"

"I don't know. He was unconscious. Walker thinks he might have broken some ribs, and it looks like his arm is torn up."

"Oh, how awful. I hope it's nothing serious. Poor Bos. What bad luck."

"Luck?" The word was spoken on a sob. "Butcher and Walker say that something was wrong with the lance."

"Yeah, the whole thing kind of shattered. I thought only the tips were supposed to do that?"

Her face was pale and had a strained quality, as though her flesh were being stretched too thin. "They are. Butcher thinks it was sabotaged. Oh, God, Pepper, who would do such a terrible thing to Bos?"

I shivered despite the heat. The horror in her eyes was contagious, leaving me sick and cold. "No one would be that inhuman; it must have been a faulty lance. Poor, poor Bos. He'll be horribly disappointed he won't be able to joust."

CJ looked at me in disbelieving silence for a moment, her eyes full of tears, her face ravaged. "You don't understand, do you? It's not just Bos who won't be able to joust—the whole team is out of the competition now. It's all over. Everything is ruined. Everything!" She burst into tears, turning to run from the ring. Butcher met her at the entrance, swinging her up in his arms, holding her close as she sobbed against his chest. I glanced over to where Fenice was sitting. She had one hand across her mouth, her face stark with disbelief. Gary, the American jouster, had his arm around her, trying to console her, but even from where I stood I could see the despair in her eyes.

"Come on, Marley. Let's get you rubbed down and I'll take a look at your leg."

Moth streaked down the stairs as I led Marley slowly by him, jumping up on the railing and watching me with his silly devil horns tipped to the side, his leash trailing down behind him. I led Marley over to him, holding up my arm to scoop the cat off the railing, but before I could, Moth decided to take matters into his own paws. He gathered himself, then sprang down and landed on my shoulder for a moment before jumping over to the deep wood-and-leather saddle on Marley's back.

"You're going on a diet, cat," I said, rubbing the shoulder he had landed on. Marley looked back at Moth, snorted twice, then evidently decided he didn't mind the cat as long as he remained on the saddle.

"You animals are too strange for me," I said softly as I led the duo past a sobbing CJ. Butcher had his face buried in her hair, but he lifted his head to nod at me as I walked Marley out of the still-hushed arena.

The despair I'd seen in Fenice's eyes was evident in the grim line of Butcher's mouth. I wanted to say something to comfort them, but there was just nothing to say.

I walked Marley back to his stable in silence.

Chapter Seven

"What are you doing?"

Marley turned his head and nuzzled my fingers as I gently probed the area around the slight swelling. I tensed for a second, relaxing as he did nothing more than snuffle my hand.

"Marley's been hurt." I shifted sideways from where I was squatting in front of the big horse's front legs. "See? Right here."

Fenice bent over to look at the spot on the left leg. "I don't see anything."

"Use your fingers; you'll feel it."

Marley blew into my hair. I prayed he was just smelling me, and not using my head as a convenient handkerchief.

"Oh, yes, now I feel it. What is it?"

"Feels like the start of a hematoma on his flexor muscle." I gently pushed Marley's muzzle away and stood up, wiping my hands on my skirt. "Who's the vet around here? You should have him look at Marley's leg before he runs a course again."

Fenice looked up from where she was still squatting, her face white with tension. "The vet? Is the injury serious, then?"

"No, not really. It's just a small swelling, but it needs to be opened and cleaned up before it gets worse. I could almost swear. . . ." I bit my lip, trying to figure out how Marley could hurt himself in that particular spot.

"What could you swear?"

I ran my hand down his leg again, weighing my words. "Look, do you see? Here—it looks almost like he's had a cut there."

She bent over to look at what seemed like far too straight a laceration to be natural. "It does look like he's cut himself."

I shook my head. "No, that would be more jagged; this looks like a straight slice, almost like . . ." I hated to say it. In the face of Bos's terrible accident, the last thing I needed to do was to start paranoia running through the Three Dog Knights.

"What?"

On the other hand, if it was what I suspected, then the horses had to be protected. I made my mind up quickly. "It looks like someone took a scalpel and deliberately nicked him in a spot where a hematoma was almost certain to occur."

Fenice gasped, her eyes huge in the shadows of the stall. "My God!"

"I could be wrong, but it's something to point out to the vet."

She stood up slowly, her eyes on Marley, but I had a feeling she wasn't really looking at him. "If we call the vet over and he sees an injury, he'll disqualify Marley."

"Oh, surely not over such a small injury. It's not very deep—it just needs to be drained and cleaned. If it's done today, I doubt if Marley will even notice it tomorrow. Barring infection, he should be fine to ride then."

"You sound terribly sure of that."

I did a half nod, half shrug. "I was going to follow in my mother's footsteps and be a vet, but I quit veterinary college after a few years. I did, however, do enough interning to know that this isn't a serious injury . . . if it's taken care of now."

Her eyes met mine. The anguish in them wrung my heart. "They'll DQ Marley. They have a rule—no horses suffering any sort of injury can joust."

"Yeah, well, that's a bit of an overreaction in this instance, but that fits with what CJ was saying about the horses' safety coming first."

Her fingers bit into my arm as I started to move around Marley, intending to put away the equipment I'd used to brush him down. "If they take Marley, we'll be a horse short."

"Don't they have to replace him?"

She looked over my shoulder, her eyes huge and dark with pain. "Butcher, Marley's injured."

The big Englishman swore colorfully as he and CJ approached, her eyes still red. Butcher frowned at Fenice. "What's wrong with him?"

Fenice pointed at me. "She's a vet. She says it's a hematoma and it needs to be drained."

"Whoa, wait a minute," I said, holding up my hands to deny Fenice's statement. "I'm *not* a vet—I said I thought about being one, but quit."

"Yes, but you went to vet college for three years before you quit," CJ said quickly. "And you worked for your mother all those summers, so you have loads of experience."

"What is the big deal with my having experience?" I asked as Butcher ran his hand down Marley's leg. His eyes were thoughtful as he glanced over to me. "I'm sure the Faire vet is very competent to deal with something so simple as a minor little hematoma. All it needs is to be drained, cleaned, and stitched back up. That and a shot of antibiotic, and Marley will be as good as ever."

"They'll remove him from competition if the vet finds out he's had an injury, no matter how slight," Butcher said slowly.

"Yeah, so Fenice says, but even if they did—and really, the injury isn't that bad; he won't notice it after tomorrow—surely the Faire people will give you another horse to use."

CJ clutched Butcher's arm. He put one gigantic hand over her tiny one, his brown eyes worried. "All of the trained horses have been claimed. There are none left that aren't being used by one of the jousting teams. If they take Marley away, it'll mean someone in our team doesn't joust."

"And if someone doesn't joust, it means the competition is over for us all," Fenice said, watching me carefully.

"That's what CJ said about Bos being injured. I'm really sorry about that. It's a damned shame that you guys don't have an alternate who can joust in Bos's place, but since that's so, what does it matter if Marley is yanked from competition or not?"

Fenice and CJ were shaking their heads even before I stopped speaking. "We do have an alternate," Fenice said.

All three of them looked at me as if I were the answer to their prayers. My eyes widened as I realized what they were implying. "Like hell you do! I am *not* a jouster!"

CJ rolled her eyes. "No, stupid, we don't mean you—Walker is the alternate. Each team has to have one alternate named, and he's the alternate for the Three Dog Knights."

Well, that was a load off my mind! "Thank God for Walker, say I! Well, so all's well that ends well—aside from Bos being hurt, of course. Walker will joust in his place."

Butcher slid a glance toward Fenice, who was still watching me with an avidity that made me nervous. "It's not going to be quite as easy as that, but that point aside, Walker won't be able to joust if Marley is DQ'd."

I looked at the huge black horse now blowing sadly into an empty grain bucket. "He's not hurt that badly.

Maybe if you tell the vet that there are no other horses—"

"There *are* other horses, but they aren't trained, and there's not enough time to train one," Butcher interrupted. "Walker's horse has to be ready to joust tomorrow in order to qualify for the remaining two jousts."

Three sets of eyes pleaded with me. I shook my head, knowing what they wanted without their even having to say it aloud. "Nope. Huh-uh. Not going to happen. What you're asking is illegal. It's against the law to practice veterinary medicine without a license."

"No, it isn't," CJ said quickly. "Lots of farmers do minor vet work themselves. Your mom said that the time you guys came up for the Calgary Stampede and she went out to help Grandpa with his sheep."

"Yeah, but there's a difference between docking sheep's tails and doing surgery," I protested, starting to feel very trapped.

"Please, we need you to help us," Fenice said, clasping her hands together.

"You said it was a minor injury." Butcher's broad face was both tired and strained. "If it's such a little thing, and if Marley won't be injured further by running a course tomorrow—which is also what you said—then you could do it for us and no one would be the wiser."

"I'd be the wiser," I said, a wee bit desperately. "What if something went wrong? What if I made it worse?"

"You've done this before?" Fenice asked.

I struggled with the urge to claim an easy out, but I knew CJ would know if I lied. "As a matter of a fact, I have, but—"

"Then you won't mess it up," CJ said triumphantly.

"And if the worst happened, we'd call the Faire vet," Butcher added. "No blame would be attached to you."

"You're not this horse's owner," I pointed out,

grasping at the last straw I could find. "Even if I wanted to help you, I couldn't without the owner's permission."

Fenice and Butcher exchanged quick glances. "If we get it, will you do it?" she asked.

"Well—"

"I'll go find the papers that have the horses' information," Fenice told Butcher, running off before I could object.

He nodded. "And I'll fetch Walker's medical kit. He has a little veterinary experience as well, but not nearly as much as you. Love, you go find Bliss and Vandal, and have them get Walker's name on the list as Bos's replacement. What do you need to do the job, Pepper?"

I raised my hands, then let them fall, too swept up in the current to fight my way out of it. "Whatever instruments Walker has, antibiotics, local anesthesia, antitetanus serum, suturing material, and someone to call the nuthouse, because this is an absolutely insane plan."

I refused to do so much as look at Marley's leg again without the owner's permission. Since Fenice couldn't get ahold of him until late afternoon, it wasn't until early evening that I was hunkered down in Marley's stall, adjusting one of the big camp lights Bliss had brought for the surgery. Geoff and Walker were still at the hospital, although Walker had sent back word that Bos wasn't seriously injured, but wouldn't be jousting for a couple of months.

"Would you angle the light a little more toward— Thanks, Bliss. Butcher, can you turn that one a little more to the left?"

"You're not going to hurt him, are you?" CJ asked, her face pale and drawn in the shadows of the stable.

"Nope, that's what the local is for." I looked down at the plastic box of Walker's tools, impressed not only with the scope of what it held, but also by the quality of the instruments. I pulled a new syringe from its package, holding the bottle of Procaine, a common local anesthetic, up to the light while I inserted the needle, setting it aside on a bit of sterile gauze. "Vandal, could you hold his head? Thanks. All right, Marley, just stand still for a few minutes and we'll get this taken care of."

I carefully clipped around the area, swabbing it down with antiseptic before picking up the syringe. Vandal was at Marley's head, stroking the horse's long face and mumbling reassurances in his ear. Butcher squatted down next to me, watching me closely, holding a flashlight on Marley's leg. CJ and Bliss and Fenice were on Marley's off side, their expressions grim. The only people missing were Geoff and Walker. Geoff was spending the night at the hospital with Bos; presumably Walker was on his way back to the Faire. I hoped he'd stay away until after I was finished with my bit of illicit surgery. The last thing I needed was him yelling at me.

"Can someone act as a nurse and hand me things as I need them?" I asked. "It's not complicated, but if I don't have to go rooting around in the clean instruments, it's much easier."

"I'll do it," Butcher said, his voice hoarse.

"Thanks. The tools in that bowl are the sterilized ones. Do you have gloves? Oh, good. Okay, well, it's showtime, folks!" Five unmoving faces stared at me. "Right. It's kind of a hard crowd tonight, Marley, but I think we can bring them around. For those of you playing the home game, I'm administering the local now. It's called infiltrating a wound, and after the first prick of the needle, he won't feel a thing." I slid the needle under the skin near the slight swelling. "There, see? He didn't even notice it. Now I'll do the other three sides of the injury . . . just sliding it along at the end of the anesthetized part . . . and voilà! Give it a few minutes and that whole area will be numb."

The light on Marley's leg wiggled. "Scalpel, please. You okay, Butcher?"

"I'm fine," he said, but I noticed there was a faint sheen of sweat beaded up on his forehead. "It's a bit warm in here, though, isn't it?"

I smiled as he carefully placed the scalpel in my hand. "Don't worry; it'll be over with quickly. Marley probably is dozing off, he's so bored with what we're doing."

He made an inarticulate choking noise as I probed the anesthetized area with my fingers, watching closely to see if Marley felt anything. When I judged it safe to incise the wound, I made a cut about an inch long, watching with satisfaction as the infected matter dribbled out of the incision, followed by a slow trail of blood.

The light on Marley's leg wavered, then dropped as Butcher, with a soft sighing noise, keeled over in a dead faint.

"Poor lamb," CJ said rather dispassionately as she grabbed the light, readjusting it to shine on the surgery area. "He's absolutely great when it comes to people's injuries, but animals . . . he'd never make it on Grandpa's farm."

"Mmm. Can someone else play nurse?" One of the two women rustled behind me. I paid no attention to them as I watched the blood seeping down Marley's leg, judging whether or not I'd need the artery forceps to clamp down on the bleeding. "Doesn't look too bad. . . . Forceps."

A familiar weight of cold stainless steel was placed across my palm. By the time I cleaned the small clot out of the wound, the bleeding had stopped, reaffirming my assessment that the wound was a minor one. Cleaning it was accomplished quickly—each time I held my hand out for more cotton wool, it was there waiting for me. I finished picking out the ugly bits, applied a dash of antibiotic powder, and used the suturing needle that was in my hands before I asked for it to place two tiny stitches.

"There you go, all right and tight, a nice clean closing. I think you'll survive to joust another day, Marley." I accepted the bandage that was handed to me, placing it over the wound so it wouldn't get dirty in the next twenty-four hours. "Ladies and gentlemen, Elvis has left the building! Did someone round up an antitetanus shot?"

I stretched my tight shoulder muscles and stood up, patting Marley's side, genuinely impressed with his ability to not stomp on me while I was working around his leg.

A capped syringe was shoved toward me. I narrowed my eyes at the large hand holding it, following the hand up to an arm, and over to a broad chest housed in a familiar red-and-black tunic. Silver eyes glittered at me from the face above the tunic.

"Oh. Walker. I didn't know you were back. Um. That's okay; you probably know how to give a tetanus shot."

"You're the expert," he said, his voice low and intimate in the close surroundings of the stall.

I said nothing to that, but gave Marley the shot in the heavy muscles of his neck, patting him again as I stepped over Butcher's prone form to collect the instruments. "I'll just go clean these things. . . ."

CJ and the others on Walker's team closed around him as I went out to wash off the tools, all of them questioning him about Bos. I wondered briefly where Moth was, but found him quite happily settled in a small wooden crate lined with a soft blanket. "Talk about spoiled," I told the cat as I washed the tools at the outdoor spigot. "Don't try to look pathetic to me; I see those two empty bowls next to you, and I recognize that sated, well-fed look on your face."

"Fenice took care of him." Walker's voice emerged before him from the doorway of the stable. He leaned against the door frame, an indescribable parade of emotions passing over his face. "You're not afraid of horses."

"Seems to me I've told you that."

"You acted like you were." He had such a disgruntled look on his face I had to squish my lips together to keep from snickering. "You made me believe you were afraid of them."

"Well, I'm not. I just don't like them stepping on me or biting me or eating my hair, all of which horses usually do to me."

He was silent for a moment as he watched me clean the instruments. When he did speak, his voice held an undertone that I could have sworn was something warm and fuzzy, like admiration. "That was good work you did. You didn't tell me you were a vet."

"That's because I'm not." Despite the familiar frown that settled on his brow, a little kernel of pleasure glowed deep within me at his praise. "You . . . uh . . . didn't just show up at the end?"

"No, I arrived in time to see Butcher pass out."

So it was he who had done such an efficient job of handing me instruments. "What I did was probably illegal," I pointed out, glancing around to make sure no one overheard me. It was getting on to the dinner hour, so most of the Faire folk were either drifting back toward their camps or were enjoying themselves at the various eateries to be found at the Faire proper.

"Fenice said the owner gave his permission."

"Yeah, well, there is still the fact that I'm *not* a vet. I'm sure the Faire vet would have done a better job." I straightened up, wiping the instruments on a clean cloth and placing them in a small surgical pan.

"Fenice also said that you think the injury wasn't an accident."

I dried my hands, gauging how upset he was at that news. "No, I don't think it was an accident. The cut was too perfect, at a spot guaranteed to cause trouble if it hadn't been spotted, which it likely wouldn't have been, what with all the concern about Bos. And speaking of him, how is he?"

"Bruised, one broken bone, two cracked ribs. They're keeping him overnight to make sure he doesn't have a concussion."

"So it's not serious?"

"Not in the life-threatening sense, no." Walker's eyes narrowed. "You're sure about Marley?"

"About the cause of the injury?"

He nodded.

I folded up the clean cloth and set it on top of the tools, closing the lid to Walker's equine first-aid box. "Reasonably certain. I take it you've had a look at Bos's lance?"

"Butcher did. He found signs that the length of the lance had been scored deeply, then doctored with wood putty to make it look whole."

I pursed my lips, the feeling of cold returning inside me. "That's a really nasty thing to do to Bos—first hobble his horse, then tamper with his lance. How would the person doing it know which lance was his?"

Walker ran a hand through his hair in a strangely endearing move. "They wouldn't know. All the lances are stored together, each group's painted slightly differently. The people putting on the competition provide the lances. We don't have access to them until it's time to enter the list."

"You don't? Then why did Bliss have a couple of lances for me to use this morning?"

"Those are our lances. We brought them for practice." His eyes were like icebergs in a sea of silver, but I had a feeling it wasn't me he was seeing. "No one could have known who would have received the weakened lance."

"Which means it could have been meant for anyone on the team?"

"Yes." He almost bit the word in two, his jaw tightening as his lips formed a grim, thin line. "Thank you for what you did for Marley. As far as payment—"

"Don't even think about it," I said, watching him closely. Considering he was a man I instinctively knew was very private, I found it incredibly easy to read his face. Right now I knew he was very angry, not only at the person who harmed Bos but also, I suspected, at himself. The silly man probably blamed himself in some way. "If it has the result of allowing me to see you joust, it'll be worth the trouble."

Walker's frown darkened as he turned toward the stable. "I will not be jousting."

"Wait a minute!" I grabbed his arm before he could retreat. "What do you mean, you won't be jousting? Fenice said you're the alternate."

His gray eyes went icy as he transferred his glare from my hand where it rested on his arm to my face. "That's merely a formality. Every team has to have an alternate. I do not joust."

"You used to."

"I don't now."

"Why? Because you got hurt? That's kind of cowardly, isn't it? I mean, doesn't taking a few blows go along with the whole 'I'm so manly I want to knock another man off a horse' scenario?"

He wrenched his arm away from my hand, heading toward the stable. "You don't know anything about it."

"I know that everyone might as well pack up and go home right now if you don't agree to joust." I followed him into the darkening gloom of the stable. Motes of dust danced lazily in the angled beams of the evening sunlight. "I know that because you're so caught up in your own pride you're ruining the rest of your team's chances at a little fame and glory."

His shoulders twitched, but he didn't stop walking down the corridor. Horses popped their heads out of their stalls, some of them whickering hopefully at the sight of him, probably wanting their dinners. "Everyone on the team knew that an injury would force us out of the competition. They agreed to participate regardless."

"That's probably because they expected that when

the chips were down, you'd come through for them, not run away from a challenge."

Walker spun around, stalking back to me, his face all hard lines and angles in the weak electric lights of the stable. "I am not running away. I am simply using a little good sense, something you obviously have only a passing familiarity with!"

I stood watching him for a moment, reminding myself that I had just called him a coward, and that I deserved whatever insult he slung my way.

He closed his eyes for a moment, then opened them and spoke through gritted teeth. "I apologize. That was rude of me. You showed a good deal of sense with regard to Marley's injury."

I gave him a little smile—just a little one, one that hopefully he wouldn't read too much into. "It was nothing. But this—your forcing the team to quit before they even get a chance to compete—this isn't nothing. It's big, Walker. I might not have known you guys for very long, but I know how much the competition means to everyone."

He took a step closer to me until I could feel the heat of him through the thin tunic he wore, his spicy Walker smell teasing my nose. I fought down the urge to throw my arms around him and ease whatever was causing the pain I saw deep in his eyes. "I appreciate your concern, but the team will be just fine having to go home early. It's a disappointment, but disappointments happen in life. This one won't destroy anyone, I assure you."

"I wouldn't be so certain of that," Vandal said, emerging from the tack room. If I thought Walker's face was stark, Vandal's was downright tortured. He glanced at me for a second, then took a deep breath and faced Walker. "There's a little matter of our future—Fenice's and mine."

Walker's eyes narrowed on his friend. "What do you mean, your future?"

For a second I saw another Vandal, not the carefree, devilish, flirtatious man with sleepy bedroom eyes, but a young man of about twenty-five who seemed to have the weight of the world on his shoulders. "Do you remember the money I told you I won in a lottery?"

Walker nodded.

"I lied. I didn't win it." Vandal straightened his shoulders and lifted his chin. "I know it was stupid to tell you that when it wasn't true, but Fenny wanted us to come to the competition this year, and you said I was ready for it, and I knew Butcher was dying to come to Canada, and Bos and Geoff worked so hard, too, and . . . I lied."

"What money?" I asked Walker in a whisper, feeling more than ever like an outsider, but one who was determined to find her way into the inner circle.

He answered me without taking his eyes off of Vandal. "Each team has to pay not only the entrance fees to the competition—which amount to well over a thousand pounds—but their travel and living expenses, not to mention arranging for insurance for all members of the team during the competition, and for the purchase of any new costumes, tack, and supplies needed. All the members of our team have day jobs, and no one had the sort of money that was needed to come here for three weeks to compete—until Vandal raised the entire sum by a lucky lottery ticket. Or so he said. How *did* you come by the money?"

Vandal tried hard to look like he wasn't about to be sick all over the floor, but he wasn't fooling me. "I arranged for a third mortgage on the house." Walker swore under his breath, his hands fisted as he turned away as if he couldn't stand to look at Vandal. "I know, it was foolish, but everyone wanted so much to go, and you said we were ready, and I thought Fenny and I would win back what we needed to pay off the bank. It's not that bad, Walker; it's not that big a sum of money. It's just that the National Trust folk are putting pressure on the bank to hand the loans over to them, and . . . well, you know what that would mean."

"Something bad?" I hazarded a guess, watching Walker struggle with the need to kick a large metal grain bucket in front of him.

Vandal nodded. "Fenny and I live in a house that's been in my family for almost five hundred years. It's a bit ramshackle at the moment, but it's home. The National Trust has been after us to sell it to them, but it's damned hard to hand over your heritage like that for a few quid. Fenice is attached to the old place. It would break her heart if we lost it."

"Ouch. That is tough."

I jumped when the grain bucket crashed into a nearby wall, Walker having given in to temptation.

"Of all the bloody stupid things you've done, that's the bloody stupidest!" he yelled, quickly dropping his voice to a low, mean hiss when the horses around us nickered in protest. "To risk your home—your sister's home—on sport! You deserve to lose it if you're so brainless as to indulge in that sort of folly."

"I didn't think we could lose," Vandal shouted back at him. "I knew we wouldn't! You might not have any faith in us, but I do. Dammit, Walker, why won't you give us a chance? Why won't you let us prove to you that we have what it takes? That we can be as good as you were?"

Farther down the corridor Butcher appeared, CJ close behind him. On the other side of the stable, Fenice and Bliss stood shadowed in an open door. All of them stood silent, watching as Vandal and Walker squared off in the middle of the stable. Even the horses in their loose boxes seemed to hold their breaths to see what would happen next.

"*I* have nothing to do with—"

"You trained us!" Vandal shouted, stabbing his finger in the air toward Walker. Butcher hurried down the aisle toward us. "*You* are the one who taught us, *you're* the one who told us we could do it, *you're* the one who made us believe in ourselves. Well, now we do, and you're trying to yank us back home even before we have a chance to prove to you that you were right all along."

Walker's jaw worked, but he said nothing. I sidled a bit closer to him, not sure how I could restrain him should the situation come to that, but feeling that it was better if I was near him.

"We've all talked," Butcher said, coming to stand beside Vandal in a show of support. "We know what it would mean to you to have to joust in Bos's place, but we'd like to stay. We think we can do it. We think we're ready."

Fenice and Bliss and CJ were silent as wraiths as they joined the two men, all five of them facing Walker, each face wearing an identical expression of mingled hope and determination. My heart went out to all of them.

"It's just a competition," Walker said slowly, looking at each of them. "No different from any other."

"Yes, it is," Fenice said, slipping her arm through her brother's. Her eyes were bright with tears, but her chin was firm. "I don't say that what Patrick did is right, but it's done, and he did it with the best of intentions. We've all spent the last two years working every bloody weekend, training, practicing, cutting costs and scraping and saving so we can compete. Even if you don't care about whether or not Patrick and I lose our house, surely you won't let us throw away our honor as well?"

"Well put, Fenice," Butcher rumbled as everyone nodded in agreement with her plea.

"Please, Walker. We just want to have our chance," Bliss said. "We have faith in you. We know you can do what you have to in order to give us that chance."

"Why does everyone want me to joust so badly?" Walker suddenly roared. Bits of dust drifted down from the ceiling, the swallows that lived in the rafters quickly vacating the noisy premises.

"Maybe because you're so good at it," I said quietly.

He spun around, his eyes spitting silver at me, his face working as he tried to contain his anger. "So good? *So good*? If I'm so bloody good, why did I almost kill the last man I jousted with?"

The faint whisper of the swallows' wings as they fled the stable was the only sound as Walker's words cut deep into my heart. I didn't even dare breathe; I just stared into his eyes, consumed by his pain. No wonder he refused to joust—it wasn't his own injury he feared; it was the possibility of harming someone else. "I . . . I didn't know."

"No, you didn't," he said quietly, his voice as hard and cold as granite. He turned to look at Vandal and Butcher. "But they knew. They all knew."

"Walker," I said, putting my hand on his arm, needing to touch him, needing for some reason to offer him whatever comfort I could.

"No," he said, and without another word, without a glance at any of the silent, frozen figures in the stable, he turned on his heel and walked out.

Chapter Eight

Where Walker went that night, I have no idea. One moment he was in the stable, his pain there for everyone to see; the next moment he had retreated within himself and walked out on his friends. No one saw where he disappeared to. He wasn't at the Faire, he wasn't hanging around other stables, he wasn't drowning his sorrow in the beer hall, and he didn't show up for dinner, which, honesty compels me to admit, was one of the grimmest affairs it's been my misfortune to attend.

"What are we going to do?" Bliss asked the silent group gathered around the grill, everyone with plates of chicken and salad in their laps, but no one with the appetite to eat. No one but Moth, who growled deep in his chest with happiness as I fed him tidbits of my chicken. "Should we tell the tourney steward that the Three Dog Knights are pulling out? Should we just go home?"

"We might as well," Vandal said, peering morosely into a large pewter stein of beer one of the sympathetic Ale Wenches had given him. "If Walker won't joust, it's all over for us."

"I never thought he'd come right out and refuse," Bliss said, shaking her head.

"Never expected him to give up without a fight," Butcher agreed, also shaking his head. "I think we all understand why he hasn't wanted to joust until now, but it's been three years, and this is a different situation—this is our one chance at doing something really spectacular. For him to walk out on us . . . well, it's just not like him."

"Well, I think he's just the biggest poop in the whole world. If I'd known he was going to be so cruel and selfish when he was truly needed, I would never have encouraged you all to come to the tournament." CJ was squished up against Butcher's side, staring blankly at the plate on her lap.

"He should be hung up by his toes. He should be drawn and quartered. If I knew where he was right now, I'd shoot him full of arrows. Not that anyone will see me shoot any arrows now . . ." Fenice, who was sitting at her brother's feet, made a horrible gulping, trying-not-to-cry-in-front-of-everyone noise before throwing down her plate and running off to a nearby tent.

"If *I* knew where he was right now, I'd be wearing testicle-shaped earrings," CJ said, fingering the dagger strapped to her belt.

"Right, I think now is the time for the voice of sanity to be heard." I sucked the tip of my finger where Moth, in his anxiety to snatch a bit of chicken breast, accidentally bit me. At least I *hoped* it was an accident. I adjusted his horns and looked up to find everyone's eyes on me. "Well, it's obvious that someone has to reason with Walker. Yes, he is a man, so genetically he's engineered to be dense about many things, but he's not stupid. If someone explains calmly and rationally why he has to overcome his reticence to joust again, I'm sure he'll agree to do it. All it takes is someone with tact."

They looked at each other for the count of three, then turned and smiled those damned sharky smiles at me.

"Oh, no—" I started to say.

"I nominate Pepper to convince Walker to joust,"

my traitorous cousin said with a particularly evil smile at me. "Despite the fact that she has little to no tact, Walker likes her. She likes Walker. She can sway him."

"Hey!" I said, unable to decide if I was more outraged at CJ's slur, or the idea that they could use me to manipulate Walker.

"I second the nomination," Bliss said.

"All those in favor?" Butcher asked.

"No!" I wailed.

"Aye!" they all roared back.

Butcher stood up and pulled me to my feet. "You are hereby unanimously voted as our designated representative. Your job is to convince Walker that he won't injure anyone if he jousts."

"Just how badly *did* he hurt the last guy he went up against?" I asked.

They all shook their heads sadly.

"Good luck," Butcher said solemnly.

"Don't let him say no," Bliss counseled.

"Tell him how much we're counting on him," Fenice pleaded.

"Tell him how miserable my sister will make my life if we lose our house," Vandal added with a bleak look at his twin.

"And don't come back until he says yes," CJ said, giving me a little shove.

"There's no way Walker is going to listen to me," I pointed out. "One of you should be talking to him. You're his friends."

"And you're the one who thinks he's sexy and smells nice," Butcher said, his eyes sad even though he smiled.

"As his potential girlfriend, it's your duty," CJ said righteously. "Besides, you're the one who discovered the plot against the Three Dog Knights."

"Anyone could see someone has it in for you guys, and . . . Oh, you big rat fink! You've been telling me for the last I don't know how many days just how *not* right Walker is for me, and now you're signing me up at the bridal registry and picking out the wedding cake? Ha! I laugh at you! Double ha with antlers on it!"

"You can laugh all you want, as long as you do it," she answered. "He'll listen to you because he likes you."

"He doesn't like me; he's mean to me. He's always arguing with me."

"That's just his gruff exterior hiding his heart of gold," Butcher said, putting his arm around CJ's shoulders. "If he really didn't like you, he wouldn't talk to you at all. That he argues with you means he likes you."

The others nodded their agreement.

"That might be so, but your belief that my opinion holds any sway shows that you're all quite, quite insane." I gathered up my things, snapping the leash on Moth's back. "And I might enjoy a good verbal tussle now and again with Walker, but that's neither here nor there."

"The fact that you and Walker get your jollies by arguing isn't anything to be ashamed of," CJ said smoothly. "Just look at Hepburn and Tracy—they were known for their witty repartee. It's true you guys aren't really trading barbs of their quality, but still, whatever turns your crank."

I lifted my chin and gave her a long look. "If I see the men in the white coats, I'll let them know you're ready and waiting. Until then, good night."

"We'll expect a full report in the morning," CJ called after me as I strode off into the soft evening air. "It's only everyone's whole life riding on this, Pepper! Don't screw it up!"

I might not be the Incredibly Brainy Pepper, but I knew there was no way Walker would give me the time of day concerning something about which he was so vehement. Still, I figured that if I happened to run into him when I took Moth out to stretch his legs before bed, it wouldn't kill me to broach the subject with him.

An hour and a half later, having searched the entire fairgrounds for a tall, dark, and handsomely furious Englishman, I staggered back to my tent with Moth, having done nothing more than avoided what looked like a Bacchanalian party at the Norwegians' camp, and won the battle to remove an empty condom wrapper from Moth, who had chased after it in the mistaken belief that it was something he should kill.

"It was a ridiculous idea to start with," I complained as I dug through my bag looking for my nightgown. "Like he's going to listen to anything I have to say? Oh, thank you, I really did so want kitty litter all over my sleeping bag!"

Moth was busily excavating a hole to China in his litter box as I pulled out the dark red nightgown that had been my birthday present to myself back in the days when I was gainfully employed. I have a weakness for negligees, and this one was custom-made by a company in England, its long, sweeping lines, bare lace-up back, and appliquéd lace giving it a faintly flamenco flavor. I always felt like I should be doing the tango while wearing the gorgeous satin-and-chiffon creation. Too bad I would have to cover it up with a long T-shirt for brief runs to the nearest toilet.

"Oh, well, the T-shirt isn't the end of the world. It's not like I have anyone to tango with," I said sadly, sweeping kitty litter off the sleeping bag. "Walker is obviously not interested in me, Farrell is too stuck on himself, Vandal is too young, Butcher's already taken, and the Norwegians are way too Viking. Guess that means it's just you and me, baby."

Moth, who preferred to sleep in a shoe box two sizes too small, settled down in the box with his furry sides oozing over the edges, and gave me one of those enigmatic looks cats do so well. I switched off the camping light, resigning myself to another night spent in lonely solitude, lying awake for a long time before

I fell asleep to the sounds of people laughing, singing, and generally having a good time outside the confines of my tent.

The tiny travel clock cast just enough of a glow for me to see that it was a little after two in the morning when Moth decided he was a mite peckish, and he'd just have a quick bite of tent before settling back to sleep.

"Cat, I swear to you by all that is holy, this had better be an emergency of 'Timmy fell down the well and is going to drown in five seconds unless you save him' importance, or else I will personally see to it that you wear those horns permanently."

I crawled out of the sleeping bag, too groggy and sleep fuzzed to get a grip on Moth before he managed to squeeze out the tiny opening at the bottom of the tent.

"Oh, for God's sake . . . fine!" I mumbled, shaking my fist at the gap in the zippered doorway. "Run around by yourself. Get trampled on or run over or picked up by vivisectionists; see if I care. You beastly cat, I'm going back to bed."

I curled up on top of the sleeping bag (it was still too warm to sleep covered with it), lying first on one side, then the other, trying to get comfortable on the lumpy ground. Then the pictures started forming in my head, pictures of Moth squashed flat by an unwary motorist, pictures of Moth choking on a bit of tent that I wasn't there to remove from his maw, Moth being eaten by a dog, Moth being kicked by a horse, and the coup de grâce, Moth being scooped up by an evil person who intended on subjecting him to all sorts of vile experiments.

"This is ridiculous," I growled as I scrabbled around the dark tent for my shoes. I couldn't find the sandals I knew I had set out for the following day, and the T-shirt I used as a cover-up had evidently completely disappeared from the northern hemisphere, so it was that three minutes after Moth escaped from the tent, I was creeping through an eerily silent tent city clad in nothing but a lacy satin negligee and a pair of scrungy, horse-trodden-upon tennis shoes. With luck, no one would see me while out making a late-night trip to the bathroom. My apparel wasn't X-rated, but I could do without the inevitable comments should someone get a gander of my choice of night wear.

Above me, nightjars and owls sang their nocturnal songs, brief gusts of wind whisking away my soft cries of, "Moth! Here, kitty, kitty, kitty! Num-nums!" as I swung my flashlight back and forth along the pathways of the tent city. Not even the sound of Moth's favorite treats being shaken in their can brought him to me. I looked everywhere I could for the cat, feeling stupid and foolish and more than a little worried as I stumbled over chairs left sitting out, boxes of foodstuffs, coolers, tables, and the other normal detritus that was generated when a large group of people camp together.

"Moth? Please, cat, I'm tired. I've had a long day. And my toes hurt. Come back and I'll scratch your back for you." I stood shaking the can of cat treats in a desultory manner, flashing the light around the yellow-and-white-striped tents. Out of the corner of my eye I saw a white shape streak across the open ground toward the farthest tent. I shot the flashlight that way, and just caught the tip of Moth's white tail disappearing into a vaguely familiar tent. "Aha! Got you now, you demonic imp in feline form."

The tent wasn't a camping model, but was one of the ovals favored by Ren Faire people. I knew it must belong to a jouster, but which one I had no idea. The doorway didn't zip or Velcro-close; it was simply a heavy panel of material that hung on rings before the split opening. I squatted down (feeling for some reason like it would be less of an invasion of privacy for whoever was in the tent if I was on my knees rather than if I were standing), turning off the flashlight so it wouldn't wake up the occupant.

"Mothikins," I crooned in an almost soundless whisper as I crawled into the tent. I pried the lid off the cat treat container and shook a few of them out into my hand, waving them around hopefully so the aroma would entice Moth over to me. In one corner I could see a long, dark shape that was presumably the tent's occupant, sound asleep. A white blob shimmered for a minute in the dense blackness inside the tent, then moved slowly toward a light patch to my left. I waved the treats toward Moth's blobby shape as I crawled toward him, doing a little knee stumble as I ran into something hard and bulky. "Ow. Stay right where you are, you little darling. Pepper has something for you."

"I'm sure she does," a deep, velvety voice spoke out of the blackness. "The question is, is she willing to share?"

A camp light flicked on, the relatively bright light blinding me for a few seconds before I realized several things all at once: The blobby shape I'd seen moving *was* Moth, the tent was vaguely familiar because it belonged to the Three Dog Knights, and the voice came from a big, broad, nicely haired, muscular chest that I couldn't help but noticing was bare of any covering.

"Holy cow," I breathed, my eyes bugging out just a bit as my brain processed the fact that it wasn't just Walker's chest that was bare—the rest of him was, too. From the long, narrow feet and the muscular calf that I was straddling to the thickly muscled line of his thighs, all the way up to a taut tummy, the aforementioned chest, and arms that looked like they were sculpted out of warm, living marble, every inch of Walker was bare. He was completely nude—except for the white and orange cat he wore across his groin. "You're . . . uh . . . naked."

"Yes," he drawled, not looking in the least bit like

he minded lying stark naked, wearing only a cat draped across his middle, while I crawled around in his tent. "And you don't appear to be wearing anything under that fancy nightdress, if you could be said to be actually wearing it."

"What are you talking about? Of course I'm *wearing* it!"

His eyebrows rose. "It looks to me as if you merely thought of covering yourself with cloth and decided instead that a bit of frothy nothingness would do the job as well. You don't camp much, do you?"

I glanced down and realized that, on my hands and knees as I was, he could see right down the opening of my negligee to my belly. "Gah!"

"Indeed," he said. I sat back on my heels, tugging the front of the negligee up as the conflicting urges to throw myself on that magnificent chest of his warred with the desire *not* to appear like Pepper the Wonder Tart. "*Gah* says it all, doesn't it? Might I inquire as to what you wanted of me at this time of the night? Was it something in particular, or did you just have a desire to take a nocturnal stroll in a scanty bit of satin that was evidently created with the goal of exploding the eyeballs of any man who saw you in it?"

"That was a compliment," I said, working my way through the comment about me not actually wearing the negligee (which was an exaggeration, since I most definitely was wearing it, even if it didn't cover up a whole lot of skin).

"How very bright you are in the middle of the night," he said dryly, his silvery-eyed gaze dropping a bit to consider my breasts, as concealed by a wisp of satin and lace.

"You said something nice to me." It was so unexpected, I figured I'd better make sure he meant to be nice.

"Do you want more? How about this: The sight of those luscious curves of yours in red satin makes my tongue cleave to the roof of my mouth."

I poked him in his kneecap. It was a very nice knee-cap, I took a moment to notice. Nicely rounded, but firm. It was sexy, too. A sexy, sexy kneecap. "You're flirting with me!"

"I've found it to be the gentlemanly thing to do when a woman calls upon me while I'm sleeping."

I eyed his cat-covered middle and wondered what it would take to pry Moth off his groin, and if I did manage that, whether the old wives' tale about the size of men's feet being proportionate to the size of other parts was true or not. One glance at the long length of Walker's feet had me salivating.

"Ahem." I jerked my gaze up as he raised an ebony eyebrow.

"Oh. Sorry. Um—what were we talking about?"

"You accused me of flirting with you, something you seem to find amazing, and yet given our current situation, I felt it was entirely appropriate."

"Oh, that's right, you're flirting. And you shouldn't be," I said, crossing my arms under my breasts.

There was a moment there when I thought Walker's eyes were going to go cartoon and bulge right out of their sockets with an accompanying *woobah!* sound, but he managed to keep them in his head. "Oh, really?" His voice was hoarse. He cleared his throat again and dragged his gaze back up to my eyes. "Why shouldn't I flirt with you?"

"Because you don't like me."

He looked genuinely puzzled at that. "When did I say that?"

"Well"—my hands did a little flutter thing—"you didn't actually *say* it, but you implied it with all the times you've yelled at me, or said mean things to me, or denied that you were sexually frustrated."

"I'm not sexually frustrated," he said.

I stared at Moth.

"Well, not much."

I pursed my lips.

He shifted uncomfortably, which resulted in Moth

extending his claws to keep his soft, warm, comfy bed
steady beneath him. "Yeearch!"

Walker grabbed at Moth, plucking him off his middle and setting him on the side of the sheet-covered
air mattress that was Walker's bed. I eyed the three
scratches that were slowly turning red with beaded
blood. "It's reassuring to find that sometimes old
wives' tales are founded in fact."

Walker sat up, brushing at the bloody scratches on
his groin.

"Want me to kiss it and make it better?" I offered
with my best Wenchish leer.

He frowned at me for a second; then his brow
cleared and he stretched out on the mattress, his hands
behind his head as he looked down the long line of
his body to where I was still straddling his leg. "Certainly, if you want to."

I dragged my gaze from where it was taking in the
sights up to his silvery-gray eyes, back to the sights,
up to his eyes again, and then pretty much did a little
tennis-match thing for a minute or so where I looked
back and forth between the two points of interest
while I frantically tried to resuscitate my mind from
where it had fallen into a faint at his words.

"Um . . . you do? Why?" His eyebrows rose. I
blushed at the stupidity of my question. Geez, you put
a particularly nice specimen of manhood in front of
me, and I turned into Pepper the Village Idiot. "That
is, I know *why* you'd like me to—most guys would—
but still, I understand *that* why, but why me? I mean,
you don't like me."

"You keep saying that." Walker propped himself
up on one elbow, his gaze nice and steady on my face,
whereas mine kept roaming all over his landscape. "I
don't know why you assume that I dislike you because
we've had a few disagreements. It's not true."

That had me narrowing my eyes at the innocent
look he was trying very hard to fit over his handsome
face. "A few disagreements? You accused me of being

afraid of horses, told me you were busy when I wanted to swoon into your arms, and spurned my advances when I wanted to kiss you. On top of that you yelled at me, and walked out when I was trying to comfort you. I think that pretty much spells dislike."

Walker thought about that for a minute. I sat where I was, his calf warm between mine, and wondered what sort of a man wouldn't feel the least bit discomfited by finding himself stark naked in front of a woman he'd known for all of three days.

A man who was starting to look more and more like the knight of my dreams, that was who.

"I suppose some of my actions might have lent themselves to an incorrect interpretation," he finally said, his eyes dipping for a second to my lace-covered breasts as I took a deep breath to dispute him. "But I assure you that on the contrary I find you very . . . very . . ."

My breasts, evidently possessing a mind of their own, did an amazing sort of sensitizing thing beneath the cool satin and lace of the negligee, my nipples suddenly going tight and hard under the effect of his gaze. His eyes widened as he watched them, which, in turn, turned my breasts into impudent creatures that brazenly shoved themselves forward as if inviting him to put his hands on them. Other, more private parts of me thought my breasts had the right idea, and they, too started clamoring for Walker and his hands. One minute I was just sitting there, straddling the lower leg of a totally naked man while having a stimulating (if not quite intellectual) conversation, and the next my entire body went up in some sort of wanton inferno of desire.

Walker, being a bright, intelligent sort of person, did what any red-blooded manly man of his generation would do in such a circumstance: He grabbed me and hauled me over his naked body, collapsing so we both fell down onto his makeshift bed.

"Hi," I said with a girlish giggle as my chin bumped his.

"Hello. Are you comfortable?" I wiggled my leg out from where it was caught under his. He sucked in his breath and clamped both hands down onto my hips. "For the love of God, woman, don't do that unless you want it to be all over before we even get started."

"Oh, are we going to start something?"

His eyes turned molten. "We already have."

"Really?" I stacked my hands together and rested my chin on them. "That's interesting, because although you're naked, and parts of you seem to be in an anticipatory sort of mood, I'm still back on that whole 'you don't like me' thing. Call me silly, but when I offer to kiss a man and he backs away, that more or less tells me he's not interested in the same thing I am. So why the change of heart?"

Surprise danced across his face. "You want to talk? Now? You want to talk now? Right now? *Talk*?"

"Yes, I want to talk." He squawked as I adjusted myself. "Oh, sorry. Hope I didn't squish anything important. I'd like to talk because despite the fact that I think you're yummy and you smell nice and I liked those little tiny kisses you pretended you weren't giving me yesterday, we don't seem to be on the same wavelength."

Walker's chest rose beneath me as he took a deep breath. It was a lovely movement, one that set my breasts alight as they brushed the thin layer of satin that was the only thing between my flesh and his. "For the last time, dammit, I like you!"

"You didn't like me earlier," I pointed out.

"Yes, I did. When you weren't infuriating me, I did." He looked very irritated. I almost pointed that out to him, but figured I'd better keep that observation to myself. "It's just that I don't do well with words. Talking and such. It's . . . difficult."

"You told me you didn't like aggressive women."

"I don't."

I tipped my head to the side to consider him. He was so cute, lying there being all manly and unwilling—or unable—to express his feelings. "But I'm being aggressive now. I came into your tent, and I've looked at all your naked bits, and now I'm lying on you thinking about just how fine those naked bits are, and how nice your chest is, and how much I want to suck on that spot behind your ear, and all sorts of other wicked, aggressive-woman sorts of things that I can't possibly do because you wouldn't appreciate such actions."

"You want to suck on my neck?" he asked, curiosity rampant in his beautiful eyes.

I put a finger on his chin and turned his head slightly so I could see the spot behind his left ear. "Oh, yeah!"

"Ah. Perhaps I need to rethink my previous stance regarding aggressive women."

"I like how you talk," I whispered against his lips, kissing my way along his jawline until I reached his earlobe. "You've got the most delicious accent, and your voice thrums through me like I'm a plucked string. Do you want me to show you why being an aggressive woman can be a good thing?"

He moaned his answer as I found the spot behind his ear that I'd been dying to taste. I sucked on it for a moment, then nibbled his neck until he was writhing beneath me, his fingers digging convulsively into my butt.

"You taste just as good as you smell," I whispered, running my tongue around the curve of his ear.

He moaned again as I gently bit his earlobe. "I've changed my mind," he said in a deep, hoarse voice that made me shiver.

"About us starting something?" I asked, going still, wondering what the hell I was doing lying on top of a man who was systematically making my entire body melt until I was nothing but a (relatively) sentient puddle of aroused goo.

He smiled then, a wicked smile, a wonderful smile, a smile full of unspoken desire and excitement and need. It was a smile that left my body smoldering, thrilled to my toenails by the dark promise that shone so brightly in his eyes. "No. About me not liking aggressive women. You may aggress me to your heart's desire."

"Oooh, such generosity! Let me see, do I want to investigate this lovely broad chest with its two impudent nipples"—I swept my hand down the planes of his chest, greatly enjoying the way his stomach contracted when I tickled his belly button—"or do I want to nuzzle my cheeks along these strong horseman's thighs"—I leaned over his thighs and gently bit the inside of one leg. Walker sucked in approximately half the remaining oxygen in the tent—"or do I want to study, in great detail, this monument to everything masculine and good?"

I leaned against his hip and considered the monument, which had been busy while I was lying on him nibbling on his neck.

"I don't care what you do, just so long as you do something soon." His voice, so tight and tense with arousal, literally sent shivers down my spine.

"You're not circumcised, are you?"

"No," Walker said, and I could be wrong, but it almost seemed as if there was also a note of desperation in his voice. "My mother felt it wasn't necessary. Does that matter?"

I made a little moue at the parts in question. "No, I guess not, I was just a little thrown by the different scenery. I wouldn't want to break any rules, so be sure to tell me if something doesn't work the same. If you're good to go, I am."

"Oh, lord, yes, I'm ready." His chest was covered with a faint layer of sweat, his hands clutching the sheet beneath us as I reached out, and with one finger, spread the little bead of happy juice that crowned his penis.

Moth, bored with us, went over to the other side of the tent, where there was a stack of long canvas bags that presumably held lances and swords. I looked down at Walker, laid out like a buffet table of orgasmic delights, and I knew I couldn't do the things my body was demanding I do. Not without explaining myself first.

"I'm sorry, but I can't."

"You can't?" His eyes popped open at that, the silver heat in them enough to steam my blood. "Why can't you? You think I'm sexy and I smell nice, don't you? You said I did! You can't deny it; I heard you tell Butcher that you think I'm scrummy."

"Yummy," I corrected him. "Scrummy is probably appropriate, too, although I'm not quite sure what it means. Either way, yes, I did tell Butcher that, and yes, I meant it, and under normal guy-meets-girl circumstances I would be, at this moment, riding you like an unbroken stallion, but this isn't a normal circumstance. There's something I have to tell you."

He stared at me with the same bemused look I knew I wore often, an act that so warmed my heart, I leaned down to kiss him. What I intended as a little peck changed the second my lips touched his into something much more heated, something profound and not at all what I expected. His hands swept up behind me, pulling me down onto his chest, the thin layer of satin no barrier at all between us. His lips parted, the hot lure of his mouth too much for me to resist. I teased his lip with the tip of my tongue, capturing his groan as I sucked his lower lip into my mouth, urging him without words to claim what I wanted so badly to give him. His fingers worked down my spine, trailing fire behind them, sending little waves of arousal flickering up my back. His mouth was hot and spicy, the taste of him just as intoxicating as I knew it would be. I allowed my tongue to do a fiery tango around his, tempting him, teasing him, the heat inside me burning brighter and brighter with each touch of his hands and mouth. The world around me spun, his mouth branding mine as his tongue surged and retreated, charging around my mouth like it owned the place.

I opened my eyes, aware that somehow he had flipped me over onto my back, and that just as mysteriously the satin of my lovely negligee was now up around my waist. Walker's chest was hard and hot against my breasts as one of his hands skimmed down my hip, tugging my underwear off.

"What do you have to tell me?" he asked, and my back arched at the way his voice stroked along my sensitized skin.

"What?" He wanted to talk? Now? When my whole body was about to explode?

His head dipped, and I shivered as his lips caressed the sweet spot behind my ear. He nibbled me just as I had nibbled him, the soft, cool silk of his hair brushing my cheek. I couldn't stifle a little moan of sheer, unadulterated pleasure as he sucked hard on my neck, his teeth scraping gently before he lifted his head. "You said you had something to tell me. What was it?"

I stared into those beautiful silver eyes, feeling as if I were standing on the edge of a cliff, about to fall into something I wasn't sure I would be able to escape. "What? Oh. That. No!" I stopped him as he was about to kiss me again. Pain darkened his eyes as he started to pull away. I wrapped my arms around his back and refused to let him move. "No, I didn't mean no, I don't want you to kiss me, I meant no, I can't think when you do that, and what I have to say is important."

The muscles in his back stiffened beneath my hands. "What is it? You're married?"

Now, that annoyed me. "Do you really think I would be here now if I were? Is that what you think,

Walker? That I'm the sort of girl who would seduce you if she was married? It's because we've only known each other a couple of days, isn't it? You think I'm Pepper the Wonder Slut because I think you're sexy as hell and my breasts love you and all that, right?"

His eyes widened. "No, I don't think you're any sort of a slut, and I'm just as attracted to you as you are to me, but you said it was important—"

"It's the jousting thing," I interrupted. "Your team asked me to persuade you to joust, and I didn't want us to get all hot and sweaty together, and later have you accuse me of trying to bribe you sexually."

He was silent for a minute, the hairs on his chest tickling my breasts as he claimed my mouth for another one of his mind-drugging kisses. "Thank you for your honesty, but your worry is unwarranted."

"Does that mean you're going to joust?" I asked when we came up for air.

"We'll talk about it later," he mumbled against my collarbone, his lips doing marvelous, amazing things as they kissed a hot, wet path between my breasts.

"But they asked me to convince you—"

"We'll talk about it later, sweetheart."

Sweetheart! He called me sweetheart! I shivered as he rubbed his stubbly cheek against my right breast. "I'm responsible for making sure you agree—"

He lifted his head, his eyes shuttered, hiding his feelings from me. "Pepper, jousting has nothing to do with you, with us. Can't we just enjoy each other without worrying about anyone else?"

My heart fractured just a little at the way he shut me out, but I realized then that he was *it,* he was the man I was meant to spend my life with. He wasn't just a romantic figure, a handsome Englishman, an exotic jewel in a world of baser mortals; he was the man who had been born just for me. He was mine, and I wasn't going to let him suffer by himself anymore. I smiled up at him, my heart swelling with burgeoning love as I acknowledged to myself that he might make me insane with frustration at times, but he really was perfect for me. "Yes, we can talk about it later. We can enjoy each other tonight, now, right now—"

Moth strolled over to where we were lying.

"—for several long, endless hours filled with nothing but sensual delights—"

He squinted at Walker, then looked at me.

"—as we learn each other's intimate secrets, and wildest, most romantic—"

Huurack! Plaaaaaaaagh! Moth vomited a hair ball right next to my head.

"—fantasies." I sighed.

Chapter Nine

"Now, where were we?"

"You were about to tell me your wildest, most romantic fantasy," Walker answered, his voice rumbling deep in his chest.

"Oh, the one about the three cabana boys and a key lime pie?"

Walker grinned and leaned down to kiss me, his lips doing the sorts of things that I was willing to bet were illegal in many countries. "No, the one about the brave knight who single-handedly rescues his lady from a dastardly blond villain from California."

"Oh, *that* fantasy," I cooed, arching my back so I could rub myself up against him. The satin-and-chiffon negligee was gone, tossed into the corner. I was thankful, the hair ball was also gone. Walker removed it just before he dumped out a box bearing leather gloves and gauntlets, throwing one of his tunics inside and plopping Moth in on top of it.

"Sit, stay!" I ordered Moth from where I had been lying seductively on Walker's mattress. Moth's orange whiskers twitched, but evidently the smell of Walker on the tunic was enough for the cat, because he curled up and went to sleep while Walker crawled back to me, stretching himself out alongside my waiting body.

"That is a very good fantasy, one of my favorites.

I especially like it when the bold knight shows me why they call him Lance-a-lot."

Those adorable manly lips of his curled into a smile as I spread my fingers through his silky black hair, tugging his head down so I could kiss the breath right out of him. His mouth started a now-familiar excitement deep in my belly. I moved my legs against him, savoring the feeling of his body against mine, wondering at the way his hardness fit into my softness.

"Why wouldn't you let me kiss you before?" I asked, pulling my knee up along side of his, reveling the feeling of his burning flesh scorching mine.

"Butcher interrupted us," he mumbled, nipping my earlobe as his hand swept up from my hip to where my breast was aching for his touch.

"Before that," I breathed, gasping a delighted gasp as his tongue licked my pulse point just as his fingers brushed against my nipple. "You said—oh, my god, that's so good—you said—"

"I told you"—he lifted his head, his eyes burning into mine—"I'm not good with words. Women like poetry and things. Compliments. I'm not good at any of that. I'm just a farrier, Pepper. Good with horses, but not with women."

"Would it make you more comfortable if I asked you to shoe me?" I teased, my heart warmed by his confidence. Silly man, didn't he know that actions spoke louder than words? Didn't he know how women fell for the strong-but-silent types? Didn't he realize that one look from those brilliant eyes had me melting into a great big puddle?

One of his eyebrows rose with wicked intent. "As a matter of fact, it would."

Before I could even think of blinking in stupefaction, he was gone, having slid down my body to kneel between my feet.

"Walker? Uh . . . what are you doing? You're not some sort of weirdo foot fetishist, are you? I mean, I know you work around horses' feet all the time, but you're not going to— Oh, my god!"

I thanked God I had the foresight to take advantage of one of the communal showers before I had tucked Moth and myself into bed for the night, because he didn't give my foot a quick smooch, as I half expected; he kissed my ankle, running his tongue around my anklebones. He nibbled a path down to the tip of my foot, his tongue flickering between two of my toes. I just about came up off the mattress as he sucked one of my toes into his mouth. His mouth was hot and wet, his tongue tickling me in a way I'd never felt. It was the single most erotic thing anyone had ever done to a very unerotic spot, and I lasted of all of three seconds before I was writhing, clutching great big handfuls of bedding in order to keep from throwing him to the ground and ravishing him the way he deserved. "Oh, my god, Walker!"

He grinned, kissing his way up the arch of my foot. "Like that, do you?"

"I don't know; does the fact that I'm humming like a harp tell you anything?"

His grin turned very male and very smug. "Then you're going to love this."

My entire body spasmed as his head dipped again, and I groaned when his tongue snaked out to trace the valley behind my knee. "Oh, yes!"

A deep, sexy chuckle rolled over me as he spread my legs apart, licking a spiral path up one thigh before stopping to give the other the same treatment. I lay before him, twitching with anticipation, my body burning for his touch, feeling exposed, aroused, and so fragile I was sure I was going to fracture into a million pieces if he touched me just one more time with that amazing tongue. . . .

I arched off the ground when he nuzzled the magic spot on my body, the one place that made me see stars, and see them I did when his mouth found me. His tongue swirled, and I clutched his hair, my body exploding into a series of waves that rippled through me until I was left weak and trembling with the intensity of the orgasm, my mind strangely at peace.

"You are the most responsive woman I've ever seen," Walker said as he pressed a gentle kiss on my still-trembling belly. "Do you have any idea what you do to me? How the scent of you fills my head? Do you know how much I want to thrust myself into you until you scream with pleasure? Do you know . . ." He moved upward, his hands skimming my hips as he took one taut peak disguised as a breast into his mouth, sucking hard, his teeth gently scraping along my nipple before releasing it. The silver of his eyes scorched my flesh as he lifted his head. ". . . how much I want to mark you so every man out there will know you're mine?"

For the life of me, I couldn't seem to manage a complete sentence. I ended up pleading. "Marking is good. Thrusting is better. Much, much better. If you have any mercy, you'll thrust. Now would be good!"

His eyes glittered brightly out of the dark shadows of his face, the line of his jaw tense and tight with desire as he rose up on his elbows, the hard, hot length of him nudging against my very own gates of paradise. I reached between us to position him, and he shuddered, his eyes closing for a moment as I stroked the soft velvet over steel.

"Do you have any condoms?"

He snarled softly and rolled off me, rustling around for a moment while I admired the line of his back. With a guttural noise deep in his chest, he was suddenly back on top of me.

He took my hands in his, linking his fingers through mine as he slowly slid into my body. Muscles I didn't know I had rippled around him as I tipped my hips upward, allowing him to fill me, stretch me, join his heartbeat with mine until the two rhythms were indistinguishable.

"Thrust?" I managed to ask, which was a minor

miracle considering that my brain had completely shut down with the sheer, utter magnificence of the feeling of his heat inside me, but it turned out to be a good choice of words.

"Thrust," he agreed, and suited action to word. He pulled out of me, but before my body could do more than weep tears of ecstasy, he was back, claiming me, binding us together, joining with me not just in body, but in my heart as well. His body moved against me faster, more aggressively, thrusting hard and deep into me, his tongue wild in my mouth. I moaned my exaltation, the burn inside of me roaring into another inferno as his strokes shortened, his body pounding down as mine rose up to meet him. I slid my hands from his, tracing the damp planes of his back, delighting in the play of muscles as he pushed us toward the moment of completion I knew would change my world. Beneath my fingertips his muscles tightened, a low, primal groan coming from deep in his chest.

I tore my mouth from the heat of his, wanting to watch as pleasure overtook him, wanting to share my bliss with him. The inferno inside me exploded, sending heat to every point on my body. My orgasm triggered his, my ears ringing as he arched upward, shouting a wordless acknowledgment of what we shared.

Eons passed. The ages of man came and went. Dinosaurs could have risen from extinction, walked the earth for millennia, and disappeared into the long, dark oblivion that ultimately claimed everything, and I wouldn't have noticed them. Making love with Walker had been the single most profound experience of my life, and I lay struggling to regain my breath beneath his damp body, his breath rough and hot on my ear as he, too, struggled for air.

After a while my legs, wrapped around his hips, began to cramp. His heavy weight pushed me down into the air mattress until I was aware of every rock and stone in the ground beneath me. Our bodies were glued together with perspiration. My breasts were smashed up against him, each inhalation forcing his chest hair across my sensitive nipples. I had to pee. And yet, despite all that, I cherished every discomfort, because the man lying gasping for air in my arms was the man I'd been searching for the whole of my adult life.

"You truly are my knight in shining armor," I whispered, kissing the curve of his ear. He mumbled sleepily into my shoulder before rolling us over so I was draped on top of him. I smiled as he fumbled for the camp light, the soft blackness of the night closing around us.

I had found my knight, and life, from here on out, was going to be absolutely perfect.

"You are the single most obstinate man I have ever met."

"And you're the most irritating woman I've ever met. Now get off me, I have work to do."

I looked down from where I was straddling Walker, having fulfilled my promise of four hours before to ride him like a stallion. After a lengthy recuperative period from a second mind-numbingly wonderful lovemaking session, I could once again summon words and speak them in a manner that made sense.

To me, at least. Walker didn't seem to be any too willing to admit anything of the kind.

I wiggled, my hands on his chest made damp with the sweat of our joint exertions. He was still inside me, and by concentrating very hard, I managed to tighten an array of inner muscles in a manner that had his fingers digging into my hips. "You don't just tell a woman who you've pleasured to the moon and back to get off you, you big oaf. Especially when you don't really mean it."

His eyes narrowed, but his fingers were now edging upward toward my breasts as they bobbed above his chest. "How do you know I don't mean it, wench?"

I wiggled again. "That's Harlot to you, and the proof, Sir Studmuffin, is growing within me—so to speak."

One corner of his mouth quirked up. "I'm not as young as I used to be, sweetheart, but I'm willing to sacrifice myself to your lustful desires."

"Why do I have the feeling you're trying to distract me with your extremely scrumdillyicious body, and why do I know it will work if I don't stop you right now?" I leaned down to kiss the manly, chiseled lips that I knew could melt me with just one touch, sliding off him with squelchy proof of the previous half hour's activity. I curled up next to him, one hand resting on his damp chest as I propped up my head on my hand. "Now we're going to talk."

Walker groaned, then started to get up. "I have work to do. The horses need feeding—"

"And someone else will do it." I pushed him back down. "Walker, this is serious. We need to talk."

His face darkened, his eyes mutinous. "I don't see why."

I drummed my fingernails on his chest. "Well, for one thing, if you refuse to joust, that means the Three Dog Knights are out of the competition, so it'll be back to England for all of you. *Without me*." I added the emphasis just in case he missed that pertinent bit of information.

He looked extremely discomfited. "Pepper, I—"

"No," I said, putting a hand over his mouth. He kissed my palm. "I'm not ready to talk about that yet. Later, after the competition is over, then we can talk about what's going to happen to us. But right now, you getting your extremely attractive butt onto a horse and jousting is what's important."

I removed my hand from his mouth, expecting him to refuse flat-out, but he didn't. He just stared at me with those bright eyes of his, and looked a tiny bit confused. "Why does it matter so much to you that I joust?"

"Because I've got you figured out, McPhail. You're a man with a very deep sense of responsibility, and when you hurt that other man, you swore to yourself never to put anyone else at risk again. Am I right?"

"Somewhat." The fingers of his left hand were tangled in my hair, gently stroking my neck. "I was . . . reckless in those days, Pepper. Stupid. Foolish. I let pride rule me, driving me to take risks that I never should have taken. When my own stupidity ended up costing a man his life, I realized how arrogant I had become. I thought I was invincible . . . but I never once realized what the cost for my success would be."

My hand covered his heart, where it was beating strong and true, my own aching for him, for the pain that was shadowed in his eyes. "This man, he died?"

"No." Walker's gaze flickered away to the wall of the tent, but I knew he wasn't seeing it. He was looking inward, to the past, to the horrible guilt he carried with him still. "He didn't die, but he might as well have for what I did to him. I broke his neck, Pepper. I did, not anyone else, not the horse, not the fall he took; *I* broke his neck and ruined his life the minute I decided to aim for his head. It's the trickiest of all shots, and the one that scores the highest, but you have to be a master jouster, a true champion at arms to pull it off." His chest rose and fell three times before he spoke the words that fairly dripped with anguish. "I didn't."

I've never been in a situation where I was responsible for evaluating someone's psyche. My mother had always been a straightforward person, and my father had disappeared from my life by the time I was two. Friends and family mattered, of course, but no one had ever really needed me, not needed me in the way I sensed Walker needed me. CJ was wrong—the woman who was meant for him wasn't someone who could comfort him and protect him from the world he had so successfully hidden from for three long years, flaying his soul with guilt for a tragic accident. No, what Walker needed was someone who wouldn't allow him to wallow in martyrdom any longer, someone who made him confront his issues, work through them, and move on with life.

It wasn't going to be easy, it wasn't going to be fun, and I had a nasty, suspicious feeling that it would take a while before Walker realized just how good I was for him, but I have never been one to back away from a challenge.

Much. Well, okay, there was that whole vet thing, but that was a *totally* different situation.

I leveled Walker a steady look, and said simply, "Then I guess you've got a lot of practicing to do before you make your qualifying runs today, huh?"

His arm stiffened beneath my head. "I've just explained to you why I can't—"

"No, you can, you just won't." I sat up, looking down at him. "But that's a quitter's attitude, Walker, and you're not a quitter. Furthermore, this isn't just about you. You have a responsibility to your team members."

He frowned and sat up as well, reaching for the black tights he wore under his tunic. "They knew the odds were against them—"

"Yeah, and you've pretty much made it a sure thing, haven't you?" I pulled my wrinkled negligee over my head, looking around for something else I could wear back to my tent. I hated to be so rough on him, but it was about time he stopped hiding from the truth.

"I don't have a responsibility to them—"

I whirled around, at the end of my temper. "Yes, you do! Why don't you see that? You're their leader. You're their teacher. I'm willing to bet you're their idol, as well—at least you are for the men. And if you don't do this, if you don't get a grip on yourself and confront your fear, you will be responsible for the ruination of two more lives. Can you live with that, Walker? I sure couldn't."

He made an abrupt, frustrated gesture, throwing me

a long white linen shirt before donning its twin. "Vandal made the choice to mortgage his house, not me—"

"And how likely is it that he would win the lottery just when you guys needed a couple thousand dollars? Come on, Walker, admit the truth, at least to yourself if not to anyone else—you had to know that there was something suspicious about his coming up with all the money needed for you guys to come to Canada, and yet you did nothing. You didn't ask questions, you didn't probe, you just accepted it because you wanted to come. You wanted to see your team compete, and probably, buried deep down inside, hidden behind the fear you hold so tightly to, you want your turn at glory again."

He was truly angry now, his eyes spitting little silver sparks at me. "You don't know anything about it."

I pulled the shirt over my negligee, walking over to stand before him. I smiled and traced my finger along his jaw. "Your muscles are so tight, it's a wonder you haven't cracked a tooth."

He stared down at me, silent, angry, and sexy as hell.

"The bottom line is that you have to do this not for Vandal, not for Fenice, not for Butcher or Bos or anyone else. You have to do this for *you,* because I truly do believe you've been living in a hell of your own making for the last three years, and it's time to move on. What happened was an accident—a horrible, tragic accident—but unless you went into the ring with the intention of wounding that man, then it was just an accident. You are older and wiser now. You've learned."

He stood stiff for a minute, and I was sure he was going to reject my comfort again, but a little tremor shook him as he bowed his head, his eyes closed. I wrapped my arms around his waist and held him. After a moment, his arms tightened around me as well, his breath brushing my ear as he spoke. "I don't want to hurt anyone again."

"I know you don't. But that's part of the chance you take, isn't it? It's part and parcel of jousting. Would you love it so much if you jousted with foam-rubber lances?"

He rubbed his chin against my head, silent for a few minutes. "What if . . . what if I'm not good enough? What if it happens again? What if I *didn't* learn?"

I kissed his jaw, my heart aching for him. "You're unbeaten, Walker. You are the most skilled jouster in all of England. How many times were you world champion?"

"Eight."

"Eight?" My mouth gaped a little before I realized what it was doing. "Eight years? In a row?"

He nodded.

"Good God, you're, like, the best jouster in the world!"

"The best jouster in the world doesn't ruin other people's lives."

"Walker." I cupped his jaw in my hands, putting every iota of emotion I possessed into my face. I wanted him to see the belief I had in him. "That man made the decision to get on his horse and joust with you. You didn't make it for him. He must have known the chances that he took doing so, and he was willing to accept the possibility that something could go wrong. Didn't you accept that every time you entered the list?"

"Yes." His eyes were dark, fathomless pools of anger and frustration. "But it didn't have to end that way."

"But it did. And you've learned from the tragedy, and now the time has come for you to confront your fear. So the real question is, are you man enough to face that fear and beat it, or are you going to let it win and spend the rest of your life hiding?"

His gaze held mine for a minute; then it dropped away. I wanted to press him, to make him agree to what I wanted, but I knew that this was a decision he had to make on his own. He had to stop running away from himself, or there would be nothing left of him.

I kissed him on his lovely blunt chin, whispering, "I have faith in you, Walker McPhail. I believe in you."

He stood silent, watching me as I gathered up Moth and his tin of cat snacks, but I didn't look back as I shoved the heavy material of the tent flap aside. I had done all that I could; the rest was up to him.

Walker's tent faced east, which explained why I was momentarily blinded as I left his tent. I put my hand up to shade my eyes, and found myself staring at five very shocked faces. Fenice and Gary, who had evidently been to a nearby Starbucks, were setting down several lattes on the table next to the lawn chairs. CJ, in a T-shirt that went to her knees, was yawning as Butcher handed her a pastry. Bliss was breaking up a large bunch of grapes. Vandal sat with his head in his hands.

I looked back at all of them, then down to where my sexy red negligee was clearly visible below the hem of Walker's shirt. "Oh. Uh. Hi. Morning. Um. Moth ran into . . . uh . . . Walker's tent, and I . . . uh . . . I went to get him. And . . . um . . . he barfed, and Walker gave me a shirt. Because he barfed. Moth did. A hairball. And I needed a shirt. Er . . . that's all."

They stared with unblinking, stunned expressions until the material behind me parted and Walker emerged fully clothed from his tent, a scrap of red lace and satin in his hand.

"Gah!" I shrieked, and grabbed my underwear. "Gotta run. Lots to do this morning! Later!"

As I lumbered off (being burdened with Moth slowed me down considerably), Vandal said in a voice rife with awe, "Bugger me, she did it! Pepper seduced Walker!"

Chapter Ten

The morning was not without its moments of irony. I fully intended to give Walker the time he needed to think things through, but despite my best intentions to avoid him, I kept running into him.

"Oh, hello," I said as he entered Marley's stall, obviously there to do the very same thing I was doing. "His leg looks great. See—no swelling, no tenderness, and the wound appears to have closed already."

As he squatted down next to me to look at the horse's leg, every atom in my body stood up and shouted a demand to throw myself into his arms. His long fingers ran lightly over the wound, and I shivered with the memory of the desire those fingers could stir up inside me.

"Good. How soon do you think we'll be able to work him?"

I got to my feet and moved back a few paces, more to put distance between myself and the temptation that Walker posed than to avoid Marley. "I'd say you could take him out for a little gentle exercise today and see how he feels. I doubt if he'll even notice it, though, if you were wanting to . . . oh, say, *joust* with him today."

"There's no need for that," Walker said, his eyes shaded.

Damn and blast the man! It sounded like he was

still being obstinate. I bit back the urge to ask him what he had decided, instead saying simply, "Well, I guess I'll be seeing you around."

He nodded.

"Today on *Pepper's Dishy Englishman Show:* alpha males and the women who fall in love with them," I muttered to myself as I walked away.

An hour later I ran into Walker again. I had fed Moth, cleaned myself up, and strapped my breasts into the red-and-black bodice before setting out for the day's Wenching. No sooner had I zipped up the tent and straightened Moth's devil horns than I heard a familiar voice.

". . . don't know who told you that, but it's false. The Three Dog Knights have not been disqualified from competition."

"But it is true that one of your team members is in the hospital?"

I scooped up Moth and hurried down the line of tents to where Walker was holding a breastplate and mail hauberk. Red-haired Claude was in front of him.

"No. He was released this morning with two cracked ribs and a broken wrist."

Claude's eyes widened. "He can't joust with a broken wrist, can he?"

"No, he can't." Walker's gaze lifted to meet mine. I didn't say anything, just held my breath and willed him to say he was going to take Bos's place. He didn't, of course. That would be far too sensible of the man. Instead he nodded at me, saying in an extremely noncommittal voice, "Pepper."

I nodded back. *Drat the beastly man.* "Walker."

Moth purred at him until he turned without another word and walked off.

"But . . . but . . ." Claude watched Walker's back for a few seconds before turning to me to ask, "Who are they going to get to replace the injured man?"

"That is the sixty-four-thousand-dollar question," I said, and hoisted Moth up higher.

"Need a ride, stranger?" I asked an hour and a half after our last run-in.

Walker, tromping alongside the road that led through town, stopped and peered into CJ's VW. He was wearing normal clothes: a pair of khaki pants and a light-colored T-shirt, the latter stuck to his back with sweat. "What are you doing here?"

I smiled as he carefully folded his long body into CJ's small car. "Probably doing the same thing you're doing—making a run to the nearest grocery store. His highness back there ran out of his favorite flavor of pricey kitty food. How come you're walking?"

He shrugged, his eyes closing in relief as the full force of the air-conditioning hit him. "No one had a car I could borrow."

"Ah." We drove the mile and a half into town in silence. I kept taking little glances at him, trying to get used to seeing him out of his knight clothes. Either way you cut it, he was mighty darn fine.

"I've decided that I like you in regular clothes," I told him as he came out of the store bearing two cases of beer, assorted barbecue fodder, and ten cans of Moth's favorite food. I had stayed in the car with the air-conditioning on because it was too hot to leave an animal unattended. "You're still handsome and dashing, but not so gorgeous that I'm worried about other women throwing you to the ground and wrestling your chinos off. I approve of you."

Walker looked startled for a moment, then gave me a once-over. I was back in jeans and a lightweight gauze shirt. "I approve of you, too."

"Good," I said.

"Good," he agreed.

*   *   *

Forty minutes after we had parted at the parking lot, I held up both hands. "Fine, I surrender. You win."

Walker's eyebrows rose as he looked beyond me at the portable toilet from which I had just emerged. "Win what?"

"Win your campaign to follow me around and try to make it look like an accident that we keep bumping into each other." I untied Moth's leash from the door and allowed the big cat to jump into Walker's arms. "Go ahead; say it: You can't resist me, and every hour spent away from me is a eternity."

A tiny little smile quirked the corner of his mouth. "I'm beginning to think I can't resist you."

"That's a start. I'll accept it." I plucked Moth from his arms (much to the cat's obvious unhappiness) and gave Walker one of my special wicked smiles. "The sooner I have you groveling on your knees before me, the happier I'll be."

I turned to walk away from him (for a change), but he called me back with one low, velvety brush of his voice. "Pepper?"

"Hmm?"

His mouth was hot on mine—arousing, enticing, everything wonderful that was Walker, hot and fiery, and spicy just as he was. Desire and an annoying bubble of happiness welled up within me as his tongue danced through my mouth.

"I never grovel," he growled against my mouth; then he was gone.

"Holy garbanzo beans," I breathed, watching him walk away, my mind fogged with the need I felt within him, a need that exactly matched mine. As soon as I gathered my wits together I realized what he had said. "Oh, you don't grovel, eh? We'll just see about that!" I bellowed after him, much to the delight of three passing Ale Wenches.

"Shield up and a little more to the left," Bliss called. I adjusted the wooden shield strapped to my left arm so it was slightly angled away from my body. "Are you sure this lance is okay?"

"It's one of ours, so stop fussing and lift the shield. You must learn to present it properly, else you'll have points deducted."

"Points? Who said anything about points? I thought I was just learning how to do this to prove to Farrell that I could?" Cassie tossed her head in protest of the tightened reins. I loosened them up, giving her shoulder an apologetic pat, which she answered by trying to eat my left foot. "Bliss, much as I appreciate you giving up your time to teach me how to joust, I have to admit that I think it's a waste— Argh! Bliss! Not now, I'm not ready!"

"A jouster must always be ready to run her course," she called as she spurred her horse forward, avoiding a large ditch in the field.

We were out in the distant reaches of the fair-grounds, the auxiliary parking lot that consisted of a bumpy grass field. Bliss had rounded me up during the two-hour lunch break between qualifying rounds and dragged me out to the field to teach me how to conduct a jousting pass at a live opponent. The first half hour was spent with us walking our horses toward each other, attempting to touch the lance tip on a specific part of the shield. Or, in my case, any part of the shield. The results were just as abysmal when the practice was accomplished at a trot—I just could not seem to hit the shield. I aimed, I watched the target carefully, but every time I hit Bliss's arm, her leg, and twice her saddle. I refused to think about the times I struck nothing but air.

"This is so stupid," I muttered as I dug my heels into Cassie. "I'm going to fall; I just know it."

Before I had time to aim, Bliss was on us. I lowered my lance and prayed that I wouldn't strike her or Miss Loretta, the pretty roan she was riding. It might not hurt her to be struck at a walk, but at a canter . . .

"Hiya!" I yelled as the lance tip connected with

Bliss's shield, shattering at the impact. I felt the shock in my lower back more than in my arm as I was thrown backward against the high back of the Paso saddle. This was no quintain, giving way easily under my blow, as both my right wrist and forearm were willing to attest. Bliss's lance struck my shield at the exact time I struck hers, leaving me surprised to find the received hit was not as hard as I thought it would be. Her lance tip shattered as well, and I was able to push the shield out so the rest of her lance slid along the curved front.

"I did it!" I yelled as Cassie cantered by Bliss. "Can you believe that? Hot damn! I did it! This could be addicting!"

Bliss laughed as she turned her horse and started back toward me. "Welcome to the world of contact jousting, Pepper."

Cassie happily turned toward our designated starting area. I grinned, feeling more than a little bit cocky and sure I was the next jousting wunderkind.

Bliss quickly took care of that notion. "This time keep your heels down, your head up, your shield more to the left, and for God's sake, don't close your eyes just before your lance strikes! You could have disemboweled me or Miss Loretta!"

And so it went. For a half hour or so I was fine—successfully striking her shield at a canter, but missing every single time when we went slower. Bliss gave up trying to figure out why and concentrated on showing me how and when to strike the shield.

It wasn't until the lunch break was almost over that I realized I wasn't any sort of wunderkind—Bliss had been holding back. That became sadly apparent when I went sailing off the side of Cassie, one moment sitting firmly pressed up against the high back of the saddle in anticipation of my lance striking her shield, the next feeling as if I had been hit by a Mack truck, one that ripped my shield from my left arm and flipped me up and over Cassie's right shoulder.

"That's what we call doing a face plant," Bliss said calmly as I raised my head and spit out a mouthful of grass. "Are you all right? How do you feel?"

"Like I was run over by a train. Ow. Dammit, horse, stop slobbering on me!" I sat up slowly, flexing my fingers and arms as I did a quick check on all available body parts. Everything radioed back as being in working order. "What happened? One second I was fine, and the next, whammo!"

"You weren't paying attention," Bliss said complacently as I pushed Cassie's face away and got to my feet. "That's a cardinal sin in jousting. One moment's distraction, and it's all over."

"Yeah, I guess." I shook my arms, pushing away the horse again as she tried to snuffle me. "What *is* her problem?"

"We train them to get treats when we fall. It makes them easier to catch if they're not running about the ring loose. She's waiting for you to give her a treat."

I ripped out a handful of grass and offered it to the horse. Cassie snuffled my hand for a moment, blowing a disgusted snort when she realized all I had was grass. I wiped my hand on my skirt, looking over to where Bliss sat on the roan. "Are we done for the year? 'Cause I think I've just about had enough jousting."

Bliss's face went blank and I realized just how whiny I sounded. "Very well. We have twenty minutes left, but if you wish to quit—"

"No." I sighed, gathering up my skirt and grabbing at Cassie's reins. "I'm not a quitter. We'll do a few more runs, and I promise I'll pay attention."

"It makes no matter to me," Bliss said stiffly as she turned and directed Miss Loretta to the opposite end of the field.

"Of course not, that's why I'm out here eating the ground," I said softly, then swore and dismounted to pick up my fallen lance. I plucked one of the remaining three lances from where we had leaned them up against a nearby horse trailer, and resumed my training.

By the time I went to retrieve Moth from CJ, my entire body felt as though it were made up of one gigantic bruise.

"Took a few falls, did you?" Butcher asked.

"Only about a thousand," I groaned as I slid into the bench attached to a wooden picnic table. "Why, does it show?"

CJ giggled and waved her roast corn on a stick at me. "You've got grass stains on your chemise, and dirt in your hair."

"Classic signs of someone who's taken a tumble or two," Butcher said with a kind smile. "How did it go?"

"Um," I said noncommittally, looking over the line of food vendors. "I'm so wiped out I don't even think I can make it to the Dragon Wing tent for some hot wings."

"Then don't, my lady. Allow me to have the immense pleasure of providing you with sustenance," a smooth voice spoke behind me.

I didn't need to see the mask of indifference slide over Butcher's face, nor CJ's sudden interest in the foil that had wrapped her turkey leg, to recognize just to whom that voice belonged.

"Hello, Farrell," I said politely.

"And greetings to you, beauteous lady of mine."

"Surely that will come as news to Walker," CJ mumbled into a glass of spiced apple juice.

"Sorry, didn't catch that," Farrell said as he slid onto the bench next to me.

"She didn't say anything," I answered with a bright smile, determined not to let Farrell bait me into admitting anything. It was because of him and his misbegotten ego that I was all banged up, after all. "So how are you? How is the qualifying going?"

He smiled. Up close, I could see the tiny little lines that networked from his eyes, the sign of someone who spent too much time in the sun. Even with that, I had to admit to myself that he was gorgeous—his eyes dancing merrily, his teeth white against the tan of his skin, the sun all but kissing his long golden hair, the black and white of his tunic showing off his physique . . . he was perfection all wrapped up in a manly package, and it left me colder than a three-day-old pile of horse poop.

"The qualifying is almost over, and I am pleased to say that every member of Team Joust! has qualified thus far, which, I believe, is something that cannot be said about the Three Dog Knights. Having a bit of difficulty with your alternate, Sittow?"

Butcher gave Farrell a cold, indifferent glance.

"Now, now, play nicely or we'll have to ask you to leave our table," I said, not wanting Farrell to get going with any digs about Walker.

To be honest, my concern had less to do with not irritating Butcher than with easing the ache around my heart. The morning's Realgestech qualifying rounds had been held—without Walker. No one had seen him for the three hours during which the morning qualifiers were run. No one knew where he was, and no one said a word as the morning passed with us in the bleachers, watching jouster after jouster qualify for the competition. Bliss qualified with no trouble, Butcher qualified after just one match by unhorsing his opponent all three times, and even Vandal qualified after being unhorsed by two different opponents. When the last pair of jousters finished up the qualifiers, the collective mood in our section of the bleachers was bleak. Even Moth seemed fretful and unhappy, periodically reaching out with sheathed claws to slap at my hand.

"Does this mean it's over?" I had asked earlier as everyone but team 3DK filed out of the arena for the lunch break. No one answered me, but they didn't have to. The hopeless looks in their eyes said it all. And now here was Farrell, gloating over the fact that Walker had not come through for his team.

"My dear lady Pepper, you cannot mean to tell me that you wish to associate with the sort of jousters who show the cowardice displayed by this team?"

"These people are my friends," I said evenly. "I'll thank you not to call them cowards."

He eyed me for a moment. "Very well, I withdraw the comment."

"Thank you. Now if you don't mind—"

"I should instead say that the leader of this team is a coward."

"Farrell!" I said, outraged on Walker's behalf.

Butcher growled an oath under his breath, his hands fisted as he half rose from the bench at the insult. CJ clung to his arm and murmured soothingly in his ear.

"That's unfair, and you know it," I said, hoping to defuse the situation despite the fact that I wouldn't have minded seeing Butcher plant one of his big fists right on Farrell's nose. I gave him the same sort of curious look he'd given me. "You really are jealous of Walker, aren't you?"

"Jealous? Me?" Farrell laughed a hard, brittle laugh.

"Yes, jealous, you. As in, you can't stand it that Walker is such a good jouster. Tell me, did you ever joust with each other?"

The laughter faded from his face, his eyes going a bit hard. "Yes, we did."

"Ah." I toyed with the end of Moth's leash, savoring for a moment the pleasure of what I was going to say next. "And since Walker is undefeated, I have to assume that he beat you."

Farrell's jaw tensed. "Beat me? No, he did not, not fairly. There was an equipment failure—"

I waved this excuse away. "So the truth is that you just can't stand it that Walker is a better jouster than you, and rather than let it go or work toward improving yourself, you go around bad-mouthing a man who's not even active in the sport anymore. I may not be an expert on the subject, but that sure doesn't

sound like any form of knightly chivalry I've ever
heard of."

"Go, Pepper," CJ cheered as I stood up, suddenly
overwhelmed with the need to find Walker and kiss
the man into a stupor—right after I gave him a piece
of my mind, of course. "You tell 'im!"

Farrell stood as well. "There is nothing—*nothing*—
for me to be jealous of where Walker McPhail is concerned."

"Oh, really?" I snapped the leash on Moth, who
was happily chewing on the last of CJ's turkey leg.
"How many times have you been world jousting
champion?"

A dull, angry red flush crept over his cheeks. "I
have been the United States Grand Champion for the
last seven years—"

"Oooh, does that mean you have a great big goose
egg on the world-championship front?" I was starting
to get really angry. No wonder Walker didn't want to
participate anymore if this was the sort of person he
had to deal with. "Enough said. I can understand why
you want what he's got if it's something you've
never had."

"There's nothing he has that I want!" Farrell all but
yelled at me.

"Not even Pepper?" a familiar voice rumbled behind me.

Farrell gawked—there really was no other word for
it; his mouth hung open and everything—when Walker
slid an arm around my waist, pulling me toward him
as I turned to smile. I didn't get a chance to complete
the smile before he was kissing me, really kissing me,
kissing me like he hadn't kissed me before. It wasn't
just his mouth at work; his whole body got involved
in the event, his arms sweeping up behind me, one
hand sliding into my hair, tugging my head backward,
while the other slid down my back to clutch one side
of my butt. His tongue went all pushy with mine, boss-
ing it around as his arm tightened behind me, pulling

me even tighter to his body. His legs were hard against mine, his chest like a brick wall, but all of him fit perfectly as I molded my body to his.

It was a kiss to end all kisses, and although the taste and feel and scent of him sent my senses reeling out of control, in a tiny dark corner of my mind I couldn't help but feel that he was kissing me that way simply to make a point. I remembered his comment about wanting to mark me so other men would know I was his, and a little of my joy faded.

"It would appear that I owe you some form of congratulations," Farrell said when Walker retrieved his tongue and broke off the kiss. I weaved a little as I stood clutching his arms, trying like mad to get my legs to support me again. "It seems you got the girl. However, I believe the lady is a bit confused about which man is worthy of her attentions—"

"Nope, not confused at all," I said.

"—a misconception that I will happily take it upon myself to correct." Farrell didn't quite leer at me, but the way he eyed me definitely wasn't polite.

Walker almost rolled his eyes. "For Christ's sake, man, she's not the competition."

"Yeah," I agreed, my hands on my hips. "And if I were, Walker would win."

"Indeed?" A tiny curl curved Farrell's lips. He didn't look like he believed me at all, but I wasn't worried. No doubt his gigantic, bloated ego would insist that he make a halfhearted play for me, but I hadn't dated unemployed geeks for nothing. I could take care of him. Farrell pointed his smug smile toward Walker. "I do hope she's *ample* compensation for not winning the championship."

"Who are you calling ample?" I asked, leveling a really quality glare at him.

"It may be your practice to award yourself a title before the actual competition—and if your past record is anything to go by, I assume that's your standard operating procedure—but the rest of us like to wait until we've actually won a title before claiming it," Walker said, his voice rumbling around in that big chest of his.

It took me a few seconds to drag my mind from contemplation of just how wonderful his chest was to understand what it was he was saying. I spun around, my mouth agape. "*Us*? As in, you being part of a group? You're going to joust?"

Walker's mouth thinned, his eyes grim and dark with unhappiness. "If I can't find anyone else to take my place, then I have no choice, do I?"

"Yes, you do," I said softly, wishing I could ease the pain I knew he felt.

"According to you, I don't," he replied, and tried to brush past me, but Moth threw himself at Walker just as Farrell recovered from the verbal blow he'd been dealt.

"So the wild man of the circuit is going to make his reappearance in a desperate attempt to regain his honor and impress a wench." Farrell's lips were smiling, but his eyes were furious.

"There had better have been a capital W on that word," I said softly.

He didn't pay me the slightest bit of attention as Walker handed Moth to me.

"Much as I would dearly love to stand here and listen to years of bitterness spill forth, I have work to do. I have no doubt that I will see you in the lists, Farrell." Walker gave me a look that could have melted marble, then gestured to Butcher as he walked past.

"*No doubt,*" Farrell parroted Walker's accent. "The question is, how many men will you destroy in your attempt to grab at the glory long lost to you?"

Walker froze for a few seconds, then continued walking as if he hadn't heard the slam, Butcher alongside him.

I wasn't about to pretend any such thing. I shoved Moth into CJ's arms and marched over to Farrell, poking him in the chest. "You really are something, aren't you? You know, I've tried to give you the benefit of the doubt, even though you really didn't deserve it, but now I see that you're nothing more than a frightened bully. You just can't stand the fact that Walker is better than you."

"He is not better than me," Farrell snapped. "There is *nothing* Walker McPhail can do better than me. He is an ignorant, dirt-grubbing farrier, nothing more. You would do well to remember that when you are comparing the two of us. As for jousting, we competed against each other only three times, and twice the results were draws."

"And the third time he tossed you off your horse, boo-hoo-hoo. Get a grip, Farrell. Oh, and just so you know, there's at least one thing Walker does a hundred times better than you." I smiled sweetly and leaned in close to whisper, "Just being near him makes my knees melt, and when he kisses me? Hooo, daddy! Get out the fire hoses and wet me down, because I'm sizzling."

Farrell bit back something that I was sure was extremely rude, then said simply, "We shall see, won't we?"

"Some of us have already seen," I answered, ever Pepper the Pithy. "But speaking of your insane jealousy, you wouldn't happen to know anything about how to doctor a lance, would you?"

"Doctor a lance? I have no idea what you're talking about. Pepper, sweet Pepper, obviously spending so much time around Walker and his Dogs has weakened your wits. You must allow me to carry your favor. I, at least, can guarantee that it will be carried to glory."

"Not a chance. Walker has all my favors, and yes, I mean that the way you think I mean it. How do you feel about horses, Farrell? Been making any unexpected and unseen visits to other teams' horsies? Just you and your little pocketknife, hmm?"

His blue eyes glittered with barely disguised anger,

the air between us positively humming with the restraint he was clamping down on himself. "Now you're making absolutely no sense. Alas, I fear it is too late for you, but if you change your mind and decide you'd prefer being with a champion rather than a has-been, let me know. I, at least, will not disappoint you."

"Sorry. I'm taken. Literally and quite happily," I answered, wondering how on earth I was going to find proof that he was behind Marley's injury and the damaged lance.

He said something under his breath before storming off with such speed that three people strolling past were shoved out of his way.

"That was subtle," CJ said as I snapped Moth's leash onto his harness and set him on the ground. "I thought you had a thing for him?"

I limped slightly as we joined the throng heading toward the big arena. "Farrell? No, but I wasn't ready to believe him to be the villain you guys all thought him to be until Marley and Bos were hurt. Now I have to admit that he fits the profile pretty well, and even if he's not responsible, I wouldn't tolerate him being so snotty to Walker. No one picks on *my* boyfriend and lives to tell about it!"

"Pepper," CJ said, her brows pulled together in a worried frown.

I didn't let her finish the warning. "I know, I know, he's not for me, it'll all end in unhappiness. I kind of figured you'd be back to the old doom-and-gloom scenario once I did what you wanted me to do. Regardless of what your gut is telling you, I'm not giving up on Walker. He needs me now more than ever. I can't believe the stupid man doesn't see how much he has to offer—"

She stopped and pinched my arm. Hard!

"Oh, I like that!" she said. "And here I was, all ready to give you guys my blessing. You think I'm the sort of person who would take back a blessing?"

I cocked the Eyebrow of Disbelief at her.

"Well, all right, so I do happen to think you and Walker are all wrong for each other, but that doesn't mean I'm going to continue to tell you over and over again, ad nauseam, what sort of a miserable, horrible life you'll have if you insist on continuing this ill-favored fling. I have some dignity, you know."

"That is debatable, and oh, joy of joys, look who's waiting for us." I smiled a smile I didn't truly feel and raised my hand in greeting to the woman standing at the entrance of the arena.

"I doubt if she's waiting to talk to me. It's you she has the hots for," CJ said, but she smiled and waved as well.

"The hots?" I stopped, grabbing CJ's arm and stopping her as well. "You think Veronica wants me?"

"Not sexually, you dolt!" CJ pulled away with a frown at me. "Honestly, just because one man likes you enough to kiss you in front of an audience, you think everyone is lusting after you."

"You are *so* good for my ego," I said dryly, but before I could ask her more about what she meant, Veronica was putting out her cigarette and walking toward us.

"I wondered if I would see you here. Your cat has sprouted some horns, I see."

Moth didn't mind walking alongside me, but there were so many people converging on the arena I was worried someone would step on him. I hoisted him up in my arms, ignoring the nasty look he gave me as I settled him on my hip. "It's the devil in him. Yes, we're here, ready to watch the last bit of qualifiers. CJ tells me it's the most dangerous style. Will you be participating?"

"Of course, I wouldn't dream of doing otherwise. Pepper, if you have a few moments, I'd like to talk to you about a subject of mutual interest."

She wanted to talk about Walker; I just knew it. By now the news about Walker and me was bound to be all over the Faire, given the gossipy, tight nature of the Faire folk. Veronica probably wanted to give me advice about what sorts of things drove him wild, or tell me about her marriage to him, or other intimate details that I didn't want to hear from her.

CJ made her excuses and went to claim a section of the bleachers for the various members and supporters of the Three Dog Knights. I allowed Veronica to steer me toward a little grassy swath that ran alongside the front edge of the building.

I decided to forestall what I could of her advice. "You know, I appreciate the fact that you take such an interest in me, but honestly, there's nothing you can say that is going to sway me."

She frowned slightly. "I'm sorry to hear that. I had hoped to persuade you into joining us. I believe the experience would do much to open your mind."

Good God above, was she talking about a threesome with her, Walker, and me? Holy cow! No, she couldn't be. I didn't have the ménage à trois look about me, surely! I must have mistaken what she said.

"I realize it must all be new to you, but I can assure you that I can do things for you that Walker could never imagine." If her lazily drawling voice didn't get the message across, the sidelong looks she was giving me did.

Oh, my god! She *was* talking about a threesome! I stared in horror at her for a few seconds before I realized my mouth was hanging open.

She must have seen the shock on my face, because she quickly continued. "I know you don't have much experience, but it will give me pleasure to teach you what you need to know."

How lovely—she was willing to take on a learner. The conversation held such a bizarre fascination that I had a hard time focusing my thoughts. "Well . . . as to that, I do actually have some experience. Not great big tons of it, but enough to get by in life."

"Surely not enough to achieve your goals."

I straightened my shoulders. "Well, since you're asking, yes. I certainly haven't heard any complaints."

"Complaints?"

"Not a single one," I said a bit righteously, two seconds before I realized I was defending my sexual experience to a woman who lusted after me. "Veronica, I'm . . . I'm . . . I'm sorry, but there's no way I could even think of saying yes to your proposition. It's flattering, but out of the question. It's not that I'm a prude or anything, but I never was one to share my toys, and where men are concerned, I'm positively territorial—"

Her frown turned puzzled. "What are you talking about?"

I gestured with my free hand, Moth taking the opportunity to dig his claws into my wrist in protest for being squished up against my side. "Ow. The . . . uh . . . what you suggested with you and me and Walker. I'm sorry, but it's just not going to happen."

"Walker? Why would you want Walker to join us?"

She wanted me all to herself? I looked down at the breast shelf flowing over the top of my bodice. "I had no idea this bodice would make me so irresistible to everyone! The power of really good boning is simply amazing. Veronica . . . I don't know what to say. Other than no, that is. I'm flattered and humbled and I appreciate what it must have cost you to approach me, but to be completely honest, I'm not . . . er . . . into girls. That way. So thank you, but no."

She stared at me in silence for a few moments, then raised both eyebrows. "Do you believe I just asked you to join me in bed?"

She wanted to have sex with me somewhere else? Somewhere nonbed? I was obviously way out of my league. "Well, usually it's done in bed, so I assumed . . . er . . . you weren't?"

She shook her head for a moment, as if she couldn't believe what she was hearing. "No, I wasn't asking if you'd like to sleep with me. I was asking you again if you wanted to join my company as an alternate."

"Oh," I said, and prayed for the earth to open up and swallow me whole. "Sorry. Just a little confused here."

"Obviously," she said.

Chapter Eleven

Once I got over the mortification of believing Veronica wanted to have a lesbian fling with me (not to mention the little pang of disappointment that I wasn't as seductive in my bodice as I had surmised I was), our conversation settled down to something a little less out of *Pepper and Veronica's Amazing Crosstalk Show.*

"What I said before is still true, Veronica. I'm not practicing to joust professionally."

"You also said that you had no intention of learning how to joust, and yet I've heard that you spent an hour and a half today learning how to do just that." She picked a tiny bit of dried leaf out of my hair as proof of my perfidy.

I raised my free hand in a gesture of denial. "I didn't *intend* to learn anything, but I sort of got myself railroaded into it. Bliss is difficult to say no to when she's got a lance in her hand and she's galloping toward you. Besides, I did kind of throw a challenge to Farrell, and I'll be damned if I give him anything more to gloat about. That man's ego badly needs to be taken in hand."

"Granted, but there is no reason why you cannot do so under my auspices. Pepper"—she smiled a persuasive smile—"a little bird told me that you and Walker have found pleasure in each other's company, something else I believe you decried. Your relationship with Walker aside, do you really think his troupe offers you the best opportunity for instruction?"

I prepared to bristle on behalf of everyone in the troupe. "Well, as a matter of fact, Bliss is very good—"

"Yes, she is," Veronica interrupted me smoothly, taking the sting out of it with another friendly smile. "But she is also relatively new to the sport, and has never taught anyone, whereas I have jousted professionally for almost eight years, and was taught by the best."

She waited a couple of beats until I couldn't help asking, "Walker?"

Her smile put Moth's smug look to shame. "I believe you will agree with me that he is a very talented man . . . in many ways."

Ding, ding, ding! We were stepping into relationship territory, somewhere I definitely didn't want to go. "Mmm. I'm afraid I'm just not dedicated enough to do your team proud. If Farrell wasn't acting like such a butthead, I wouldn't be learning to joust at all, so it really wouldn't be fair to the rest of your team to have me hanging around their necks as an alternate when everyone knows I'm a rank novice at the sport."

"You underestimate your natural ability," she said, clearly wanting to talk about it some more, but I hoisted Moth higher on my hip, ignoring his growl of unhappiness as I scooted around Veronica toward the door.

"And I think you're overestimating it. Thanks for the invite, but I just can't do it. Good luck with your runs today. I'll be rooting for your team."

I escaped without further argument, but I couldn't help mulling over Veronica's strange request as CJ, Fenice, Geoff, and a newly released Bos watched the last of the jousting qualifiers.

"Why on earth would someone with a professional

team want an untrained know-nothing like me hanging around? It just doesn't make sense."

"It does if you are Ronnie," Fenice said, flinching as both jousters on the arena floor took simultaneous headers off their horses, their broken lances falling beside them. All the teams' lances had been double-checked by the jousting society sponsoring the competition, but no other weakened ones were found.

"What on earth does *that* mean?" I asked, my mind not on the sabotage but on why Veronica was so interested in me.

Bos, sitting next to me with his arm encased in a blue sling, grimaced as Moth suddenly had a spaz attack and attacked the fringed end of the leather belt that lay along Bos's thigh.

"Please excuse him; he's deranged," I said as I carefully pried Moth's claws from Bos's tights. "Back to Veronica—"

Fenice—minus her attendant jousters, since they were due in the ring in a short while—half turned on her bench to cast me a knowing look. "Do you know what she does when she's not doing charitable good works?"

I shook my head.

"She's what they call a cannibal."

My mouth dropped open.

"Headhunter, not cannibal, Fenice," Geoff corrected. "She finds people for high-placed positions in posh companies."

"Oh, a headhunter. That makes sense . . . no, it doesn't. What does that have to do with her wanting a person who doesn't know how to joust acting as an alternate on her team?"

"Boy, you're just really looking for the strokes today, aren't you?" CJ asked, whapping me on the arm and dropping her voice to a whisper as the next two jousters were announced. "She thinks you have talent, stupid!"

"Oh." I thought about that for a minute, then realized that it was a very good compliment. Undeserved, but still good. "Oh! That's very nice of her."

"Shh, Bliss is next."

The afternoon slipped by in a flurry of knights taking dives off their horses. I understood why the majority of the jousters considered the Southern Italian style the most dangerous—with no shields, and passing each other on the right side, the jousters more often than not went flying with the impact of the blows from the lances.

After an hour of watching, I felt the time had come for a little basic explanation. "Okay, explain to me why Vandal qualified when he was knocked off his horse, but the guy from New Zealand didn't qualify."

"It's all to do with the scoring," Bliss answered. She had joined us, having qualified easily, and was sitting at Bos's feet, leaning back against his legs. "If your lance touches anywhere between the saddle and the neck, but doesn't break, that's half a point."

"If it breaks, then you get a point," Geoff said.

"Touch but no break between neck and crest of helmet, two points," Fenice added.

"Break with a touch between the neck and crest of helmet, three points," Bliss said.

"Unhorsing, four points," Bos and Geoff said together.

"Unhorsing as the result of a touch between the neck and crest of helmet, five points," they all chanted.

"Vandal was unhorsed only once, but he scored more points by going for the higher-scoring shots than his opponents, who played it safe," Fenice explained.

"Then there're the penalties," Bos said, raising his good arm and holding up his fingers as he counted them off. "Hitting any object besides the knight is minus two points. Hitting the saddle is minus one point. Hitting anywhere on the knight but the target areas is minus three points. Sweeping the lance sideways is also minus a point. Striking the horse is disqualification and banishment from the tourney circuit, not to mention a probable lawsuit by the horse's owner."

I looked at Bliss. "Right, that's it, I'm not even going to practice with you anymore. I might not be overly fond of horses"—I ignored the hissing gasps of surprise at that admission. "but I don't want to accidentally hurt one of them."

"Don't be stupid; you're almost a vet," CJ dismissed my concern. "You help animals; you don't hurt them."

I glared at her, giving her arm a little pinch. "I write software; I'm *not* a vet."

"Shhh! Your ex-boyfriend is up next."

"He is not—"

"Shhh!"

"—my ex-boyfriend. He never *was* my boyfriend."

"You dated him; thus he was a boyfriend."

"One dinner does not a date make . . . ow. That had to hurt. Guess Farrell has a bit of a chip on his shoulder because of the whole Walker thing. You think that other guy will be able to beat his helmet back into shape?"

"Probably not," Bliss answered my question. "That was a very skilled head shot Farrell made. I'm just worried. . . . Ah, there, you see? He's conceded the victory to Farrell. Poor man was obviously not up to going another two rounds with him. Well, that qualifies Farrell."

The man who had done a very impressive swan dive off his horse hobbled out of the arena, flanked on either side by tournament officials, probably making sure the jouster hadn't been seriously injured. Farrell rode around the ring taking bows and waving at the women who were leaning over the railing yelling to him.

"What a hambone," I muttered under my breath. "Just wait till he sees what a real jouster can do."

Fenice looked back and me and smiled. "For someone who hasn't ever seen Walker joust, you certainly do have a lot of faith in him."

"She's seen him wield a lance of a different sort," Bliss said.

I lifted my chin and gave them both a lofty down-the-nose look. "I simply have faith in the man, nothing more."

"Ha!" CJ said.

"Hush, both of you, there he is."

Walker rode into the ring on the back of Marley, who was looking very full of himself, prancing a little sidestep that Walker effectively nipped in the bud. Obviously his leg wasn't bothering him in the least.

I leaned over to whisper in Bliss's ear, "What are you guys doing about watching the horses?"

She slid a quick glance at me before answering. "When we aren't around to keep an eye on them, Walker arranged for a couple of Four-H kids to stay near the stable and make a note of anyone who goes near our horses."

"Good plan." I sat back, relieved, prepared to enjoy the experience of watching the man of my dreams joust. Truthfully, if I hadn't recognized Marley, I might not have known Walker was under all the steel plate. His helmet was closed, and his arms, chest, and legs were all covered in black armor, while his hands were encased in leather-and-steel gloves. Only his boots were unprotected.

"Oooh, isn't he manly in all that armor," I cooed, watching as he stopped Marley to bow his head at the marshal, sitting in the judging area. "He has black armor just like Butcher!"

"That *is* Butcher's armor," CJ said. "Walker didn't bring his own, and there's no time to have it sent, so he's using Butcher's spare set. It's just lucky that they're about the same size; otherwise Walker would be in a world of hurt."

"Oh. Can't he have some made? There are armor guys out on the vendors' row."

CJ shrugged. "Too costly," Fenice said, resting her chin on her hands as she watched Butcher and Vandal accompany Walker, both evidently acting as squires.

I was a bit surprised when the knight of my dreams rode to the farthest side of the list, but before I could ask what he was doing, Bliss lifted her hand in a warning for silence. Overhead the tinny loudspeaker announced that Walker had appealed to the joust marshal, and due to having to bring Bos back from the hospital, he was being granted a chance to qualify for the jousting that was run during the morning, following which he would make the Southern Italian runs.

The arena, half-filled as it was, buzzed with comment at that announcement. Bliss sucked in her breath and looked meaningfully at Bos. He just shook his head and leaned against Geoff, his eyes worried. Most people were talking about Walker jousting again, but I had a suspicion that his surprise reappearance wasn't what caused all the talk.

"What?" I asked, my warning system going into full "Danger, Will Robinson!" mode. "What's wrong? It's good that Walker talked them into letting him qualify for the Realgestech, isn't it?"

"Yes," Bliss said slowly, her eyes on Walker as he took his lance from Vandal. "It is good . . . but that means he'll have to either unseat the first jouster in both matches in order to beat them, or he'll have to joust four matches back-to-back."

"That's twelve jousting runs," I said softly, fear gripping my stomach and giving it a vicious twist. "That's unfair—no one else has to joust four matches in a row without a break! He hasn't jousted in years; he'll hurt himself! Someone has to stop the foolish man!"

I stood up to do just that, but CJ and Fenice pulled me down. "You can't stop him now; it's too late. If he leaves the ring, he'll forfeit the match."

"But what about that thing you told me about

earlier—the forgetfulness or something. Can't he do that?"

"Forgiveness, and no, it's not applicable in this instance. A knight can call a forgiveness only if the horse's head is in the way, or if the tip on his lance falls off, or something like that. He can't just decide not to run after he's said he would. To do so would be cowardly."

"Whatever happened to discretion being the better part of valor?" I asked, watching with worried eyes as the list marshal gave the signal for the jousters to start by yelling out, "Lay on!" "*Lay out* is going to be more like it. This is insane. He's going to get hurt, seriously hurt. He hasn't trained for this in years. He can't possibly— Oh, no!"

"Sit down; you can't help him," CJ hissed as she pulled me down onto the hard metal bench. "Stop making a scene! He's used to this."

I sat, my stomach twisting with fear for Walker. What had previously seemed like fun suddenly took on grim overtones. I knew it was irrational, but I couldn't help it. That was *my* man down there being pummeled! "This is hard to watch. I don't know how you can stand it with Butcher."

"I have faith in him. You need to trust that Walker knows what he's doing."

"Easier said than done," I said softly, sick with worry. CJ was right. I was going to be a candidate for the nearest insane asylum unless I got control of myself. What I needed to do was to be more like CJ. She was supportive. She stood at the sidelines to yell and cheer Butcher on. She never once fainted from sheer, unadulterated horror whenever he took a hit.

What CJ could do, I could do. I rallied my pride and put on a brave, supportive face.

"You look like you're going to barf," CJ whispered. "Stop worrying. There are five judges watching every joust. If the Aussie does something wrong, they'll say so."

"It's all right, Pepper, really it is. Walker is used to taking falls," Fenice said sympathetically. "He's not hurt. See? He's up and about already."

I nibbled on my thumbnail as Butcher helped Walker to his feet, dusting him off and giving him a hand in remounting Marley. Vandal had a fresh lance ready, placing it in Walker's outstretched hand. "Oh, God, why did I think this was such a good idea? He could get himself killed!"

"Not our Walker. He's the best there is," Bliss boasted, but there were tension lines around her mouth that belied her concern.

The second run was much better, at least as far as my nerves were concerned. Both Walker and the Aussie jouster kept their seats, both of them shattering their lances. The third and fourth ended up with touches, but no broken lances. The fifth time Walker unhorsed his opponent, and the sixth ended up with them both losing lances.

"What's his total score?" I asked, too worried to add the points up. "Does he qualify? Tell me he qualifies!"

"We won't know that until the end," Bliss said. My heart clenched like a fist.

While the second jouster entered the ring, I turned to Bos. "Will they let Walker qualify for the jousts you did yesterday?"

He shook his head. "It won't be necessary—as an alternate, he assumes the points of the person he replaced, namely me. Since I qualified for Northern Italian and French, as my alternate he's automatically entered."

"Oh, good." I gnawed on my lip a little more while watching the new knight. There was something about his green-and-taupe surcoat that was vaguely . . . "Oh, my god, he's jousting one of the Palm Springs team!"

"Not just one of them," Fenice said, pointing to the electronic scoreboard at the far end of the arena. The scoreboard was used to show the number of points earned by the jousters on each pass. On one side of the scoreboard was Walker's name, while the other side read: TYLER, V.

"What? He's jousting *Veronica*?"

Bliss sighed.

"Of all the people to get in the draw . . . Ronnie'll make mincemeat out of him," Fenice predicted sadly.

I stared in shock as the two jousters rode to the opposite ends of the list, positioning themselves so the barrier running the length of the list was on each knight's right. "What? She will? Walker? Are you sure? Why? I thought he taught her!"

"Yes, he taught her, but he'll also allow his emotions to interfere and will pull back rather than attack her the way he should," Fenice said in a low whisper.

"*Attack?*" I asked, beyond worried.

"Jousting-wise, she means," Bliss explained. "The problem with Walker is that he's just too nice—he's afraid of hurting her. We've told him time and time again that we can take the hits as well as any man, but he does tend to pull his punches when he jousts against a woman."

"And that's not good," I said, my fingers tightening around Moth's thin leather leash.

"No."

"Are you saying he's going to lose because he won't joust as aggressively as he should?" The words croaked out of my mouth, which, considering that my heart was thumping away like mad in my throat, was a minor miracle in itself.

Bliss glanced back at Bos, then returned her gaze to the arena floor. "If the judges see he's deliberately going easy on her, there's a chance of exactly that, yes."

"Well, hell," I said, handing Bos Moth's leash. While only a few women were at the railing calling for their champions and waving the colorful strips of cloth that served as the favors, I decided that Walker needed every last bit of encouragement he could get, and accordingly stepped over Bos's and Geoff's legs, leaping down the stairs with the sound of CJ calling after me. Cheerleader Pepper to the rescue!

I ran to the end of the arena, where Walker was just reaching down to take the lance from Butcher. He couched it on the lance rest, nodding to the marshal that he was ready. Just as the marshal opened his mouth to give them the signal to start, I leaned over the railing and bellowed, "Knock her on her butt, Walker! No mercy!"

His head turned in my direction, but I doubted if he could see me, since the helm didn't allow him much range of vision.

"Lay on!" the marshal yelled, and Marley leaped forward. I watched for a moment to make sure he wasn't favoring his leg, but quickly yanked my attention back to the jousters, holding my breath as Veronica lowered her lance toward the man with whom I was now hopelessly in love.

"This is the stupidest sport I have ever seen," I growled to myself as Veronica's lance slammed into the left upper side of Walker's chest. His hit her at the same time. Although she rocked backward in her saddle, she stayed in it.

Walker wasn't *quite* so fortunate.

"That was a good try; she just got lucky," I yelled down as he got to his feet. "You'll get her on the next run!"

Vandal led Marley over to him, but Walker didn't climb back onto the huge black horse. Instead he walked slowly over to where I was leaning precariously over the railing, tilted back the face plate of his helm, and glared up at me. "What the bloody hell do you think you're doing?"

"Encouraging you. It's called being supportive. You can thank me later."

"Support is fine, but I'll thank you now to not distract me the second before the run is called," he snapped, and started lowering his visor.

I leaned down even lower, realizing that I was about a one-thirty-second of an inch away from popping completely out of my bodice. "Walker?"

He raised his visor again. "What?"

"I think I'm falling in love with you."

He froze.

"I just thought you'd want to know that. Good luck!"

He stood there absolutely still for another three seconds, then lowered his visor and spun around on his heel, marching resolutely back to Marley.

Butcher handed him the lance, and before I could add my voice to the others screaming their support, he was off and thundering down the list.

"That was a good shot," I yelled out helpfully as Butcher got him upright from where Veronica had knocked him off Marley. "I have faith that the next one will do the trick! Go get her, tiger!"

Halfway across the ring as I was, I could still hear him muttering under his breath.

"You're doing really well," I said as he passed by me. "I'm so proud of you. You're not hurt anywhere, are you?"

"No, I'm not hurt," he growled, but before I could reply he marched past to where Vandal was holding Marley.

I chewed my lip, pushing down all the worry and fear that roiled around inside me so that all that showed was my belief in him. "You da man!" I yelled loudly to be heard over the screaming of the other fans.

Butcher's shoulders shook as Walker swung his leg over the saddle, snatching the lance from his burly squire.

"Who wants to do the wave?" I turned to ask the crowd behind me just as the marshal yelled "Lay on!"

I spun around, the fingers of both hands crossed tightly as Marley and Veronica's gray pounded down the arena, the high overhead lights shining brightly on Veronica's shiny, bright armor. The lances were lowered and held for the count of three before both slammed into the oncoming person's armor, the tips shattering in suitably dramatic style. Veronica listed heavily to the left, and I thought she was going to go off for a second or two, but she clung to the horse's mane and managed to drag herself upright again.

"I think he needs to change his strategy," I told CJ, who had come to stand at the rail with me. "Maybe I should tell him that."

"Maybe you shouldn't and say you did," CJ advised.

"You're the one who said I should be supportive," I pointed out as Walker limped over to Marley. "You're the one who said I should have faith. I'm doing both."

"I know, and I'm sure he appreciates it, but he has to focus right now. Come on; you can be supportive and full of faith with the rest of the group." CJ tugged on my arm.

I heaved a sad little sigh as I watched Walker re-mount Marley. If only the darling man knew how much he needed me!

"No, you go. I'm going to stay here."

CJ went back to sit with the rest of the Three Dog Knights team, all of whom sat with grim faces.

Their obvious concern added to my worry. "How many falls did you say a person could take before they were disqualified?"

"Four," Bliss answered.

I straightened my shoulders as I turned back to the railing, taking my place with renewed determination.

"Butcher!" I waved him over as he walked a few feet away, heading toward Walker with an unbroken lance.

"What?" he asked, pausing.

"I want you to tell Walker something for me. Tell

him I know he can do this. Tell him he's the best there is. Tell him that we all believe in him. And tell him that later tonight, I'll let him shoe me again."

"Oooh, kinky," CJ said from five rows up.

Butcher grinned and waggled the lance at me. My fingers were white as I clutched the railing when Butcher put the lance in Walker's waiting hand. "You can do it, Walker; I know you can." The words turned into a mantra, whispered in time to the pounding of my heart. Walker couched the end of the lance onto the saddle rest, then nodded to the marshal. "You can do it, you can do it. Please, just hang on for four more runs."

"Lay on!"

"You can do it, you can do it." The words were louder now as Marley sprang forward straight into a full canter, charging down the list at a speed that had bits of dirt and sand flying from his huge hooves.

"You can do it, you can do it!" I said over the roar of the crowd as everyone surged to their feet. Walker's lance began its downward arc at the same moment Veronica got him in her sights.

"You can do it, you can do it!" I screamed, jumping up and down as the two opponents charged with apparent deadly force at each other. Veronica's tip slammed into the piece of armor that covered Walker's throat, lifting him up and out of the saddle. His lance slid across her chest plate, nailing her on the right rather than the left side. I screamed meaningless words as Walker battled to stay in the saddle, and then with a huge crack of the lances, he was past her, still in the saddle, holding a lance that was broken in the middle.

Veronica flew backward over the rump of her horse, landing heavily on her butt, just as I predicted. I yelled my happiness with the rest of the crowd, everyone cheering Walker on, no doubt because everyone there was aware of just how important that pass was.

The two remaining passes were draws—both Veronica and Walker breaking lances, but neither of them taking a dive.

"He did it, he did it," I sang as I danced up the steps to where the rest of the team was sitting. Walker and Vandal and Butcher were leaving the ring, followed by Veronica and her team. I picked Moth up and kissed him right between the horns, ignoring the cat's disgusted look as I plopped myself down beside Bos. "I'm so happy, I could burst into song! In fact, I think I will. Hey, guys, sing with me! 'Happy days are here again . . .' "

No one was singing. In fact, no one would even look at me. They were all watching the scoreboard like it was about to burst out into a pair of legs and go for a gallop around the arena.

"Uh—guys? Why aren't you singing? Why aren't you happy? Walker won, right? He didn't get DQ'd?"

"He didn't get disqualified," Bliss eventually said, her mouth still tense. "But that doesn't mean he has enough points to qualify."

"Those three falls hurt him." Bos nodded.

I stared at them, each one in turn, and felt my happiness shrivel up and turn to lead in my stomach. "But . . .not so much that he couldn't qualify, surely?"

"Only the top eighty percent make it to the competition," Geoff said softly, his arm around Bos. "The bottom twenty percent, those with the lowest scores, don't compete."

"Oh, god," I moaned, my stomach doing an unpleasant somersault. I turned to watch the scoreboard as well, sucking my lower lip as I waited for the list of people who qualified to be displayed.

Voices were subdued during the five minutes it took for the scores to be listed. People didn't wander around chatting as they usually did, probably because by that time, all the jousters had run and were waiting to see if they would make the cut. I clutched Moth until he protested with a particularly penetrating yowl.

"Sorry," I apologized to him.

He bit my knee.

At long last the announcer said the judges had verified the scores, and the names of the jousters who had qualified for Southern Italian and Realgestech would be posted.

The number one spot went to Farrell.

"Yeah, well, he probably cheated," I said softly.

Number eight was Butcher.

"Yay!" CJ crowed. I waited until she looked away to mouth, *He's bigger than everyone else,* to Bos. He snickered.

Tenth was Veronica. "She's sneaky," I said as her name scrolled by.

Twelfth was Gary, Fenice's guy. "He'd just better stay out of Walker's way, that's all I'm saying."

She grinned.

Bliss's name came up fourteenth. "Well . . . you're okay, I guess," I allowed.

"Thank you *so* veddy much," she said in a rich upper-class voice.

Twenty-fifth was the Norwegian Tomas. "He smells like cheese."

Geoff spewed soda pop out his nose.

Twenty-eight was Vandal. Fenice leaned back and cocked an eyebrow at me. "He's nice," I said, mindful that she was a very good shot with her bow. Satisfied, she turned around to look at the scoreboard again. I added, "In a flirty, can't-keep-it-in-his-pants sort of way."

"Pepper!" CJ gasped.

"Sorry. I meant that in the nicest sense, of course."

"It's okay." Fenice shrugged. "It *is* true."

Various other jousters appeared on the list, and with each name there were occasional cheers and scattered applause from the other jousters and their supporters. As name after name scrolled by the big screen, all names that weren't Walker's, the tension inside me tightened and tightened until I couldn't breathe.

"How many jousters will there be?" I asked Bliss

quietly as everyone in our section of the arena went quiet.

"Forty-six."

I looked at the board. Number forty-five scrolled up. It was one of Farrell's team. My guts lurched, imploded on themselves, and dropped to my feet. He wasn't going to do it, he wasn't going to do it. . . .

The occupants of the arena held their collective breath as the last name scrolled up from the bottom of the screen. I clutched Moth, sick to my stomach, sick with dread that I had forced Walker to do something he didn't want to do, only to have him fail at the attempt. I knew just how frail an ego could be when it came to feeling worthless. . . .

"Oh, thank God." Bliss sighed.

It was there. Number forty-six. The lowest-scoring man to qualify—Walker McPhail.

As I slumped in relief, a tingle on the back of my neck heralded the fact that Walker was nearby. I looked to my left and saw him, his face utterly blank as he watched his name scroll off the board.

Chapter Twelve

"Now, we are going to have a very romantic dinner, so I don't want you misbehaving. Don't snap at your food, don't talk with your mouth full, and don't go potty while we're eating! There's nothing less conducive to romance than the smell of poop wafting everywhere."

Moth, sitting on the cooler next to my sleeping bag, gave me one of his indignant looks, as if the last thing he would do would be to use his litter box while we were dining.

"And don't give me that look," I said, shaking my finger at him. "I know you too well, cat. Just behave yourself. This is my first real date with Walker, and I want everything to go well."

I looked around the tent to make sure everything was perfect. I had cajoled two chairs and a small table from neighbors, covering the table with a big red shawl CJ had packed. Camp lights were set low, dim enough to be romantic, but bright enough to see what we were doing. The pizza and salads I'd ordered from a delivery place had arrived, and I had a bought a bottle of wine off a couple who strolled through the tent city selling libations. It was a bit cramped even in CJ's huge tent, but I felt privacy was more important than legroom. I was in the sexiest of all the garb CJ had brought me, something called a Guinevere gown, a dress that had a low scoop neck and easy-to-undo side lacings. "We're as ready as we're going to get. What do you think—do I look sexy?"

Moth gave me a yellow-eyed stare before proceeding to do a little personal hygiene on areas prone to such care.

"Gee, thanks. You're so good for my ego. Whoops, that sounds like the man himself. Remember, you're to behave or there will be no pepperoni and sausage for you!"

I shoved aside the unzipped door of the tent and struck a provocative pose next to it. Walker had been stopped just outside the tent by one of jousters who was congratulating him on his reentry into competition.

"Hi," I said as the jouster drifted away, suddenly feeling shy. "I hope you're hungry."

He eyed the Guinevere gown. "For you or food?"

"Ideally both." I held open the tent flap and gestured inside. "Look! I made room for a table in here. Dinner awaits, good sir knight."

He glanced longingly into the tent, but shook his head. "I should check on Marley's leg—"

"Already done. His leg is fine—no swelling, no signs of infection or tenderness, and it looks to be healing extremely well."

"Ah. That's good." He looked tired, his shoulders slumping a little as he hesitated. The fact that he was still outside rather than inside being smothered by my kisses—or eating the dinner I had provided—was explained in part by his fatigue, but not wholly.

The thought occurred to me with a swift rush of horror that perhaps his sudden reticence to be alone with me had something to do with my reference earlier to my falling in love with him. That had been nothing but a joke, of course, something to take his mind off the fact that Veronica was kicking his butt. I may have told CJ that I wanted to experience love at first sight with my ideal man, but I never expected it to happen. So it was all a joke. Not seriously meant. I couldn't fall in love with someone after just a few days, after all.

How pathetic is it when you try to lie to yourself?

I sighed and waggled the tent flap. "What's it going to be, Walker? Are you dumping me after a one-night stand, or are you coming in and letting me feed and molest you?"

His eyes glittered in the setting sun. "What sort of molestation is involved?"

"I thought I would give you a full-body massage. I figured you've got to be a bit sore after falling off your horse so much."

His mouth tightened, but at least he entered the tent. "I didn't fall off my horse. I was knocked off."

I shrugged and offered him a glass of wine. "Same difference. Oh, all right, stop glaring at me; it isn't the same thing. After jousting with Bliss, I know just how hard it is to take a hit and stay in the saddle. Now will you stop being all prickly, and sit down and allow me to woo you into a romantic mood? This dinner didn't come cheap, you know!"

He frowned at the pizza box.

"No, it isn't haute cuisine, but I did get wine!"

Walker slumped into the closest chair, raising his hands as if he wanted to protest something, then letting them fall. "I'm sorry, Pepper. I'm just not very good company tonight."

My heart, that volatile and sometimes fickle organ, shriveled up at his words and turned to something that resembled a runty lump of coal. "Oh. I see. Gotcha. You don't want to . . . well, you don't have to. But since I got a large pizza, you might as well' eat that before you go back to your cold, lonely tent and your cold, lonely bed."

A little tiny smile quirked the corners of his mouth. "I doubt if anything is cold in this heat."

"Fine," I said, turning my back to him so he wouldn't see the tears filling my eyes. The poop. "Go back to your lonely hot bed. Whatever. Makes no difference to me."

"Sweetheart, don't cry. I didn't mean it to sound like that." His voice shivered down my back as his hands settled on my arms, warm and strong.

"I'm not crying," I lied, trying to shake off his hands. "I'm . . . I'm allergic to Moth! That's why I couldn't be a vet. Allergic to animal dander, I am. Oh, great, now I'm starting to talk like Yoda!"

"Pepper," he said, his breath warm on my neck, his voice rich with laughter. I allowed him to turn me around and sank bonelessly into his embrace. His lips nuzzled my neck as he said, "I'm just not very good company tonight. I wouldn't want to disappoint you."

"Disappoint me? *You?* I don't think that's physically possible," I said, giving his Adam's apple a little kiss just to let it know I liked it.

"Not just sexually." I pulled back to look at him. There was something in his voice, a note of despair that I didn't like. His eyes were dark and haunted, and as soon as I looked into them, he turned away, his hands dropping from where they had been caressing.

"What do you mean, you're not good company?" Hope flared to life within me. "Are you bummed out because you're last on the qualifying list?" He flinched and returned to the chair, his body language shouting defeat. I knelt in front of him, sliding a hand up each thigh until I was caught between his knees. "Are you depressed because you've made the right decision, but don't want to admit that to yourself? Is that what's making you so glum?"

A very disgruntled look—one almost identical to the expression Moth had adopted the first time I strapped his horns on—flitted over Walker's handsome face. "You don't have to look so bloody hopeful about it."

I leaned forward and nuzzled his chest. "I'm sorry; I can't help it. I thought you were being skittish because of that bit about me falling in love with you. I'm sorry you're stressed and unhappy because of the jousting, but I'm am relieved that it's not a relationship thing between us. A sore ego is no fun, but it's *nothing* compared to the horror of trying to fix a broken relationship. Hey, what are you wearing beneath this tunic? Do you have a codpiece? Can I see it?"

I lifted up the hem of his tunic to peek, but he hauled me up until I was leaning against his chest, my hands braced on his heavily muscled thighs. "It was a joke? When you said you were . . . er . . . *you know*?"

"Was falling in love with you? What is it with men that they can't say the word *love*? It's just four little letters, Walker. It won't hurt you to say them. I promise."

He shook me—gently, but still, he shook me. "Was it a joke, or were you serious?"

His eyes, truly one of his best features, were warm pools of liquid silver. Did I want to admit to him that I wasn't joking as much as I would like to think I was, or would he run screaming into the night at that thought? Walker didn't seem to be the kind of man to do that, but I hadn't really known him for all that long. "Serious? Me? Ha. So can I see your codpiece?"

He tipped my chin up so my face was open to his, vulnerable to his all-too-clearly seeing eyes. "You weren't serious about what you said?"

I turned my head and pressed a kiss to his palm. "I was in earnest when I said I had faith in you, that I knew you could qualify. You can do anything you want to do, Walker."

Was that a flicker of pain I saw in his eyes?

"I see," he said, and I felt him withdraw from me. Not his body—that was still there warm and hard and reassuringly solid under my hands—but a barrier suddenly appeared between us, and I knew that it was there because of what I'd said.

But what was I supposed to say? my Inner Pepper wailed. Misery twisted in my belly as I watched him, wanting to tell him what was in my heart, but aware that my feelings for him were so new, I didn't even know for certain what I felt. Other than that I liked him. A lot. And I wanted to be with him. Also a lot.

I stood up with a little sigh for the tangled mess my life had become, and popped open the lid to the salad. "Look, I don't know what I think anymore, other than I'm hungry and I assume you are too, so why don't we eat? If you still want to talk about this later, we can. Or you can take off all your clothes and allow me to rub a fabulous frankincense-and-myrrh massage oil that I found at one of the vendors into every available square inch of your body. The choice is yours."

His eyes did the cutest little bugging-out thing I'd ever seen. "Do we have to eat first?"

"Yes," I said, a whole lot more firmly than I felt. "You've had a hard day, physically, what with squiring everyone, then jousting twelve times in a row, not to mention getting tossed on your butt innumerable times."

"Five," he said, frowning as I served him a plate of salad. "Five isn't innumerable. Five is very numerable."

I took the seat opposite him and poured the wine. "All right, then it's 'not to mention getting tossed on your butt five times.' So we'll have dinner; then I'll massage those poor, aching muscles of yours while we discuss just exactly what this relationship is all about, and then after that I'll take off all my clothes and lick off that massage oil, and we'll have wild, unbridled sex. Sound doable?"

He choked on the sip of wine he'd just taken.

"I'll take that as a yes. Here. Have some food. You're going to need the energy later, if you know what I mean."

He stabbed his fork into the salad, shaking a piece of lettuce at me. "You're incorrigible, Pepper. Just when I think you're nothing but a sweet, sincere, slightly mad, but loving woman, you say something lecherous like that to me. I've told you before, I do not like aggressive women."

"Well, drat, I guess that means you won't want to wear the studded dog collar, or call me Mistress Pepper?"

"You know what I mean," he said, munching a mouthful of salad.

"Yes, I do," I answered, wondering just how much of what he was saying was a little courtship teasing, and how much was ingrained into his psyche.

We talked about his life in England, mine in Seattle, and a lot of trivial subjects, but beneath the easy conversation there was an unmistakable sense of anticipation, a kind of electric excitement that left us both periodically silent.

"Why are you looking at me like that?" Walker asked after one such moment.

I smiled. "I told you before—I like looking at you. I like listening to you. I like pretty much everything about you, although sometimes you're a bit frustrating, what with that whole obstinate male thing going on. But even that I've learned to like—you just wouldn't be the same wonderful Walker if you weren't quite so stubborn."

He set down his glass of wine with exaggerated care. "One moment you're arguing with me, trying to boss me around, and the next you say something like that."

"Argue? *Moi?*" I tried hard to look innocent. "I don't argue. I debate."

"Ha." He snorted.

"Well, all right, maybe just a little, but only because it's so much fun with you. I love it when you get indignant. I can't help but want to kiss you when you have that outraged look on your face."

He gave me a long-suffering look, shaking his head. "I never know what you're going to say next."

"It's the element of surprise—it keeps you off balance," I said, grinning and waggling my eyebrows suggestively. "The better to sweep you off your feet."

He tried to look stern, but failed miserably. "That's my job, Pepper. I'm the strong knight; you're the delicate, gentle lady. Thus, if anyone is going to be swept off her feet, you will be. Once you have that straight in your mind, there won't be anything to argue about."

"*Gentle.*" I giggled, putting away the remains of dinner in an ice-filled cooler, wondering when was the last time anyone had ever applied either description to me. "*Delicate.* Sounds more like *downtrodden,* which I certainly am not. Take off your clothes and lie down."

Moth, having spurned his own dainty bowl of cat food in favor of eating the pepperoni off of three pieces of pizza, lay curled up inside his shoe box, watching us with interested eyes.

"There, you see? That's exactly what I'm talking about!" Walker glowered at me, his nostrils flaring dramatically. "You may think that dominating me in such a fashion is a sexual turn-on, but I don't find it so. And I think you'll agree that both of us have to be aroused in order for either party to benefit."

"Oh, for heaven's sake . . . I wasn't telling you to strip so I could jump your bones! Sex, sex, sex, is that all you men can think about? I told you I was going to give you a massage! If you prefer I do it through your clothing, I will, but I can tell you from experience it works better if I can rub my hands over your bare, oil-slicked flesh."

A little tremor shook him, but he managed to peel off his tunic without too much trouble. "I apologize. I didn't mean to snap at you."

"It's okay; I know you're tired after the long day. Hmm. No codpiece," I said sadly, eyeing the manly bulge in his tights.

"Have you ever ridden in one?" he asked. "It's like a hamster rattling around in an exercise ball."

"Now there's an image I'm not soon going to forget. Vandal wears one and he rides."

Walker blinked at me. "How do you know Vandal wears a codpiece?"

"He showed it to me. I think I was supposed to be impressed by its size."

"Don't be. He stuffs his with socks."

"Really? That's interesting, but not as interesting as you. Come on, McPhail, strip. I'll turn my back if you've suddenly gone shy." In fact, I did turn my back as I poked through the duffel bag of my things, looking for the bottle of massage oil I'd bought earlier.

"I'm not shy, I just didn't realize that you were serious about a massage." Clothing rustled as he stripped off his boots, tights, and blocky white underwear.

"We need to get you some seriously sexy undies." I allowed my eyes to go wild on him for a few seconds, just long enough to start all sorts of fires in my belly.

"These are quite functional," he answered, folding his clothing and laying them nicely on the chair.

The muscles in his back rippled as he moved, sending a sympathetic ripple of pleasure down my own back. "You really are beautiful, Walker."

He frowned, turning to me, touching a spot high on the left side of his chest. "I am not anything of the sort. I have scars. Right here, I broke three ribs the first time I was thrown from a horse. And here, this is from when I fell into a line of barbed fencing and was cut up."

I stood clutching the bottle of massage oil, warming it between my hands as my eyes feasted on the magnificence of his body. "Scars aside, you're absolutely gorgeous."

His frown darkened. "I am not."

"You take my breath away, you're so beautiful."

"Stop saying that!"

I walked a slow circuit around him, eyeing him from every possible angle. "You're like a god come to life. Your feet are nice feet, big but attractive in a feet sort of way, and you have great legs, not in the least bit scrawny or otherwise chickenlike."

Walker sighed and crossed his arms over his bare chest. "Do you plan on cataloging all of me?"

"Yes. Stop interrupting. Your calves are nice and bulgy. You have adorable knees, strong and yet not too bony. Your thighs are a work of art—"

"For the love of God, woman!"

"You have an adorable stomach, with just a lovely bit of belly so that you aren't too perfect."

His hands closed over his stomach protectively. "I've been working out. It's getting better."

I pulled his hands away, bending over to bestow a little kiss on his tummy. "No, no, it's not a criticism; I like it like that. Don't do anything to change it. And then your chest! Well, Walker, I've seen a few chests before, but I have to say that yours—broad, masculinely hairy without putting you into the realm of Walker the Ape Boy, and with the two most adorable nipples I've ever seen—is truly the king of all chests."

He relaxed a little, one side of his mouth quirking upward. "I'm glad you approve."

"Oh, I do approve." I smiled and kissed the quirk. "And as for the rest of you, your arms are nicely muscled but not bigger than my thighs—always a plus!—and your hands are marvelous. I like big hands." I made a little tour to the back side of him. "Your back is particularly nice, and your butt positively makes me drool; it's just that wonderful."

"Thank you," he said, trying to look over his shoulder at his behind.

"I like it very much."

"Ah. That's nice."

"I just want to take it in both my hands and squeeze," I said, flexing my fingers and thinking about doing just that.

"Bum squeezing doesn't sound much like a massage to me," he said.

I sighed and returned to face him. "No, I suppose not, but perhaps later you'll indulge me. You know what I think about the rest of you—your eyes are beautiful, and I love your chin, and you have the nicest ears I've ever seen."

"Really? And you're a connoisseur of the male body, are you?"

"No, but I know a nice one when I see it. On your belly, gorgeous, and let me at those muscles of yours."

He shot me another one of his quasi-peeved looks, but at least he lay down on my sleeping bag. I hiked up my skirt and spread his legs in order to sit between them.

He looked back at where I was rolling the bottle of massage oil between my hands. "You're smiling at my bum."

"I know, I just can't help it, it's so adorable. It's even more adorable when you tighten it like that. I don't suppose you have a quarter handy? I'd like to see if I could bounce it off your butt."

"Are you going to get on with this, then, or talk all night?"

"Testy, testy," I said, flipping open the lid to the oil and squeezing a line of it from his ankle to the back of his knee.

"I know I am," he said, sighing into the sleeping bag. "I'm sorry, Pepper. I told you I wasn't very good company tonigh— Oh, lord, that's good!"

"Told you it would be. Boy, your calf muscles are really tight." I drizzled the oil up the back of his thigh, spreading it around so his skin was wonderfully slick before digging my thumbs into the tense length of muscles. For a few minutes the only sounds were those of Moth snoring in his box and Walker's soft whimpers of pleasure into my pillow as I loosened the muscles in both his legs. "So, while you're lying there moaning and groaning, would you like me to tell you just what I'm going to do to you once the massage is over?"

"I don't know—oh, god, yes, right there. Again!— will it kill me if you tell me?"

I added a little extra oil to the small of his back and used the heels of my hands to sweep long lines upward. I knew how tight my back was after spending an hour practicing with Bliss, so I could imagine that indulging in the bat-out-of-hell style of jousting Walker had had to perform with Veronica had left his back tight and sore. "Kill you? I sincerely hope not, because I have most definite plans for you after the massage is over."

He stopped moaning for a second and half rolled onto his side, tipping me off his butt and onto one knee. "What? What do you want from me?"

I frowned at his frown. "What do you mean, what do I want?"

"All women want something—even I, with my limited skills with females, know that. So what is it you hope to get from me?"

I slapped my hands on his back and pushed him down flat again, gripping his hips tightly with my knees as I resumed rubbing the muscles in his back. "Boy, you really know how to make a girl feel good. I don't *want* anything from you, Walker. I have no ulterior motive other than the fact that I receive a great deal of pleasure in being with you, and I had the impression you felt the same."

He mumbled something.

"What? I couldn't hear you; you're talking into the pillow."

He lifted his head. "I said, I do feel the same way, but I still want to know what you want. Sex? Is that it? You're another groupie who wants to say she's laid a jouster? Well, you've done that, so hurrah for you."

My first instinct was to smack the back of his head, so temptingly close before me, and chew him up one side and down the other, but I reminded myself that not only was Walker in a crappy mood, but the reason he was in that crappy mood was because he was filled with self-doubt and a horrible belief that he was likely to injure someone in his attempt to save his teammates' honor. Anyone would lash out under those cir-cumstances. It was all part and parcel of his alpha-male he-man makeup. If I was serious about him—and despite the fact that sometimes he drove me nuts, it was getting quite hard to pretend I wasn't—then that meant I had to take the bad with the good.

So instead of smacking him as he deserved, I said simply, "You know, you're perilously close to insulting me to the point where I kick you out of my tent, but despite the urge to do just that, I'm not going to. And do you know why? I'll tell you why—I won't because I know that this is your defense system kicking in. I matter to you, and you just don't want to admit that, because if you do, then you'll have to deal with me on an intimate, personal level rather than how you might treat a normal jousting groupie. I'm not going to let you insult me to the point where I leave you, just so you can crawl back and lick your wounds, and tell your-self that all women are alike, and what a lucky thing it was that you found out about me before you got in-volved. Like it or not, McPhail, you're involved."

He said nothing as I moved up onto his shoulders, not even groaning with pleasure as I worked the heavy muscles.

I sat back on his butt. "Oh, this is a waste of time."

"Me, you mean." It wasn't a question; it was a state-ment, a statement that wrung my heart because I knew he truly believed he wasn't worth any woman's time and trouble.

"No, not you. I meant it's a waste of time massaging your shoulders when you are lying there tense as a bowstring. I want to help you, Walker, I really do. But you have to unbend enough to meet me halfway. Either relax and enjoy this, or go back to your own tent."

He went perfectly still under me for a couple of seconds. I held my breath, unsure of whether the bar-riers he'd erected around his heart would cause him to reject me, but after a few moments in which I was beginning to believe he would, he relaxed.

"Good choice," I told him. "So, would you like me to tell you, in excruciatingly glorious detail, exactly what sorts of things I'm going to do to make your eyes roll back into your head and that wonderfully big, broad chest of yours heave with the attempt to suck enough oxygen into your body so you can survive my attentions?"

He mumbled something incoherent that I took to be assent.

I dug my fingers into the muscles of his shoulders, rolling and compressing and working out all the knots. "First of all, I'm going to lick every inch of you, from the tips of your toesies to the sweet spot behind your ear. Then I'm going to nibble. Legs, arms, nipples— they'll all be nibble fodder. Following the nibbling comes the teasing with hair, whereupon I pick particularly ticklish spots and allow my hair to drape over them, inciting you to thrash around in an attempt to escape the sweet torture. After that, I'm going to spend a good hour or so exploring your naughty bits, seeing exactly how much more sensitive that foreskin is supposed to make you. Once I have you bucking beneath my hands and mouth, pleading with me to end your torment, begging me to allow you to grab the brass ring, so to speak, why, then I'll just up the ante by totally ignoring that part of you that will be hot and hard and near to bursting, and I'll kiss you for a while. I'll teach your tongue to boss mine around—yes, I will—and when you are properly submissive, then, and only then, will I sink slowly down upon your rampant nether parts, moving up and down, up and down, slowly, so I can feel each inch of you sinking into my body, pleasuring myself at great length and numerous times before I finally allow you to seek your own moment of sheer, unadulterated ecstasy."

In a blink of an eye I went from sitting on his butt

rubbing his shoulders to lying flat on my back, Walker's eyes molten with passion as he spread my legs and settled himself on top of me.

"Or we could just do it right now and to hell with my grandiose plans."

"That was my thought," he rumbled as he nudged himself forward into me.

"Wait! Condom!" I gasped, my body lunging upward to meet him even though my mind knew it wasn't a good idea.

He froze, the tip of his penis inside me, all my inner muscles trying to grab him and welcome him back home where he belonged. "Are you on birth control?"

"Yes," I said, writhing around, my hands going wild on his slick, oil-coated back.

"I don't have any diseases. At least, I didn't four years ago when I was tested, and I haven't been with a woman since."

"Welcome to the party." I sighed, lunging my hips upward to capture him. He sank into me with a groan that I felt all the way to my bones, the hot steel of him piercing my burning flesh, firing me to greater heights than I thought possible. "Do you have any idea what it feels like when you do that?"

"Probably it's similar to the effect you have on me," he groaned into my ear, our bodies making all sorts of wet, slicky noises that just made me wilder.

"Tell me." I gasped, pulling my knees up higher around his waist. "I know you like to be on top, which is just fine by me, because I like the way you squish me, but tell me what else you like."

"I like the way your body welcomes me," he said as he thrust his hips forward. "It feels like I'm diving in pool of fire, sweet fire, fire that burns under my skin."

I locked my ankles around his back and nibbled on his neck and jaw, my body moving in time to his, our pace quickening as our breath grew shorter, the sweat on his chest mingling with mine, our joining more than just physical. I bit his lower lip until he opened for me. "More," I whispered.

He levered himself up on his hands, my legs still locked around his hips, changing the angle of his entry. I moaned and ground my hips against his, too overwhelmed with the tension he was building with every touch of his flesh to mine to manage words.

"You fit me perfectly, every curve meant for me, every soft part of you a pleasure to touch." His head dipped and he took my nipple in his mouth, his teeth scraping along its tautness as his body thrust into mine, his strokes growing shorter, stronger, quicker.

"Oh, god, yes," I moaned, arching my back and clutching desperately at his shoulders. The tension inside me was so tight I knew it was going to explode at any second. With the tiny fraction of my mind that was still rational, I slid my hands down his back, digging my fingers deep into his gluteus muscles as I pulled him even tighter, needing to feel him as deep in me as possible, so deep that no matter how much physical space there would be between us, we'd never really be parted again.

"You're heat and warmth, like a sun burning only for me." The last words were spoken on a growl that turned into a shout of triumph as his back arched, his face locked in an expression of purest joy.

"Yes," I whispered as my body spasmed around him, my soul crying with happiness even as the tears snaked down the sides of my face. "Only for you, Walker. Only for you."

Chapter Thirteen

The first day of the actual jousting competition (as opposed to just qualifying rounds) dawned, I was told, as bright and brilliant as it had the last few weeks. I didn't know, having spent the morning lying smooshed up against Walker's side, wonderfully at peace and happy as his breath ruffled my hair in regular, even breathing tinged with the slightest hint of snoring.

"What do you think, should I keep him?" I asked Moth, who lay in meat-loaf mode on Walker's belly, reaching out a paw occasionally to bat at my fingers as I drew lazy circles on Walker's chest. "He's bound to be trouble, what with that whole obstinate male thing going on."

Moth's whiskers twitched.

"No, I'm not saying he's not worth the trouble, it's just that I had this idea of everything working out easily, and look at him! He's everything I don't like in a man—stubborn and pigheaded, way too handsome, and blind about so many things that should be obvious to him."

Moth yawned.

"Well, that is true; he does have many fine qualities." I scratched Moth behind his ear, making the big cat's eyes close in pleasure. "He's brave, honest, generous, and caring, and he has a lovely soft heart under that misanthropic exterior. I just wonder if I'll ever see the real Walker, the one he was before the accident, or if that dashing, carefree, adventurous man is gone forever?"

"I hope to God he is; he was a right pain in the arse," Walker's chest rumbled pleasantly beneath my ear. "Talking to the cat, are you?"

I kissed the nipple that rose so pertly next to my face. "Only because you were snoring the morning away."

"I never snore!" he said, outrage dripping from his voice. "And for someone who says she dislikes animals, I certainly do find you around them a great deal."

I made a face at Moth, who was now drooling on Walker's adorable belly as I scratched under his collar. "I've told you, I'm stuck with him. It's not a matter of my choice at all."

"Why didn't you become a vet?" Walker asked suddenly.

I looked up at his face for a second, then pulled my body away from his. "Breakfast first, or shall we fight our way through the hordes to the showers? I say showers first. I'm a bit sticky from last night."

He wrapped his long fingers around my arm as I tried to scoot out from under the sheet that served as a blanket. "Why didn't you become a vet? CJ said you were well into the program when you quit. Is it because you don't like animals?"

I pulled my arm away, tugging the sheet until it was wrapped around me in toga fashion. "Come on, don't be such a lazybones. If we don't hurry we won't get any hot water. Those Norwegians are such shower hogs."

"Pepper," he said, sitting up after carefully removing Moth from his stomach. "Why won't you answer my question?"

"Why do you care? Is it so important a question that I have to answer it?" I shrugged into a pair of jeans and grabbed a T-shirt.

"I didn't think so, at least not until you avoided answering it. If it wasn't the animals, why didn't you become a vet? You certainly had the family background for it."

"Oh, yes, I had the background," I said, mentally wincing at the bitterness in my voice. "There've been vets in my mother's family for almost ninety years, going all the way back to my great-grandfather, who was one of the first vets in Scotland. Veterinarians we have aplenty in our family. Software engineers, however, are notably scarce. There's just me, you see."

"So you quit vet school because your heart wasn't in it? You preferred computers to animals?" Walker probed, pulling on his tights and tunic.

"Let me just add 'tenacious' to your list of qualities," I grumbled, sticking my feet into my sandals and grabbing my bag of shower things. I tossed Walker a towel, taking another one for myself. "So! What are you going to do about finding out who vandalized—no pun intended—Bos's lance and Marley's leg?"

"I've told you, I'm looking into both. Is the reason you quit vet school because your heart wasn't in it?" he asked again, ignoring my blatant attempt to distract him.

"Looking into how? Are you grilling people? Asking questions? Hiring a private detective? I can help, you know, I've read lots of detective stories. I cut my literary teeth on Agatha Christie. My family used to call me Pepper Poirot. I want to detect with you."

"Pepper . . ." His thinned lips told me he wasn't going to let go of his infuriating curiosity about something that had no relevance.

My teeth ground for a moment, keeping back the reply that wanted to burst out, but after a couple of seconds' thought, I decided, What the hell. He'd find out sooner or later. "No, it's not the reason. I quit vet school because there was no use in continuing, okay? Happy now? Good. I'd like to find a shower and wash off the proof of our activities, if you're done with the third degree. Moth, you move one paw from this tent and I swear I'll be wearing a cat-shaped hat before the day is out."

I unzipped the door to the tent and strode out into the still-cool morning air, ignoring Walker until he caught up to me, stopping me with one big hand on my arm.

"What is this about?" he asked, turning me so I was facing him. Around us, the Faire was coming to life, people milling around the tent city, going to or from the bank of showers and toilets, feeding horses and themselves, talking, chattering, laughing— everyone happy to be alive on such a glorious, promising morning.

Everyone except me.

"This is about nothing, all right? Nothing—which pretty much sums up my career had I stayed in vet school. Now, if you don't mind, I'd like to get cleaned up." I turned and marched off to the low building that housed the showers and toilets.

"Why would you think your career would have been nothing? If your whole family are vets—"

I stopped and put my hands on my hips as best I could while holding the shower things. "What did your father do? Was he a farrier?"

Walker shook his head. "No, he sells insurance. What does my dad have to do with this?"

"Pretend for a minute he is a farrier. Not just any farrier, though—a world-class farrier, one who works for zoos and international wildlife organizations. Imagine he's the sort of guy who gets asked to international conferences to speak on . . . oh, I don't know, hoof welfare."

"Pepper—"

I held up a hand to stop him. "I'm not finished. Now stretch your mind a little and imagine that your grandfather was also a farrier, but he, too, was a one-of-a-kind farrier, a man who came up with unique ways of shoeing horses, a man who embraced every aspect of horse care, a man who not only rode in the Olympics, but who pioneered a method of treating injuries in racehorses' feet."

"I see," Walker said, his eyes steady on me. I had the oddest sense that he did see, that he was looking deep into my soul, seeking to bare all my secrets. It was an extremely unwelcome sensation.

"Do you? There's more. Let's take this make-believe scenario a little further—imagine that your great-grandfather was a man who was a world-renowned researcher at a time when there was no research being done into animal welfare. Imagine that he was one of the creators of a drug that revolutionized hoof care. Imagine all that, and ask yourself if you still would want to be a farrier. I think your answer will help you understand why I didn't become a vet."

I left him standing there as I walked toward the showers, my gut roiling at my having to admit something so painful.

His voice was positively icy. "So you quit because you felt like you weren't good enough? That's rather hypocritical of you, don't you think?"

I stopped at his words. I didn't want to—I didn't want to talk to him about such an insignificant bit of history anymore—but there was enough anger in his voice that it fired up my own ire. I turned to look back at where he was still standing. "Hypocritical? You don't know what you're talking about."

"Don't I?" Slowly he approached me, his eyes mirroring the scorn in his voice. "You lectured me for the last two days about this very same thing."

"No, it isn't the same thing—"

"Yes, it is. You said I didn't have the confidence in myself to succeed. You rubbed my nose in my own insecurities, and I let you because I believed you were superior, and now I find you're doing the exact same thing I'm accused of doing—namely, of being a coward."

Now *that* stung. I lifted my chin and glared at him, mindless of the people strolling past and around us, calling greetings to us that weren't answered. "I might be a lot of things, Walker, but knowing that I could never be as good as my mother or grandfather or great-grandfather does not mean I'm a coward. It just means that I know my own limitations."

"That's what you tell yourself, is it?" His jaw was tight, but he didn't frighten me. "That's what you say to get through the periods of self-loathing and misery, isn't it? Don't forget, according to you, I'm a coward, too. I know what I'm talking about."

"You don't know squat about me," I answered, furious but unwilling to admit why.

His beautiful silver eyes narrowed. "Answer me this, Pepper—do you want to be a vet? In an ideal world where nothing but you matters, do you really want to be a vet?"

"There is no ideal world," I said, refusing to take his bait.

He grabbed my arm and hauled me up close, not in an embrace, but so he could glare down at me in an attempt to intimidate. "That's not an answer. Do you, in your heart, want to be a vet?"

I gritted my teeth and refused to answer.

He let my arm go and stepped away, as if he were disgusted by my nearness. I didn't blame him. At that moment I disgusted myself. "What a fine pair we are. You too frightened of failure to even try to get what you want in life, and me all too aware of my failures to risk trying again. Do you know what the difference is between us?"

"No," I answered, my throat tight with unshed tears. "What is the difference?"

"Nothing," he said, turning on his heel and marching off toward his tent.

*   *   *

"There you are!" CJ called, waving me up to sit next to her on the section of the bleachers she had claimed with several red-and-gold blankets embroidered with the Three Dog Knights emblem. The arena was packed, this being the first official day of competition, probably a good 70 percent of the audience in garb, with another 20 percent families making an attempt to get into the spirit of the thing by donning bits and pieces of rented garb for the day. Women in T-shirts and shorts wore padded head rolls and veils, small children in expensive tennis shoes ran wild with plastic swords and Robin Hood hats, and guys of every shape and size wandered around in leather jerkins and gauntlets. "We saved you a spot. You haven't missed much, just a couple Americans taking headers."

"Crunchies," Fenice said, Gary flanking one side of her.

"I beg your pardon?" I asked as I settled Moth onto the blanket next to CJ, giving him his favorite catnip toy to keep him occupied. "What's crunchy?"

"Who, not what. Or should it be whom? It doesn't matter—the term applies to knights who spend more time on the ground than in the saddle. They crunch when you step on them, do you see?"

"All too well, thank you," I said, the piece of leftover pizza I'd shared with Moth as breakfast doing a backflip in my stomach. "So when is everyone on?"

CJ shoved a piece of paper into my hands. I glanced at it as the speaker overhead burst into song, a rock anthem used with gleefully anachronistic disregard, the announcer calling for the next two participants to enter the ring. Two men on bays entered, one horse in a fancy yellow-and-black drapery, the other in blue and green. They rode a promenade around the ring, bowing and waving and generally playing it up to the crowd as the announcer related their name, affiliations, and jousting wins. Women and girls (and a couple of enthusiastic guys) leaned over the railing waving the premade cloth favors sold by a couple of vendors, scarves, homemade favors, and even a pair of panties as the jousters rode the ring.

"Good God, they really go whole hog for the competition, don't they? This is nothing like the qualifying. Is that woman waving what I think she's waving at that knight?"

"Looks like a G-string to me. Qualifying is for serious jousters—this is for the public," CJ answered.

"Yeah, but this is the competition." She shrugged. I leaned forward and touched Fenice on her arm. "Do you guys have the fancy horse blankies like these knights?"

"They're called caparisons, Pepper," she answered with a grin. "And yes, we have them, too."

"Butcher's is a full caparison of green with silver fleur-de-lis on it. Walker just has red and gold cruppers that can adjust to different-size horses," CJ said.

"Cruppers as in the straps that hang over the horse's rump?" I asked absently, reviewing the day's schedule of jousting. Walker had told me in pillow talk that each morning that names were drawn randomly to pair up jousters, with the list of who was going up against whom posted immediately thereafter.

"Yes, those sorts of cruppers."

"Ah. So Bliss is first at a little after nine against one of the Norwegians, then Walker and an Aussie at ten thirty, Vandal versus one of the Palm Springs ladies right after that, and Butcher and one of the Whadda Knights at three."

"Colin. He'll cream Butcher," Gary said loudly of his teammate. CJ, never one to take criticism (implied or not) of her gigantic lamb, pulled off her gold velvet muffin hat and smacked the back of Gary's head with it.

I frowned at the schedule. "What happens if someone draws their own teammate as a competitor?"

"In team competition, the chief marshal would throw the name back and pull another until someone who wasn't a teammate is pulled. In individual competition, it's luck of the draw, and quite often you do draw your own teammate," Gary answered with a shrug.

"I didn't realize there were team and individual jousts," I said slowly, flipping over the day's schedule to look at the overall tournament schedule, only to choke at what I saw. "Good god! The winner gets two hundred thousand dollars? *Two hundred thousand?* No wonder people have come from all over the world to participate!"

Fenice nodded as CJ grinned and said, "That's just for one event. The winning team of the four jousting events gets two hundred grand to divide. Each winning person in sword and archery also gets one hundred thousand. Then the jouster who wins the individual competition gets another two hundred thou, and finally, the one person who has the highest individual score in jousting and the skill games is the tourney champion, and he or she gets another two hundred thousand."

"Wow! That's a whole lot of money—almost a million dollars!"

"It *is* a million—there are lesser amounts of money offered to people in the first four places of each competition. This is the largest purse ever offered to jousters. It's unprecedented."

No wonder everyone on Walker's team was so frantic to have him joust, thereby keeping them in the competition. If they won even one event, they'd stand to walk out of there with a pretty big chunk of change.

"It's an experiment to see if jousting has the support to become an Olympic event," Gary added as the crowd applauded the two jousters, now taking their places at either end of the list. "Of course, they have to get past the politics first, which frankly I think is a lost cause."

"Politics?"

"Shhh!" CJ ordered, the crowd roaring as the two knights spurred their horses forward.

I gave the two men in the ring the briefest glance, more interested in what Gary had said. I leaned forward and tapped him on the shoulder until he turned to look at me, saying softly, "What sort of politics?"

"There are four different jousting organizations, each supposedly better than the others, but really they're almost the same, with a few key differences. There's the American Jousting Association—your friend Farrell is the head of that—and the International Tournament Organization, who are mostly the Aussies and Kiwis; then there's the World Jousting and Combat Association, which is predominant here in Canada and Europe, and finally there's a new group called the Federation of Armed Combatants set up by people who didn't like the restrictions in the other three—they're the bad boys of the jousting world."

"Ah. So each organization does what—holds its own jousts?"

He nodded, glancing toward the ring for a moment as the jousters threw down their broken lances and rode back to their starting points. "They hold their own tourneys, award their own titles, keep different scoring systems, and have different rules for jousters. Each one names their best jouster as the world champion, so it can get confusing when you have four world champs at one time. The real reason that jousting isn't in the Olympics has nothing to do with the question of public support, as the tourney organizers claim— it's because there is no one international organization. Until there is, jousting won't be anything but an amateur sport, even at this level of competition."

"Hmm," I said, sitting back, my attention suddenly caught by the sight of a familiar figure standing just outside the arena. Walker and Butcher were dressed in identical red tunics and black leggings, the three golden dogs on their tunics blazoning the team's emblem. Walker held an armload of red-and-white-striped lances, while Butcher carried a couple of painted shields, both evidently waiting to squire Bliss at her turn. "What a poop." I sighed, my eyes on the dark-haired man of my dreams.

"Trouble in paradise?" CJ leaned over Moth to whisper. "Walker doesn't look very happy."

I raised both eyebrows and tried to look haughty. "I gave the man a full-body massage last night and fulfilled his every wanton desire, and let me tell you, he has quite a few. That doesn't sound like trouble to me."

"No, but the way he was muttering and snorting your name when he came around the camp this morning did. I'd say I told you so, but I'm not the sort of person who gloats over another's troubles." I gave her a narrowed-eyed look. She grinned. "Oh, what the hell—I *told* you so!"

"Shut. Up."

"Oooh, touchy!"

I ignored her and her smugness for the next half hour, thinking all sorts of confusing thoughts of a dichotomeus nature, one moment doing an inner swoon at the sight of Walker handing Bliss a lance, the next recalling how annoyingly perceptive he could be, and what I could do to distract him from probing any further at something I didn't want to talk about. The heinous plot against his team would do, to start.

"The best defense is an offense," I muttered to myself as the crowd rose to their feet, screaming as Bliss and the Aussie ran the last of their three jousts. I began to plot accordingly.

Fifteen minutes after Bliss's jousting run (for which she scored a perfect fifteen, having struck what amounted to a bull's-eye on the outside upper quarter of the shield) she was at the bottom of the bleachers waving me down.

"Go on; she probably wants to do some training

with you. I'll watch Moth until you get back," CJ offered.

I sighed as I handed over his leash and dug his can of kitty snacks from the leather pouch that hung from my belt. "I don't know why she thinks anyone cares whether or not I prove myself to Farrell. . . ."

"Stop complaining and go." CJ shoved me.

Bliss had already started toward the stable as I hurried after her. She was still clad in breeches and tunic beneath a thigh-long chain-mail hauberk that she wore for jousting, but despite her being so burdened, I had to run to catch up with her.

"Don't have much time before I have to squire Walker. I want to work you on the shock quintain this morning. We'll work on your accuracy skills; then this afternoon before Vandal's match Butcher will take you through your paces."

"I hate to take you away from watching the joust—" I started to say, but clamped my teeth closed at the look she shot me. Nothing but outright refusal was going to get her to budge from her plan to train me, drat the woman. I sighed and gave in as gracefully as I could, even allowing her to arm me.

"What's this?" I asked as she handed me a navy-blue quilted vestlike object that laced on the side. At her request I'd gone back to my tent first and gotten into a pair of jeans and one of the short shirt-length chemises that CJ had brought for me.

"It's a gambeson. An arming tunic. It protects you from the chain mail."

I gnawed on my lower lip for a few seconds. "Bliss, I don't have any chain mail, and although I know there's a guy on the vendors' row who'll make it for you, it's pricey."

"Very pricey," she agreed, and held out the gambeson.

"Then why am I putting this on?"

"You're going to wear Bos's armor."

I straightened my shoulders and prepared to level

a glare at her. "I might be sturdy, but I am not as big as him!"

"Just his mail, not the plate armor," she agreed. "That would take some padding, but you might be able to wear it if you had to. Put this on, and then I'll show you the easiest way to get into a mail hauberk. Did you bring your gloves? Good."

I slid into the padded gambeson, tying the sides as she held out two more blue quilted pieces. "These are the padded cuisses. They go on your legs and tie onto your belt."

"Oh. Sorry, I left that behind."

She frowned at my waist for a second, then shrugged. "Just tie them to the belt loops on your jeans. Do you have a pair of sturdy hose? If not, you'll need to get a pair. It's all right for you to wear jeans today, but the sooner you're properly kitted out, the quicker you'll accustom yourself to the feel of the equipment."

I pulled the cuisses on and tied them to my jeans. "Do I really need this?" I held up my hand quickly, forestalling the lecture about my honor and the dignity of women jousters the world over. "Not do I need to learn how to joust; I'm becoming resigned to that. I mean the leg thingies. I'm not really going to be using my legs, am I?"

She just smiled. "Tell me after today's session whether or not you need them."

Oy. That sounded ominous. I took the thin scarf she handed me, wrapping it around my head as instructed.

"That's to protect your hair while you're getting into the mail. The men don't do it, but with your long hair, you'll not want it snagged on the mail. On your knees, arms straight up, please."

I knelt before her as she held the long mail garment above my head, slipping into it as she lowered it down onto my arms. As the weight of it settled on my shoulders, I was thankful for the gambeson, since it helped distribute the weight of the thirty pounds or so of chain mail.

"I hope to heaven this is it," I said, getting awkwardly to my feet. "Because if there's anything else I have to wear, I doubt if I'll be able to hold the lance at all. Man, I thought Farrell's mail was heavy—this stuff is wicked."

"This is all you'll need today. If you were jousting in competition or performance, you'd have a surcoat or jupon with your coat of arms on it, but it's not necessary for training. You'll need a helm eventually, though. We'll have to see how mine fits you, but for now you can make do with just the mail."

I gave her back the scarf, then grabbed the shield she indicated and followed her out to the stable, feeling like a slow, cumbersome sloth as I struggled to keep up, sweating heavily under the bright August sun. "Is your mail lighter than mine? How on earth can you walk so fast in it?"

She didn't even slow down, blast the woman. "Practice. You should wear that mail as long as you can each day. Your muscles will build up in response and soon you won't even notice that you have it on."

"Ha!" I laughed, walking around to the field behind the barn. Vandal was there with my archenemy Cassie, flirting with twins dressed in identical low-cut bodices and flowery layered skirts. At the far end of the field a white quintain had been set up, although it wasn't the same one I'd gone up against (and defeated, go me!) earlier in the week.

"Mount up. That's a shock quintain," Bliss said abruptly, frowning at the twins until they murmured excuses and fluttered off with many a backward glance at Vandal. "I don't think we'll even bother trying you at a walk and a trot; let's see you hit it at a canter."

Bliss turned to where a stack of lances lay alongside a small ditch. Vandal held Cassie for me as I got my foot into the stirrup. I gave him a pathetic smile. "You look smashing, Pepper. Mail becomes you. Eh . . . do you need a push up?"

"Oh, I don't know; I kind of like bouncing up and down on one leg like this," I said breathlessly, trying to hoist myself up and onto Cassie's back. "Hey!"

He grinned as I settled into the saddle, the feel of his hands on my butt still fresh. "Just giving you a helping hand."

"Next time try somewhere else."

"Come along, Pepper, we don't have all day! Vandal and I are to squire Walker. Let's see you make a run at the quintain."

I will admit to being a bit cocky as I took the lance from her, couching it against the saddle as I rode Cassie to the end opposite the quintain, turning her and lining her up with the white wooden structure. "Quintains are old hat," I told Cassie as I took a deep breath and focused as Bliss had instructed me the day before. "I've jousted with a real person. This is gonna be a piece of cake. Hah!"

Cassie jumped forward at the yell, my legs tightening against her sides, the lance clamped down in my armpit with my hand directly behind the protective vamplate. As I approached the quintain, I lowered the lance into the couched position, holding it steady as Cassie cantered easily toward the wooden target.

I think I was smiling when the lance tip touched the shield nailed onto the quintain. I wasn't smiling a minute later when I managed to shake the stars from my head and sit up.

"Wha' happened?" I asked, dazedly noting that Cassie had stopped a few feet away and was happily cropping the grass. "What's wrong with that quintain? Did you nail down the swing arm or something? Isn't it supposed to swing when I connect with it?"

"This is a shock quintain," Bliss said neutrally as she hauled me to my feet. I clung to the stirrups for a few seconds just to make sure my legs were going to hold me. I wasn't hurt, other than a slight bruising on my right hip, but the . . . well, there's no other word for it but *shock* of the blow left me mentally reeling. "It doesn't move. Your goal is to hit the quintain hard enough to knock it all the way over onto the shield on the back. We use them to get jousters accustomed to taking a blow, and to hone their targeting skills."

I glared at the quintain. It did indeed have two shields, mounted on either side, about seven feet off the ground. Four sturdy legs were bolted onto a wooden platform that sprouted two wooden braces projecting horizontally on either side. I gathered it was supposed to rock back under a blow, but my still-tingling fingers and sore armpit were testament to its not having much give to it at all. "You could have warned me," I groused, rubbing my side. "I think I broke my armpit."

"You're holding your lance wrong," Bliss said, bending down and putting her hands out for me to step into. "You also were using an incorrect seat, your grip on the lance could easily have broken your wrist, and you jerked back on Cassie's mouth when you struck the quintain. We'll have to work on all of those things. Get on; we don't have much time before we have to go."

"Huh-uh," I said, shaking my head and backing away from both the horse and the monster in Bliss clothes. "That thing is evil. I like jousting against you better. It doesn't hurt nearly so much."

"I can't joust with you until after the competition is over. It's too chancy; I can't risk your making a wild blow and taking me out of the competition. Butcher said he'll take the chance and joust with you later, but I won't until you've had more training."

I shook my head. "Then I'll just wait until you have more time—after the competition is fine by me. . . ."

"Quitting again?"

My spine snapped from its "this mail is heavy" slouch into a perfectly vertical line as I slowly turned and faced the owner of the deep voice that slipped over me like silk.

"I am *not* quitting. I'm simply going to wait until a time when Bliss can joust with me personally."

"She'll have to go home after the competition," Walker said evenly, his eyes shaded by the period black wool hat he wore. It had a curved brim, and made him look like something out of a medieval tapestry—a *sexy* medieval tapestry. He was leaning against a sign warning people not to drink the water out of the attached tap, looking handsome and masculine and very, very scrumptious in his gold-and-red surcoat and black mail. I swallowed down the thrill of excitement my traitorous body gloried in whenever he was near, and reminded myself that although he was everything wonderful, he was also a very large pain in the patootie. *My* patootie. "Which means that you're quitting. That's a rather *cowardly* act, don't you think?"

I let my nostrils flare at him for a second, just so he'd know how peeved I was with him, then spun around and marched over to Cassie, hauling myself onto her back on the first try. "Lance," I said, holding out my hand for an unbroken lance.

Bliss handed it to me, snapping out a series of orders. "Hold the lance from the underside rather than the top. Lean in a little more than what you've been doing. The minute the lance touches, drop the reins so you won't harm Cassie's mouth, and push through the target. Aim a bit high—the closer you are to perpendicular, the more shock you'll feel. Leave a little more lance behind you, and it'll be easier to hold— eighteen inches is about right. The reason you went off the last time is because you struck the target lower than your armpit, which pushed you back and up, out of the saddle, so keep your aim higher than what you've been doing. And don't fight the saddle—use the high back to brace you, but don't forget to use your knees and thighs to grip Cassie against the shock. Ready? Go ahead."

I gave Walker a long look as I turned Cassie, trotting her to the far end of the field. Damn Walker, he just stood there watching me, a slight smile on his lips as though he were anticipating my fall before it happened.

"What a big poop. Why did I have to pick him to fall in love with, Cassie?" The horse's ears moved as she shook her head, mouthing the bit in an excited way. "Right. Whatever. Let's try to make this a good one, 'kay?"

I dug my heels in, leaning forward and deliberately loosening the reins as she cantered toward the target. I adjusted my hold on the lance, raising it and leaning forward, trying to remember everything Bliss had just told me. The lance connected with a loud splintering, crashing noise that reverberated down my arm into my back, twisting me slightly in the saddle. I dropped the reins, cartwheeling my left hand for balance as I leaned even farther forward, throwing my weight into the lance. The shock quintain rocked backward on its base, teetered on the projecting braces for a second, then suddenly gave and fell onto its back.

A victorious cheer rose in my throat. I'd done it, and Walker had seen me! *Coward, ha!* I sure showed him who lacked the courage to try something difficult!

Cassie, feeling no pressure from the reins and no doubt seeing the quintain fall, decided that she'd done her part, and such good behavior deserved an appropriate reward. She stopped suddenly and dropped her head to graze. Unfortunately, I was still leaning forward, throwing my weight into the lance as it pushed through the quintain . . . which was no longer there.

I went right over her head, landing spread-eagled on my face in the dirt and grass.

Chapter Fourteen

"Pepper? Are you in here? Dammit, where has she gotten to?"

I stood up from where I'd been crouched next to Marley's leg, examining the wound. "Keep your shorts on; I'm here. What's up?"

CJ, half turned to leave the stable, marched over to me and thrust her pugnacious face in mine. "*What's up*? We have a Wench Promenade in three minutes—that's three minutes—and you've spent the whole day hiding because you and Walker are on the outs. Well, you can just knock it off and get your butt in gear, cousin, because this Promenade is an important part of Faire tradition, and I'm not going to allow you to screw it up! Thank God you've got your garb on. Come on; we don't have any time to waste."

"But Ceej," I whined, grabbing Moth from where he was sitting in Marley's feed bucket. "I don't want to Promenade!"

"You'll do it and you'll like it," she said grimly, walking so fast that even I with my long legs had to hurry. "You've sulked all day long because Walker saw you fall off your horse when you were trying to impress him, but it's time you grew up and stopped thinking only of yourself."

"Oh, yes, my selfishness is legendary," I huffed,

hoisting a disgruntled Moth higher as I scurried after my cousin. It wasn't easy, since the Faire was in full swing, and the walkways were crammed full of Faire-goers, some decked out in full garb. Trailing CJ as she headed for the Promenade starting point at the far end of the vendors' row, I shook my head at a woman whose dalmatian was wearing an Elizabethan ruff and saucy feathered hat. "Imagine making that poor dog wear a hat. Some people have absolutely no idea of good taste."

"What?" CJ asked without stopping.

"Nothing, other than that I am *not* selfish. A selfish person wouldn't have this cat glued to her every friggin' day."

"I'm not going to talk to you when you're being impossible," CJ said, dodging a couple of girls in Celtic wear who had evidently decided to give an impromptu demonstration of Scottish dancing. "Hurry up, we're going to be late! Honestly, I can't imagine why someone with legs as long as yours walks as slow as a slug. Fairuza! Is everyone gathered?"

I grumbled to myself as CJ and Fairuza consulted for a moment, hastily taking my place with the gathered Wenches as CJ turned to scowl at me. "I am not selfish," I muttered as I snapped Moth's leash onto the gold-and-amber jeweled and beaded harness I'd purchased for him earlier, setting him on the ground and giving his horns a quick tweak before straightening up. If I had to Promenade, he had to Promenade, too.

Fairuza and CJ, finished with their whispered consultation, turned to face the ten gathered Wenches. "Wenches, we are about to commence the first Promenade of this season."

"Huzzah!" the women around me yelled.

"Yay," I said without much fervor.

Moth licked his privates.

"For the benefit of those new Harlots amongst us,"

CJ said with a pointed glance at me, "we will briefly cover the rules of the Wench Promenade. First of all, does everyone have their lipstick?"

"Yea, verily," the assorted Wenches cried, everyone quickly pulling tubes of lipstick from their pouches or pockets and waving them at CJ. She glared at me until I rooted around in my leather pouch and dug out my lipstick. "Excellent. Wenches, apply lipstick!"

I shared the tiny pocket mirror belonging to the Wench next to me, applying dark bloodred lipstick that clashed horribly with my hair.

"Teeth check!" CJ ordered.

My neighbor Wench bared her teeth at me.

"You're good," I said, then did the same.

"As you know, the purpose of this Promenade is to mark likely-looking lads. Please remember that this is a family venue, and keep your marks confined to above the markee's waist. Also, last year we had some trouble with particularly lusty Harlots racing down targets." The twins in the low-cut chemises whom Vandal had been flirting with earlier in the day giggled. "Wenches are not cats in heat! We do not run; we saunter saucily. When you see a potential mark, saunter up to him, announcing as you do, 'What ho, my sisters in Wenchdom, yonder I spy me a likely-looking lad/lord/rogue. Methinks he's ripe for a marking, what say you?' To which the rest of you reply, 'Verily, 'tis the truth yonder lad/lord/rogue is ripe! Have at him!' At that point you may proceed to mark your lad, but please remember to do so in a manner that will not embarrass the gentleman."

"And please confine wubbies to those lads who indicate they'd like to be the recipient of one," Fairuza added, which caused the Giggle Twins to snicker. "I won't remind you all of the incident last year when the visiting English archbishop was wubbied by a Wench, but suffice it to say that wubbies are to be given only to those individuals who first give their consent."

"What's a wubby?" I asked my lipstick friend, remembering Walker saying something about one the first time I had met him.

"It's when you pull your mark's face to your cleavage and rub it around."

I looked at the two fleshy mounds of boob that swelled over the top of my Black Watch plaid bodice (CJ felt I shouldn't alienate the Scots by ignoring them in my garb-wear), my entire body tingling at the thought of Walker rubbing his stubbly cheeks between my breasts. Then, of course, I imagined what it would be like for him to rub his cheeks everywhere else, and lost as I was in those thoughts, it took me a minute to realize that the Wenches were singing a lusty song.

"Sing!" CJ hissed an order to me during the chorus, shoving a small photocopied list of lyrics into my hands, and I joined in the song about the bald red-headed man and his love for dark places.

A crowd started to gather as a troupe of Rogues marched up, singing their own song about a wench with an unquenchable thirst, the men dividing to form a guard on either side of the Wenches. Fairuza made a pretty medieval-speak announcement that the Wenches were about to Promenade, and quicker than you could say, "God's teeth, the Wenches have plentiful breasticles," we were off.

The Wenches who were experienced at Promenading carried those of us who hadn't a clue (which turned out to be only a short, shy little brunette and me). The crowds seemed to like us, though, laughing and applauding both the Rogues who accompanied us (pretending to keep back the thundering herds of men who were accused of wanting to dally with us), and the Wenches themselves as the ladies sang relatively PG-rated songs, pausing to pick out men they passed for marking and wubbying.

"You're not participating," CJ whispered furiously to me as we made our way down the now-packed vendors' row, heading for the beer garden. The jousting was over for the day, but the evening's entertainment—various singers and a Scottish bagpipe band—was about to begin. "Stop embarrassing me and get into character! Mark someone!"

"I am not going up to a strange man and kissing him," I whispered back. "I'm not that kind of a Harlot."

She pinched my arm. "You'd better become one, and fast. Everyone is looking at you because you aren't joining in! They'll think you're making fun of us if you don't play along."

I spied a familiar big shape lurking in a nearby leather maker's tent. "Fine, you want me to mark a guy, I'll mark a guy." I raised my voice and shouted over the din, "Hey, there, Wenches, in yon leather guy's tent lurketh a very big rogue. Methinks I'll sashay thither and marketh him. How say you?"

CJ rolled her eyes and said in an almost inaudible tone, "You are rotten at Faire speak!"

"Verily, 'tis the truth, yonder rogue is ripe for marking. Have at him!" the Wenches responded.

I handed CJ the leash, snickering to myself that she was too disgusted with my attempt to join in to realize who it was who stood in the tent.

"Rogue, prepare ye to be boarded by the good ship *Kissylips,*" I called loudly as I tapped Butcher on his shoulder. He turned around, a long leather belt in his hands. I grabbed his head and pulled it down enough so I could plant a few lipstick kisses on his cheeks, grinning when CJ squawked loudly behind me.

"Thank you, I think." Butcher grinned back at me.

"Nothing like a little jealousy to spice things up," I told him, then did my Wench walk (exaggerated hip action and heaving bosom) back to where the ladies were gathered, curtsying to the crowd when they applauded.

"Of all the . . . I have never . . . You have *some* nerve. . . . Just because you aren't getting along with *your* man doesn't mean you can have *mine!*" CJ threw Moth's leash at me and stormed over to where Butcher stood covered in lipstick kisses, grabbing his ear and hauling his head down so she could scrub the marks off his face.

Fairuza, deciding to overlook this obvious breach in Promenade policy, herded us onward. It wasn't until we reached the beer garden that it struck me that almost everyone at the Faire had lined up to watch the Wenches Promenade . . . everyone but Walker.

We continued on our way, pausing when the Wenches spied Farrell posing for a newspaper camera. Three Wenches swarmed him, kissing every available stretch of skin. He shot me a triumphant glance over the head of the nearest Wench.

I thought about ignoring him, but decided that since there was a chance Walker would be facing Farrell in the list, it would behoove me to make nice in an attempt to tone down Farrell's manic sense of competition and determination to pound Walker into the ground. It wasn't that I believed he could actually do it under normal circumstances, but Walker was a bit delicate, emotionally speaking. Although he'd jousted well enough with the Aussie—both of them scoring points, neither unhorsing the other—I had the sense that his heart wasn't in it. He'd been too hesitant, too cautious.

"You look positively edible." Farrell leered when I separated from the Wenches while they snacked on his teammates.

"I'd return the compliment, but I'm sure you know that you're the handsomest man here," I answered, reeling Moth in when he started gnawing on the fringe of Farrell's boots. "So how's tricks?"

"Tricks, my lady fair, are very fine, very fine indeed, which, alas, I fear you cannot say." He made a show of eyeing my face, *tsk*ing at the faint smudge of a bruise under my left eye. "That facer you executed earlier today did your beauteous face no good. I warned you about the knave Walker's training methods, did I not?"

My intentions to be nothing but polite to him flew away on a breeze of irritation. "You did, but it wasn't Walker who was training me. And besides, you know I take everything you say with a huge grain of salt, what with the inferiority complex you have around Walker."

"Inferiority complex!" he sputtered, and I bit back the urge to tell him exactly what I thought. I'd done that already, and it would do no good to express *that* opinion again. "I do not have an inferiority complex, not about Walker or anything else. It may have escaped your attention, but I am the reigning U.S. champion here, not the man you so generously allowed to plow your belly."

"Jealous?" I asked, amused rather than offended by his crudeness. I'd never before had a man jealous over my relationship with another, and I found I rather enjoyed it. So long as Farrell didn't do anything to harm Walker, that was . . .

"Only of the attention you pay that gor-bellied, clay-brained gudgeon," he said smoothly.

"Oooh, you do Elizabethan insults, too! That was a favorite game around the office before we got laid off. How about this: Thou art a spleeny-tongued, pottle-deep hedge-pig."

A sudden flash of humor lit the fair blue of Farrell's eyes. He put both hands on his hips and said in a loud voice, "And I say you, lady, are a dissembling, spur-galled canker-blossom!"

Heads of the people nearest swiveled to look at us. I considered the gauntlet Farrell had thrown down, and decided that *this* was a challenge I could win.

"Oh!" I said loudly, tucking Moth under my arm so I could circle Farrell, giving him an appropriately scathing look. "Says you! Your words are but the purest drivel upon mine ears. I find you nothing but a claver-headed, fat-gilled moldwarp!"

More people turned to face us.

"Scold!" Farrell sneered, his eyes lit with unholy glee.

"Malt worm!" I answered promptly.

"Oooh, it's an insult-off!" someone in the crowd cried, and immediately Farrell and I found ourselves in the center of a circle of bodies.

I faced him with a smile lurking around the corners of my mouth.

"Lady, you are nothing but a quaky, onion-eyed dewberry."

The crowd oohed appreciably. "That's one for Sir Farrell," David, Fairuza's Rogue, said.

I smiled prettily at Farrell and waggled my eyebrows. "Alas that you'll never taste the dew on my berries, you unmuzzled, pox-warted, boiled-brained pustule on the buttock of a skainsmate!"

"Ho! The maid strikes hard with that one." David laughed. "Three points to Lady Pepper. How answer you, good Sir Farrell?"

"This is all I have to say," Farrell said, preening himself as the crowd groaned in anticipation. I cocked a brow at him, thoroughly enjoying myself. Back in my days of gainful employment, I was the office queen of Elizabethan insults. No one could top me, but I had a suspicion that Farrell's pièce de résistance was going to be difficult to beat. He bowed to me, one hand on his chest as he said, "My lady, thine eyes are as a layer of whey-scum on curdled milk, thy skin is as pox-mangled as the most loutish of privy-scrapers, and thy hair, oh, lady, thy hair is as shard-borne as a rump-fed harpy lying spitted on a scurvy-tongued horn-beast."

The crowd gasped. I pursed my lips and considered my store of Elizabethan words.

"Lady, the good and brave knight hath issued his

challenge most heinous, worth an extraordinary five points. Do you have an answer for him, or will you cry quarter?" David asked.

Everyone turned to look at me. I smiled, set Moth on the ground, and looked at Farrell. His eyes twinkled at me, and I was aware of an odd a sense of companionship with him. How could a man who was willing to trade insults with me be such a complete boob about other things? I gave Farrell a little curtsy, then clutched my hands together and said, "Good sir knight, my heart fails me in the face of such glib-tongued barbs as you have let fall."

The assembled audience groaned at my apparent surrender. "Don't let him win, Pepper!" CJ cried. "A Wench never gives up, and God knows you can talk a person's ear off, so get to it!"

"However," I said before my cousin got any more digs in, "I find myself driven to say that in all the years that I've been graced to walk upon this earth, I have never seen such a fobbing, guts-griping, mewling, pribbling, puking, excrescent-brained, spittle-scuttled, earth-vexing codpiece of a bladder-headed ball-less puxion! You are toad-spotted! You are urchin-smirched! You are a beslubbering, foul-tainted, dung-worm-scented pile of offal spewn from the rump of a flap-dragon, and I will suffer your countenance, swaggish and bum-bailied as it is, no more! Begone, Sir Ratsbane, and never darken my horizon again!"

The ladies around me, Wenches and otherwise, cheered. The men groaned, and I bowed to all four quarters, accepting the accolades. David pronounced me the winner, and commanded me to set a boon upon Farrell.

I considered Farrell as the Faire people fell silent, most of them aware of the history between Walker and Farrell, not to mention the fact that I had spent the last two nights personally polishing Walker's sword. "The only thing I ask of Sir Farrell is that he abide by the code of chivalry at all times."

Farrell's smile slipped a notch.

"Lady," David said, looking nervously at him. "It is an insult to suggest a noble knight would do otherwise."

"Perhaps," I said, my eyes holding Farrell's suddenly wary gaze. The spirit of fun generated by our mock battle melted away, leaving me once again extremely aware that Farrell was very jealous of Walker. "But it can do no harm to remind him that where chivalry is concerned, a man's honor is everything."

He said nothing, but made me another one of his flashy bows.

"Wenches, ho!" CJ yelled, hustling me back into the Wench group. We continued down the line of vendors in what was now a veritable parade of Faire folk and visitors, so that by the time we sang the closing song (a ditty about a Wench and the sheepherder who stole her chemise), half the Faire was crowding into the area set aside as one of the three ale gardens.

Released from my Wenchly duties, I picked Moth up and wended my way through the jolly crowd, still engaged in singing Wenchish songs and toasting the bosoms of every woman present with large tankards of ale. Everyone was there—jousters, archers, swordsmen and -women, visitors and performers, children, elderly people, and hundreds in between. All of the Three Dog Knights were present except their erstwhile leader, but no one seemed to know just exactly where he was.

"Haven't seen him for a few hours," Butcher yelled over the nearest boisterous singers.

"Doesn't that worry you?" I asked, also in a yell, since it was impossible to hear otherwise.

He shook his head. "Not with Walker. He's prone to disappearing for hours. Moody bugger, he is."

"Lovely," I said too quietly for him to hear, then yelled my thanks and pushed my way through the human sardines to the less crowded fairway just as a Scottish band was firing up their bagpipes. I hoisted

Moth up so I could see into his beady yellow eyes. "I don't suppose if I waved a bit of Walker's clothing in front of your nose you'd be able to pick up his scent?"

His ears flattened.

"I didn't think so," I said on a sigh, and wandered back to my tent, wondering all the way there where Walker could be.

I fed Moth, let him use his facilities, and donned the dark forest-green tights and matching tunic I'd bought earlier using the last tiny bit of credit left on my now maxed-out card. "It's worth it if Bliss'll be off my case for wearing jeans," I told the cat when he sauntered over to examine the soft ankle boots I had managed to get for half price. "I don't suppose you'd like to stay here and sleep off that dinner while I go hunt for the dishy Mr. McPhail?"

Moth shot me a disgusted look and marched over to the door of the tent, his tail twitching irritably while I struggled into the gambeson and mail hauberk. I forgot to wrap my head first, which had me yelling out all sorts of creative Elizabethan oaths as my braid snagged repeatedly on the mail before it settled down onto my shoulders.

"Right, here's the game plan—we'll take a quick look around to see if we can find where Mr. Pouty Pants is hiding, and if not, we'll saddle up Cassie and have a little extra practice at that evil shock quintain. I'll be damned if I let Walker see me falling on my face again. A girl has to have some dignity."

Moth sneezed on my boot before turning to sharpen his claws on the nylon tent door. I gave in to the inevitable and took him with me as I headed for the Three Dog Knights' tents. There was no one there, although that was difficult to see at first, since Walker's tent was crammed full of jousting equipment—striped lances without their balsa tips, a big trunk containing two swords in scabbards and a black painted suit of armor (probably Butcher's spare that Walker was using) that Moth played on until I pulled him

away, a beat-up high-backed saddle straddling a chair,
suitcases, boxes of foodstuffs, and a large plastic case
of medical supplies that included several elastic ban-
dages, sports tape, and various ointments intended for
the relief of chafing. Glancing around the tent turned
up several interesting facts: Walker had a hitherto un-
suspected addiction to salt-and-vinegar potato chips;
he was very tidy, his clothes being folded nicely and
not wadded up in his suitcase like mine were; and
Butcher's spare chain-mail hauberk was nowhere to
be found.

"What do you deduce from this very interesting
fact, Watson?" I asked Moth as I emerged from Walker's tent with a couple of lances and a handful of
unpainted balsa tips shoved into my belt.

"I thought its name was Moth?"

I jumped and stifled the scream that wanted to burst
from my throat at the unexpected voice. "Geez, Lou-
ise, Veronica, do you think you could warn me the
next time you're going to sneak up on me? You almost gave me a heart attack!"

Veronica was dressed in a lacy white poet's blouse,
crimson tights, a sword strapped to a belt slung low
over her hips, thigh-high boots, and a big black pirate's hat complete with fwoofy white feathers. The
feathers bobbed in the late afternoon breeze as she
tipped her head to the side while she considered first
me in all my mailed glory, then the lances. "It would
defeat the purpose of sneaking up on you if I warned
you first."

"Yeah, I guess, although I'd prefer it if you didn't—
Moth! Spit that out, it's not your sock!—didn't sneak
up on me at all. Are you looking for Walker, too?"

"Walker? No."

"Ah." *Crap*. That meant she was looking for me.
And there I was, obviously going off to have a little
jousting practice. *Oh, joy.* "Look, I appreciate your
belief in me, but I'm really not interested in being
your alternate—"

She smiled and patted me on the shoulder. "Don't worry about it, Pepper. I'm not going to badger you about joining our team."

"You're not? Oh! That's good. I mean, it's not that I'm not horribly flattered and all, but—"

"I know, you're not interested in anything I have to offer, not even if it means fame and glory." Her head tipped a little to the side again. "Tell me—would you be quite so uninterested if it was Walker we were discussing, not you?"

Apparent stupidity had its charms, one of which was to get you out of answering tricky questions. "Walker? What do you mean? He's already on a team."

"Yes, but will he win?"

I opened my mouth to tell her of course he would, but closed it up again. Walker had jousted moderately well today, but not with what Bliss called any of his usual brilliance. Even to my inexperienced eyes he had looked uncomfortable and stiff in the saddle. It was entirely possible that if he continued as he started, he'd finish way out of the money, ruining the rest of the team's chances.

Veronica nodded, patting my shoulder as she turned to leave. "I thought not. You have the look of a woman who would do anything for her man, no matter what the cost. Will we see you later at the Swashbucklers Ball?"

"Maybe. I'm not sure. It depends . . ."

She paused, giving me an odd look before she said, "Keep me in mind if you find yourself in trouble and need a friend. Unlike others, I am not afraid to do what needs to be done."

She left before I could ask her just what sort of trouble she envisioned me being in, not to mention what the cryptic "doing what needs to be done" part of her message entailed, or question her regarding Marley, and Bos's lance.

"Well, she's up for suspect number one based on that conversation," I told Moth. His face donned its martyred look as I slung him up onto my hip, heading for the stable. The two teens who were watching the shop told me everyone had gone off for dinner.

"Ah," I said as I ran my hands over Cassie, checking for any signs of injury, not that I expected to find any. "I'm just going to take Cassie out for a little exercise. No one's been messing around with the horses, have they?"

"No one's been in the stable at all except the Three Doggers and the Jousting Jesters," Tim answered. He was the oldest of the two hired to watch over the horses, and looked like a reliable kid.

I nodded at the mention of the other team who shared the stable and settled the saddle blanket over Cassie's back. "Good enough. Make sure you watch anyone who comes near. The competition is only just starting."

It wasn't easy to get Moth, the lances, and Cassie to the distant field where the shock quintain had been set up, but in the end I managed it by plopping Moth onto Cassie's deep Calvary saddle. I spent the long walk out to the field figuring out how I'd brace the lances up on their butt end so I could grab one without having to dismount, but in the end it was all moot.

"Well, I'll be a milk-livered gudgeon," I told Moth as we rounded the corner of the outbuilding next to the field. "Lookie what we found. Sir Hottie himself. Holy cow!"

Walker and Marley went thundering down the field, Walker in full armor with a shield on his left arm as he lowered the lance, couching it just before it slammed into the shield bolted onto the quintain. I knew from experience just how heavy the shock quintain was (about two hundred pounds, according to Bliss), but Walker didn't just tip it over; he blasted into it with such force that it flew backward about six feet before crashing onto its back.

"My God, that must have hurt." I gasped, noting how Walker's body recoiled backward against the high back of his Paso saddle. It was then that I saw that he was riding without touching the reins that hung loosely around Marley's neck, using instead leg and voice cues to direct the big gelding. "Now *that's* impressive training in just one week."

Walker didn't spy us coming toward him until he dismounted in order to pull the quintain back onto its legs.

"What are you doing here?" he asked with a familiar scowl. I tamped down ruthlessly on the various parts of my body that woke up and started cheering at the sound of his voice. I hadn't forgotten how mean he had been to me earlier.

The truth can be painful when you refuse to admit it, a traitorous voice in my head said softly. I squashed it down, too.

"Looks like the same thing you're doing—practicing, although if that's how you normally hit, it's pretty obvious you don't need much practice."

"Everyone needs practice, even experienced jousters," he said dismissively, grunting a little as he hauled the quintain onto its wooden platform. I watched him rub his neck where the metal plate had rubbed a raw spot on the flesh just above his collarbone.

"That looks nasty. Aren't you supposed to be wearing something underneath the armor to protect your skin?"

"The problem isn't with the gambeson; it's this armor. It wasn't made for me. I'll fix it tomorrow, between matches. Where's Bliss?"

"Come on, your highness, you get the seat of honor," I told Moth, setting him down on the metal barrel, having first placed one of my towels down. "Bliss is probably partying with everyone else. We had a Promenade and everyone went crazy afterward. What do you mean, you'll fix the armor? Won't that require something like an anvil? Blacksmith stuff?"

"Yes. The metalsmith said I could use the forge he has set up to demonstrate smithing."

"Isn't that kind of dangerous?" I asked, visions of hot blobs of molten steel flying onto Walker's adorable face. He might be the most irritating man in existence, but he was *my* irritating man, and I didn't want him hurt.

"I'm a farrier, Pepper. I know how to use a forge," he said, giving me a hot glance before striding over to where Marley was dozing in the early evening sun. "Were you planning to practice by yourself?"

"Yup. Now you can watch and tell me what I'm doing wrong, and I'll do the same for you." I didn't see it, but I just *knew* he rolled his eyes at that suggestion. "Then maybe after we've practiced for a while we can joust together? Mano a . . . uh . . . femo?"

"No," he snapped, sliding smoothly into the saddle.

"Oh, come on—dammit, Cassie, stand still!—don't be such a poop. I hit Bliss's shield almost every time yesterday when we jousted."

"That wasn't jousting; that was training. You'd be dead in a real joust," he said dismissively, and watched with one eyebrow cocked as I hopped up and down a half dozen times before managing to hoist myself into the saddle. I adjusted the girth, fiddled with the stirrup length, and rearranged my mail until it was to my liking, all forms of procrastination. The truth was that part of me really didn't want Walker around to watch me hit the dirt again, but the other part, the girlie part, went all giggly around him and wanted to patch things up and live happily ever after.

Instead of giving in to that desire, I straightened my shoulders and told myself that I'd brazen it out. "Yeah, well, I might just surprise you. So, you going to stand there all day, or are you going to nail the quintain?"

He gestured a graceful hand and moved Marley to the side. "Ladies first."

"That's Sir Lady to you, buster," I said haughtily, taking one of the lances to which he'd already fixed the breakable balsa tips. As I turned Cassie toward the other end of the field, I called back to him, "We brave knights of yore demand respect from common folk. We're virtual gods upon the earth, just you remember that."

Walker said nothing, but sat easily on a bored Marley, both of them watching as I lined Cassie up with the dreaded shock quintain.

"All right, old girl, let's refrain from snacking until Pepper is steady in the saddle, hmm?" I took a deep breath, got a good grip on the lance, and dug my heels in, gripping Cassie firmly with my knees.

"What was that you were saying about being a god?" Walker asked twenty seconds later while I spit out grass and dirt, groaning just a little as I got up on one elbow to glare when he dismounted and started toward me.

"I mentioned earth," I grumbled. "This is a form of worship."

"Ah, is that it? I could have sworn it was a form of inexperience."

I let him help me to my feet, taking the opportunity to throw a clump of grass at Cassie as she grazed. "You great big four-hoofed traitor! I said *no* snacking!"

"The sign of an inexperienced knight is one who blames the horse rather than himself," Walker said, his hands still on my arms.

I threw grass at him, too. "Oh, yeah?"

"Yes," he said, his eyes impossible to read in the creeping evening shadows, but his jaw was tense and tight as he ground out the word. "Everyone knows that. Give it up, Pepper. You can't do this."

"Never!" I swore, glaring at him, alternating between the desire to strangle him, and throw him to the ground and have my way with him. "Bliss says I can do this, and do it I shall."

"Bliss is wrong," he said roughly, moving closer to me. "She's never trained anyone before. I have. You don't have what it takes to be a jouster."

"Says you." I snorted, my body taking a step forward until my mail brushed with a metal whisper over the surface of his plate armor. "I say I can."

"You can't," he hissed, his breath hot on my face, his eyes glowing with a molten light.

"Are you as aroused as I am?" I asked, unable to resist the offer his body was making me.

"More," he growled, jerking me forward, his mouth claiming mine to the sound of chain mail scraping across steel armor.

Chapter Fifteen

"This is ridiculous," I complained, my fingers working desperately on the buckles holding Walker's armor on. "We'll hurt ourselves. Or someone will see us. Or the horses will run off. Or Moth will eat my gambeson. Stupid buckle!"

Walker snarled something as he ripped at the leather buckle on the shoulder of his breastplate. Truly, what we were considering doing was idiotic in the extreme. Voyeuristic aspects aside, it was ridiculous to think we could possibly make love while one or both of us was covered in protective armor.

That didn't stop me from ripping my mail hauberk off, though. I had it, my gambeson, and my tights off before Walker had the first buckle of his pauldron—the shoulder armor—off. I stood in nothing but my tunic fighting with his buckle until I realized just how foolish we were being to give in to our passion this way. There were better, more comfortable, sensible ways to do this. "Stop! This is silly! You'll hurt yourself, and you're breaking the armor!"

Walker was panting with frustration as he ripped the second pauldron off. His eyes met mine, and any further protestations dried up as his mouth descended on mine again, the heat and taste of him enough to drive me wild with need.

"Screw sensibility," I muttered into his mouth.

"I second the suggestion," he answered, his tongue swirling over mine. While I kissed him with everything I was worth, he managed to get the breastplate and armpieces off without once taking a lip off me.

"Mail," he murmured against my mouth as I writhed against him.

"Yes, you are *very* male," I cooed, reaching for the proof of just that.

"No, chain mail. Let me get it off—"

"No time!" I shrieked, grabbing his shoulders tight and jumping up, wrapping my legs around his hips, using one hand to jerk his mail and arming tunic out of the way. Walker lurched a few steps to a small stand of fir trees that would give us a modicum of privacy, not that I really feared anyone would discover our illicit activities. Everyone was too busy toasting the Wenches' breasts to wander out in a distant, seldom-used field.

"Pepper—oh, god, sweetheart, this is going to be fast. . . . Can you reach my hose?"

"My darling, I will always be able to reach your hose," I said in between scattered kisses to his lovely mouth.

"Not that hose, love." He groaned as pressed me up against one of the tree trunks. "Lord, the way you taste—can you reach me? I'm going to burst if you don't—"

"Just a sec. Ow!" I dug a branch out of my back before reaching down between us, jerking at his tights. "Good god, were you this big last night? You haven't been taking Viagra or something, have you? Because I don't remember you being so . . . *gigantic*!"

I couldn't see that particular part of him, but the way he pressed up against me was a bit intimidating.

"I'm just the same as I was before," he groaned, shifting me a bit against the tree. I wrapped both arms around his neck, kissing his neck and jaw. "Christ, I'd like to do this slowly—"

"Never mind," I said, squirming around as the tip

of him teased all my squishy parts, my legs tightening around his hips. "Boy, these last few days of horse-back riding have done a lot to increase my thigh muscles. Up just a bit, my darling. Now to the left. No, no, not your left, my left. Your right. No, Walker, that's my leg; you're not going to get anywhere if you start thrusting away there—"

"For Christ's sake, woman, help me!" Walker all but sobbed as he lunged upward.

"I'm trying to help you, but you're not listening! Left! I mean, right, right! Go right!"

He leaned his forehead against mine, his breath as rough and ragged as my own. "Pepper, love, would you please use your hand to help me? Not that I don't appreciate your directions, but if I have to rely upon your navigation to do this, we'll be at it all night."

"Well, that doesn't sound too awful," I said, giving his lower lip a quick suck, just so he'd know how much I adored it. I reached between us again, grabbing his now seemingly humongous penis and directing it to where it was sure of a hearty welcome. He surged into me, filling me, nudging himself into areas that were all but quivering with anticipation of his arrival, and I almost let go of his neck, the feeling was so over-whelming. It was good, it was right, and when he started to move within me, it was the most beautiful thing in the whole world.

"Are you all right?" he asked as he nipped my ear, his tongue soothing away the sting.

"'All right' is a bit of an understatement, my lusty knight. Oh, yes, do that again!"

He surged upward, and my muscles rippled around him, the breath caught in my chest. Pressed as I was against the tree, I was limited in my movement, but I managed to do a little swivel that damn near had him singing with pleasure.

"You're so good, so hot, like liquid fire around me," he gasped into my ear. I couldn't answer; my brain had stopped working by that point. All that was left was the knowledge that there was nothing in my life that would be as important as my decision to take this man into my heart and keep him there forever. I twisted my arms around, grabbing his hair with both hands and yanking his head back.

"You're mine, Walker, and I'm never going to let you go. Do you understand?"

His eyes crossed as I tightened every muscle I had around the long, hot, velvety-slick length of him.

"Pepper, my sweet, fiery Pepper, you warm me when no one else can—oh, god!"

"Yes, yes, I know it's good, isn't it? We fit so perfectly together." Walker's hips went wild against me, his body all but dancing as he thrust into me again and again. The pressure was building within me, my muscles cramping in anticipation of the big moment.

His back arched, thrusting his hips even harder against me. "Oh, god, I can't—"

"Yes, you can, my darling," I answered, sucking his neck, trying to reassure him with the tiny fragment of my brain that was left lucid. "I know it's overwhelming, but just stay with me a few minutes longer. . . . Merciful heaven, you feel so good inside me!"

"Moth, no!" Walker's voice was hoarse, his face caught between a grimace of pain and a stultifying look of the ecstasy that I sensed he was within seconds of reaching.

"Moth? My name is Pepper, you deranged and yet adorable man! Don't stop!" I yelled, moving against him as his fingers bit into my thighs, shifting me against him. "Not now, not yet, please not yet!"

His eyes blazed at me as he writhed, but he didn't stop his heroic attempt to send me to heaven and back, no, sir, not my Walker. Tears collected in the corners of his eyes, tears that I kissed away as I gave in to the red wave of rapture that crashed over me, filling me and binding me to him in a way so profound, it shook me to my core.

"Walker!" I yelled, my nose touching his, my body

consumed with everything that we were together. I wrapped my fingers into his hair and shook his head until his teeth rattled. "I love you!"

He shuddered, his back arching even harder as he, too, surrendered his soul to the amazing, wondrous entity we had become. His eyes went wild as he shouted my name to the heavens while I melted against him, one great big puddle of Pepper goo, mindless to everything but the man who had so effectively filled my heart.

I gasped into his neck, his breath as rough as mine as he collapsed against me, pinning me to the tree. Beneath my hands a fine tremor shook his body, but whether it was from the stress of holding me up or from the power of our joining, I didn't know. I kissed his neck, wanting to stay in his arms forever, but knowing that even hidden in the trees as we were, it was too exposed a spot to linger.

"My darling, my dearest love, my scrumdillyicious Walker, we have to . . ." I lifted my head from his sweaty neck, only to come nose-to-nose with the most annoying cat in the western hemisphere, a cat that evidently thought nothing of scaling Walker while we were making love. No wonder the poor man was twitching and writhing—I knew from experience just how sharp Moth's claws could be. "Stop puffing your breath on me, you horrible beast. You smell like cat food!"

"I do?" Walker asked. "I don't know why I would. I haven't been eating any."

"Very funny, Mr. Comedian," I said, turning my head and giving his adorable chin a little love bite. "You know I was talking to this damned cat. Why didn't you tell me he was climbing you?"

Walker also turned his head, this time to meet Moth's inscrutable cat eyes. "It didn't seem very important at that moment. We really have to do something about him. I've never been one for a ménage à trois."

"Don't worry," I said, one finger beneath his chin turning his face so his lips were back within range of mine. "I have a plan."

The next five days passed in utter and complete bliss, or at least a reasonable facsimile thereof. My days were spent watching Walker and his team perform in the competitions, rooting on the Three Dog Knights during the competition hours, training with Walker in the off hours, spending my nights with my knight . . . and falling deeper and more irrevocably in love with each beat of his heart.

The time wasn't without moments of lunacy, however. When I trained with Walker, he ceased being my adorable dream knight, turning into Walker the Hun, scourge of my life. We argued about everything, from the way I held the lance to the fact that I had stolen his favorite black Venetian hat and claimed it for my own (it was a very cool hat and looked good on me, a fact Walker had to admit one night when I stood before him wearing nothing but it). After spending ten minutes with Walker instructing me at jousting, I understood completely why Veronica had warned me against training with him.

"Are you deaf, woman?" Walker yelled at me the third day into training. "I told you this morning not to brace the lance against your shield, and yet you just did it again!"

I squinted at Walker and thought seriously about running him through with the pointy end of my lance. Surely it was justifiable homicide? The only thing that kept me from throwing down the lance and quitting was my audience.

Word had gotten out that not only was Walker jousting again, but he had taken a new pupil under his wing. I didn't realize until then just how well respected the man was in the jousting community, but the fact that every morning before breakfast, and every evening after the day's competition was over, a

group of ten or so squires—and occasionally even a
couple of jousters—gathered to watch Walker put me
through my paces said something about how highly
valued his instruction was.

I glanced at the gang of usual suspects, giving them
a little wave of my lance to let them know I wasn't
going to take Walker's bullying. They liked it when I
argued with him.

"Try it again, and this time keep your lance steady,
and do *not* rest it on the shield. Only amateurs do
that."

"Who are you calling an amateur?" I yelled as he
turned to walk over to the spot he claimed as his
viewing stand (it was a lawn chair with a cooler of
beer). "I won't take that sort of a slur, you scurvy
knave! You've insulted my honor. I challenge you to
a joust!"

The squires cheered and looked hopefully at
Walker.

"Stop playing around, Pepper, and get to it. We
don't have all evening to waste."

Those squires who were married or in long-term
relationships pursed their lips and shook their heads.

"Waste? Excuse me, who insisted that Bliss stop
training me just so he could take over the job?"

Walker crossed his arms over his chest, which would
have been a nice intimidating move if Moth wasn't
lying draped over his shoulders, his tale flicking lazily
across Walker's mouth.

Two or three of the squires began to make wagers.

"Get on with it, Pepper."

"I challenged you to a joust," I said, waggling the
lance at him. "You can't refuse a challenge."

The squires all nodded.

"Yes, I can."

They shook their heads.

"No, you can't. It's illegal. It goes against the code
of chivalry."

Three nodded, four shook their heads, two pulled out a pack of cards and began to play a game.

Walker frowned and spit the end of Moth's tail out of his mouth. "You don't know what you're talking about. If you don't want to joust—"

"But I do, with you, but you won't. And that's not fair!"

"Dammit, Pepper, I'm not jousting with you," Walker bellowed.

The squires, to a man, froze.

"Why not?" I bellowed back.

"Because I'll break your bloody neck, that's why!" he roared.

It was at that moment that I realized he loved me, but he hadn't yet admitted it to himself. Oh, I knew he didn't want to break *anyone's* neck, but it was the way he stood there yelling at me, a vein on his neck bulging, his face red with anger, his eyes icy slivers of silver cold enough to burn liquid oxygen. Only a man in love would get so upset.

That knowledge warmed me through the following two days, and despite the blissful moments I spent in Walker's arms, I couldn't help but worry about what was happening to him. The Three Dog Knights finished twelfth in the team competition, well out of the money. No further accidents had happened, nothing out of the ordinary, and everyone seemed to relax, feeling the worst was over. Walker's covert investigation—which he refused to share with me, the beastly man—got him no farther than my own interviews of anyone and everyone who could have reasonably been around the stable the days before I noticed Marley's leg. I had given up trying to find out anything about the lances—those were stored in a shed next to the arena, the shed locked and supposedly secure, but I suspected it would be all too easy to sneak inside.

No, what had me worried wasn't a horrible plan against the team; it was worry about one man who filled my heart. Walker had continued to joust moderately well, but not nearly up to his past standards, according to a whispered conversation I had with Vandal, Butcher, and Bliss the morning of the swordplay competition.

"He's holding back, that's what it is," Vandal said, plucking a latte from the cardboard holder that Bliss carried. "Did you see him in Realgestech? It was like *he* was made of steel, not his armor. He sat on Marley's back like a great big lump."

Butcher shook his head, carefully holding a latte for CJ and his own cup of tea. "He's afraid, Vandal. Fear will do that to you sometimes."

"The question is, what are we going to do about it?" Bliss asked, biting her lower lip as she glanced toward Walker's tent.

"He's taking a shower," I reassured her.

Her shoulders slumped. "It's not that I don't have the fullest respect for him—I know how he can joust. We all do."

Vandal and Butcher nodded their heads.

"Top drawer," Vandal said.

"Best there is," Butcher added.

"And we all know what hell he went through after the accident, but we're not going to stand a snowball's chance in a Scotsman's kilt if he doesn't snap out of it." Bliss's forehead wrinkled as she thought of something. "Did you see his face when Farrell walked off with the team trophy? There was nothing there—no anger, no sorrow, nothing. It was as if he doesn't care anymore."

"He cares," Butcher said slowly. "It's buried deep, beneath all the self-hatred and fear that he'll hurt someone else, but it's there. He would have gone home if he didn't care."

"It's not enough," Vandal said, his voice mournful. "He's ruining all our chances just because he's lost his nerve. Everyone knows that we would have come in the top three if Walker's low scores hadn't pulled us down. *Someone* has to get him to shake out of it. *Someone* has to bring the old Walker back to life."

Bliss turned to me. "Pepper, couldn't you—"

I choked on the sip of latte I was taking. "Not a chance. You've seen him whenever I talk jousting— he goes Joust Nazi on me."

The three shared a glance before turning back to me.

"Oh, no," I said, snatching Walker's cup of coffee from Bliss before backing away from them. "I know that look. You're not getting me to do anything else. Walker and I have an unspoken peace treaty going on, and I don't want anything to ruin it."

"You're the only one he'll listen to," Vandal whined, grabbing my sleeve to keep me from running.

"Bull! He's known you guys much longer than he's known me," I said, still trying to make my escape.

"He's not sleeping with us," Butcher pointed out.

"So? The act of sexual congress does not give the congressee magical powers of persuasion."

"Oh, I don't know. There's an Ale Wench who could have me painting myself blue and dancing naked on the green if she put her mind to it."

Butcher shot Vandal a scathing glance. "You did that last year at the French championship. No, I agree, Pepper is the logical choice. She can talk to Walker where we can't. He knows how we feel; we've all talked him blue about the way he's been jousting." For the first time since I'd met him, his eyes held none of the gentle amusement that was normal. Instead, his usually warm eyes were bleak and flat. A cold shiver rippled down my back at the look. "We aren't getting through to him. Only you have the ability to do that."

The three of them looked at me with such hope in their eyes that I couldn't just walk away as I wanted. Instead I went back to Walker's tent to feed Moth, wondering how on earth I was going to broach the subject without Walker going ballistic.

That was the thought that consumed me most of the day. While the Three Dog Knights sat in the small outdoor arena to cheer on Butcher, Fenice, Vandal, and Geoff during their matches, I let my mind dwell on the problem at hand.

How was I going to tell the man I loved to throw away caution and joust like the maniac he used to be? At first I had thought his reputation had been exaggerated, but after listening to some of Walker's tales about past tourneys, I had a new appreciation for just how he had earned the title of Walker the Wild. The key was to get him to make a sincere attempt to win the competition without endangering his—or anyone else's—life, which meant I had to polish up that tarnished self-image he held.

"Easier said than done." I sighed as we watched the competition.

"What is?" Walker asked, his voice a low velvet rub against my skin, his breath hot in my ear. I relaxed into his side, stroking Moth where he lay on Walker's thigh.

"Nothing important. I'll tell you later."

"Later? When you're naked and writhing beneath me and begging me to spread your thighs and—"

I put a hand over his mouth, allowing my fingers to do a little caressing before removing them. "Yes, thank you, Walker, just in case there was anyone left at the Faire who didn't know exactly what was going on, that should clear up the confusion."

He grinned at me, my heart turning a somersault at the look. When he wasn't being Walker the Hun, he was everything I had ever wanted in a man—witty, charming, intelligent, mostly respectful of my opinion when he wasn't telling me what to do, and sexy as hell. The last few days he'd started to open up to me, sharing his thoughts and feelings in the dark, warm hours of the night when we lay sated in each other's arms, our bodies tangled together in drowsy completion. The thought that his trust in me might be shattered by the conversation I needed to have came close to breaking my heart. *How could I risk losing everything I have with him, our entire future together, just for a stupid competition?* I asked my Wise Inner Pepper.

How can you believe you have a future with him if he won't conquer the darkness he hides inside? WIP answered back.

I ground my teeth and tried to tell myself Inner Pepper had clearly lost her mind, that Walker and I would be just fine if he never lifted another lance for the rest of his life. The following day I watched him covertly as he followed the swordfighting. His muscles twitched in time to the fighters' bold sweeps of the swords, his arms tightening and releasing as he anticipated a blow, his body swaying and jerking as he countered a near-fatal lunge.

My heart sang a hopeless dirge as I admitted that maybe Inner Pepper wasn't so wrong. Fighting was in Walker's blood; he loved it so much that even in his darkest moments, he couldn't separate himself entirely from the combat community. The man was born to be a knight. He'd even chosen a livelihood that would feed his addiction, keeping him around horses and their owners, many of whom were also part of the jousting society.

"Vandal's up," Walker said, interrupting my dark musing by wrapping his arm around my waist and pulling me closer. The lovely, spicy Walker smell of manly man sank deep into my blood, and I couldn't help but wonder if we could bottle whatever it was he exuded. "Now you'll see some real fighting, not the feeble bit of sparring that we've seen so far."

There was pride in his voice, pride and satisfaction and pleasant expectation, as if he were anticipating a precious gift. I gnawed on my lower lip as Vandal swaggered into the swordplay ring, calling out taunts and slurs against his opponent (one of the Canadian team). Would it change his relationship with his teammates if I turned him back into the old Walker? Would he resent them for demanding he give his all for them, or would he see them as innocent, ladling all the blame onto my head?

"Vandal!" one of the Ale Wenches yelled, waving a pair of undies at him. He saluted her, waving to the crowd as the announcer read off his name and history. Both men were in full armor, the heavy plate stuff, not just mail. Vandal's helm had a scarlet plume that bobbed in the wind for a few seconds before the ring marshal shouted the cue to start.

"Holy cow," I couldn't help but say, my mouth hanging open just a bit as I tried to keep my eyes on the blur that was Vandal.

"He's good, isn't he?" Walker asked, his voice warm and happy. "Best there is in England."

"Did you teach him that?" I asked, not taking my eyes off Vandal as he danced around the Canadian, his sword flashing in the sunlight.

"Me? No, his father did. He was a master fencer."

Crash! Vandal landed a blow on the man's shield. *Whammo!* Another to the guy's sword arm. *Screeeeeauck!* Metal slid along metal as Vandal cracked the poor Canadian right across the middle of his breastplate.

"I can believe it."

With each blow, Vandal's opponent got slower and slower with his responses, his strikes against Vandal all easily parried by the far more talented Englishman. In a matter of two minutes or so, Vandal had the Canadian backed up to the boundary of the circle in which they fought.

"One," Walker said.

Vandal swung backhanded, landing a blow on the Canadian's side. The man stumbled backward.

"Two." A smile flirted with Walker's lips as the Canadian raised his shield in an attempt to deflect Vandal's spinning slam to his head. It didn't work. He fell to his knees, the toes of his boots just touching the white line of the circle.

"Thre— Urgh! What the hell!" Walker lunged to his feet along with half the crowd, the rest of us too stunned by what we'd seen to do anything but watch in horror.

Vandal's opponent, obviously realizing he was about to lose, made a last-ditch effort to gain a few points by throwing himself, sword first, at Vandal.

The curved wooden shield Vandal used to defer the blow suddenly went flying under the assault. Vandal stood for a moment looking down at his arm where the two upside-down U-shaped metal prongs that held the shield to the arm still embraced his forearm, barely leaping back in time to avoid being impaled on the tip of his opponent's sword.

"Oh, no! Why aren't the judges stopping them? Can't Vandal call a time-out or something?"

"Not for faulty equipment, no, not without conceding the match," Walker answered grimly.

"What's he going to do?" I asked, flinching as Vandal's opponent, realizing he had the advantage despite having almost been beaten, slashed at Vandal's armor.

"Fight."

"That armor can't be pierced by a sword, can it?"

"No, but he can still be hurt," Walker answered, his hands fisted as the opponent lunged forward, intent on skewering Vandal. He parried with a spinning backhanded move, then before the Canadian could recover, caught the man full on the chest with his booted foot, throwing him backward four feet, well out of the circle. The crowd erupted in cheers.

I sagged into a relieved blob. "Thank God it's over."

"The match might be over, but that's about the only thing that is," Walker growled, stepping across my legs.

I grabbed the back of his tunic, pausing only long

enough to scoop up Moth from where he was sleeping in an empty nacho tray. "Oh, no, please tell me that move Vandal did was legal, and he won't get DQ'd!"

"It was legal. Anything is legal in the sword ring except blows below the waist. He won't be disqualified." Considering the long two-handed broadswords the men were using, the rule made a lot of sense, if nothing else for their unborn children's sakes. I scrambled out of the bleachers after Walker, knowing his words should have made me a happy camper, but the look in his eyes chilled me to the bone. I knew what he had referred to as not being over, what all the Three Dog Knights were thinking—the saboteur was back.

Vandal, I had to admit, handled the whole thing with great aplomb. After helping the man he'd defeated to his feet and making sure he was all right, he swaggered around the ring, bowing to the men and blowing kisses to the ladies just as if nothing untoward had happened.

Walker and Butcher stood together examining the broken shield. CJ, standing next to Butcher, looked frightened by something he pointed out. Once more I was aware of a feeling of isolation, as if I were looking in from the outside, not a stranger, but not part of what amounted to a family. Even CJ seemed distant when it came to the team—she'd brought me, but I knew her heart lay with Butcher and the team. And oh, how I wanted to belong, too.

Maybe there was a way I could earn a spot in their group. Maybe if I figured out who was behind the attacks, they would view me as more than just Walker's Faire girlfriend.

My mother always said respect was best earned, not handed over undeserved. "Obviously it's time for Sherlock Pepper and Dr. Moth to do their stuff," I told the cat tucked under my arm. "I hope you're part bloodhound, because I have a feeling we're going to need all the help available to nail whoever's responsible."

I stood back from the crowd, watching as people streamed up and down the wooden bleachers on either side of the uncovered ring. The Three Dog Knights—Vandal excluded, being busy with his adoring gang of Ale Wenches—huddled together around the shield, their faces guarded.

"Let us review the suspects, shall we?" I whispered, hoisting Moth up so he was cuddled against my chest, his soft felt horns bumping against my chin. Along the far side of the ring, Farrell and two of his men—both swordfighters—stood in conversation. As I watched, a woman in obviously rented garb and a man bearing three cameras approached the threesome. A few seconds later Farrell was posing with his men. "Suspect number one: the handsome Farrell Kirkham. Motivation: intense jealousy of Walker spreading to encompass any member of his team. Opportunity: loads of it where Marley is concerned, unknown but probable for the lances, and as for Vandal's shield . . . hmmm. Unknown there, too. What do you think? Guilty or not?"

Moth reached up and patted my lips with his paw.

"What is that supposed to mean? Yes, I speak the truth, or no, what I'm saying is all wrong?"

Moth just looked his mysterious, all-knowing cat look at me. I touched the tip of my finger to his little pink lips. "Oh, that's helpful. If I touch your mouth, you"—he sank fangs into my finger, and I jerked it back—"you'll bite it, that's what you'll do, you mangy beast! You know, you totally suck as a spunky sidekick. Right. On to suspect number two."

Veronica applauded from where she sat at the bottom of the closest bleacher. She was surrounded by her teammates, all there to cheer on their swordfighters, one of whom was in the ring now up against a giant Aussie. I watched the woman fight for a minute, then transferred my gaze back to Veronica. She looked as perfect as ever, her hair tousled in that expensive, "takes an hour to achieve" look of careless fashion, her tights emphasizing the long line of her legs, her tunic tailored to make the best of her rangy, athletic shape. She was professional, in control, and clearly wore the mantle of leader well, demanding respect from everyone who knew her. She was also covertly watching her ex-husband as he and his team congratulated Vandal. "I say she's guilty. I wonder if Canada has the death penalty for horse abuse?"

Moth's left ear twitched.

"Stop looking at me like that; no one likes a smart-aleck cat. All right, suspect number two's motive is a bit weak, I'll admit. She doesn't seem to hold any grudge against Walker, nor vice versa, but that doesn't mean she wants to see him in one of the top couple of spots, although that comment about asking me if I'd do anything to make sure he did kind of hints that she wouldn't be averse to the idea. And there's definitely some backstory there that no one is telling me."

Veronica must have felt my gaze on her, because her cool eyes flashed in my direction, giving me an assessing look as she nodded and smiled. It was a short glance, her attention once again fixing on the swordplay in the ring.

"As for opportunity, she had *that* in great huge gobs. Anyone could have gotten to Marley before Walker set up a watch on the horses, and you remember the way she was slinking around his tent a few days back—what was to stop her from slipping into Vandal's and messing with his shield? And I just bet you she could sweet-talk her way into any building on the fairgrounds, so messing with the lances wouldn't pose too much of a challenge. I just wish I had a motive for her."

Moth declined to comment on that.

"And last, but not least, we come to suspect number

three—which could pretty much be anyone else in the jousting community who has a grudge against Walker or the rest of the team, and given how successful he was years ago, that could be just about anyone."

Moth's head snapped around to look at Walker as he slapped Vandal's back, obviously praising his skill at getting out of a sticky spot.

"Talking to Mothly again?" CJ asked behind me, startling me out of my dark thoughts.

"Mmm. Better than talking to myself, like some people I know."

"Not bloody much better," she answered, coming to stand beside me, her head reaching as high as Moth's.

I considered her. She looked happy, even with the latest near tragedy, her eyes sparkling with an inner light, her face aglow with love and contentment. "You sound like that bulky Englishman of yours. When are you two going to stop playing around and get married?"

"Just as soon as I get the research job with the BBC. We can't afford it any other way. When are you going to marry your knight in borrowed armor?"

"Walker?" I shrugged, refusing to think about it. We'd fallen into an easy peace the last few days; I think neither of us wanted to shatter it with talk of the future. "No one's said anything about marriage, Ceej. I think you'd better brace yourself for the thought that your matchmaking skills might fail this time."

"I didn't matchmake you and Walker," she pointed out, giving me a searching glance I had no intention of meeting. "What's wrong, Peppidy? You look . . . sad."

"It's Vandal's shield. It gives me a terrible feeling to know that someone is purposely trying to harm them. I take it the consensus was that the shield had been tampered with?"

She nodded, her smile evaporating. "The bolt heads holding the arm grips had been sheared away. You couldn't notice them because of the way the grips hung, but Butcher said it was a miracle it held together as long as it did."

Walker handed the remains of the shield to Vandal, the team turning as one to reclaim their seats. The show of solidarity was telling—they would stand by each other, fearless in the face of adversity. I clutched Moth tighter, my eyes on Walker's hard profile. What would it take for them to consider me one of them?

Chapter Sixteen

"Did you get a bottle of champers so we can celebrate?" CJ asked Walker and Butcher as they returned from hitching a ride with a local couple to a nearby store, her VW being temporarily out of commission. It was Tuesday, the day of the archery competition, which I was grateful had gone off without any of Fenice's or Bliss's arrows exploding, bows snapping and taking out an eye, or any of the myriad other disasters I had spent the night before imagining.

"No, we didn't get a bottle of champagne," Walker said. The dark circles under his beautiful eyes gave his long English face a haunted look that wrung my heart.

"We bought two!" Butcher announced, bringing both bottles out from where he had been concealing them behind his back. "It's not every day we have *two* members finishing in the money!"

The tight, worried looks on the Three Dog Knights' respective faces relaxed as the bubbly was popped and poured. Butcher watched Walker in a meaningful sort of way for a moment, but the love of my life was in an abstracted, introspective mood I knew was focused on his concern about the sabotage. I nudged him.

"Hmm? Oh, it's you. Does your arm hurt?"

Without thought I rubbed the spot on my elbow where I had smacked it against a rock earlier in the afternoon when Butcher sent me flying off Cassie's back. "No, it's fine. I think they're waiting for you to say something about Vandal and Fenice in your official capacity as head Dog."

He shot me one of his (soon to be patented) long-suffering looks that I knew really meant he was amused, and raised his plastic glass of champagne. "Tonight we honor Fenice, for her skill at archery, and for coming in second in a very difficult competition."

"You were robbed!" her boyfriend, Gary, said, giving her a squeeze.

"To Fenice!" we all said, sipping the lukewarm champagne.

"And more important, to her fifteen thousand Canadian dollars!" Vandal added. She smacked his head.

"And we also honor Vandal—"

"Who is *not* so big he can't be taken down by his older sister," Fenice said with mock ferocity.

"You're only older by six minutes!" Vandal protested. "And that's because you shoved me out of the way while we were being born. You always were a bossy thing."

She pinched his arm until he yelped.

Walker cleared his throat and continued. "—Vandal, who performed in an outstanding manner despite the handicap of faulty equipment, finishing a very respectable fifth."

"And his six thousand dollars!" Fenice added.

We toasted the twins, commiserated with Butcher and Bliss for finishing out of the money, and settled down for a celebratory dinner of take-out fried chicken.

"Will you wait a minute and let me pick off the coating, you great big greedy cat?" Moth slapped at my hand and growled deep in his chest as I stripped chicken meat onto a plate for him. I gave him a tiny bit of macaroni and cheese to add a bit of variety to his diet, turning back to face my human companions. Chat was lively as the last two days' combatants recounted particularly telling blows or targets, everyone relaxed and happy. Even Walker seemed to shake off his self-absorbed mood and joined in the talk, his eyes brilliant with warmth and something that looked very much like happiness. He sat close to me, his leg touching mine, his arm brushing against me in a casual way that left me breathless with tingly awareness of him.

Seeing him happy and laughing, the burdens he so assiduously shouldered melted away for a few minutes, had me swearing an oath to myself: I would not let whoever was trying to ruin the team succeed. No matter what it took, I would find him, her, or them, and stop the evil plot. I had to, or else Walker would never be free of the shadow of failure.

It was time to unleash Pepper, Warrior Princess. *Aiaiaiaiaiai!*

"So what are we going to do about these sabotage attempts?" I asked in a momentarily lull in the conversation. "The individual jousting starts day after tomorrow, and if someone really wants to hurt you guys, that's when they're going to strike. So what's the game plan?"

A hushed, wary silence fell over everyone (except Moth, who kacked up a small piece of chicken).

"What?" I asked, looking from person to person, finally ending at the silver eyes I knew and loved so well. "You aren't going to tell me you're not doing anything to catch the person who thinks he or she can ruin your lives, are you? Because if you are I won't believe you. At the very least I know Sir Shoulder the Woes of the World will do something."

Walker glared at me. "I do not shoulder the woes of the world!"

"Yes, you do."

"I do not!"

"Oh, really?" I set my plate down and swiveled on the bench we were sharing to cock an eyebrow at him. "Perhaps you'd care to share what you were thinking about when I nudged you and made you give the toast for Fenice and Vandal?"

Dismay flashed in his eyes. "Perhaps I do shoulder a few woes, but only those meant for me. I assumed women like a man who faces his responsibilities rather than shirks them."

"Sure we do, but no one likes a martyr, Walker. You are not responsible for Bos being laid out or Marley being injured."

"No, absolutely not," Bos said loudly. The others voiced their agreements.

"I never said I was responsible for that," Walker said hotly, but I interrupted him before he could continue.

"No, you didn't say it, but you thought it, I know you did. I see the guilt and remorse in your eyes every time you look at Bos. I know that you think you're paying the wages of your past sins."

"You know nothing of the sort." He snorted in a manly, dishy-Englishman sort of way. It was a snort that thrilled me to my toenails, and I had to bring my wandering brain strictly to order to keep myself from lunging at him and kissing the scowl right off his face.

"I do, too. You talk in your sleep. So you can just stop thinking that you're responsible, because you're not, unless you sheared the heads off the bolts on Vandal's shield."

"Not bloody likely." Walker allowed his nostrils to flare at that suggestion.

I smiled at his outraged nostrils. As hard as Walker worked, and as much as he fought for the team's success, he'd have to be insane to harm his teammates. "Regardless, you aren't to blame for what's going on, but someone is, and I for one don't intend to sit around and allow that person or persons to ruin all your chances to blow everyone's boots off in the individual competition. I have expensive tastes. Walker is going to need oodles of money to keep me happy, and I expect the rest of you would like to go home with your pockets full, too."

Walker growled in my ear.

"She's right," Bliss said, her eyes serious as she looked around at all of us. "We all stand a good chance of winning the competitions. We would have come into the money with the team competition, but for . . ." Her voice trailed off.

"For me, yes, I know, you needn't tiptoe around the issue," Walker said, pulling away from me. I grabbed his arm and pulled him back, refusing to allow him to play Mr. Martyr anymore. "I would gladly lay down my arms in favor of anyone else—"

"There is no one else as good as you," I said, greatly enjoying being plastered up against his side, his warmth penetrating not only his thin linen shirt, but my chemise and bodice. I gave myself a few seconds of just breathing in his scent before continuing. "And you know it, so stop being humble and put that wonderfully complex mind of yours to work on what we can do to find out who's pulling the nasty tricks."

Wicked silver eyes glared at me. "You're going to make my life hell, aren't you? I know you are; I can see it in your eyes. I just want to be left in peace, and you're not going to let me, are you?"

"Nope," I said, leaning forward to capture his lower lip between mine. "I'm making it my duty to drag you back into the human race, no matter how much you kick and scream."

"Wench," he said, his eyes going shimmery with passion.

"Rogue knight," I answered.

"Can you two keep your hands off each other long enough so we can figure out what to do?" CJ asked. "Sheesh! The newly in love. What a pain in the ass."

"Technically, I think it's their lips that are on each other, poppet," Butcher said.

I smiled against Walker's mouth and gave his lip a little love nip before releasing it. "All right, Miss Smarty-braes, you have the floor. What's your idea?"

"Smarty-braes," Geoff laughed, snorting a little as he prodded Bos. "Smarty-braes. Get it? Instead of pants? Braes?"

Bos rolled his eyes good-naturedly. Vandal made a rude joke *sotto voce*, but not *sotto* enough for Fenice, who threw a roll at him. He stuffed the entire roll into his mouth and grinned at her as he ate it. CJ, who had evidently been thinking, pursed her lips and effectively stopped the silliness by saying, "I say we set a trap."

We all considered this.

"A trap how?" Bliss asked.

CJ shrugged. "What, I have to think of everything? I thought up the idea of a trap; you guys have to figure out what sort of a trap it is. I have to go to a Wench Madams' meeting. Let me know what you decide."

"We could leave some equipment lying around with something that will dye the hands of the person who touches it," Bos suggested as CJ gathered up her bag and departed.

"Won't work. Anyone might touch it, you wouldn't necessarily get the person who is trying to bring us down," Vandal said.

"How about one of us hides in the building holding the lances, and waits to grab the person when they're having another go at them?" Geoff asked.

"Too chancy," Walker answered. "It's not likely anyone would try to damage a lance again. After Bos's lance shattered, the officials decided to check the ones used each day."

Bliss frowned. "What if we were to make it known that one of us—I'd volunteer—was going to be practicing late at night on the quintain, leaving myself open to an attack? The rest of you could hide in the area, and grab the person when an attempt was made on me."

"A person would have to be insane to want to tackle you," Vandal joked.

"None of you will do anything," Walker said firmly. "This is my problem, and I will take care of it."

The group all voiced their disagreement, saying it was an attack on all of them, not him.

Walker was adamant, refusing to allow anyone else to claim responsibility. "Regardless, I am the leader of this troupe, so I will be the one to take care of it."

"You?" I asked, startled by what he said. "Why you? Why not the whole team? Everyone has a stake in this, Walker."

"I am responsible for everyone. It's my team, my job."

I rolled my eyes at that bit of profound stubbornness, but didn't argue with him. Walker truly did think he was responsible for his teammates. It was just part of his character, and I realized that if I tried to make him any different, we'd both end up miserable. "I don't know how those medieval women lived with their bossy knights without beaning them on the head now and again," I murmured.

"They learned to appreciate the warrior mentality," Walker answered, just as softly, his lips twitching.

I leaned into him, smiling to myself. The discussion went back and forth, but after listening for a few minutes I stopped paying attention, enjoying instead the warmth and solid feel of Walker next to me as I mulled over a plan of my own that I had been considering for the last two days—infiltration into the enemy camp. Despite conjecture of who at the fair would have it in for the Three Dog Nights, I knew there were only two real suspects. No one else had even the remotest sense of a motive. Given that, there was only one person present who was uniquely qualified to be a covert spy, and that person was me. It would mean I'd have to consort with Farrell and agree to be Veronica's alternate—assuming she hadn't found one by now—but I was willing to make those sacrifices in order to help Walker.

Nothing, I thought as I snuggled even closer to him,

reveling in the way his arm tightened around me and he nuzzled my hair before turning back to the conversation, nothing was as important as he was.

"Mail chausses."

"This is silly."

"No, it's not. And gamboised cuisses, Marc."

"I don't need a gamboised anything; I have a gambeson. Bos won't mind me using his—"

"But I mind," Veronica said, giving me a thin-lipped look that had me biting back my objection. "No member of the Palm Springs Jousting Guild appears in borrowed equipment."

"Yeah, but this stuff is expensive." I waved my hand at the armorer, who was delightedly pulling out bits and pieces of armor in between taking my measurements. I stepped closer to her and lowered my voice. "I told you I'm unemployed. I just can't afford to pay you back for all this."

"Then you'll have to pay me back with your time," she said abruptly, frowning down at a list. "Marc, we'll also need steel schynbalds and sabatons. How are you fixed for vambraces?"

"I have steel."

"Good. Also steel rerebraces, aillettes, a standard coat of plates—"

I groaned. I was going to have to be her lackey for a year in order to pay back the cost of the equipment she insisted on ordering for me.

"—steel hourglass gauntlets, besagews, and an early manifer for her left hand—"

Not a year, a lifetime!

"The mail coif and helm you have ready, yes?"

"Yes, I have a helm that will fit her."

Me and my fat head—what did it say about me that I could wear an off-the-rack helm?

"Excellent. As I told you, we'll need everything as soon as possible, and I am willing to pay for your undivided attention."

Marc the armorer almost salivated as he nodded. "You'll have it. Er . . . about the down payment . . ."

I gritted my teeth as Veronica unbuckled her belt pouch. "You take plastic?"

Marc smiled a wolfish smile. "Lady Visa and Master of Card are welcome here."

Veronica flashed him her platinum card as I had one last attempt to make her see reason. I'd been trying since the previous evening, when I offered myself up as a sacrifice (Saint Pepper—has a nice ring to it) in order to find out whether she was the one behind the attempts on the Three Dog Knights.

"You know, just because Walker says I'm not bad at jousting doesn't mean I'm ready to jump into competition. When I said I'd be your alternate, I had no idea that you intended for me to compete. Just the thought of it is ludicrous—I've only been jousting for a little over a week! There's got to be someone else who can replace Jill."

Veronica gave Marc a couple more instructions, tucking her credit card away as she swept Moth and me forward, out of the armorer's cramped quarters and into the heavy stream of Faire-goers who were strolling the vendors' row. "We've been all over this, Pepper. Jill has a hairline fracture in her wrist. It's not safe for her to continue jousting. Since this is individual, not team competition, your inexperience won't harm the team's standing."

"I guess I don't quite understand why you need an alternate for the individual competition," I said, feeling more than a little overwhelmed with the enormity of what I was doing.

"The jousting organization has rules regarding the number of team members who must compete in both team and individual combat. It's to prevent teams from using their best jousters for just one competition, and not the other. All we need is a warm body to replace Jill—your skill, or lack thereof, will affect only your own standing."

"Ah. That makes sense. I'm not planning on doing this again, so it doesn't matter how badly I do so long as I'm on your team."

"Just so." She paused for a moment as we made our way past the busy vendors, clearly waiting for me to say something more, something she expected to hear.

"Obviously any team who can come in second in the team competition as yours did is very talented," I dutifully said. "It's a shame Farrell's team beat yours, but you can take pride in the fact that it was only by a few points."

She snorted and continued forward. "Pride, schmide, he stole first place from us, but it won't happen again. Regardless of that, you replacing Jill will be a very good experience for you. It will give you a taste of real competition without negative repercussions on the image of the Palm Springs Jousting Guild."

And that image, I had quickly learned, was a god to Veronica. Pride in your team I understood, but Veronica's "image is everything" attitude went even beyond Farrell's recognized shallowness.

Veronica was speaking but was too far ahead of me to hear. Moth lunged toward a chicken-on-a-stick vendor who was grilling kebabs, throwing himself on the counter where an innocent patron had set his kebab down for a second.

"I'm so sorry; he's always a bit peckish in the morning. . . . Sir? Could you get this man another one? Two dollars? Thanks."

I picked up the cat and his gnawed-upon kebab, running to catch up to Veronica.

". . . have to agree it's for the best." She stopped and gave me an unhappy look. "Pepper, I appreciate the fact that you feel responsible for the cat, but must it accompany us everywhere?"

"Yes," I said, hoisting Moth higher on my hip. He sank his claws into the back of my hand until I waggled the kebab where he could tear bits of chicken off the stick. "He must. I'm sorry; I missed what you were saying."

She sighed, then turned and wove her way through the crowd until we were free of the worst of it, walking quickly toward the cream-and-green tents at the boundary of the tent city. "I said that now you've joined the guild, it's only right you should take your instruction from me, and not your *lover*."

I ignored the emphasis she put on the last word. If she had issues with Walker and me, that was just tough. They'd been divorced for almost five years, certainly long enough for her to work it all out. "Uh . . . Walker is the man who taught you, so isn't it just kind of cutting out the middle man to have him continue to train me?"

She froze for a second before slowly turning to face me. Moth ate the last of the chicken and started gnawing on my thumb knuckle, watching Veronica with slitted yellow eyes. "One of the few requirements I have of my team members is that they have the utmost belief and confidence in their team members, myself included."

Whoopsie, stepped on her toes. "Sorry, I didn't mean that to sound rude. It's just that if you learned how to joust from Walker, I don't see why—"

"You're on *my* team now, not his," she said calmly, but there was a note of steel in her voice that convinced me that Fenice and the others were right about her having an overly proprietary nature.

I wanted to tell her what she could do with her team, but I wasn't there for my own pleasure. I had a job to do, and do it I would. "Right. Sorry. You're the boss."

"It would be best if you kept that fact uppermost in your mind," she agreed pleasantly, then continued toward her tent, towing Moth and me along by the sheer force of her personality.

I met the remaining nine members of the team, (Veronica could get by with fewer members, but insisted on the full team) had a bit of a skirmish with her when she insisted I wear the guild uniform rather than my Wench wear (we compromised with me wearing the tights and tunic, but my Wench pin and accompanying favors, etc.), and sat down for an hour-long pep talk and general indoctrination into the ways of the Palm Springs Jousting Guild.

"How was it?" CJ asked two hours later after I had made a temporary escape from Veronica Land.

"Let's just say that if Martha Stewart ever decides to take up jousting, she'll have a ready-made team," I answered with an exaggerated shiver.

"Ew." Her nose wrinkled at the thought.

"You said it."

She eyed me before turning back to the suitcase she'd left in our tent. "I see she was quick enough to brand you. I take it your new friends won't let you Promenade with us lowly Wenches?"

I turned my back on Moth as he strolled toward his litter box, plopping myself down onto the folded sleeping bag. Moth and I had taken to sleeping with Walker in his tent, using this one as more or less a changing room and feline potty stop. Likewise CJ spent her time in Butcher's tent. I sighed a particularly martyred sigh as she shook out a royal-blue chemise and added it to a stack of garb. "Not you, too. Walker is going to be bad enough when he hears about my signing up with Veronica, but at least you understand why I'm doing it."

"Because you plan on infiltrating Veronica's group in hopes of finding proof she's behind the attacks," CJ said in an irritatingly neutral voice.

"Yes, and you don't have to say it in that tone—you know full well that it's the only way to find out what's going on."

"Do I? Hmm." She stripped off the chemise she was wearing and donned the blue one. "I just don't think it's a good idea. I think you made a mistake going behind Walker's back."

"I'm not going behind his back, per se. If I told him what I was going to do, he'd stomp around and forbid it, and then we'd have a big argument about him going alpha on me. I'll tell him later this afternoon. It's too late for him to do anything but rail at me now, anyway."

She slid me an odd look. "I would think a woman who cared so much for a man wouldn't want to do anything that made him mad. I know you want to find the person responsible for the sabotage, but I just don't understand why you are so eager to join Veronica's team to do it."

She had me there. I couldn't tell her about my secret longing to be more than just a temporary bit of fun for Walker. I'd seen how solid the bond of friendship within the Three Dog Knights was, and I badly wanted to be a part of something so wonderful. I shrugged, making light of her question. "Someone has to do the dirty work."

"Hrmph." She didn't look like she believed me. "I think the truth is that you're taking the easy path again."

I picked a bit of dried grass off my tights. "Easy path? Are you insane? What on earth is easy about jousting when you've been doing it for just a hair over a week?"

"Not easy physically, stupid." CJ shot me a chastising glance before slipping her arms through a gold and purple bodice, turning her back to me. "Tighten the back lace, would you? I meant easy as in avoiding that whole success issue with Walker."

"You are insane. I have no issues with Walker. I talked to all of Veronica's team today, and unfortunately, none of them sounds like they have the slightest interest in Three Dog Knights other than the normal competitive concerns. And every time I brought up the subject of Walker with Veronica, she shrugged it off. She knows he and I are . . . *you know* . . . and doesn't seem to mind that, either, so it's not like she's going after him because of me. So what's her motive?"

CJ shrugged and turned around so I could finish tightening her laces. "Maybe she just wants to win."

"Everyone wants to win, but they don't try to hurt other people in order to do it. No, if she has a motive, it has to be compelling enough for her to take such extreme chances, and I just don't see that in her. In fact, I think she's just the opposite—very cautious, and doesn't like to leave things to chance."

"Anal, you mean," CJ said as I tied the laces in a knotted bow.

"Well, yeah, that too."

CJ grumbled as she adjusted first her bodice, then her hair, quickly tying on a blue-and-purple metallic snood. "If you had any brains in your head you'd let the guys deal with it and instead practice your jousting. You're going to need practice if you intend to join the competition."

"Trust me, it's not what I want to be doing," I said with a sigh, realizing that lunch was over and I'd have to go watch the afternoon's competition. Not that it was a pain—as serious as the jousting was, the skill games were sheer fun, ones the knights participated in for amusement as well as for monetary reward. What bothered me was that I hadn't clued Walker or any of his team in to the fact that I had signed on with Veronica, and I dreaded having to explain my reasoning to him. "He's so damn stubborn about things."

"Walker?" CJ examined herself in a tiny mirror propped up against the back of the suitcase, decided she was good, and stopped primping.

"Yes." I stood up and snapped the leash onto Moth's harness. "You saw him yesterday, Mr. 'I am in charge of this team, and I will investigate the matter' just as if no one else has a stake in it."

CJ pulled the cloth door open, zipping it up behind

us as Moth and I started toward the arena where the afternoon's events were held. "He's always been that way. He takes his role as team captain very seriously. But don't worry; Butcher will be helping Walker make sure no other accidents happen to the team. Everything will turn out all right."

"Mmm." I wasn't convinced.

"So what are you doing later this afternoon? The Wenches are hosting a Drink Till You Spew ale tasting, and your company is requested."

I took a deep breath and tried to block out the mental image of Walker's face when he found out what I was up to. "Much as I hate to miss a good spewing, I won't be able to. I asked Farrell for a little help with the quintain. He said he'd be happy to show me whatever I wanted, and yes, the innuendo that you imagine present really was there."

She sucked in her breath as we skirted two huge bay Percherons who were waiting outside the arena. "You asked Farrell for help? Walker isn't going to like that."

That was the understatement of the year. "Can you think of a better way to get close to Farrell without him thinking I have the hots for him?"

"Why on earth do you want to get close to— Oooh, look, there's Butcher! Lamby-kins! You go!"

I froze for a second, doing a "deer in the headlights" sort of horrified statue thing when Walker, mounted on Marcy in front of Butcher and Vandal, turned his head to look back at us. He wasn't wearing a helm, since there was little chance of injury, thus I could see when the slight smile that curved his lips disappeared as he noticed the tunic I was wearing. Even at the distance of forty-some feet I could see the pain in his eyes before he swung around to face forward.

"Dammit, I knew this was going to happen. Walker!"

"Shhh," CJ said, grabbing my arm and hauling me

and Moth toward the bleachers. "Listen, they're announcing him. Don't make a scene."

"I'm not going to make a scene, but you saw the look on his face. I have to explain—"

"You made your bed; now you can lie in it," she said callously.

"CJ!"

"Oh, stop giving me that look. You can talk to him later. Now sit down and do the girlfriend thing."

"What girlfriend thing?" I asked, my eyes on the man in the black armor as he rode into the ring, the crowd applauding him. Why hadn't I explained to him what I'd done earlier in the day, when I would have had a chance to make him understand my reasoning? Now Walker would be tormented by the thought that I had abandoned him, sold out to a more financially successful team. No doubt his already lackluster performance would take a nosedive with the blow to his ego.

"Smile and act like nothing's wrong. Yay, Three Dog Knights!" CJ stood and shouted out her support as Walker and Butcher were announced to the crowd.

At least everyone in the arena was cheering for them, but I knew with a twist of my gut that Walker wouldn't care about the public's support. "The poor, darling man. Please just don't let him do anything crazy," I prayed in a whisper that was lost in the rumble of the crowd and the tinny voice of the announcer.

"Welcome back to the *Knight's Bane World Jousting Grand Championship and Renaissance Faire* skill games! This event consists of five games—the quintain, which you can see at the south side of the ring, running the rings, the Saracen's head, spearing the boar, and the gauntlet. Points are awarded to each knight for successful targeting count in the final total for tourney champion, so be sure to cheer on your favorite."

"I would, but my favorite would probably plant his spear in me rather than that bale of hay that's representing the boar," I said, sinking into a great big pit of self-pity.

"I warned you, didn't I?"

"There you are! Mind if I sit with you? Bos and Geoff have been sucked into the Norwegian contingent to wager on who'll do better at the Saracen's head. . . . Good god!" Fenice stopped in midstep over a bleacher, her eyes huge as she stared at me. "Why on earth are you wearing that? Does Walker know? He'll be furious! You have to get out of here quickly, before he sees you and goes ballistic!"

I slid my cousin a glance. She looked smug.

"Pepper? Why are you wearing it?" Fenice asked in a whisper as she sat down next to me. She frowned, giving me a look as if she'd never really seen me before.

My heart sank. How on earth was I going to get someone as temperamental and touchy as Walker to understand my plan when happy-go-lucky Fenice obviously viewed me as a borderline traitor, not to mention CJ predicting doom and gloom?

With no hope for it, I started to explain my plan to infiltrate Veronica's team, but the announcer cut me off as he explained to the audience the goals of each of the five games. I told Fenice I'd fill her in later and sat back to watch, trying to push down the worry about Walker, but every time I glanced at him, it surfaced.

Walker kept Marley at a muscle-warming trot at the opposite end of the ring, but he never once looked my way, a fact that had my stomach wadded into a minuscule ball.

"Just look at Walker the Wild go!" the announcer crowed a few minutes later as everyone in the arena surged to their feet, yelling and screaming as Walker sent Marley into a full gallop, racing down a staggered line of melons atop six-foot-tall poles. Half the melons wore painted happy faces, indicating friendly foot soldiers; the other half bore frowny faces and snarling mouths—those were the Saracens, the foe to be struck down. Points were given for each foe whose head was demolished by the sword-wielding knight, and taken away for each friend who was accidentally "slaughtered." The one with the most amount of points in the least amount of time won the event.

I was on my feet with the rest of the audience, watching in amazement as Walker and Marley raced through the field of melons, Walker's sword flashing in the overhead lights.

CJ turned to me with a grin as the crowd erupted into cheers.

"God, it's good to see him back," Fenice cheered, jumping in excitment. "Yes! The wild man is back!"

"Lovely," I said, sinking to the bench, so confused I didn't know what to think. I stayed that way for the next few minutes while Walker challenged the quintains, getting a respectable ten revolutions on the quintain, and blasting the shock quintain onto its back. He gored the boar (stabbed the hay in its painted heart), was the fastest running the gauntlet, and by the time he and Butcher had gone to the opposite ends of the arena for the running-the-rings race, I was more or less numb with shock. The man on Marley's back wasn't Walker, not *my* Walker, not the careful man who was haunted by the demons of his past—the man out there was a manic crazy-man facsimile of Walker.

"It's a wonder he lasted eight years before he came to grief," I said in a quiet voice to CJ. She nodded, her attention on the men, her voice hoarse from cheering nonstop. She was now yelling for Butcher as he and Walker were poised to race around the arena starting at opposite ends, each with the goal of snatching as many rings as possible from the brave squires who stood along the perimeter holding out four-inch straw rings.

"*Allez!*" the judge in the center of the floor yelled, and once again the entire audience of the arena leaped to its collective feet to scream for their favorites, me right along with them.

Walker flattened himself to Marley's neck, his long fifty-inch sword a silver streak as it danced in front of the squires, each one successfully coming away with a straw ring. Three of the squires were evidently more than a little intimidated by the sight of Marley and Walker thundering down on them, for they all fell backward as soon as Walker snatched the ring at sword tip. On the other side of the arena Butcher was doing the same, but his horse wasn't flying as Marley was. By the time the fifty seconds allowed for the race were up, Walker had lapped Butcher.

"He's back, he's back, we don't have anything to worry about now!" Fenice sang, clapping her hands and doing a little dance as the announcer praised both men, giving the point total for Walker (which was almost perfect). "Life is good, life is wonderful, we have our Walker back! We can't possibly lose now!"

"No," I said quietly, my gaze on Walker as he rode from the ring without acknowledging his victory, never once looking over to where he knew we were sitting. "We can't possibly lose anything . . . except maybe our future together."

Chapter Seventeen

"Walker, will you slow down and let me explain?"

"There's nothing for you to explain," the infuriating love of my life snarled as he led Marley toward the stable.

"Yes, there is, you obstinate man! I want to tell you why I agreed to join Veronica's team. I owe that much to—"

Walker whirled around so fast Marley did a startled little sideways dance. Silver eyes blasted me with cold that would be at home in the Arctic. "I've told you, there's *nothing* you have to explain to me. You don't owe me *anything*. Debt indicates an interest on the grantor's part, and I assure you, I have no interest whatsoever in your actions."

Ouch. That hurt, and how. Walker's face was tight and hard, almost as hard as his eyes. I swallowed back a lump of pain and reminded myself that until he understood my actions, they were open to misinterpretation.

A man who loved you would give you the benefit of the doubt, Evil (formerly Wise) Inner Pepper whispered. I ignored that thought as I put my hand on his arm. "You may not have interest in me, but I have a great deal in you, and I want to explain why I've done what I've done."

"I don't want to hear it," he snarled, snatching his arm away and storming off toward the stable.

"God, why does everything have to go wrong for me?" I entreated the afternoon sky, quickly picking up Moth and racing after Walker. "I really don't want to have to bellow this across the fairgrounds so everyone hears, but if you insist on it, fine. I love you! I love you more than life itself, you annoying, irritating man! Now will you just stop and let me tell you what I've decided?"

"No."

He didn't even slow down, damn it all. I sighed and trotted after him, a bit breathless by the time Walker tied Marley up outside the stable in order to brush him. I had seen Butcher and Vandal doing the same as we approached, but they quickly took their horses in and effectively disappeared, leaving me and the man who was breaking my heart alone with one three-ton horse and a cat that was presently chewing on the sleeve of the tunic Walker had just stripped off and tossed onto a bench.

I dragged my eyes from the wonderful land made of up the rippling muscles in his back to plead my case. "Please, Walker, just hear me out. I know you're upset—"

"Upset?" He shot me a hot look as he wrenched the heavy jousting saddle off Marley's back and all but threw it onto a nearby box. "Why would I be upset? I have nothing to be upset about. The old Walker, *he* might be upset by his woman using him the way she did, but not me, not Walker the Wild. Haven't you heard? I don't care about anyone but myself."

Oh, god, what had I done? I stared at him in dismay as he ripped off the saddle blanket, tossing it in the dirt. He never treated equipment like that!

"What's wrong, *love*?" I flinched at the way he said that last word. There wasn't an ounce of gentleness in it. "Don't like the new me? Or rather the old me, the old Walker you so desperately wanted me to become? Congratulations, you've succeeded."

"I never wanted you like this," I said cautiously.

"No? Well, you sure fooled me. I thought you wanted a real man, a man who wasn't afraid to face anything. You wanted me to be a champion, a ruthless warrior who doesn't give a damn about the consequences, and here I am."

I bit my lip as he yanked a brush out of the bucket, pouring a cup of grain for Marley.

"I never wanted you to become anything you weren't. I know you have it in you to be anything you want to be—"

"Face the facts, Pepper," he interrupted, splashing water into another bucket and setting it next to Marley. "You know nothing about me. Nothing!"

I raised my chin. "I know I love you."

He grunted and turned away to brush Marley.

"I know you're a good man who values honor and faithfulness." He spun around, his eyes coming close to scorching me. I lifted my chin in answer to the look of fury he was firing at me. "And I know that you love me, only you're too caught up in your own hell to admit it."

"Love," he snarled, his lip curled in derision. "You honestly think I love you?"

My heart, which was clutching its little hands hopefully, praying Walker would at last admit to what I so desperately needed to be true, threatened to keel over in a faint. I swallowed again, harder this time, since the painful lump of unshed tears had grown. "Yes, I think you love me. I couldn't love a man as much as I love you and not have the feeling reciprocated."

His eyes narrowed for a moment, and before I could blink, he was on me, pressing me back against the hard, rough wood of the stable, his body hot and hard and aggressive. "Do you think this is love then?" he growled, grinding his hips against me as his mouth descended upon mine. There was no tenderness in him, nothing but domination as his body ruthlessly used its knowledge about me to quickly set mine raging with desire.

His hands were everywhere, not in the least bit gentle as they tormented me, demanding a response as his tongue swept into my mouth and carried away any objections I had to his rough handling. His body was rigid and unyielding, the muscles beneath my hands tight with tension, every inch of him expressing the pain and outrage he felt at what he perceived as my betrayal. I bit back the urge to struggle, deliberately softening myself against him, cushioning his hard tension with every ounce of love and understanding and gentleness that I could muster.

"Yes," I whispered against his mouth when he wrenched his lips from mine. My fingers trailed a serpentine path up the muscles of his bare back, my touch as light and tender as his was hard and angry. "This is what I call love. You're everything to me, Walker. You fill my life. You make me happy in ways I never knew I could be happy." The grim line of his mouth softened as my hands slid up his arms to his shoulders while I pressed little kisses along his tense jaw. "I want to be with you. I want to know what you're thinking, what you feel. I want to bind myself to you so that we'll never be apart."

His eyes were still glittering brightly at me, but the icy disdain was slowly turning to a shimmering silver flame. His body language changed, as well, going from dominance and aggression to an erotic wooing. I doubt he even noticed the change, but I did, and my heart rejoiced. I allowed my softness to cradle him as I tugged his head down so I could press gentle kisses to his adorable, manly lips. "I will never leave you, Walker. My heart will always belong to you, always. I'm yours, body and soul. I love you, and I will until the day I breathe my last."

"My sweet Pepper," he murmured, his voice sinking

into my skin and wrapping itself around my heart as his lips claimed mine in a much different kiss from the one that had just bruised my lips.

"Tell me you don't feel the same thing I do," I said as I gave myself up to his passion, pressing myself closer to him.

"Pepper, is that you being squashed to death against the wall?"

Walker's body, which was starting to curl enticingly around mine, froze at the voice that spoke behind him. I groaned to myself, my heart shattering into a gazillion infinitesimal pieces at the look of pure, unadulterated fury that flashed in Walker's eyes.

Not only did I have the rottenest luck imaginable; Farrell had the world's worst timing.

"I've been looking for you. I'm ready to help you with the quintain. Or is this a bad time? I'm afraid I'm a bit booked, but as I told you earlier when you asked me to tutor you, I'm happy to do what I can to give you the help you need and so obviously aren't getting elsewhere."

"Walker—" I started to say, knowing it would do no good. I could explain until the moon was blue, but if he truly had no faith in me, it would be useless. It was bottom-line time, with our future at stake. Either he trusted me, or he didn't. "I know what this looks like, but I truly do love you—"

"Don't." It was just one word, but the anger and desolation and anguish that were packed into it would qualify it as a dictionary of misery. He pulled away from me, his hands clenched but his face impassive as Farrell held out a hand for me.

"Well, it seems we're right back were we started— Pepper preferring my company to yours," Farrell told Walker.

"History has a nasty way of repeating itself," Walker said softly, his eyes flat and cold. "Fortunately, I don't care anymore."

Farrell looked startled for a moment, and was about

to answer, but I couldn't stand the hard, uncaring mask that Walker wore. My heart was bleeding; my *soul* was bleeding at his rejection. *This* was why it never paid to take risks—the pain of failure was worse than anything I could imagine.

Giving up so easily? Inner Pepper mocked.

I looked at Walker, really looked at him. He was just a man—a wonderful, warm, caring man—but still just a man. Was he really worth the heartache, the frustration, the risk of losing myself even more in order to win him back?

Damn straight he was!

Inner Pepper cheered as I looked Walker dead in the eye and willed him to understand. "A week ago you told me that only by learning to trust myself could I achieve what I wanted in life. You were absolutely right. I trust not only myself, but you, too. I just hope you can do the same."

He said nothing as I scooped up Moth and walked past Farrell, heading for the far exercise ring where I had first challenged Sir Quintain.

"So if I change the angle of the lance a little, what will that do to the quintain? Will I hit it harder, or does a steeper angle deflect the blow?"

"Has anyone told you that your hair is like a molten river of fire?"

"Farrell, please, no hair similes. We're here to practice, remember?"

"Are we?" Farrell smiled, picking up my free hand and bestowing a kiss on my fingers. I fought the urge to clench those very same fingers and smash his nose. No matter how much my heart was breaking, no matter how miserable Walker was making me, I had a job to do, and the only way to salvage the shreds of our future was to do it. Successfully. Which meant Farrell didn't get a knuckle sandwich. "I thought perhaps you were simply trying to be discreet in your pursuit of me."

I stopped walking, retrieving my hand to hoist Moth higher on my hip, glaring against the setting sun to pin Farrell back with what I hoped was a stern, unbending, meaningful look. I may have had to make nice with him, but it didn't mean I had to let him slobber on me to find out what I needed to know.

"Just so you know, I'm madly in love with Walker. I like you, Farrell," I said, not even stumbling over the untruth, "despite the fact that you're as nasty as you can be around Walker, but don't expect anything from me other than friendship."

"Really?" Curiously, Farrell looked interested rather than put out by my statement. "So it's the real thing then, not just a little Faire fling?"

He turned toward the collection of Team Joust! trailers rather than the small practice ring. I followed without protest, figuring I could get more out of him in a casual situation than on the back of a horse.

"No, it's not a fling. Just out of curiosity, how long have you known Walker? I mean, how many years did you two compete together before Walker's . . . hiatus?"

"Two years. Claude! Where the devil are— Oh, there you are. Here, take Pepper's cat for a stroll, will you?" Farrell plucked Moth from where he was snuggled up against my side, thrusting the big cat and his leash into Claude's arms. "Pepper and I want to be alone for a bit."

"He really does like to go for walks," I told the startled squire, ignoring the innuendo Farrell had tossed out. "Just don't let him eat anything but grass. He's had his dinner, and if he eats too much, he barfs. And try to keep him from chewing on his horns. He ripped the last pair up thinking it was some sort of odd-shaped toy."

Claude looked in horror at the cat overflowing in his arms. Moth gave him a long, considering look.

"Come, let us have a little wine before we get to your *tutoring,*" Farrell said.

I ground my teeth against the urge to let him have it, instead gritting out a smile as I climbed the stairs into the trailer.

"Two years isn't very long for you to be carrying so much animosity toward Walker," I said, blatantly steering the conversation where I wanted it. "I thought you said he beat you only once, and that your other jousts together ended in draws?"

"There were only two draws," Farrell said easily, fetching a bottle of wine from a tiny refrigerator built into the wall of the RV. "The truth is, Walker is so consummately the whipped dog, he takes all the fun out of baiting him. You wouldn't know it from his present demeanor, but we used to have a very lively relationship. We made quite the show out of our rivalry, building on it until the fans were screaming for us to have a match—but that was in the days before he crippled Klaus. After that, the heart seemed to go out of him, and he went from Walker the Wild to Walker the Whipped."

I clutched the stem of the wineglass he handed me, slowly, finger by finger, loosening my hold so I wouldn't snap the delicate glass. "He's not whipped, Farrell—"

"Oh, not in the sense you think I mean, no. The light was gone out of that marriage long before the accident. Of course, there were those who found it more than a little suspicious that it was the man Veronica had left him for whom he crippled, but I knew Walker hadn't destroyed him for that reason. He was simply going after a target, nothing more. The fact that it was Klaus really was nothing but coincidence."

I stared at him in openmouthed surprise. "The guy whose neck was broken was Veronica's . . ."

"Lover?" Farrell nodded and settled himself back against the plush burgundy couch, his blue eyes amused as he sipped his wine. "One of many, I'm afraid." He must have seen my eyes widen as I digested this information, because he gave a little laugh.

"Oh, yes, the lovely Veronica has never been one to keep her favors for just one knight. She even tried to share them with me."

Absently I sipped at the cold white wine, embracing its mellow burn down my throat as I tried to readjust my mental image of Veronica and Walker of five years ago.

Farrell rubbed his chin, his face thoughtful as he leaned forward. "In fact, I wouldn't be surprised if that's what Walker meant with that comment about history repeating itself."

There were so many pieces to the puzzle, I was having a hard time seeing the big picture. "Oh," I said absently, shuffling and moving around the facts until they fit together. Sort of.

"For some reason, Walker took it into his head that Veronica ran to me rather than Klaus. I assume that all these years he's thought I was her partner in infidelity, but the truth is, I wasn't. Still, it's an amusing thought that he imagined himself cuckolded by me when I never laid a finger on the lady."

His words penetrated the cloud of abstraction that held me in its confusing grip. I gave up fact shuffling to focus on the here and now. "What? Why not?"

"Why *not*?" he asked, setting his glass down in order to sprawl back against the velvet cushions. "I prefer my women warm and willing. Veronica's taste ran heavily to revenge, and that, my sweet, is a bitter dish, indeed."

"Fine words from a man who's made it his raison d'être to revenge himself against Walker." My chest was tight, as if iron bands had been tightened around my lungs.

"Me? Oh, no, I'm not the one who wants revenge — I just want another chance at jousting against Walker. That's all I've ever wanted."

I stared down at the glass of golden wine, the puzzle pieces of information I'd been trying to force together suddenly looking all wrong. "But . . . but . . . you're always saying mean things to Walker—"

"It's called goading, darling, and if that man of yours had a shred of dignity, he'd throw down the gauntlet and accept my challenge, but since that day five years ago, he's ignored every attempt I've made to get him into the list with me."

"You just want to joust with him," I repeated, now staring deeply into his blue eyes. He held my gaze easily, not even the faintest whiff of deception present. "My God, if it's not you who's after Walker's blood, then it must be—"

"If anyone is trying to seriously harm him, it would probably be ex-Mrs. McPhail. You look shocked, Pepper. Don't tell me you didn't know about the streak of revenge in the lovely Veronica? Lord knows it's a mile wide. How can you be working for her and not know of it?"

"I . . . I . . ." I shook my head, too overwhelmed to know what I was thinking. "I didn't know! Why doesn't anyone tell me these things? Life would be so much easier if I didn't have to pry every single fact out of everyone."

"How could you *not* know? Everyone knows!"

"I didn't! No one said a word about her. I've got to tell Walker. . . ." I started to stand up, setting the glass of wine down on the tiny table.

Farrell pulled me back onto the curved couch, shaking his head sadly, as if I had disappointed him. "Walker knows all about her."

"Don't be silly, he can't know. If he knew, he'd be doing . . . something . . . about . . . oh." The penny dropped. *At last.* "That's why he said he knew he was the real target of the attacks. Damn him, he knew it was her, and he didn't tell me!"

I stood up again, intent on finding Walker, poking him once or twice in that wonderful chest of his, and asking how he dared keep something so important from me.

Farrell was still shaking his head. "I doubt if it will do any good, not with Walker. Especially in the light of your defection."

I stopped at the door, flinching slightly as if the words themselves had struck a blow. *Defection.* No wonder Walker was so angry with me—he thought I had gone to join the woman who was bending all her energies to destroying him, repeating the pattern of his past.

And why wouldn't he think that? In his eyes, I had trodden the very same path she had. All the team probably thought the very same thing . . . that would account for Fenice's coldness earlier, during the games. I cursed myself for not explaining my plan to Walker earlier, but deep down, I knew I hadn't because he would never allow me to investigate. All I wanted was to be part of the team, to belong, really belong, and now I'd blown what I suspected was my only chance.

In the midst of that horrible contemplation, Farrell spoke. "As a rule, I don't take other men's leavings, but if you find yourself without a bed for the night, you're more than welcome to mine."

I spun around and walked quickly back to him. He must have thought I was going to belt him, because his head jerked back when I reached for him.

"Underneath all that ego, there's actually a nice guy," I said, pressing my lips to his tanned cheek. "Thanks, but no thanks. If I can't have Walker, I'll just spend the rest of my life miserable and lonely, rattling around my mother's big old house until the neighborhood starts to refer to me as Crazy Old Lady Marsh who talks to herself and lives with a gazillion cats."

Farrell raised an eyebrow and gave me a dashing smile. "I thought you didn't like animals?"

"Yeah, about the same way you don't like Walker." I smiled and started toward the door.

"So I take it you're not interested at all in having me tutor you at the quintain?"

"Do I need tutoring?" I struck a pose next to the entrance, the very picture of a jouster so naturally talented, she didn't need anything so mundane as instruction.

"Hell, yes!"

So much for my wunderkind status. I gave him half a smile as I opened the door. "Maybe later, after I superglue together the shattered remains of my life. Thanks for everything, Farrell. You really helped me out when I needed it."

Claude was lurking around outside the trailer, frantically trying to dab at the bits of blood welling up on the scratches on his hand, while at the same time amusing Moth with a frayed piece of rope. "You're going to work the quintain now?" he asked, his voice all but weeping martyrdom.

"No, that's off. Moth! Bad kitty!" Moth flattened his ears, both at the scold and the fact that I rubbed his nose on Claude's injured hand. "Bad! We do not injure those who take care of us!"

"It's all right," Claude said lamely. "I'm kind of used to being—"

"Abused?" I asked with a nod toward the trailer.

"Taken for granted," he suggested.

"Really?" I gathered up Moth and his leash. "Then why do you put up with it? I'm sure there's any number of people who'd welcome an experienced squire on their team."

Claude shrugged and rubbed the back of his hand with a less than pristine bit of tissue. "It's part of my apprenticeship. I want to be trained by the best. Walker wasn't accepting students, so he asked Farrell to take me on as a squire. Since he's the second-best jouster around, he was the best choice."

"Walker *asked* Farrell to take you on?" I asked, astounded by that fact, then surprised that I was astounded. No one was turning out to be who I thought they were.

What does that say about the wisdom of falling in love with a man you don't really know? Evil Inner Pepper asked.

I ignored her.

"Oh, yes. They go way back."

"Well, poop, why didn't anyone tell me it was all just a display?" I grumbled to myself as I nodded good-night to Claude before heading out into the soft purple haze of the falling evening.

My talk with Farrell was anything but warm and fuzzy, but it left me feeling hopeful, if a bit naïve about what everyone else knew. I formulated a plan of attack as I walked quickly through the tent city, greeting people whom I'd come to know over the past ten days, turning down invitations to dinner, ale tasting, a singalong of medieval ditties, and the chance to see if I could French-kiss a jouster for five minutes straight without passing out (that offer came from the Norwegians). It struck me as I was wending my way in and out of the pools of light around each tent that I was strangely comfortable with these people, enjoying not only a sense of camaraderie, but something that made me feel like I was walking up the path to my mother's house after a long journey.

Ironic that in the middle of a different country, surrounded by people I'd just met, I felt a fragile sense of kinship. I just hoped I hadn't destroyed the same with Walker and his team.

"Hey, guys, wait up. Where are you going?"

The entire group of Three Dog Knights—minus the head knight—was heading off toward the parking area. CJ and Butcher, bringing up the rear, stopped as I ran up with Moth. CJ waved Butcher on before turning toward me.

"It's Bliss's birthday. We're taking her to dinner at the steakhouse in town."

"Oh," I said, a bit hurt that no one had mentioned

the birthday dinner to me. "Why didn't you tell me? I've got plans, but—"

"It's a secret. No one is supposed to know," CJ said, her gaze avoiding mine. "We don't want people to know that we're all going off. For security reasons, you know."

"Oh. Security. Yeah, I understand." It didn't lessen the pain that no one had thought of clueing me in to the plans, though.

Evidently something of what I was thinking must have shown, because CJ suddenly looked away. "I would have looked for you to join us, but I assumed you were busy with your new boss."

"She's not my boss, but . . . er . . . I can't come anyway. I've got some things to take care of here, first."

"He's not here," CJ said flatly, looking back at me with an unusually hard stare. "He went off God knows where, saying he wanted to be by himself."

"Who? Walker?"

She was silent for a few moments before answering. "You messed things up royally, didn't you? You hurt him, Pepper, really hurt him. I'm not saying you meant to—I know your intentions were good—but you did hurt him. You're my cousin and all, but I have to say that I'm sorry I ever thought of bringing you with me." I opened my mouth to protest, pain settling with a dull heat in my chest as she continued. "You're not right for him, Pepper. I've told you that and told you that, but you wouldn't listen. I know you both had a physical thing going on, but there's more to a relationship than a good lay. And now you've crushed the life out of Walker, and that's hurting the entire team. We took a vote, and we all think it would be better for everyone if you stayed away from him. From us."

I staggered backward a step, unable to believe I was hearing correctly, tears burning the backs of my eyes and throat. "I . . . I . . . "

"Leave him alone, Pepper. Just leave him alone!"

"But I want to help. You know why I'm doing this—"

She looked at me long and hard. "I thought I knew you, but after seeing what you did to Walker, I wonder if I really do."

Her eyes were shiny, as if she too were fighting tears. That wrung my heart even harder.

"I was just trying to help," I said simply.

"Don't you think you've done enough already? How much more of your *help* can the poor man take?"

I stood there silently. What good would protesting do? My cousin, my own cousin, had decided my motives were less than honorable. I just stood there watching as she ran after the others, my happy "I belong" feeling shattering into a thousand pieces and turning to dust at my feet.

That was it. It was all over. Everything was ruined.

A picture of Walker rose in my mind, his eyes dark with pain.

"Like hell it is," I snarled at Moth, spinning on my heel and marching back the way I'd just come. "I'm not giving up on him this easily. He wanted me to fight for what I wanted—well, I'm fighting!"

A surprised group of minstrels agreed to watch Moth for me for an hour or so, two little girls belonging to the head singer descending upon the big cat with cries of delight and plans for dressing him up.

I headed back out into the night, determined to find Veronica and have it out with her. Then I'd go find Walker and straighten him out on a thing or two, after which I would sit back and graciously allow CJ to beg my pardon.

"But only after she grovels a lot," I said to myself as I stepped into the circle of light outside Veronica's tent.

"Pepper? Are you looking for Vee?"

Teri, one of the Palm Springs Jousting Guild members, looked up from where a small group of her team-mates and a couple of Farrell's men were barbecuing ribs. She wielded a barbecue brush as I answered.

"Yeah, I am. Has she gone?"

Teri nodded. "She said something about going off to a birthday dinner for another jouster. She should be back in a couple of hours."

"Oh, okay. No, thanks, it smells lovely, but I've got . . . uh . . . other arrangements. Night."

A birthday dinner for another jouster? Just how many of the forty-some-odd jousters present had a birthday on the same day as Bliss? I retraced my steps quickly, my thoughts no longer jumbled and confused. I could see it all, see everything with remarkable clarity. Shadows from the camp lights wavered and reached out like warning fingers as I jogged toward the low red building that housed Marley, Cassie, and the other horses of 3DK.

Walker was off having his hissy fit somewhere alone. The rest of the team had gone off to celebrate Bliss's birthday.

But the horses are guarded by the teens Walker had hired, Evil Inner Pepper pointed out.

"You're right," I said aloud, veering to the right toward the familiar cluster of tents. Veronica would never try to harm one of the horses, not with guards hanging around the barns watching for any unauthorized person. But the team's equipment was another matter. There were any number of things that could be done to swords, saddles, and armor, all of which would guarantee the item to fail just when it was needed most.

I found her just where I knew I would—in Walker's tent, hunched over his Paso saddle, silver flashing as the blade of her dagger caught the thin beam of her pencil light.

"Right," I said, fumbling for a moment with the camp light I knew Walker kept on an overturned box.

Bright bluish-white light flooded the tent. "You can just stop right there, Veronica. At the risk of sounding melodramatic, the jig's up."

She stood up slowly and faced me, her face in its usual placid and smooth lines, not even the least shred of surprise or remorse evident. "Good evening, Pepper. I see you've changed out of your PSJG tunic. I must insist that as a representative of the guild, you wear it at all times while at the Faire. It's a little thing, but it promotes team unity."

"Team unity?" I asked in a disbelieving snort. "You're worried about team unity at a time like this?"

"A team's reputation should be guarded at all costs—"

"Excuse me," I interrupted with a gesture toward the wickedly sharp dagger she held in her hand. "But don't you find it the slightest bit incongruous that you're lecturing me about something like a team's reputation when I caught you in the act of trying to sabotage Walker's saddle? That is what you were doing, isn't it?" I moved around her to the opposite side of the chair that held the big wooden saddle. The big leather girth had been twisted up, exposing the underside of it and the cinch strap that connected it to the saddle.

I bent over the cinch strap, seeing nothing wrong with it until I angled the camp light.

"Very clever," I said as I set the lamp down. "No one would think of examining the underside of the cinch strap, not that high up. And you didn't score the leather all the way through, so it won't snap the first time the girth is tightened. Very, very clever, Veronica."

"I thought so," she said, her manner complacent, almost bored, just as if I hadn't found her in the process of trying to ruin Walker's chances at the joust. I knew from experience what sort of pressure was put on the saddle when I took a blow, and had no doubt

Walker's saddle wouldn't stand a chance after he took a couple of hard hits.

"Your vengeance against Walker ends here. There will be no more revenge of any sort." I held my hand out. "Dagger."

She looked at my hand curiously for a moment, a little smile turning the corners of her mouth up. "Surely you don't expect me to just give you the dagger?"

"Yes, I do. Give it to me."

She cocked her head on the side. "And if I do? What then?"

"Then you swear to me that you will make no more attempts on Walker or his team. After you've written out a full confession, of course. If he has no more accidents during the competition, I won't do anything. If he does, I'll go to the joust marshals, the competition's backers, and every media source I can find and tell them everything I know about you—how your fun with the lances injured Bos, how you hobbled Marley, and made certain Vandal's shield would fail when he needed it. Honor is everything to these people, Veronica—you'll be finished, your team will be ostracized, and you'll be the laughingstock of the jousting circuit."

She said nothing for a moment, but I wasn't deceived by the calm mask she wore. She had to be seething inside.

"Very well," she said on a sigh, placing the dagger handle first across my outstretched hand. "But you're a fool if you think I've relied solely on a little fiddling with equipment. I have a much more powerful weapon in my arsenal against Walker and his team."

She strolled slowly toward the open doorway of the tent, the flap having been pushed back when I arrived.

My fingers closed over the smooth mahogany handle of the dagger. Like everything else connected with Veronica, it was expensive, highly polished, and without even a hint of warmth. I knew she was baiting me, knew she wanted to have a killer parting shot, but I couldn't help myself from asking: "And just what would that be?"

Her chilly, controlled smile blossomed until it was reflected in her eyes. I shivered under the impact of so much joyous malice. "Why, you, of course. You've done more damage to Walker than I ever could have. I can only revenge myself on his body—you alone have the power to destroy his heart and soul."

She must have heard the wordless sound of protest I made because her smile got that much brighter. "I knew that first day I saw him look at you that you would be the one; you would provide me the means to revenge myself on him. I can't tell you what a pleasure it's been to watch you destroy him little by little."

"Why?" I asked, sick at heart, the hard wooden handle of the dagger biting into my palm. "Why do you hate him so much? What has he ever done to you?"

She raised her eyebrows in earnest surprise. "I thought you knew—he destroyed the man I loved. I swore the day I learned that Klaus was nothing more than a helpless crippled shell of a man that Walker would pay. I have been patient, biding my time. I knew that sooner or later he would find something that mattered to him, and when he did, I would destroy it as he destroyed my love." She did the little head-tip thing again as her eyes positively sparkled malice. "How ironic is it that in the end, you did the job for me? Good night, Pepper. Don't stay up too late—tomorrow is a very big day for you."

"If you think I'm going to joust on your team—" I sputtered, stopping when she held up a hand.

"You have to. There's a little matter of the contract you signed." Indignation, fury, frustration, the desire to hurt her as she hurt Walker—it all roiled around in my stomach as she patted me on the cheek. "Didn't

you read the fine print? You really should have. It
obligates you to joust under the Palm Springs banner
unless you have a documented medical injury or are
otherwise excused by the team leader—who is, of
course, me. And since I see no reason why you should
not joust, I shall hold you to the terms of the contract.
I suggest you abide by them. Lawsuits can be so
nasty."

She started to turn away, but I grabbed her arm,
tussling a bit with my conscience. It won—I *didn't*
plant the dagger in her black heart. "You might think
you have me by the short and curlies, but you can't
stop me from taking a header and breaking an arm
or something guaranteed to keep me off a horse for
a long, long time."

"You, the proponent for honor, do something so
cowardly as to purposely inflict an injury on yourself?"
She shook her head. "Someone else, perhaps, but not
Saint Pepper."

I tried to laugh it off, but I knew she'd read me
right. My laughter came out harsh as she sauntered
out the door. "Maybe not, but don't expect me to
cover myself in any glory, Veronica. If I decide to
compete, it'll be for myself, not for your team."

She waved an uncaring hand and disappeared into
the blackness of the night.

I swore profoundly for a few minutes, calling myself
every name I could think of. If I hadn't taken it into
my head to rescue Walker, I'd be happily sitting next
to him drinking to Bliss's birthday, not standing here
feeling as if my heart had been torn out and stomped
on by an enraged Marley.

Why hadn't I looked at that contract more closely?
Why hadn't I realized that I was being used by Veronica? Why didn't I listen to Walker when he said to
leave the situation with the sabotage alone?

"Because the man needs me to take care of him,"
I snapped out loud, pulling the girth back so I could
see if the cinch strap could be salvaged, or if the whole

thing would have to be replaced. The scoring Veronica had done on the underside bit too deeply into the leather to repair it, which meant the entire strap piece would have to be removed and a new one sewn on. Thank heaven there was a saddle maker at the Faire. If I got the saddle to him tonight, and promised him whatever money I could beg from family and friends, perhaps he'd get the saddle done by the morning. I flipped the dagger around and started sawing at the damaged leather, figuring I'd pull it off and save the saddler that much trouble. "I don't know why I bother. No appreciates anything I do around here."

"I wouldn't say that," a deep, dark, velvety soft voice rumbled through the tent. "I imagine Veronica is very appreciative of everything you've done."

Startled, I spun around, the dagger and leather cinch strap clutched in my hands. People filled the doorway of the tent—CJ, Butcher, Bliss, Vandal—all of them watching me with silent, harsh faces, the faces of a jury that had made up its mind about the guilt of the accused. But it wasn't the sight of them that stripped the air from my lungs and stilled my beating heart.

The flat, lifeless look of Walker's eyes did that.

Chapter Eighteen

"I don't suppose there's any chance you would believe that I didn't come here to destroy your saddle while you were all gone to Bliss's birthday party?" I asked, which was pretty amazing, considering my brain had frozen up at the sight of him, more or less leaving my mouth on its own.

Butcher pushed past the silent Walker into the tent, instantly reducing the available space by approximately 25 percent. "That's a little difficult when you're holding a dagger and a bit of saddle. I'm ashamed to admit that when I suggested making everyone think we'd left in order to catch the saboteur, I never thought it would be you. I think it's better if you leave, Pepper."

I looked from Butcher to the others as they crowded in the doorway of the tent. A couple of them looked away, unable to meet my searching gaze. Others, like CJ, stood with accusation rampant in their eyes, their body language telling me everything I needed to know.

"How nice you all have such faith in me." I let my eyes go back to the lodestone that stood so silent in front of them. "No trial, Walker? Am I not even allowed to present my defense?"

He shook his head. "I don't believe that's necessary."

That was the moment I understood just what that saying about the straw that broke the camel's back meant. With one shake of his head and five simple words, I had reached my limit. I had fought harder for Walker than I had ever fought for anything in my life. I had sacrificed myself in order to help him, and rather than have someone—anyone—realize that fact, I was vilified and denounced, damned without regard to my innocence.

I faced my accusors, so hurt and angry I could barely speak. "How can you think I would do anything to harm this team?"

"We saw you with the knife, Pepper," Vandal said almost apologetically.

Almost didn't do it.

"I'm CJ's cousin!" I said, my throat sore with unshed tears.

"A close relationship isn't always a reliable indicator of someone's intentions," Bos said, looking at the ground. "Veronica herself proved that you can't always trust people near to you. And now you're on her team."

I bit my lip. "I've trained with some of you. We've eaten together, laughed together. I thought we were friends."

Bliss held my glare long enough to shrug.

"I'm in love with your leader, for god's sake!" I yelled, trying against hope to make them see reason.

Butcher looked uncomfortable as he glanced at me. "Are you? All we know is that you're sleeping with him, Pepper. And with due respect, there have been women who've used Walker before."

Tears of mingled fury and pain filled my eyes until I was almost blinded by them, but I would be flayed alive before I allowed any of them to see how much they had hurt me. I elbowed Butcher aside, dodged Walker's hand as it reached for me, and ruthlessly shoved Vandal and Bos out of my way as I burst out of the tent at a full run, tears snaking down my cheeks as I raced into the night.

Walker shouted my name, but I couldn't take any more of his anger and pain. I had too much of my own. I needed to be alone, somewhere they wouldn't find me, somewhere no one would bother me as I beheld the irreparable remains of my miserable life.

An hour later, having sobbed out the worst of my grief on Marley's strong neck, I brushed the straw off my tights and sneaked out of the stable.

Oddly enough, the sob fest provided me with blessed relief, leaving me rather numb as I picked my way through the tent city toward the minstrels' contingent. Oh, sure, my mind shied away from thinking about a certain Englishman, and there was a fresh, gaping hole in my chest where he had ripped my heart, but other than those facts, I was doing pretty well.

I stopped by the minstrels' tent, thanked them for cat-sitting Moth, admired the doll clothes the girls had forced the big cat into, and oversaw the removal thereof (much to Moth's relief).

"Just so you know," I told the now-naked cat as we walked toward my tent, "we will not be going to the other tent, the one inhabited by the nice-smelling Englishman. I have a sucking chest wound from where he's destroyed my heart. My life is over. I plan on falling into a decline just as soon as this nightmare of a trip is over. I may even become an alcoholic and dic loncly and alone in a ditch with nothing but a few tadpoles to mourn my passing, assuming they would care in the first place, which, given my popularity, isn't at all likely."

Moth refused to join me in my pity party, which just made me feel that much more pitiful. By the time I shoved the door to our tent aside and hustled the big cat in, I was too depressed to do anything but remove his harness.

I didn't even turn on the light, not wanting to see

anything that would remind me of— I stopped my mind before it could say his name, morosely peeling off my tunic and tights, wondering if the leaden weight I carried in my chest would ever ease.

"Doubtful," I muttered as I gave up groping for my lovely silk nightie.

"What is?" a voice asked just as I dropped onto the sleeping bag in nothing but my undies. "*Urf!* Christ, woman, you shattered my eardrum," the voice said again as I screamed at the unexpected surprise of finding my sleeping bag inhabited. My forehead had banged into something hard when I landed, making me see bright yellow stars in the darkness. One of the two arms that had wrapped around me shifted, and then the stars disappeared as Walker turned the camp light on. He rubbed his chin, scowling up at me as I lay halfway across his chest, too stunned to care much about my aching forehead.

"What are you doing here?" I finally gathered up enough wits to ask.

"I assumed you wouldn't be paying me a nocturnal visit, so I came here instead."

"Wait a minute; you're looking disgruntled," I said, leveling a finger at him. He kissed the tip. I snatched it back, trying to pull myself off him, but he had both arms around me now and I wasn't going anywhere. Part of me went all swoony over that fact, but I reminded that part that the warm, tempting, sexy man beneath me had just broken my heart and destroyed my life. "Why are you looking disgruntled? You have no right to look disgruntled; *I'm* the injured party here. If anyone is going to look disgruntled, it's me. And just what do you mean, you came here instead? You think I'm going to have sex with you?"

"Sex? No," Walker said, his arms tightening, pulling me inch by inch down until my mouth was just above his. "I don't expect you to have sex with me, but I hope—I fervently pray—you'll have your wicked, wanton way with me and make love to me until I fall into a limp, boneless heap beneath you, satisfied to the point of stupor, well loved and hard ridden."

I shook my head, too stunned to figure it out. "Someone must have taken away the real Walker and substituted Walker Lite. I appreciate the offer, but I prefer the real man, warts and all."

"I don't have warts," he said, and I had to concentrate very hard to ignore both the feeling of his hands stroking down my back and the tempting lure of his warm mouth, just an inch below mine.

"Maybe not, but you do think I sabotaged your saddle. You think I betrayed you. You think I joined Veronica's team rather than be with you."

"You did join Veronica's team," he pointed out so seriously that I just had to have a quick nibble on his chin. Just for old times' sake.

"Yes, but not because I wanted to. I was trying to get the proof I needed that she was—"

Fingers laid across my mouth stopped me from talking, fingers that were quickly replaced by a warm, gentle mouth that teased my lips and pressed sweet kisses all over my face.

"I know, sweetheart. CJ told me what you did."

"You knew?" A great big lump of unshed tears rose in my throat, making it ache with tightness. "Then why did you think I'd help Veronica sabotage your saddle?"

"I never did," he murmured as he nuzzled my temples. "I didn't understand at first why you joined Veronica's team, but once I spoke to CJ, I figured it out. You said you loved me, and once I understood your plan, I believed you. I just didn't find out until after you ran off."

I pushed back on his chest, well aware of his chest hair as it tickled my nipples. "Oh, no, you don't, you might have believed me tonight, but what about today?"

Remorse filled those lovely, shadowed silver eyes. "Yes, well . . . I should apologize about that. I went a little mad. I thought it was happening all over again—me not being good enough to keep a woman happy. I thought you . . . erm . . . "

"Was using you? Betrayed you? Didn't love you?"

"Yes," he said, lying still, not trying to distract me or hide the fact that he knew he had wronged me. "I haven't had good luck with women, and I'm afraid it was easier to think the worst of you than to accept what you were willing to give me. I'm sorry for that, Pepper. I'm sorry I didn't have strength to admit that you were right about us. About me."

"About you *what*?" I asked, deliberately turning the screws a little tighter. It wasn't nice, it wasn't pretty, but I was the one who had offered my heart and been spurned. I figured he owed it to me to say the words.

He sighed, a tiny little frown appearing between his eyebrows. "You want me to say it, don't you?"

"Yes. It's requisite to any further actions on my part of the kissing, nibbling, and general touching nature."

He pulled my hips up and onto him, wiggling me around on his hardness, the satin of my underwear making us slide together with a sensuality that sent shivers down my back. "How about if I just show you instead?"

I shook my head, doing a little squirm when he peeled my underwear off. "Nope. You have to say the actual words. And in English, please; no saying them in Esperanto or Moldavian or something I won't understand."

He pulled me upward, catching the tip of my nipple in his hot mouth, his tongue doing a swirl over it that had me arching my back in an attempt to shove my entire breast in his mouth. "What if I were to mime it?" he asked, his breath steaming its way over to my other breast.

"No mime. Please, God, no mime!"

I melted into a big old puddle of Pepper goo when his teeth tugged ever so gently on my other nipple, his mouth and fingertips raising goose bumps on every inch of skin he touched. I tried to spread my fingers across the wonderful chest that was heaving so enticingly beneath me, but his hands slid along my arms, his fingers twining with mine as I leaned down to kiss the words out of him.

"Do you forgive me?" he asked once he retrieved his tongue from where I had sucked it into my mouth. With a twist of his hips I was on my back, the soft hair of his chest teasing my overstimulated breasts as he nibbled the shivery spot behind my ear.

"Not until you say the words." Molten silver eyes peered down at me for a second before disappearing from view. For one brief, horrible moment I thought he'd left me. Again. "Walker?"

"Right here, my lusty little wench. Just looking for . . . ah, here it is."

"Here what is—oh, my god! Walker, I am not into S-and-M! I don't want you to hit me with anything, let alone your belt!"

His sexy chuckle rubbed up the length of my body as he stretched out next to me, his long leather belt clutched in one hand, the other closing around the nearest breast. "As if I would want to mar this beauty. The belt is for your hands, Pepper. I've decided that actions speak louder than words, and thus I am going to have to demonstrate to you—at great length, spanning several hours, leaving you so sated your eyes will be crossed—just exactly how I feel about you. Hands, please."

I thought for a moment—did I trust him? Did I want my hands bound so anything he did would be completely out of my control? Did I want to relinquish my body up to him so he could ravish me until my eyes crossed?

Was there any question? I held my hands together so he could wrap the leather belt around my wrists, tight enough that I couldn't get them free, but not so tight that it hurt.

"There are unexpected kinky depths to you that I'm

going to have to explore in great detail," I told him as he looped the free end of the belt through the handles of three stacked suitcases beyond my pillow, handing me the end. I clutched it tightly. Tied as I was, my arms were stretched over my head, not too hard, but with a pleasing sense of wickedness and utter lack of control. "I'm thinking that I'll be paying Bern the Barbarian's booth a visit and pick up the pair of leather fleece-lined manacles I saw a couple of days ago. They have a pair that will go really well with your eyes. And I saw some wonderful slicky lotion at Bawdy Mary's Love Hut that heats up when you blow on . . . Ooooh!"

Walker plucked a small plastic bottle from under the pile of his clothes. "Raaaaaspberry," he drawled with a particularly lascivious leer as he flipped open the top, eyeing my body like it was a playground. I rubbed my leg along his as he knelt next to me.

"Can I pick where you raspberry first?" My breasts, which wholeheartedly approved of the raspberry plan, thrust themselves up in a wanton display of bosomage.

"No," Walker said, his hot gaze working its way up my legs to the part of me that proved I was a natural redhead. "I am the man. I am the one in charge. You are merely a body spread out here for my enjoyment."

I pursed my lips and thought for a moment about letting go of the end of the belt, but knew it would ruin Walker's fun. Not to mention *mine*. "For a man who was all but begging for my forgiveness a few minutes ago, you've gone awfully medieval on me."

"Sweetheart, I'm going to go medieval *all* over you," he said cheerfully, plying the raspberry lotion.

Oh, man, did he!

"Have I shown you how I feel?" he asked who knows how many minutes later, lifting his head from a raspberry-soaked breast, gently blowing over a nipple that was so tight, I worried it might implode from the sheer bliss of his attention. "Do you know now?"

"Not yet." I gasped, twisting against my bonds and

shivering as he drizzled a line of raspberry lotion down my quivery belly, my muscles clenching with anticipation.

"Then I shall just have to try harder," he murmured as his fingers spread wide, drawing a serpentine pattern that led straight to my personal gates of paradise. His mouth followed the pattern, the heat from his tongue licking along my skin and sank deep within me, firing my blood until I writhed beneath him.

"How about now?" he asked, his voice deep and rough with passion, the sound of it as erotic as the site of him kneeling between my legs, his body hard and aroused and magnificently male. "Now do you understand?"

"No," I said, vaguely aware the word came out as a sob as he reached for the bottle of lotion, gently baring all my secrets, warm breath steaming my thighs as he teased oil over all the center of my aching need with light, flicking touches of his fingers. I clutched the belt end with everything I was worth, the muscles in my legs cramping with tension as I waited for it, waited for the touch that I knew would send me flying. "More. You need to do more."

One long, thick, lotion-slicked finger slipped inside me, causing my belly to contract as my muscles tightened in their attempt to grip him.

"Now? Do you know now?" His finger withdrew, then returned with a friend. My hips bucked upward as he leaned over me, pressing kisses to the red raspberry-scented curls. I closed my eyes and gritted my teeth, still holding the belt, mentally pleading with him to touch me where I wanted to be touched.

"No."

"Ah," he said, his breath hot on the hidden parts of me, the touch of his whiskery cheeks on the sensitized skin of my inner thighs sending streaks of lightning straight up my torso. "Then maybe if I were to try this, you would understand."

He lowered his mouth to me and licked up every

last atom of raspberry goodness. I arched up, wrapping my legs around him, giving myself up to the magic of his touch. The lightning within me turned to a fireball and exploded in my belly as his fingers joined his mouth. Without realizing I had let go of the belt, I clutched his head with my still-bound hands and shouted his name.

Before the echo of it had died, he lunged upward, spreading my thighs and thrusting into me with one smooth move that left him surrounded by my still-quivering muscles. My wrists were bound behind his head as he captured my mouth, his tongue mimicking the thrust of his hips, his chest sliding along my breasts, the lotion providing a wonderful friction as his body moved with mine, the two of us joined so tightly there was no end of him and beginning of me; we simply were, together, one.

"I love you," he said, his quicksilver eyes burning as his hips moved faster, short, hard moves that sent me soaring a second time without even having come to earth. "God, how I love you. I want you now. I'll want you tomorrow. I want you in my life always, arguing with me, yelling at me, driving me crazy. I want you forever. Now do you understand? I love you so much it's killing me."

"Yes," I gasped, tasting the salt of his neck as I bit him when my orgasm swept over me, an all-encompassing wave of wonder and joy and rapture that I knew had its origins in the man I held in my arms. "Forever and always."

We slept with arms and legs and other raspberry-scented parts entwined, but before I drifted off I told Walker things were going to be different from here on out.

"Good morning, Three Dog Knights," I said as I strolled into camp bright and early on the thirteenth day of competition.

"Pepper, good morning," Butcher said, jumping up from a folding chair and offering it to me.

"Latte?" Bliss asked as I settled into Butcher's chair. "I've been keeping it warm for you."

"Thank you." I accepted the offering with a sunny smile.

"I brought you the pastries you like," Vandal said, hurrying over with a paper plate of the lemon turnovers I'd quickly grown addicted to.

"That's very thoughtful of you." Graciously I took a pastry and the proffered napkin, giving Vandal a smile in return. He beamed back at me.

"Day looks like it'll be another nice one," Bos said conversationally. "Perfect for jousting."

I glanced up at the cloudless blue morning sky overhead. "Perfect."

"Oh, for God's sake, you're all making me sick," CJ snarled, kicking a clod of dirt at me. "How can you can stand having her queen it over us because we made one tiny little mistake in judgment—"

I pointed at CJ. "That's it, cousin or no cousin, I've had enough of your lip. Off with her head!"

Everyone in the camp froze, staring at me with mouths open in horror. Vandal's eyes widened as he slid a glance at his twin, who was just offering me a bowl of freshly washed grapes. "Can she do that?"

CJ rolled her eyes. "Of course she can't do that! All this groveling has gone to her fat head."

"Hey!" I said.

"Why do you do it?" CJ was facing the team now, hands on hips, glaring at even her beloved Butcher. "Why do you act like she's some princess who has to be kowtowed to?"

"We have to," Vandal said in a near whisper. "We treated her badly."

"We didn't believe in her," Butcher said. "We grossly misjudged her."

The others nodded.

"I didn't think she'd done it, but Vandal convinced me she did," Fenice said, punching her brother in the arm. "We were wrong to think Pepper would sabotage us."

"For which we've all apologized," CJ pointed out.

I sat back, grinning, knowing the days of Walker's team treating me with kid gloves as penance for their wrongful assumptions were drawing to a close. It had been an enjoyable two days; there was no denying that.

"You look like Moth after he's stolen my lunch," Walker said as he strolled into the cluster of people, the aforementioned cat draped like a great furry orange-and-white stole over his shoulders. He clamped a protective hand over Moth as he bent to kiss me, his fingers trailing a gentle caress on my cheek. "What are you smiling about?"

"Well, there's the two hundred grand you won by beating Veronica and Farrell to the Realgestech and French titles, for starters." I waggled my eyebrows as everyone laughed. "I like a man who can keep me in style."

"Knowing you, that won't go very far," CJ said sourly. "Besides, Walker's wins were easy. It was Butcher's third place that was hard-won."

"And my fourth," Vandal said, raising his latte to Walker. "Our share of the pooled money should go far in paying off the mortgage."

"I told you before—we'll pay off the mortgage first, then divide up what remains," Walker said, giving Vandal a meaningful look.

"We can't accept that," Vandal protested.

"You can and you will," Walker said, all manly and determined and every inch a knight. Everyone voiced their agreement. Vandal gave in with a relieved nod of his head.

"And let's not forget Bliss and her amazing tie for second yesterday when she went head-to-head with Farrell," Bos said.

She held up her hand, now encased in plaster. "It'll be a long time before I forget it. If only the blasted vamplate hadn't been bolted on, I would have taken Walker next, and he would have found his arse on the ground—"

Everyone groaned as the familiar argument had started as to whether or not Bliss would have been able to take Walker if she hadn't broken her wrist in her last run with Farrell.

I glanced up at the man who filled my days with happiness and my nights with wonder. There was something about his eyes that had me suspicious. "What?" I asked while the others argued about Bliss's chance in the list with Walker.

"*What* what?" He raised an eyebrow in an attempt to look innocent, but I wasn't fooled. I set down my latte and got to my feet, sliding a hand up the scarlet-and-gold tunic, the familiar rush of excitement giving my smile a wicked glint as I examined his face. His lips were their usual seductive selves, slightly curled up on the ends, his chin just as bluntly obstinate as ever, and his eyes . . .

"Uh-oh, I know that look. It's the 'I bought something new at Bern the Barbarian's and want to show it to you' look. What are you up to?"

"About eight inches, if your measurements last night were accurate." His voice was a soft growl in my ear that sent ripples of awareness down my chest.

I pinched his arm. "I didn't measure you to pump up your ego; I just wanted to look into having one of those satin codpieces made for you, and it was hard to tell if you needed the plain old beefy model, or the roomier stallion one. Now spill whatever it is that's making the corners of your mouth curl up in the way that makes me want to rip off all your clothing and molest you shamelessly."

With a grand gesture Walker bowed to me (without spilling Moth, who had learned he could hook his claws into Walker's chain mail without fear of repercussion), and pulled from under his tunic a piece of paper.

"Fair ladies and scurrilous gentlemen, I give you this, the last day of competition's match schedule."

"Oooh, who does Geoff get in my place?" Bliss asked, elbowing Vandal and Butcher aside. "Tell me it's someone good!"

Poor Geoff turned pale at the thought of having to joust. He'd jousted only a couple of times before he decided he didn't have the stomach for it, but according to the rules, if a team member or his designated alternate didn't joust, the entire team was removed from competition.

"I got Tomas again, ten thirty this morning." Vandal handed the sheet to Butcher, grinning as he rubbed his hands together. "Good, I'll be able to take care of him easily, and still have time to meet with the delectable Hanson twins."

I gave Geoff a reassuring smile. He was clutching onto Bos's good arm looking like he was going to be sick.

"Don't worry, Geoff; it's not that bad. If I can survive jousting after only a week's instruction, so can you."

"You came in dead last both days," CJ pointed out.

"Yes, but the point is I survived," I said, giving her a look that should have stripped the hair from her head, but it had little effect on her. My looks seldom did. "Despite being burdened by the requirement of jousting for Veronica the Villain, I did my best, and survived the last few days. And I finished forty-fifth yesterday, so I wasn't dead last."

"That's only because the other jouster had a concussion and had to be taken away to the hospital and couldn't complete his matches," she countered.

Butcher looked up from the sheet of paper, his lips pursed. "I drew Farrell. Two o'clock."

"Goody! Your turn to cream him, lamby-pie. Oh, but that means Walker won't get him."

"There's always the melee tomorrow," Butcher replied. "Walker can finally show Farrell that a little thing like five years out of the list hasn't affected him."

I glanced back at my brave knight, who was watching me with that curious half smile on his face. "What? Don't tell me I drew you?"

His lips curled even more as he shook his head. "I've already told you that wouldn't happen. They match jousters together by skill level. They'd never put a new knight up against an experienced one."

"Okay, then, who did I get?"

"Let's see . . . four o'clock, Pepper Marsh and Candy Roman."

I frowned for a second as I thought. "Candy . . . oh, she's Aussie, isn't she?"

He nodded.

"Good draw," Bliss said matter-of-factly. "She's new at it, too. Her husband jousts, so she thought she'd take it up. She leans to the left, Pepper. If you keep that in mind when you hit her, you *might* just end up beating her."

"Thanks for the vote of confidence. All right, then, if it's not me, it's got to be you. Who are you jousting? Butcher says he drew Farrell, and there's no one else. . . . Oh, no!"

Butcher, holding the sheet, started to laugh. "Here it is, four fifteen. It'll be the mister versus the missus."

I crossed my arms over my chest and thinned my lips at him.

"Erm . . . that's mister versus the ex-missus."

"Thank you. I bet Veronica's thrilled," I said, watching Walker. There were no more shadows in his eyes, no more signs that he was caught on the self-destructive path he'd started down five years ago. He certainly had jousted brilliantly the last few days, aggressive but not wildly foolish, and he was well on his way to winning not only the hat trick of all three individual jousting titles, but the big one, the whole enchilada, the title of tourney champion. All that remained after today's joust was the free-for-all melee tomorrow, and then the points would be totaled and the champion named. "Just watch yourself with her, and don't be nice like you were the last time. She has a serious emotional problem where you're concerned, and won't stop at anything to beat you."

He leaned forward, his lips a warm if too brief caress on mine, his eyes liquid with happiness and love. "Thank you for the warning. I'll keep it in mind."

"I think I might just have a little flutter on the wild man," Butcher said. "It's a sure thing he'll beat that she-witch and take the Southern Italian title as well."

"Oooh, excellent idea, I'm good for a hundred quid," Bliss said.

"Me too," Vandal jumped up. "We can pool our money and lay down a big wager on him."

"You're jousting, stupid," Fenice pointed out.

Vandal grinned. "I know a sure thing when I see it. Don't worry, big sister, I won't bet against myself . . . I'll just bet on Walker."

I turned my back on them as Fenice tried to make Vandal understand that the two things were the same.

"Have I told you today how madly in love I am with you?" I asked, sliding my arms around Walker.

"Three times, which means you owe me twenty-two more," he answered, the low, silken rumble of his voice thrumming deep within me as I offered up my lips in wordless penance.

Chapter Nineteen

The wonderful warm glow that wrapped around me whenever I was near Walker remained with me during the day. Geoff went down after two runs, but didn't get seriously hurt. Vandal defeated his opponent in all three runs, moving up to joust against the winner of the following joust. Butcher and Farrell tied twice, finally going to a third tie-breaking match, which Farrell won, only to be defeated by his next opponent.

It was a glow heightened by the excitement of the last day of competition. The Faire was at capacity crowds, each jousting run getting the entire audience on their feet yelling and screaming for their favorites. Everywhere we went there were people, kids with snow cones, babies in strollers, dogs, a couple of cats, parrots, and even one goat. It was wall-to-wall people, everyone gawking, taking pictures, asking for autographs, and just generally having a good time. The Faire folk geared up to accommodate the crowds, donning their brightest, flashiest garb, sunniest smiles, and hammiest acting tendencies.

The horses were equally gorgeous, brushed by the squires until they were glossy, each horse decked out in beautifully decorated finery, everything from jeweled headstalls and caparisons to metal and leather warhorse armor that was as impressive to look at as the mounted knight's armor.

Despite my reticence to joust, somehow I had been caught up in it all. Although I had as little to do with them as possible, the excitement of Veronica's team and support staff was contagious. Sukey, a sweet eighteen-year-old art major who was acting as squire, shined up my new armor until it was almost blinding under the big arena lights. I still wasn't used to wearing an additional twenty pounds of armor strapped to my arms, legs, and chest, but I had to admit that the armor did cushion the falls a bit.

"You remember everything I told you?" Bliss said as she walked me and Tansy, one of Veronica's horses, to the rider's entrance of the arena. I was in my armor, the cream and green of my surcoat covering the plate armor matching Tansy's headstall (a fancied-up bridle), saddle cloth, crupper (crisscrossed leather straps over her hindquarters, painted green and cream), and a jeweled peytral, or breast strap. I felt pretty spiffy in my duds, but Tansy positively sparkled. "Candy leans to the left, so it's important your hit is accurate. None of that wild scything that you did yesterday. Use the saddle and your legs, and for heaven's sake, don't forget to drop the reins before the strike!"

"I will. Bliss?" I leaned down and gave her a quick peck on the cheek. "Thanks for everything."

"Do me proud, girl," she said in a gruff voice. "You've got it in you to be a world-class jouster if you just stick with it."

I glanced over to the right to the practice ring, where Walker and a couple other jousters were warming up their horses. He raised his hand high in a victory sign, turning Marley to leave the ring. I waved and started up the long ramp into the arena, stopping at the gate. Veronica was talking to one of the competition officials, the long-haired, bearded man who was acting as list marshal, her hands gesticulating despite the fact that she was in full armor. The official protested something, but she cut him off, spinning on her heel to walk over to Gladiator, the sharp-tempered Friesian who was Tansy's twin as far as caparisons went. To the left was the Aussie I was going to joust against. I gave her a friendly smile and nod, which she answered just as happily. Inside the arena the crowd roared as one jouster took down another.

"Don't drop the lance until the last minute, aim a bit high and to the left—no, wait, to the right; she leans to the left—and remember to drop the reins," I muttered to myself, more than a little bit nervous at the upcoming joust. It wasn't the first one I'd done without the familiar shield to take the blow—Bliss and Walker had been working me for long hours the last couple of days—but it was the first time I had jousted Southern Italian with a stranger, someone who didn't give a fig about setting me down gently rather than just blasting me off the horse.

Tansy moved to the side as the two jousters exited the ring. I looked behind me to see Walker waiting at the bottom of the ramp, talking with Butcher, but watching me. I reminded myself that although he wouldn't stop loving me if I were so nervous I barfed in the middle of the arena, I really didn't want to end the competition on a note of vomit.

"Save the lance till the last minute, aim high and to the right, and drop the— Huh?"

The voice of the announcer, tinny and somewhat drowned out by the buzz of the crowd, was supplemented by a crier who stood outside the entrance, bellowing the names of the next combatants.

"Candy Roman, of Joust for Fun, and Veronica Tyler, Palm Springs Jousting Guild, in the arena, please."

"Veronica?" I asked, looking at the crier, then back at Walker. He was too far behind me to hear, and obviously didn't know what was going on, but I knew. Oh, I knew—Veronica had somehow convinced the list marshal to switch our positions. I was willing to bet everything I had that there was some sort of weird rule allowing team members to switch spots—which meant I'd have to joust against Walker.

My mind balked at the thought of just what that would mean.

"I won't let that happen," I swore. "I will not destroy him now that he's finally found his feet. She will not beat us!"

Veronica gave me a horrible smile as she waited for Candy to ride into the arena. Unsure of what she should do (and no doubt terrified of the thought of going against the much more experienced Veronica), Candy remained poised at the entrance.

Her husband raced to the judging area and began arguing vehemently with the marshal, but he was having none of it, waving the Australian off as he strode toward the center of the arena. The Aussie looked at his wife helplessly for a couple of seconds, then ran after the marshal to try again.

"Second call for Candy Roman and Veronica Tyler."

Candy looked around nervously. I turned Tansy's head and nudged her over to where Veronica sat on the handsome black. "Tell me, Veronica, just what sort of blackmail did you have to resort to in order to get us switched?"

"Blackmail is such a harsh word," she said with another sharky smile. "I prefer persuaded. It's all perfectly legal, you know. As the team captain, I have the power to change the order of jousts should I feel one of my team members is in a position to move up the ranks. Congratulations on your promotion."

"You heartless bitch," I said softly, without any heat.

"Third and final call for Candy Roman and Veronica Tyler. If you do not enter the list now, ladies, your match will be forfeit and your teams disqualified."

Candy bit her lip, hesitated for a second, shot Veronica a look of loathing, then urged her horse into the arena.

"Have a lovely joust, dear," the she-witch of Palm Springs said as she followed Candy.

I turned in the saddle to gesture to Walker, but he was bent to the side, signing autographs for a crowd of teens and a couple of squires. He was too far away to hear me over the noise of the arena, and the squires and grooms dashing back and forth blocked my path so I couldn't turn Tansy and ride to him.

"Hey, you!" Sukey was already in the arena, serving Veronica, so I yelled at an empty-handed squire. I beckoned the lanky teen over, awkwardly dismounting and shoving the reins into his hands. "Hold my horse for a minute."

The judges loge was midway down the ring, on a raised platform on the arena floor. It was hard work stumbling in full armor through the soft dirt-and-sand mixture that was gentle on the horses' hooves. I skirted the edge and was halfway across the ring when the marshal called, "Lay on!" into his microphone, and the two horses jumped forward.

Candy never stood a chance. The crowd yelled their approval as Veronica sent her flying backward over her horse's rump.

"Marshal? Can I talk to you for a minute?"

The list marshal, wearing a crown and fancy purple robes, frowned as I staggered up to him. "What are you doing here? Jousters are not allowed on the field unless they are acting in the capacity of squire."

"It's about what my team captain did—whatever she told you, it wasn't true. I'm not so improved that I'm ready to joust Walker McPhail."

"My decision is final, Miss Whatever-your-name-is. If you wish to file a grievance, you may do so after the joust." He dismissed me without a thought.

"But that won't do me any good *now*," I argued.

"My decision is final," he said again, turning away

from me. I knew then that Veronica really had black-mailed him somehow. Probably she'd slept with him, too.

"Your decision sucks, and you can just bet your bottom dollar I'll be filing that grievance, and one against the dubious ethics of a list marshal who allows himself to be blackmailed."

He didn't even look at me as he said, "I believe they are calling for you. It is preferred that jousters enter the list on horseback, but if you wish to joust on foot . . ."

I swore as I ran back toward the opening. Veronica was just leaving after taking her victory lap around the ring, waving and smiling at the yelling fans. Candy limped past me, having bowed out of the remaining two runs of the match, yielding the win to Veronica. Walker dislodged his gang of adoring teens and was next to where Tansy stood.

Veronica blew him a kiss as she rode by, Walker watching her in surprise for a few seconds; then his head snapped around to me. I knew the moment he realized what she had done—his hands went tight on the reins and Marley reared in protest.

"Walker McPhail, Three Dog Knights, and Pepper Marsh, Palm Springs Jousting Guild, in the arena, please."

Walker's roar of protest had both horses dancing nervously, and several squires covering their ears.

"Help me up," I ordered the squire who was trying to calm Tansy. With a boost to my rear, I managed to get into the saddle.

"Pepper!" Walker bellowed, heading straight for me.

"Shush," I ordered when he got close enough to hear me. "Walker, I talked to the list marshal; there's nothing we can do."

"Yes, there is. I won't joust with you."

"You have to," I said as quietly as I could and still be heard. Tansy didn't like being so close to Marley, tossing her head and laying her ears back, but I told her to get a grip and reached across for Walker's hand. "I don't want to do this any more than you do, but Walker, we have to. If you forfeit this match, your titles and the prize money will be stripped from you and the rest of the team."

"I don't care about the damned money. I will not joust with you."

"*I* care about the money. After Vandal's mortgage is paid off, you all share the remainder of the winnings equally, right? Of your sixth share, half of it is going to go to the government in taxes, so that leaves you with only a twelth, which means we're going to need you to win today in order to have enough to start a life together."

"We can have a life together without it," he snapped.

"Second call—Walker McPhail and Pepper Marsh."

"But we'll have a better one with the money. I can go back to vet school. We can go to Central America so you can meet my mother. We can buy a house."

His eyes were dark, but I could see the panic in them as he leaned close, his breath hissing along my face. "Pepper, I could kill you. I could cripple you for life like I did the German five years ago."

"But you won't," I said, squeezing his hand, throwing every ounce of love and confidence I had into my eyes so he would see how much faith I had in him. "You're not the same man you were then, Walker. You're better. You're smarter. You won't hurt me."

His teeth ground together for a few seconds. "There's nothing to stop *you* from forfeiting the match."

"Nothing but my honor," I said softly, pushing aside his mail coif so I could touch my gloved hand to his cheek. "I wouldn't mind stripping Veronica of her wins and prize money, but I can't do that to the rest of her team. They're innocent. If I quit now, they all lose. That's not fair to them. They worked hard."

"Third and final call for Walker McPhail and Pepper Marsh," the crier yelled, looking directly at us.

"We have to do this, Walker. There are too many other people counting on us."

He pulled away from me, reaching for his black helm, jerking it over his head as he dug his heels into Marley's side. "Nothing says I have to joust well."

"I say you do! Those judges will be watching you extremely closely. If they see you deliberately pulling your blows and taking it easy on me, they're not going to give you the points. Farrell is only a little behind you. If you don't get the full points for jousting seriously, you'll be out of the money. We *need* that money, Walker!"

He ground his teeth at me, but said nothing, turning Marley toward the opening of the arena.

I muttered to his back a couple of rude things about men who were too chivalrous for their own good as he rode into the ring. I was still muttering as I took the shiny helm from Sukey, jerking on my cloth cap before easing the helm over my head. Tansy danced forward a few steps into the arena. I reined her in at the opening as Walker's music, the *Triumphal March* from *Aida,* blared throughout the arena.

Marley pranced forward, the big horse showing off for all he was worth. Rather than take his processional ride around the ring so everyone could cheer him on and throw favors at him, however, Walker went straight to his end of the list. The crowd, hyped up to see Walker the Wild joust, didn't know quite what to think of that, and everyone sat down while the remainder of Walker's music played.

My music ("Saturday Night," by the Bay City Rollers—it was the only tape I could get my hands on in a short time) started. Tansy didn't need any urging to trot into the ring, her neck arched beautifully as she, too, played up to the crowd. Following Walker's lead, I didn't circle the arena, but rode straight to the man I loved.

With one gloved hand I flipped up my visor when

I was close enough to yell over the noise of the music and cheering audience. "Listen here, you great big adorable man! Stop giving up! You wouldn't let me quit, and I'm not going to let you."

He shoved his visor up, too, his mercurial eyes blazing at me from the shadows of his helm. "I will *not* hurt you!"

"Damn straight you won't; you're too talented to hurt me. But if you pull your punches, I'll know, and I'll never forgive you, so put that in your helm and smoke it!"

I slammed down my visor before he could reply, wheeling Tansy around and cantering her down to the end of the list.

Before I could so much as reach for my lance, Walker was upon us, bellowing over the music and the audience, "I love you, you infuriating woman!"

"I know," I yelled back, then realized he couldn't hear me with my visor closed, so I opened it and yelled even louder, "I love you, too, but if you don't win this match, I'll make your life a living hell, and don't you think I can't do it!"

"The next woman I fall in love with is *really* going to hate horses," he swore before sliding his visor down and spinning Marley into a turn.

"The *next* woman? Oh, you wish," I yelled to his back, closing my visor and reaching for the lance. The announcer pumped the crowd up with Walker's exploits and wins, including a detailed list of all his tourney wins. He was noticeably silent about me, but I didn't care. I was too busy praying to as many deities as I could think of to survive the joust without injury. I didn't care so much for my own sake—although I truly didn't care for the idea of being pummeled by Walker—but I knew that if he injured me, his jousting career would be over. Worse, I'd spend the rest of my life trying to get him to believe in himself, and he'd spend the rest of his convinced he was a miserable failure.

"Lance up until the last minute, aim dead center on the grand guard, drop the reins, let go of the lance as it falls," I murmured. Tansy's ears twitched, a fine tremor running through her as she waited. Veronica had trained her well, I had to admit, Tansy was extremely responsive to leg cues and loved to run. I was grateful that at least one of us knew what she was doing.

"Lay on!"

The audience surged to their feet with a roar as Tansy sprang forward, taking me by surprise for a second before I realized she was cantering down the list. I gritted my teeth against the coming impact, sighted Walker's black grand guard, and lowered my lance.

"Pepper? God, love, tell me you're all right. Pepper?"

I opened my eyes to find Walker leaning over me, his helm gone, his eyes haunted.

"Hi, Walker. Have I told you how much I like your eyes?"

He looked up and spoke to someone else. "She's delirious. Dammit, get the paramedic over here now!"

Paramedic. Delirious. The joust! I struggled to a sitting position, pushing Walker away. "I'm not delirious, just in love. I'm fine, not hurt at all."

"You were unconscious," he accused, putting a restraining arm on me.

"Like hell I was," I lied, slapping at his shoulder armor until he let me up. I thought I was going to pass out again when I sat up, fighting hard to keep my voice and face from showing just how hard I had been hit. Bravado, that was the key; I'd just brazen it out and he'd never know. "What's the matter, you afraid to joust with me again?"

"Pepper, I am *not* going to—"

I lurched to my feet, my chest as sore as if someone had kicked me. "Sure you are, 'cause I am, which means you have to, or all these fine people will think the man I'm going to marry is a coward."

"Marry?" he asked, his frown a fearsome thing to see as he followed me to where Sukey held Tansy.

"Well, yes, I assumed you'd want to marry me." It took every last muscle I possessed, but I managed to clamber into the saddle without either vomiting or passing out. I took the helm offered to me and bit my lip as I looked down at Walker's face, his adorable face, a face now wearing a mingled expression of anger and guilt. "You *do* want to marry me, don't you?"

"Yes, I do, but that's not the point. We've had one run; now you can concede the win to me without jeopardizing the rest of your team."

A little of the tightness across my chest eased. "I could, but I'm not going to. My honor's at stake here, Walker, but more important, yours is as well. I trust you. I believe that you can joust without harming me." I looked down at the dented section of my armor. "Much. So get that adorable butt of yours back onto Marley and prepare to defend yourself, because this time I'm taking off the kid gloves. It's war now, buster."

It was all bravado, of course. I didn't relish taking another blow like the one he had dealt me, but it was important that Walker triumph over his fears. One run wouldn't do it, but three might.

"Pepper, dammit, I'm not going to joust against you again. You can't make me."

"I love you, Walker."

I could see his teeth grinding together. "I know what you're doing. You're trying to shame me into another run, and it's not going to—"

"I love you more than anything in the whole world."

"I will not be manipulated like this—"

"I love you so much, I trust you with my life."

He snatched up his helm and shook it at me. "Fine! But when I break your damned fool neck and you spend the rest of that life crippled because you insisted I joust, I just hope you'll be happy!"

"Hugs and smooches," I called to him as he stormed over to Marley, muttering and swearing the whole way.

Walker rode to the end of the list, and I sent up another quick prayer to protect us both from injury, barely getting it completed before the audience exploded in cheers as the list marshal called the start.

"Well, this is getting to be humiliating," I said a moment later as I raised my visor and shook the dirt and sand from where it had permeated my helm. "I don't think I even touched you this time. You don't have an extra-long lance, do you? And no, I don't mean your manly eight inches."

Walker pulled me to my feet, his gaze frankly assessing as it ran over my dented armor. "Are you hurt?"

"No, just a little winded. That passing on the right side really takes the breath out of you, doesn't it?"

"Yes," he lied. He wasn't even sweating despite wearing all that armor.

I pushed his visor up high and leaned forward to brush my lips against the thinned line of his mouth. "You're a rotten liar. I'm fine, Walker. Your accuracy is dead-on, and you're setting me down much gentler than even Bliss does."

Pain flashed over his face, thickening his voice. "You're killing me, Pepper. My heart stops each time I think of what could happen."

"Then think instead about how good you'll feel when I give you your reward for jousting with me."

The frown I had come to love pulled his ebony brows together. "What reward?"

"I bought out Bawdy Mary's selection of lotions. I thought tonight you could be my smorgasbord," I whispered, then limped back to Tansy.

"Pepper—"

"Come on, I want one more shot at knocking you on your handsome butt. On your horse, McPhail."

I smiled to myself as he shook his head and walked back to Marley.

"There goes the man I'm about to make deliriously happy," I told Tansy. She snorted and jogged to the side when Sukey shoved the lance into my hand. "I just hope I live to appreciate his gratitude."

Time seemed to do that weird "flashing your life before your eyes" telescoping thing as Walker turned Marley at the far end of the list. The roar of the crowd dulled to a distant white noise as I stared through the narrow eye slit of my visor at the figure of the black knight facing me, my breath rasping hard in my ears as it echoed in the steel confines of the helm.

Beneath the steel plates, mail, cloth gambeson, and thin linen shirt, my heart was thumping madly, so hard I could feel it in the tips of my fingers as I gripped the lance. Tansy must have felt the excitement too. She positively danced in anticipation, but her movements seemed slow and laborious; even the sound of her harness jingling seemed to be slowed as it penetrated the shelter of my helm.

From the very corner of my eye slit I saw the list marshal raise the cloth pennant. Although I couldn't hear the words, the second his arm started its downswing I clamped my legs tight on Tansy's sides, my breath coming out in a shouted exhalation that deafened me as the horse lunged forward.

Walker was quick off the start as well, but even so, each second seemed to take five times what it normally did; the only sound audible was my own breathing, hard and fast as Tansy pounded down the list. Walker and Marley suddenly seemed to speed up as I lowered my lance, clamping it down between my side and arm, my eyes on the curved black plate that was bolted to Walker's shoulder piece.

I dropped the reins just as his lance slammed into

my grand guard, knocking me backward against the high back of Veronica's McClellan saddle. Splinters from the shattered tip flew up, blinding me and blocking my view of Walker, but the shock I felt as my lance connected with him twisted me to the right, my left leg coming out of the stirrup. I clung desperately to the horse and threw myself into the lance in an attempt to keep from being thrown.

There was a tremendous pressure in my chest that had me falling into a pit of blackness, but just as I started losing my grip on both consciousness and my lance, a thunderous *crack* reverberated through the air. The pressure miraculously disappeared, and Tansy was flying past Walker. I looked down, surprised to find myself still in the saddle, my right hand numb, but still there, gripping the remains of a lance broken in the middle.

"We did it," I said, still staring at the lance, Tansy having turned to trot docilely back to our end of the list. "We did it. I don't believe it—we did it!"

There was a flash of black to my left, and suddenly I was ripped from the saddle and slammed up against a brick wall. A black brick wall, one made up of plate armor and an extremely dishy knight.

"We did it," I told the knight as he ripped my helm and arming cap off. "I can't believe it. We did it. It was a draw because we both broke our lances, right? So I didn't lose? Man, was that amazing!"

"You are never doing that again, do you understand?" He shook me a little as he spoke. "My heart won't stand for it! I forbid you ever to joust. I refuse to go through that hell again—promise me you won't do it again!"

I looked up into the silver eyes I loved so much, smiling through my tears of happiness at them, pausing only to pull off my gloves before I cradled his face in my hands. "You look furious and relieved and happy all at once."

"I could have killed you." His voice was so low I felt rather than heard it.

"But you didn't. You, my brave knight, have proven your worth and won the fair maiden. So what are you going to do about that?"

"Take you back to my tent and make love to you for the next three hours," he growled against my lips. His mouth was hot on mine as he kissed me, hot and fiery, aggressively demanding, but at the same time impossibly gentle. Around us the audience cheered, but we didn't hear them as our lips parted reluctantly. My dream man, my knight in shining armor, the man who made me see that I, too, could do anything I wanted. . . .

"Best five out of seven?" I asked brightly.

Epilogue

I hung up the phone and looked at the bodies scattered around me. "All right, you mangy mongrels, get off me and let me get up. I have to go find your daddy."

"I'm right here," Walker's voice rumbled from the kitchen, the door slamming behind him. I pushed Searcher the greyhound off the pad of paper that lay next to me on the couch, digging through the blankets to find the pen I had been using before the call. Walker loomed up on the doorway in his black leather duster, pulling his gloves off as he eyed us. "You look comfortable. You were right about the sofa—it does go well with the house."

"Farm," I corrected, wrinkling my nose when the elderly spaniel curled up against my hip emitted a sign he'd been into the compost heap again. "We have a farm, thanks to your winning the tourney championship, not that we got to see a lot of the money—what is it with your government taking so much of it for taxes? You won it in Canada, you shouldn't have to pay English taxes on it—"

"Pepper," he interrupted what was fast becoming my favorite rant.

"What?"

"Is there something you wanted me for?"

"Other than wild, unbridled lovemaking, you mean?"

He grinned. "That goes without saying."

I slid my foot out from where Baskerville the bloodhound was lying on it, wriggling my toes to restore the flow of blood. "Yes, as a matter of fact, I did want you for something else. When CJ explained to me that you had three dogs, I thought, 'Okay, so the man has three dogs. I can live with that.' But this"—I waved my hand at the canine carcasses that were spread out on and around me—"this appears to be *five* dogs."

He grinned. "They just seem to find me. They all needed homes, and, well . . . I couldn't leave them."

The blanket on my lap moved. I pushed it aside to uncover the three steel-gray balls of fur that Walker had brought home the previous day. "And the kittens?"

His eyebrows shot up in mock horror. "You wouldn't have liked it if I let old Ferguson drown them, would you?"

"No, of course not, but that didn't mean *we* had to take them."

"You're good with animals," he pointed out, squatting down next to me to tickle one of the kittens' tummy. "Who better to have animals than a vet?"

"I have been at vet college exactly one week, buster. Nothing says I have to stay there! Besides, we have a situation that may mean I have to leave."

"A situation?" He leaned in and kissed me, his lips cold from the chilly November weather. "What sort of a situation?"

"A family one," I said.

His eyes widened until they were silver disks. "Pepper! You don't mean you're—"

"No! Not that. I'm not ruling it out, but not now, not when we're just getting settled, and you're starting the jousting school, and I'm trying to figure out the British veterinary world. It's . . . well, there's just no easy way to say this. My aunt called and she wants us to go back to Ontario."

"She does?" His brow wrinkled. "Why?"

I sighed. "It's Moth. Evidently he's been in a decline ever since you left. He's pining for you. He won't eat; he won't play with his toys—not even wearing his devil horns cheers him up. My aunt wants to offer you visitation rights. She knows he can't come here because of the quarantine laws, so the only solution is for you to go back to Ontario every other month and jolly Moth out of the doldrums."

Walker laughed so hard he fell back onto his butt, taking me, the blanket, the kittens, and four of the five dogs with him. We sprawled over him in a glorious confusion of fur, legs, and tails.

"Welcome to my world, Mrs. McPhail," he said, his lips teasing mine as he plucked a kitten from between us.

"Thank you, Mr. McPhail. I think I may just stay awhile."

And so I did.

Author's Note

Every author walks a fine line when incorporating factual content such as details about a sporting event into a novel. We balance the need to be realistic with readers' demands to be given an entertaining story. With that in mind, when writing this book I took a few minor liberties with the subject of international competition jousting. One such liberty is the creation of a fictional international jousting competition with a $1 million purse. Although there are many competitions with generous purses to be won by the victors, I am not aware of any that have reached the level described in this book. Participants of the competition jousting world believe that they will one day be possible, however.

Other aspects of jousting competition presented in this book are as factual as I could make them, although the existence of several international jousting organizations, each with their own rules, own style of jousting, and own award system, makes it difficult to standardize specific details. For that reason, the rules of my tourney are an amalgamation of existing tournament rules, with a few little twists thrown in to make them fun.

I owe a huge debt of gratitude to Dameon Willoch of the Seattle Knights (www.seattleknights.com) for his limitless patience in answering my questions regarding styles of jousting, international rules, and myriad other queries covering everything from horse injuries to how it feels to take a fall in full plate armor, as well as for inviting me to watch his training classes and jousting demonstrations.

I'm also grateful for the support and camaraderie of the International Wenches Guild (www.wenches. com), a group of wonderful women (and men) who wholeheartedly throw themselves into the spirit of Wenching at Renaissance Faires and events across the globe. Although my version of the Wenches doesn't begin to encompass the truly awesome nature of the IWG, I hope it reflects some of the generous and fun traits of IWG members. I take great pride in being an official Wench.

Katie MacAlister